ALSO BY STEVE BEIN

THE FATED BLADES SERIES

continued . . .

"Bein excels beyond any history lover's wildest imagination with exceptionally researched, vivid depictions of ancient Japan." —*RT Book Reviews*

"[Bein is] not a one-book wonder. *Year of the Demon* is a darker story that excoriates its characters much more than was thought possible . . . a good follow-up to one of my favorite debuts of all time." —Fantasy Book Critic

"Part thriller, part police procedural, part historical, and part urban fantasy, *Year of the Demon* is simply a book for people who like to read. . . . Bein does an amazing job of weaving them all together into a fascinating story." —All Things Urban Fantasy

Daughter of the Sword

"A noir modern Tokyo overwhelmed by the shadows of Japanese history . . . a compelling multifaceted vision of a remarkable culture, and a great page-turner." —Stephen Baxter, author of *Ultima*

"The interweaving of historical Japanese adventure and modern police procedural, Tokyo-style, caught me from two unexpected directions." —Jay Lake, author of *Kalimpura*

"An authentic and riveting thrill ride through both ancient and modern Japan. Definitely a winner." —Kylie Chan, author of *Demon Child*

"*Daughter of the Sword* reads like James Clavell's *Shōgun* would have if it had been crossed with high fantasy by way of a police procedural." —Otherwhere Gazette

"Magic swords and samurai set alongside drugs and modern Tokyo and all blending in together to produce an engrossing and original story." —Under the Covers

DISCIPLE
OF THE
WIND

A NOVEL OF THE FATED BLADES

STEVE BEIN

A ROC BOOK

ROC
Published by New American Library,
an imprint of Penguin Random House LLC
375 Hudson Street, New York, New York 10014

This book is a publication of New American Library. Previously published in a
Roc trade paperback edition.

First Roc Mass Market Printing, March 2016

Copyright © Steve Bein, 2015
Penguin Random House supports copyright. Copyright fuels creativity,
encourages diverse voices, promotes free speech, and creates a vibrant culture.
Thank you for buying an authorized edition of this book and for complying with
copyright laws by not reproducing, scanning, or distributing any part of it in any
form without permission. You are supporting writers and allowing Penguin
Random House to continue to publish books for every reader.

Roc and the Roc colophon are registered trademarks of
Penguin Random House LLC.

For more information about Penguin Random House, visit penguin.com.

ISBN 978-0-451-47021-8

Printed in the United States of America
10 9 8 7 6 5 4 3 2 1

In memory of Kane and Buster

JAPANESE
PRONUNCIATION GUIDE

Spoiler alert: you're going to find a lot of Japanese words in this book. Three general rules tell you most of what you need to know about how to pronounce them:

1. The first syllable usually gets the emphasis (so it's DAI-go-ro, not Dai-GO-ro).
2. Consonants are almost always pronounced just like English consonants.
3. Vowels are almost always pronounced just like Hawaiian vowels.

Yes, I know, you probably know about as much Hawaiian as you do Japanese, but the words you do know cover most of the bases: if you can pronounce *aloha*, *hula*, *Waikiki*, and *King Kamehameha*, you've got your vowels. Barring that, if you took a Romance language in high school, you're good to go. Or, if you prefer lists and tables:

> *a* as in *father*
> *ae* as in *taekwondo*
> *ai* as in *aisle*
> *ao* as in *cacao*
> *e* as in *ballet*

> *ei* as in *neighbor*
> *i* as in *machine*
> *o* as in *open*
> *u* as in *super*

There are two vowel sounds we don't have in English: *ō* and *ū*. Just ignore them. My Japanese teachers would slap me on the wrist for saying that, but unless you're studying Japanese yourself, the difference between the short vowels (*o* and *u*) and the long vowels (*ō* and *ū*) is so subtle that you might not even hear it. The reason I include the long vowels in my books is that spelling errors make me squirm.

As for consonants, *g* is always a hard *g* (like *gum*, not *gym*) and almost everything else is just like you'd pronounce it in English. There's one well-known exception: Japanese people learning English often have a hard time distinguishing L's from R's. The reason for this is that there is neither an L sound nor an R sound in Japanese. The *ri* of Mariko is somewhere between *ree*, *lee*, and *dee*. The choice to Romanize with an *r* was more or less arbitrary, and it actually had more to do with Portuguese than with English. (If linguistic history had gone just a little further in that direction, this could have been a book about Marico Oxiro, not Mariko Oshiro.)

Finally, for those who want to know not just how to pronounce the Japanese words but also what they mean, you'll find a glossary toward the end of this book. If you have trouble keeping all the Japanese names straight, poke around my website (www.philosofiction.com) to find a list of characters showing who's related to whom.

BOOK ONE

HEISEI ERA, THE YEAR 22

(2010 CE)

I

Mariko would never forget where she was when she heard the news.

She wasn't all that likely to forget that afternoon anyway. It wasn't every day that she met with the top brass. She saw her commanding officer, Lieutenant Sakakibara, almost daily, but this was her first meeting with his superior, Captain Kusama. And since Sakakibara was also in attendance, things were about to get either very good or very, very bad.

There were only so many reasons a captain called one of his sergeants into his office, especially with a lieutenant in tow. She might be promoted to head up a special detail. On the other hand, they might advise her to seek a legal counsel in advance of an IAD investigation. Her partner, Han, had recently endured such an investigation, and come out the other side stripped of his detective's rank. He and Mariko worked closely together, and he'd strayed outside the lines; was she implicated too?

Maybe, but the captain was smiling when he opened the door. Kusama Shuichi was one of those men who only grew more handsome with age. His hair wasn't thinning, he paid a lot of money for his haircuts, and he kept his office and his uniform as immaculately as he kept his hair. He'd earned an office on the top floor of the Tokyo Metropolitan Police Department headquarters, with a wall of floor-to-ceiling windows overlooking the heart of the city. His desk was polished teak, twice as big as it needed to be, and empty but for his phone and a sleek black laptop. Others might have arranged the desk to face the windows, but Kusama's desk was perpendicular to them, so that both he and his visitors could admire the view. Mariko didn't miss this detail, and neither did she miss the subtext: either Kusama was unusually considerate of his visitors—or else he wanted to make sure they knew how important he was. Mariko couldn't say which.

"Detective Sergeant Oshiro," Kusama said, "Lieutenant Sakakibara, so very good of you to come. Would you like something to drink?"

"Coffee for me, nothing for her," Sakakibara said, his tone characteristically gruff. "She won't be staying long enough to get thirsty."

Mariko swallowed. Was that good or bad? With Sakakibara it was so hard to tell. A line of vertical furrows creased his bushy black eyebrows, but he always looked like that. On this particular afternoon he was especially enigmatic, because even he couldn't help but take in the view. He crossed the room in three long strides and looked out across the city he'd sworn to protect. Mariko wished she could see his reflection in the window. She was more interested in reading his face than enjoying the Tokyo skyline.

"Captain Kusama," she said, "thank you so much for putting us into your schedule at such short notice. I know you must be a busy man."

"Think nothing of it," Kusama said. "It's my duty to be available to those under my command. To be honest, I had already planned on calling you in to my office. Imagine my surprise when I came in this morning and my secretary told me you'd requested a meeting! I suppose you want to speak to me about the Jōko Daishi case, *neh*?"

Mariko gulped. "I wasn't aware you were following my work, sir."

"You? Of course. You were our media darling for a time. Oh, do relax, Sergeant. This isn't a military tribunal."

Mariko breathed a sigh of relief. "I'm glad you said

that, sir." He waved toward a chair in front of his sprawling desk and Mariko sat. "Begging your pardon, sir, but it's not easy for me to relax when it comes to Jōko Daishi. He's dangerous."

"And due for release today. I assume that's why you asked to meet with me."

"Yes, sir."

Kusama nodded. "I'm afraid what's done is done."

"Sir, you've got to do *something*. This guy isn't just an ordinary perp. Better to think of him as a cult leader."

Captain Kusama sat forward in his seat. "I think you'll want to watch your tone with me, Sergeant. I don't take orders from my subordinates." His smile soured. "I've read your reports, and frankly, I think 'cult leader' underestimates how dangerous this man is. 'Terrorist mastermind' is the description I'd have chosen—but perhaps you're aware that I was the one who orchestrated the public relations campaign that kept any mention of terrorism out of the press."

Mariko winced. She hadn't known of Kusama's involvement, but she supposed she understood the logic behind his decision. It was damn cold logic, though. Koji Makoto, known better by his self-appointed religious title, Jōko Daishi, sent a massive bomb into the Tokyo subway system. Mariko and Han spearheaded the manhunt for him, but they'd always been a step behind. Then Mariko ended up on a subway platform with Jōko Daishi's lieutenant seconds before he detonated the device. Mariko put a bullet in his brain and saved the lives of fifty-two civilians, but the department had quashed any mention of the explosives. Better for the press to report a police shooting than a major terrorist threat thwarted at the last instant.

It might have been good PR for the department, but it destroyed Mariko's reputation. She could have been the hero, but since no one knew of the bomb, instead she became the hot-blooded cop who gunned down an unarmed man. Even at the time, Mariko thought it was the right decision to quash any mention of the bomb, however much that decision stung. Now that she sat across from the man who had made that decision, she felt that sting again.

"You do understand," Kusama said, resting back in his chair, "it pained me to see you dragged through the mud like that. Even if I had no sympathy for my officers, from a public relations standpoint you were a godsend. The first woman in the department to make sergeant. The first woman to make detective. The go-getter cop with an addict for a sister, working your way up to Narcotics so you could save your family. The stories write themselves."

Now the sting jabbed Mariko in the heart, the lungs, the gut. "How do you know about my sister?"

"I know everything about you, Detective Sergeant Oshiro. Maintaining this department's good reputation is what I do for a living. It's why I got the office with the best view. It's why I wear captain's stripes, and it's why I'm concerned any time one of my officers takes a life. So yes, I know your sister has been in and out of rehab. I know you placed ninth in your division in last year's Yokohama triathlon. I know your English is flawless, and I'd hoped to use that fact to our advantage with our city's *gaijin* population. But that was before you shot Akahata Daisuke in the forehead. Bomb or no bomb, cult or no cult, that's not the way we do things here."

"Sir, it's not like I had a hell of a lot of choice—"

"Tone, Oshiro-san. This is your second warning. Watch it."

Mariko swallowed. "Yes, sir." She put her hands in her lap and balled them into fists, trying to keep them below Kusama's sightline so he couldn't see her whitening knuckles.

It didn't work. "May I see your right hand, Sergeant?"

"Sir?"

He gave a little smile as if to say, *indulge me*, and motioned toward her hand with his own. Mariko felt awkward but she had no choice: she placed her maimed right hand on the desktop.

It was still ugly to her, though she'd had a few months to get used to it. The last thing she expected was for him to reach across the desk and pull it a little closer. His skin was soft, softer than hers. That was a detail Mariko would rather not know about a commanding officer. She certainly didn't want him feeling the *kenjutsu* calluses on her tomboy hands. She didn't become a cop because she was fond of intimacy.

"I'd heard you lost your trigger finger," Kusama said, "but you've still got a little nub of it, haven't you?"

Mariko felt her ears and cheeks grow hot. "Yes, sir."

"You shot Akahata left-handed?"

"Yes, sir." Her breath fluttered in her throat.

"But when you stabbed Fuchida Shūzō, it was with the right hand, wasn't it."

It wasn't a question. The incident with Fuchida was the one that first put Mariko in the spotlight. A crazed yakuza butcher with a sword was enough to make the news by himself. So when Mariko was forced into a sword fight with Fuchida, when he maimed her hand and stabbed her through the gut, when she stabbed him through the lungs in return, when both of them flatlined and the paramedics brought Mariko back . . . well, Kusama must have been delighted. She wondered whether he was the one responsible for the headline SAMURAI SHOWDOWN, which had led every major news program for days.

Mariko, the samurai cop. Mariko, the narc with the junkie sister. Mariko, the woman in a man's world, fighting tooth and nail to get what she wanted. She could have been the crown jewel of the TMPD—a thing of beauty, in Kusama's mind, glamorizing his beloved department. But a thing of beauty was still a thing.

He released her hand and sat back in his chair. "You do understand," he said, "I had such high hopes for you. But what can I do with you now that you've killed two suspects?"

"Zero suspects," Sakakibara said. They were the first words he'd spoken since he'd entered the room.

"Excuse me?" said Kusama.

"Oshiro never once fired a shot at a suspect. She did kill two *perpetrators*. In the line of duty. Acting in both cases in self-defense and the defense of innocents."

Kusama inclined his head. "True enough. But in the public eye, there's very little difference."

In the public eye I'd still be a hero, Mariko thought, if only you made different choices about what the public eye was allowed to see. But Sakakibara had a different point to make. "Maybe not in the public eye, Captain, but in this office there ought to be a hell of a lot of difference. You want to kick her ass, you go right ahead. But do it because she gets lippy, not because she did her damn job."

Mariko wanted to jump out of her chair and give him a high five. She made a vow to discover his favorite brand of cigar and smuggle a few into one of his desk drawers.

Captain Kusama wasn't quite so enthusiastic. "Your lieutenant makes a good point," he told her. "But the fact remains: you were once of great use to me, and now you're a facial scar I have to figure out how to cover up."

"Do what you have to do," Mariko said. Seeing Kusama's hardened glare she immediately subdued her tone. She remembered her two warnings. "I beg your pardon, sir. What I meant to say is, I think my record shows I'm willing to make sacrifices for the team. If I have to take another hit to keep the department looking good, that's fine—but that's not really what I came here to talk to you about. Jōko Daishi's due to be released today, sir, and I have to ask you not to let that happen."

Kusama shrugged. "There's nothing I can do about that."

"With all due respect, sir, you're a captain in the TMPD. There's very little you can't do."

That earned her a tiny smile. "You're learning, Sergeant. Flattery will get you farther than belligerence. And you're right: I've spent a career building the right connections. I've tapped every last one of them to keep this Jōko Daishi in custody as long as possible. You might have done me the service of presuming I'd do exactly that, but you're not one to assume the best of your superiors, are you? You may think of me as a bureaucrat, but I assure you, Oshiro-san, I am a policeman first."

Mariko nodded, duly reprimanded. He shouldn't have had to remind her to respect the badge. Loyalty to the force had to count for something, even if some members of the force cared more about image than results.

Kusama gave her a chastising look, and softened it when he saw she'd gotten the point. "You said it yourself, Sergeant: this man has a cult of personality. He also runs a terrorist cell with dozens of zealots who will do whatever he asks. One of them has pled guilty to every charge your suspect is facing, and that means we have no argument to hold him without bail."

Mariko felt her face flush. She heard a ringing in her ears that threatened to drown out the world. It was just as she'd feared: Jōko Daishi wielded too much influence to stay in prison. His cult, the Divine Wind, had all the power of a yakuza clan. He had a lawyer slicker than Teflon, a network of illicit connections that probably included moles within the police department and the DA's office, and a string of volunteers who would take the fall for him no matter what the legal system threw at him. That was to say nothing of fanatics like Akahata Daisuke, who were willing to become suicide bombers at Jōko Daishi's command.

There was one last recourse Mariko could think of to keep the cult leader from reclaiming the power she'd stripped from him when she brought him down. "Sir, he has a mask," she said. "Very old, something you'd be more likely to see in a museum. He believes he gets divine power from it."

"Yes, the devil mask. I saw photos of it in his case file. You impounded it as evidence, *neh*?"

"We did. He had everything he needed to carry out the subway bombing well before we were onto him. He didn't pull the trigger on it because he was waiting for a holy day in his cult, their equivalent of New Year's, except they call this year the Year of the Demon. He stole the mask right before the celebration—and by 'celebration,' I mean bombing that subway station. That was just the beginning, sir. We've investigated every lead we have on the Divine Wind, and assuming our lab guys did their estimating right, we've seized about half of the cult's explosives."

Kusama gave an appreciative nod. "I'm impressed."

"It's not good enough, sir. Jōko Daishi intends to burn this city to the ground. He says the Divine Wind will deliver the Purging Fire. It's a holy quest for him. He believes the mask gives him divine sanction."

Kusama gave her a quizzical frown. "What's that supposed to mean?"

"He thinks he can't be killed, so long as he holds the mask."

"Ah. As I recall, you tested that theory."

Mariko could only nod in affirmation. She'd ripped Jōko Daishi off his motorcycle at a hundred kilometers an hour, yet somehow he'd walked away from it. Mariko didn't like to believe in magic, but she'd seen some things that just weren't natural. The only other word to use was supernatural.

But in this case, it didn't matter if the mask was magical. It only mattered that Jōko Daishi believed in it. "Sir, the mask is legally his property, and his lawyer is going to argue that it was material evidence only in the case we had against Jōko Daishi. Since he's got a proxy to take the fall, his lawyer is going to try to have the mask released to Jōko Daishi as soon as he gets out. Please trust me, sir: you've got to keep that mask out of his hands. He's at his most dangerous—"

"Spare your breath, Sergeant. He's already got it."

Mariko couldn't keep herself in her seat. "What?"

"I told you from the beginning: there's nothing more I can do. We released him this morning, mask and all. And don't you look at me like that. Do you think I want a terrorist loose in my city? Of course not. My hands are tied."

"With due respect, sir—"

Now Kusama was on his feet as well. "Due respect is *exactly* what you owe me, Oshiro-san, and you should count yourself lucky that I gave you two warnings to that effect already. You are insubordinate, obstinate, and now that I've met you myself, I see you're clearly prone to outbursts."

"Sir, that's just not true—"

"And now you *interrupt* me? Stand at attention, Oshiro."

Mariko snapped to attention, instantly silent. She risked a quick glance at Sakakibara, who closed his eyes and shook his head. It was a tiny movement, almost imperceptible, but it communicated massive, soul-crushing disappointment.

Kusama walked out from behind his desk, stood face-to-face with Mariko, and removed her sergeant's pin.

It hit her like a bullet in the gut. She felt like she should want to cry, like that should have been an urge to repress, but there was only a hollowness instead. He might as well have pulled out one of her lungs.

In the most casual act of cruelty, Kusama set the pin down on the edge of his desk, facing her, right where she could reach it. It reflected in the polished teak: a tiny plate of gilded copper, with a cluster of leaves in the center and triple bars on either side.

Kusama walked back around to the other side and took his seat. "Sit down," he said. "Let's talk like civilized adults."

Mariko looked over at Lieutenant Sakakibara, who still stood at the window with his arms folded across his chest. He gave her a tiny nod toward the chair. His face was as stern as ever, as inscrutable as ever; she couldn't tell whose side he was on.

She had no alternative but to drop herself back in her seat. She started to speak in her own defense, then thought better of it and shut her mouth.

"You see?" said Kusama. "You *can* behave yourself."

He shifted in his seat and adjusted his tie. So softly that she could hardly hear him, he said, "I don't care for raising my voice, Oshiro-san. It's unbecoming. So are these little tantrums of yours. I find you to be moody, temperamental, and far too aggressive for this line of work. I wouldn't be surprised if you killed those two men only after your emotions got the better of you."

And now it all comes out, Mariko thought. He's a misogynist, pure and simple. Yes, she'd blown her top with him. Yes, she shouldn't have. But if Sakakibara had been in Mariko's shoes, forced to kill in self-defense, no one would ever have called his *emotions* into question. He would have done his duty, period. And if Sakakibara had made the same argument Mariko had about Jōko Daishi, using the same words and the same tone, Kusama would never have called him moody or temperamental. Assertive, perhaps, but for men of Kusama's generation, women weren't afforded the luxury of being assertive. Their vocabulary for "assertive woman" was "bitch."

Mariko had no safe way to react. If she objected, she'd only become more of a bitch in Kusama's eyes. If she remained silent, she'd be a docile bitch who accepted her punishment. Her best option was to remove herself from the situation before she dug herself any deeper, but getting up and walking out was, once again, typical of a petulant bitch.

She squared her shoulders, sat back in her chair, and pressed her lips shut. Strong but not assertive. Her sergeant's bars stared back at her, along with their doppelganger reflected in the wood.

"You've killed two men in the line of duty," Kusama said. "So far this year, that's two more than the rest of the department combined. Now you tell me what I'm supposed to do with that."

Mariko said nothing; she only made a face as if she were thinking carefully about the question. That wasn't bitchy. In truth she only had thoughts for her stripped sergeant's tag. It was hard to believe such a little thing could be so heavy, so laden with meaning.

"Ah," he said, "so you do understand." He'd misinterpreted her silence, but Mariko wasn't going to correct him. "You've given me reason enough to put you behind a desk for the rest of your career. Don't think I won't. I can suffocate you with this job. I can make you spend your days dreaming of some prince on a white horse to marry you and whisk you away from all of this."

That was something else he'd never have said to Sakakibara. Still Mariko said nothing.

"I had such high hopes for you," Kusama went on. "It's a shame that so many people saw you shoot Akahata. If only you'd found some other solution, there might have been a better way to spin this."

"I'm backing her play on this one," Sakakibara said. "If you're facing someone packing his own bodyweight in high explosives, you don't spend a lot of time looking for 'other solutions.'"

Mariko wanted to say the same thing, though her language wouldn't have been quite so polite. She didn't care for being the damsel in distress, and Sakakibara wasn't much of a shining knight, but so long as she was banned from speaking in her own defense, it came as a great relief when he dipped his shield in front of her to ward off an attack.

"I appreciate your lieutenant's point," Kusama said. "But you understand what I mean. If only it had been your partner to shoot Akahata, all of this would have been so much easier."

Mariko nodded, though in truth the more rational choice was to strangle him. Did he think she *wanted* to be the one to take a life? She'd have been perfectly content to switch places. Even Han would have preferred it; he wasn't vexed by the moral problems that kept Mariko up at night. Besides, only blind luck had put Mariko on the scene instead of Han. Had the coin flip landed the other way, the headline would have been that Han shot first and asked questions later, and no one would ever have known that Mariko was involved. Instead it was the other way around: Han still enjoyed his anonymity, and Mariko was the one who went to sleep thinking of that gunshot echoing off the tunnel walls.

"As it stands," Kusama said, "my hands are tied. We operate within a system, Detective Oshiro, and the rules of that system are designed to protect the public without trampling anyone's civil rights. If the rules are flexible, they can't do what they were created to do. So as much as I might like to, I cannot bend the rules. It's not for lack of will; it's for lack of muscle. The rules themselves are too sturdy."

Or petrified, Mariko thought. But the truth was more complex than Kusama made it out to be. On the street, law enforcement had more to do with creative thinking than rote memorization. Even a simple traffic stop was never simple. Sometimes you let the driver off with a warning. Other times you looked for any excuse that would allow you to search the vehicle. Some drivers struck you as innocent and out of their depth; others were hiding something and both of you knew it. You might have reasonable suspicion in both cases, but that didn't make the cases the same.

In Jōkō Daishi's case, Mariko had logged a week's worth of overtime helping the DA's office dig up charges to level against him. No doubt he had followers willing to plead guilty to all of them. But there was at least one charge that left no wiggle room. "Captain, this man tried to run me down with a motorcycle. The last time I checked, that's attempted murder."

Kusama gave her a parental glare, warning her about her tone. Mariko lowered her gaze, softened her voice, and went on. "You're good police, sir. I know you're not the type to let this slide. Never mind that it was me. The guy tried to kill a *cop*. Please tell me that still means something in this town. Tell me we can hold him without bail."

Kusama shook his head. Mariko opened her mouth, but Sakakibara cut her off before she could say something to get herself suspended. "His lawyer's pushing for involuntary manslaughter," he said. "Says his client was high on psychedelics at the time. Says he didn't see you standing in front of him."

Mariko was happy to direct her frustration at someone else—someone who wouldn't threaten to strip her of her detective's rank as well. "Sir, that's bullshit."

"It sure as hell is."

"Can't we just tell the DA not to push for manslaughter? Let's call it aggravated assault and add the narcotics charge to it. He's admitting he was high at the time, *neh*?"

Sakakibara snorted in disgust. "The damn lawyer claims his client didn't take the drugs willingly. Says it was a part of a religious ceremony. The MDA was forced on him."

"So what, it's a normal part of church for these people to force-feed drugs to their priest?"

"That's the story, yeah."

Mariko wished she had a *bokken* in hand and something to smash with it. She managed to keep herself from hammer-fisting Kusama's desk, choosing to hit her own thigh instead. "So no narcotics charges, a big fat no on the attempted murder, and another prime suspect on all the terrorism and conspiracy charges?"

"Looks like it."

"And since Jōko Daishi has no record—"

"Involuntary manslaughter isn't enough to hold him without bail. Yeah."

Mariko slammed her fist on her thigh again, then remembered what Kusama would infer about her violent tendencies. That made her angry enough to want to hit something again, but this time she managed to bottle it up—barely. Swiveling to face Kusama, she said, "*Please*, Captain, you've got to do something. I'm telling you, if this guy isn't Tokyo's number one security threat, I don't know who is."

"I want you to listen to me very carefully," Kusama said, his voice low and cold. "You and I operate within a system. So does the district attorney who pressed to hold our perpetrator without bail. So does the judge who said that wasn't warranted for a suspect with no priors. He's not wrong, by the way. If it had been some kid driving drunk who almost hit you, they'd have released him on bail too."

Mariko could hardly sit still. Her rage writhed like an animal trapped inside her skin. "Sir," she said, keeping her voice as quiet and cold as Kusama's, "if the drunk kid deliberately aimed the car at me, I think we'd keep him locked up for as long as we could hold him."

"Yes. And we kept Koji-san as long as we possibly could, and then some. I'm told the bail was astronomical, but as you said, he has people willing to make extraordinary sacrifices on his behalf. He was released this morning, and his mask with him."

"Then something awful is going to happen," Mariko said, "and I hope to hell I don't have to say I told you so."

Kusama glared at her, inhaling like he was about to breathe fire. But just at that moment, his phone rang. "Please excuse me," he said. He donned a smile the way Mariko put on lipstick: it wasn't a part of him, just something he wore to make the right impression. He wore the smile in his voice too, and transformed seamlessly from pissed-off CO to genteel public relations rep. Whoever was on the other end of the phone could never guess that he was ready to eat Mariko alive.

But whatever he heard over the phone made his face go green. His eyes turned to those big, beautiful windows, as if he might catch sight of whatever it was that made him sick to his stomach.

He hung up the phone without a word. Looking at Mariko and Sakakibara, he said, "There's been an incident. Haneda Airport. We need to go."

2

At long last, Koji Makoto was reunited with his father. This time they would not easily be parted.

They sat together at a writing desk in the home of Makoto's lawyer, friend, and worshipper, Hamaya Jirō. It was a tidy desk in a tidy two-floor condominium in a high-rise Meguro apartment complex. The second floor of the condo was not supposed to exist. There was only one entrance, a stairway from below, though on the upper floor there was a false door. There were also neighbors up there who, had they been ordinary tenants, would have wondered why no one ever came or went from the apartment between them. But they were not ordinary neighbors; they were Makoto's worshippers and concubines, nuns of the Divine Wind. Neither was Hamaya's apartment ordinary. It concealed the hidden staircase that led upstairs to Makoto's sanctum sanctorum. None of this was in the building's floor plan.

The sanctuary upstairs was for worship. Since listening to his father was not worship, Makoto sat at the writing desk in the study downstairs, hunched over his notebook and scribbling furiously. His father looked at him, mute because they did not speak in words.

Makoto didn't take his time with his father for granted. Sooner or later the law would separate them, perhaps permanently. Before that happened Makoto wanted to record every last drop of wisdom. His father never commanded him, never prescribed what to do. Rather, he dared Makoto to go further, to think on a grander scale, to express the truth in ways Makoto hadn't dreamed possible. That was why they would be separated: because his father's vision was so grand. That was also why the condominium was not leased in Hamaya's name, and why it was not the only one of its kind, and why Makoto and his father never stayed at one address for more than a couple of nights: because otherwise it would be far too easy for law enforcement to track them.

There was no doubting that the law would come, for Makoto's sermon at the airport would unsettle them beyond words. Of course that was the object of the sermon. Being settled was an obstacle to their enlightenment, and Makoto's calling was to enlighten all beings. But Makoto had many more sermons to deliver before his time was up, and that meant he had to stay clear of the police, at least for a little while.

News of his sermon at the airport had already reached the television. Makoto could not watch it with the sound on, for without exception the reporters only reacted with delusion and fear. Even the wordless cameramen were deluded. They chose to film all the tear-streaked, fear-stricken faces, not the smoke rising from the hollowed terminal. Why could they not see the truth? Fright was the reaction of the undisciplined mind, the mind that wanted reality to be other than what it was. Why broadcast such a senseless emotion when they could film something like smoke? Evanescence was truth; fear of it was sickness.

Makoto had learned that long before he was reunited with his father, but he could talk about the truth with his father in a way that no one else could comprehend. Even now he wrote with all the urgency of a medic performing CPR, trying to record everything his father was telling him before it was too late. "One thousand," Makoto said. "Three hundred. Four." He scribbled the numbers in kanji, drew them in big numerals, repeated them aloud. He did not yet know what they meant.

He and his father were so dissimilar. Makoto had long, flowing hair; his father was bald. Makoto had a thick black beard; his father had no lower jaw from which to grow a beard. Makoto was a man of flesh; his father had iron skin, iron horns, iron fangs. Yet their commonalities were uncanny. Makoto was possessed of second sight; his father was clairvoyant. Makoto was the only one who could hear his father, and his father would speak to no one but Makoto.

"One thousand three hundred four," his father told him. Makoto wrote it down again. Was it an address? A date? A code? He didn't know, but he knew his father could not be rushed. Makoto would have to be patient— no easy thing, given the success of his sermon at the airport. He wanted to do more, to say more, to deliver the light and the truth to as many as could hear it. It broke his heart to see so many people in fetters. But his father spoke only when he had a mind to, so Makoto had to wait.

He heard a knock behind him, but then his father was speaking again and Makoto could not answer the door. "Rope," his father said. "Razor. Children."

"Yes, children," Makoto said, and proceeded to sketch them in his notebook.

"Daishi-sama," Hamaya Jirō said softly. "Your disciples have come to call."

"Not disciples," Makoto said. He'd seen these men coming before their arrival. His father had too.

He picked up his father and pressed him to his face. They were a perfect fit for each other. His father's rust-brown fangs nestled into Makoto's wiry beard; the interior curves of his iron cranium were precisely the size and shape of Makoto's forehead. The two of them perceived the world through the very same eyes.

Footfalls and creaking floorboards tracked the passage of a small group through the apartment. They followed Hamaya upstairs, through the meditation room, and into the small audience chamber behind it. Makoto bound his father to his face with leather thongs, then ascended the stairs, meditating on every step and every breath. He smelled warm candle wax and incense, and enjoyed the reflection of flickering flames on the serene white walls. From a closet he retrieved his vestments: a heavy yellow mantle to don over the thin white robes he already wore; a long, thick stole crosshatched yellow over white; eight beaded bracelets on his wrists. With these, Koji Makoto became Jōko Daishi, Great Teacher of the Purging Fire.

When he entered the audience chamber, he found four men waiting on their knees. As soon as Makoto stepped into view, they immediately prostrated themselves. "Praise be to Jōko Daishi," they all said.

"And may the light shine upon you. Tell me why you have come."

"We saw what you did at the airport," said one.

"It was so . . . *profound*," said another.

"We came because we want to be a part of whatever comes next," said a third.

"You are all liars," Makoto said. "Better to cut out your tongue than to lie to one who hears the voices of demons."

He stepped closer to them, his hands at heart center, his eyes downcast. He noticed an ink stain on the cuff of his white robe, and made a mental note to scrub it out before it set. His father told him all four men were armed, and showed him where they wore their pistols. "You have no faith," he told them. "Your paymasters decided I have crossed a line I ought not to have crossed. They lack vision. Now they have decided to remind me there is no place the Wind cannot reach. But who knows that better than I?"

The false acolytes exchanged glances, perhaps hoping for a cue to act. "Ah," Makoto said. "You were not told I am of the Wind? You were told, perhaps, that I do not know the Wind exists? Rest easy, my sons. I know the breast from which you suckle. I was once a cub like you. And those of the same family should not fight among themselves."

They shifted on their knees. One of them seemed relieved. The others were harder to read, but Makoto's father could read their minds. They were ready now to hear the truth.

"I have transcended the Wind," Makoto told them. "I am become the light, the brightest fire. Behold, now, the teaching of Jōko Daishi."

He kicked the first man in the face, snapping his spine, killing him instantly.

The other three reacted with the speed and assurance of pack hunters. The closest of them dove straight in, attempting a takedown, as the other two jumped to their feet. Makoto simply hopped over the man shooting the takedown, using him as a stepping-stone. With his left palm Makoto trapped the third gunman's elbow against his chest before he could completely draw his pistol.

The fourth gunman was smarter, and tried to increase the distance between his target and himself. But the audience chamber was small; there was nowhere to go. Makoto pushed the third man into the fourth, driving them into the corner.

The third gunman's right arm was still stuck in a crossbody draw, and pinned across his centerline as it was, he could not move it until Makoto let it go. The fourth gunman was trapped behind him, face mashed against the wall, unable to bring his weapon to bear.

The second gunman, the one who had attempted the takedown, looked up to see Makoto immobilizing two trained Wind assassins with only his left hand. Perhaps the man also noted Makoto's adamantine stance, perfected through decades of kung fu, tai chi, aikijujutsu . . . but no. These were young men, no older than thirty. Young men no longer had the taste for martial art. That required discipline, and that was sadly lacking in this generation. They would just as soon assassinate through one of their video games.

The second gunman gaped at him, then scrambled for his pistol. "Draw that weapon and you shall die on your knees," said Makoto. "I would rather have you sit and listen."

The two pinned men struggled, but Makoto's stance

was strong and his *ki* was stronger; their combined efforts only managed to make the beads of his bracelets rattle a bit. "Your paymasters lack vision," Makoto said, "or else they would see the wisdom in my sermon this afternoon. They lack vision, or else they would have known they cannot kill me. It is not yet my time."

He reached into the third gunman's jacket—the one who was caught in mid-draw—and relieved him of a sleek automatic pistol fitted with a long, matte black silencer. "Weapons such as this are of no use against me," he said. "I have foreseen the manner of my death. I shall die by the sword."

He buried the silencer's muzzle in the belly of the third gunman and fired three times. The assassins trapped against the wall twitched and grew still. He removed his left palm and both of them slumped to the floor.

"Do not feel ashamed," he told the only remaining gunman. "An assassin does not come into his prime until his fortieth birthday. You still have so much to learn."

His father glimpsed movement in the other room, a faint presence glowing through the very walls. Makoto's face broke out in a smile. "Oh, *very* good. You're not bunglers after all; you're a distraction."

He put a bullet in the young man's eye, and bent down to retrieve a second pistol from one of the dead assassins. A fusillade of bullets ripped through the wall where his head had been just a millisecond before.

"I told your companions already," he called. "Your weapons are of no use against me."

The newcomer was professional enough not to answer. He was also professional enough to stop shooting. He'd probably fired his first shots only as counterfire to Makoto's, and now that Makoto had stopped shooting, so had he. This one was better trained than the last four.

Makoto looked into the next room, heedless for his safety because he knew he could not die. His father would protect him. His destiny would protect him. In the mouth of the stairwell, on the far side of the meditation room, a nondescript man in nondescript clothes aimed a silenced automatic pistol at Makoto's center body mass. He did not fire—nor did he need to, or so he must have thought. There was but one way out of this room, and Makoto was three or four strides away, more than far enough for the assassin to gun him down.

"What have you done to Hamaya-san?" Makoto asked.

"He'll live," said the assassin.

"So that you can question him later?"

"Yes."

"How did you find me here?"

"There is no place the Wind cannot reach."

Makoto smiled and took a step forward. "Your bullets cannot harm me."

"We'll see."

The muzzle flashed. A sledgehammer struck Makoto in the chest, slamming him backward. He put a crater in the drywall behind him. His body wanted to fold in on itself, to fall to the ground, but Makoto would not indulge it. Pain and death were insignificant. Fear of them was powerful, but in and of themselves they were just states of being. He pressed his shoulder blades against the wall to stabilize himself, then stood up to his full height.

The assassin cocked his head and narrowed his eyes. "Body armor? You?" He smirked. "O ye of little faith." He took aim at Makoto's throat and pulled the trigger.

The shot went wide, but only because something grabbed the assassin's ankle and pulled. Hamaya. He'd recovered from whatever the assassin had done to him. It was a feeble effort—the assassin kicked his foot free almost instantly—but an instant was all Makoto needed.

The assassin fired a third round and a fourth, but Makoto got his shot off first. His assailant grunted and dropped to the floor with a bullet in his hip. The double-tap meant for Makoto's skull cracked two holes in the crown molding instead.

Makoto strode forward, firing alternately from each pistol. One shot obliterated the assassin's right hand. The next shattered his shin, where to his credit the man was reaching for a little double-barreled derringer in an ankle holster. Makoto allowed the assassin to draw his derringer, take aim, and fire.

The first bullet hit him in the belly, well off center. It felt like a white-hot knife in his gut. Makoto staggered back, then resumed his forward stride. "I told you before," he said. "I have foreseen the hour of my death. It is not yet at hand."

The assassin's eyes widened. Blood bloomed like a red poppy blossom across the belly of Makoto's white robes. It joined the first wound, which seeped through the stole and the over-robe just over his heart. "No," he grunted through gritted teeth. "No armor—"

"None. I have no need of it. You cannot kill me, for I am the light. What use are bullets against a being of light?"

The man pointed the gun at Makoto's face—at his *father*—and pulled desperately at the trigger.

The derringer's second shot was a misfire.

Makoto laid down his weapons, knelt beside the man who had just tried to kill him, and took him by the hand. With a sympathetic smile he raised the double-barreled mouth of the derringer to his lips. He kissed the muzzle as if he were planting a kiss on a baby's forehead, then laid the weapon back on its owner's chest.

The assassin stared at him in awe. One tear rolled down his cheek. Makoto nodded and smiled. The man had seen the truth.

A misfire was a dangerous thing. Sometimes they never went off. Sometimes they did, and there was no telling when. It might well have fired just as Makoto was kissing it. The bullet might *still* go off, but now it was resting on the assassin's chest, aimed at the underside of his chin. More to the point, the kiss was a tiny testament to the power of Jōko Daishi. Two bullets had struck him. Both should have been fatal. Their combined effect was to slow him a little. A third round should have killed him but simply refused to fire.

"You are rationalizing," said Makoto. "You are thinking about the caliber of your little palm pistol. You are wondering whether my priestly vestments are thick enough to serve as a bulletproof vest of sorts. *Neh*, my child? You seek reasons. Answers. These are the fetters of rationality."

The assassin shook his head. "You're insane."

"Ah. Perhaps as insane as your paymasters insist, *neh*? Perhaps I am so deranged that in my delusions I can fail to perceive even my own pain. *How*, you are asking yourself, how does he still live? But I have told you already: your bullets cannot kill me. This is not my appointed hour."

He pressed the derringer to the assassin's chest and willed heat into his hand. *Ki* began to flow. "Fear not," he said. "It comes soon, my son."

When the misfired bullet went off, it filled the narrow stairwell with thunder.

Makoto reclaimed the two silenced automatics, handed one of them to Hamaya, and helped his lawyer and worshipper descend the stairs. "We must go," he said.

Even as he said it, the condo's front door flew open. This time it was not assassins; it was the concubine-nuns of Jōko Daishi, eight of them, all dressed in diaphanous white. They flooded the room in a panic, except for one. One of them was calm.

"Daishi-sama, Daishi-sama," the women wailed, paling at the sight of his blood. They cloyed to him like iron filings to a magnet. Except for one.

She had a derringer exactly like the assassin's upstairs. The .22 Magnum round popped like a firecracker when she fired it into Hamaya's shoulder. His pistol cartwheeled across the floor. As he fell, the concubines flew into a panic. Some ran. Some shrieked and froze stiff. Some threw themselves over Makoto's body to shield him.

The traitorous woman took aim at Makoto's father.

"Your weapon cannot harm me," he said.

"I believe you," she said, and she pulled the trigger.

Makoto's world went dark. He could not hear his father's voice anymore.

3

Mariko didn't know how Tokyo International Airport came to be known simply as Haneda. She'd never actually been there, despite the fact that she'd flown in and out of the city dozens of times. She'd spent much of her childhood in Illinois, and had flown back home to see her grandparents twice a year like clockwork. But all the flights to Chicago originated out of Narita, some sixty kilometers to the northeast, so while Mariko knew Narita like the back of her hand, her first impression of Haneda was as an oily, gritty, bombed-out shell.

The centerpiece of Haneda's Terminal 2 was a rotunda of shining blue-green glass, an iconic background dressing in any number of movies and TV shows. Now every pane was blown out, leaving only a lattice of steel window frames twisted like chicken wire. It was a gaping wound four stories tall, leaking greasy black smoke into the bright blue sky. The sight of it froze the breath in her lungs. Seeing it made it real. Tears welled in her eyes, and the only reason she forced them back was that she didn't want Captain Kusama or Lieutenant Sakakibara to know she could be vulnerable.

She'd come in the same patrol car as Kusama and Sakakibara, plus four other officers crammed in cheek by jowl. By the time they arrived, it seemed every squad car in Tokyo was already there. Ambulances too, and fire engines, and private airport security vehicles, all forming a stroboscopic chaos of flickering lights. No one was directing traffic—everyone present had something more important to do—so between the emergency vehicles and the TV news vans, the road labeled DEPARTURES was so congested that Kusama's squad was frozen like an insect in amber. Mariko couldn't stand it anymore; she got out of the car and just ran the rest of the way.

As she passed by a news correspondent she overheard the woman confirming the death toll at forty. Perhaps that should have stopped Mariko in her tracks, but it didn't. There was nothing she could do to help the dead. Somewhere there were people she could help. She was going to find them and help them, and that was all there was to it.

When she finally reached the bomb site, she was surprised by what impressed itself most deeply on her mind. Streaks of blood didn't register for her—or rather, they did, but they didn't strike her as out of place. Neither did the miasma of blue diesel smoke that choked her, or the rasping background chatter of walkie-talkies. Those things were normal in her line of work.

No, what drew Mariko's attention was the abnormal. The thin layer of grit that made every footstep crunch as if on ice-encrusted snow. The bitter film clinging to the roof of her mouth—probably halon from all the exploded fire extinguishers. Here and there she saw something totally incongruous: a shoe, a can of coffee, an itinerary printed from someone's inkjet printer. These things were completely pristine, though everything around them was in ruins. How had they come to be there? Clearly they weren't thrown by the blast, or they'd be dusty, burned, blood-spattered, just like everything else. They didn't fit, yet there they were.

Her senses captured all of these details, but her mind still hadn't caught up. Her city was under attack. Someone had bombed her city. *Her* city, and now it wasn't hers anymore. It was like someone had slashed her face with a knife and now she didn't recognize herself in the mirror. Everything was familiar, yet everything was different.

She accidentally met the gaze of a wizened old man sitting silently on a suitcase, holding a wadded T-shirt to the side of his head. Blood matted his hair. On any other day, a silver-haired grandfather with a bleeding head wound would have been the sole focus of everyone in sight. Today he was just waiting where someone told him to wait.

Something about him struck Mariko as odd. She stopped where she stood, unwilling to go farther until she sorted it out, because maybe the whatever-it-was would require her attention. As Mariko stood watching him, she saw a grown woman being carried like a child, both of her legs striped with blood. She saw someone lying flat on his back with six people huddled around him—maybe family, maybe strangers. Nine or ten meters beyond him, a small horde of travelers and airline personnel had formed a sort of spontaneous rugby scrum, putting their shoulders into an ambulance whose driver had attempted to cross the terminal lobby, only to set off a fault line in the floor and get his vehicle trapped.

Mariko finally figured out what was so odd: none of these people were bystanders. The crowd that inevitably formed whenever there was a house fire or a downtown car wreck hadn't formed here. These were average civilians, not gawking but forming teams and getting down to business. That's what was strange about the old man with the head wound: he was alone, doing his part to aid in the relief work, without a mob of rubberneckers surrounding him. His part wasn't much; he only had to keep pressure on a wound. But he was doing his part.

Mariko wondered how long she'd been standing there, staring. Only a few seconds. She'd scarcely crossed the threshold into the lobby and already she felt so overwhelmed she feared she might drown. This was so much bigger than anything she'd been trained to handle. But no one had trained any of these civilians either. If they didn't have time for gawking, neither did she.

She made it two steps into the terminal when the whole world went to hell.

One moment she was on her feet. The next she was airborne, then flat on her back. Her head spun. She couldn't hear. She couldn't see. She couldn't breathe.

It took a few seconds to realize she wasn't blind. A cloud of white had enveloped her, leaving nothing else for her to see. Mariko smelled smoke and dust and blood. Another explosion. What else could it have been? It had knocked the wind out of her, and now that she was gasping for air it shoved its gritty, smoky fingers down her throat.

For a while she could concentrate on nothing other than getting her breath under control. Mercifully, the cloud began to dissipate almost immediately. By the time Mariko was breathing normally, the smoke had risen, the dust had settled, and she could see again. A ringing still flooded her ears. She felt a constant rumble, and knew instinctively that she should have been able to hear it. She couldn't. She was deaf but for a high-pitched ring cloying in her ears. Whatever it was, the rumbling pressed against her back and it was very warm.

Still punch-drunk, she tried to roll herself to her feet. Instead she fell about a meter and landed on her hands and knees. She'd thought she was lying on the ground. Now the world sorted itself out: the explosion had thrown her onto the hood of a squad car. The engine was still running; that explained the warm rumbling she'd felt. It also explained why the back of her head hurt so much: she'd left a skull-sized depression of spider-webbed glass in the squad car's windshield.

Now that she'd had a chance to register her injuries, everything else in her body spoke up. Her back was a cacophony of pain. Every muscle hurt like hell. The backs of her arms too; she guessed she'd probably performed a breakfall on the hood of the squad. The TMPD's aikido instructors would reprimand her for forgetting to tuck her chin.

Once she was on her feet the world slowed its spinning. She made her way toward the terminal, staggering across the five-meter expanse of rubble between her and the blown-out doors. Inside, the ambulance was a black, flaming skeleton of its former self. Of the people who had been pushing it, nothing recognizable remained.

A car bomb, she thought. She'd only seen images before, on the news or in gangster movies. Now, standing amid the wreckage, she recognized this for what it was: a double bombing. She'd heard of the tactic—always in some far-flung country, never in Japan, but it made sense in its own warped, sadistic way: the first explosion drew all the first responders and the second one blew them to bits. After that, everyone on-site would have to wonder if a third bomb was about to go off.

Mariko looked for the old man with the head wound. He was dead too, laid out flat and staring at the ceiling. At least he seemed to have died peacefully. Closer to the bomb, victims were hit so hard that it was impossible to tell where one body ended and the next began. The mere sight of them made Mariko throw up.

The taste of vomit was no better than the taste of halon. Mariko had the absurd thought that she could really use a drink of water to wash her mouth out. She dismissed it, ashamed of her selfishness. The ringing in her ears had subsided somewhat, and now she could hear someone screaming for help.

Mariko headed in that direction. More than once she tripped over the scattered debris. She'd left the apartment in her dress uniform this morning, nervous about her appointment with Captain Kusama but certain that she'd make her best first impression if she showed up in her Class A's. Now her jacket was torn, her slacks were bloodstained, and she hadn't the faintest idea what had become of her cap. In this environment her polished leather oxfords were about as useful as a pair of stilts.

She didn't dare go barefoot—too much broken glass for that—but she had half a mind to go rooting through all the scattered suitcases until she found a more rugged pair of shoes. Was that an absurd thought too? Or was she finally thinking practically? She couldn't say for sure.

At last she found the person who was yelling for help. He was pinned under the tangled remains of what used to be a clock tower of sorts. It was a decorative metal frame six meters high, with a clock and a big sign on top indicating the location of the security gate. The car bomb had taken out the base of the tower, and now the top half lay across the back of a man barely old enough to drink. He was on all fours, muscles quivering as they strained against the weight of the sculpture. A little girl huddled under him as if her father was her turtle shell.

The man looked up at Mariko with terror-stricken bloodshot eyes. Tears striped his cheeks. "I can get out. I can get out, but I can't—I can't—"

"You can't get your daughter out with you," Mariko said. "It's okay. I've got her."

Mariko pulled the girl out from under him, and once it was clear the man could slide himself free of the wreckage, she congratulated the girl for not leaving her daddy alone when he was in danger. "You two get out of here now," she said. "If you see anyone on the way, tell them to get clear of the building too."

The only intelligent thing to do was to follow those two outside, and then put as much distance as possible between herself and the terminal. Mariko knew Jōko Daishi's mind. A third bomb was exactly his style. But the only reason she knew his mind was that she hadn't put a bullet through it when she had the chance. Now a lot of people were dead and a lot more were injured, all because Mariko didn't have the guts to pull the trigger. If there was a third bomb, she was damn sure she'd get as many people clear of the blast as possible.

She watched these two go and saw a couple of cops on the street waving them to hurry outside. Once the man and his daughter were clear, the cops kept on waving. Finally Mariko got it through her thick skull that they were waving at *her*. It was as she suspected: everyone was worried about the possibility of another explosion.

She could see them shouting but couldn't make out the words over the ringing in her ears. Their body language was clear enough, but Mariko put a hand to one ear and shook her head, pretending she didn't understand them. Then she went deeper into the destruction, looking for anyone she could help—looking, in fact, for any way to ease her aching conscience.

4

An airport terminal was mostly wide-open spaces, but the relief effort ate them up one by one. Now there were rubble fields and there were places commandeered to serve some other function. The whole north side of the terminal had become a makeshift morgue. The body bags hadn't come yet. Unwilling to leave the dead simply lying in the dust, someone had scrounged up a few boxes of little fleece blankets, the ones the airlines gave passengers for free. Now the north end was pixelated with rectangles of red and blue, much too cheery for the gruesome reality they concealed.

Mariko hadn't been up that way in hours. There were more important things to do than stand and stare and cry. She'd been assisting paramedics, slinging debris, moving the wounded, and most recently—because she was too damn tired to do anything else—directing supplies. A steady stream of trucks now flowed in from the city, carrying everything from tarps to trauma surgeons. Since all the main roads to the airport were jam-packed, some high-ranking disaster management expert in the Self Defense Force had rerouted everything onto the airstrip and up through the departure/arrival gates. From there it was herding cats. Everything had to get to its proper place and none of it arrived in any logical order. Mariko was one of the cat-herders.

When she saw the boxes marked CORONER GRADE VINYL BAGS, she knew where they had to go. The image of all those red and blue blankets had never fully escaped her. She rolled up in one of those electric airport carts, ready to tell the guys carrying the boxes to hop aboard, and had to brake before running smack into another vehicle. She was surprised to see she recognized the driver.

"Han?"

Mariko hardly recognized her former partner. The electric cart wasn't his style, but more jarring was the regulation haircut he'd been subjected to when he was reassigned from Narcotics to general patrol. Working undercover had been the only reason he was allowed to grow his hair out and keep his sideburns in the seventies. And of course his hair wasn't just shorter; it was white now, too, as was Mariko's—as were their shoulders, the tops of their shoes, and every other horizontal surface in the blown-out terminal. Gypsum, pulverized cement, fire extinguisher propellant, cigarette ashes from the scores of relief workers, all stirred up in a bitter, chalky concatenation that billowed up with every footstep. Mariko couldn't see it in the air, but it coagulated on her skin as soon as she worked up a sweat. She'd given up trying to wash it off.

Han was wearing the same gritty mask, with a powdered wig to match. Even so, she could see how tired he was. Like hers, his mask was cracked in places. Every time he'd pinched his eyes shut to rub at them, every time he'd frowned or winced, wrinkles had formed, channeling away the sweat and dust and leaving little flesh-colored creases behind. Mariko knew she looked the same: weary and ready to crumble.

"Women drivers," he said, shaking his head in mock disgust. "Who lost his mind long enough to give you the keys to that thing?"

Mariko couldn't help but smile. Her white mask crackled in new places, and she realized this was the first time she'd smiled since arriving at Haneda. Not that there had been much cause for mirth.

"You look like hell," he said. "Wild guess: you haven't taken a break since you've been here, have you?"

"No."

"You want to grab something to eat? I hear they set up a breakfast buffet in the food court."

"Breakfast . . . ?" That didn't add up. "Han, what time is it?"

"About six."

"Six in the *morning*?" Mariko sagged in her seat. "No wonder I'm tired."

"Come on, let's eat. Someone else can get these body bags where they need to be. I've been avoiding the north end anyway."

Mariko nodded. She and Han had always thought along similar lines. That was one of the things she liked best about him.

He insisted on driving, not because he had to be the man in their relationship but because she was teetering on the brink of exhaustion. There weren't many guys in the department who treated her like just another cop, guys who could be friends without also thinking of her as a little sister or a nice piece of ass. Mariko slumped in her padded seat, grateful that she'd crossed paths with him and no one else.

At the food court, Mariko gorged herself on greasy American food, a childhood staple. Prior to that moment, she'd never fully grasped what the Americans meant by "comfort food." Then the first salty McDonald's French fry broke crisply between her teeth and something deep inside of her got permission to relax. She gobbled down an entire packet of fries before turning to anything remotely healthy. Han waited until she had a bowlful of rice in her belly before he offered the real delight: a little glass bottle of Chivas Regal. Mariko could have kissed him. "Where'd you get that?"

"Are you kidding? All the airport cops are on disaster detail. Those duty-free shops are wide open for looting."

"Seriously?" She punched him in the arm. "You could lose your badge for that!"

"Ow!" He laughed at her and rubbed where she'd punched him. "You make it too easy. I got it from a manager of one of the shops. She was just giving them away. Said it was the least she could do."

"You're an asshole, you know that?"

"Guilty as charged."

"And that manager deserves a Nobel Peace Prize. She's a humanitarian if ever there was one." Mariko took a swig. It was heaven. "When did you get out here?"

"I came as soon as I heard. Took me three hours. The whole city's on lockdown."

"You heard a death toll?"

Han closed his eyes and nodded. "By the time I got here they were saying eighty. Then ninety. Last I heard, maybe an hour ago, it was a hundred and twelve."

The number hit her like a punch in the mouth. She couldn't speak. Han's eyes pinched tight and he pressed a fist to his lips. Mariko could see he was trying not to cry. Apropos of nothing, he said, "Your mom called me."

"Huh?"

"I've still got her in my phone. From when we were partners, just in case—well, you know."

"Yeah." Mariko fished her phone out of her pocket. It was a mangled mess, probably crushed when she put her thigh into moving something heavy. She didn't even remember it happening. "She okay?"

"I guess. Worried sick. Said she heard from you around midnight but not since. I told her you were all right."

"How about you?"

"Me?" Han sniffled. "Yeah, sure, I'm fine."

He was lying. Both of them knew it, and both of them knew why. No one was fine. The whole damn city was turned upside down and Mariko felt like she was hanging on by her fingernails. The only way to hold on was to not think about what she was feeling. Han was the same way.

So he changed the subject. "They're saying two bombs."

"I know. The second one went off in my face."

"No shit?"

"Yeah."

He looked at her probingly, as if he could diagnose wounds on sight. "I'm okay," she said. "I mean, not *okay* okay. I'm beat to shit and my ears are still ringing, but that's the worst of it. I don't suppose you happened to overhear anything from the bomb squad."

"Nope. But I know what you're thinking. Hexamine."

Mariko's skin went cold. She and Han shared the same suspicion: if the Divine Wind was responsible for this attack, they'd likely have used the same explosives used by Jōko Daishi's lieutenant, Akahata. One of the key ingredients in Akahata's bomb was a chemical known as hexamine. If analysts found traces of it in the blast residue here, it would go a long way to corroborating Mariko and Han's theory. But what Mariko had never thought of before, and what now had her heart racing, was that if Akahata had managed to detonate his bomb—if Mariko hadn't stopped him a split second before he hit the trigger—that subway platform would have looked a lot like this terminal. So would Mariko. There wouldn't have been enough left of her to identify her through dental records.

The thought that she'd come so close to death—and a death as violent as this—gave her goose bumps and made her stomach lurch. Now just sitting here made her feel guilty. It was a stupid reason to cry, but only now did she find herself crying. She'd made it. A hundred and twelve people hadn't, and she had. She'd never been at serious risk here. She'd faced a far greater risk facing Akahata. That was when she should have cried. But she hadn't, and now she was, and she felt like a little girl but she couldn't help herself.

No. As soon as the thought struck her, she refused to accept it. She turned off the waterworks. "Goddamn it," she said, accidentally reverting to English. "I'm just tired. Give me another—" She switched back to Japanese. "Give me another swig of that Chivas."

It wasn't healthy, medicating herself like this, but she needed to put a little fire in her belly to keep herself from total collapse. As long as she kept working, she'd been able to suppress her exhaustion, but now that she'd stopped, she wanted nothing more than to go to sleep. If her mother had been there, she'd have said it was perfectly natural; if fourteen hours of hard labor wasn't a good excuse for a nap, nothing was. But Yamada-sensei, her late *kenjutsu* instructor, would have told her exhaustion of the body leads to clarity of the mind. He'd have reminded her that it was only when her arms were so tired she could hardly hold her sword that she learned her best technique. This was no coincidence; it was *because* she couldn't use physical strength that her technique had to be perfect.

Similarly, it was because she'd been working her ass off for fourteen hours straight that she could now sit in a Zen-like state of calm. Six o'clock in the morning, she thought. On a Wednesday. The bomb went off on a Tuesday afternoon, and notably *not* on a Sunday, the busiest flying day of the week. This attack wasn't meant to run up a body count; it was meant to deliver a message.

Akahata's attempt at bombing the subway was supposed to send the same message. And Mariko realized that if Kusama buried the Divine Wind's involvement in the Haneda bombing the same way he covered up their connection to Akahata, he'd be playing right into Jōko Daishi's hands. Mariko couldn't stand aside and let that happen.

"Han, have you seen Captain Kusama?"

"Hell, everyone's seen him. He made himself the media point man on this thing."

"Damn."

"Don't write him off. He's doing a good job. You should hear him play those reporters. For hours he had all of them saying 'explosion,' not 'bombing'—"

"Because explosions aren't necessarily attacks," Mariko said. "They can be accidental."

"Smart, *neh*? Controlling public perception from the get-go. Now he's saying 'bombing' and so are they."

"Yeah, but I'll bet you ten thousand yen he's not telling the whole truth. Has he mentioned Jōko Daishi by name?"

"No. But we've got a lot of evidence to collect before we jump to that conclusion."

Mariko gave him a stern look. "Come on. You're sure too."

"Yeah. I guess I am." One hand scratched his cheek where his sideburn used to be. "But I don't get how he could have ordered this from prison."

"He didn't have to. We let him go this morning." She told him all about her meeting with Captain Kusama, and about Jōko Daishi's release along with his mask. "Han, I think I know how he picked his targets. I need to talk to the captain—and I could use your help in explaining things to him. Every time I open my mouth around him, I just piss him off."

"You? Piss off a CO? No way."

He chuckled and offered her a hand. She didn't mind letting him help her to her feet; she was more tired than she'd ever been. So much the better, she thought. If she didn't have the emotional energy to explode at Kusama, she couldn't get herself suspended.

5

Finding Captain Kusama was easy; they just had to look for the reporters. Mariko spotted CNN and BBC in the herd now, and Deutsche Welle, and a host of other *gaijin* correspondents as well. They and their Japanese counterparts formed a tight semicircle around Kusama, out on the sidewalk just outside what used to be the main entrance to Terminal 2—Ground Zero, everyone was calling it now. There really wasn't a better name for it. Kusama had chosen his backdrop well, and not because the dramatic background would emphasize his own importance. The floodlights from the cameras killed all the shadows and made everything around him seem unnaturally white. There would be no lurid, high-contrast images of Ground Zero beaming back to all those foreign news networks. Even under attack, Japan would appear neat and orderly.

Mariko found Lieutenant Sakakibara not far from where she found Kusama, and though he and the captain had arrived in the same car, they looked like they'd come from different planets. Kusama was energetic in front of the cameras. Somehow he'd even kept his uniform immaculate. Sakakibara was as pale as a ghost, dusted head to toe just like Han and Mariko. He'd rolled up his sleeves, and red teardrops stood out all up and down his forearms. Mariko didn't ask how he'd spent the night, but whatever he'd been up to, he'd sustained dozens of tiny lacerations doing it.

He sat in the lee of a disaster management truck the National Police Agency had parked where the terminal doors used to be, a giant Mercedes Unimog painted in stripes of blue and white. Sakakibara sat on one of the big, knobby tires, elbows on his knees, his head and hands dangling toward the floor like heavy fruit from thin branches. "A little pick-me-up, sir?" Han said. He proffered a little bottle of vodka he'd stowed in his pocket.

Sakakibara unfolded himself and stood up to his full height, which was considerable. "Bribing a peace officer is a serious crime, Buzz Cut. I'm confiscating this as evidence."

Sakakibara rarely called anyone by their real names. He assigned nicknames on the fly and never bothered to explain them. The name Han was a Sakakibara creation; Han's real name was Watanabe, but just as his Han Solo hairstyle had earned him one nickname, his new regulation haircut now earned him another. Mariko wondered what Sakakibara called himself. Sonny Chiba, for his thick black hair that sat on his head like a helmet? Yao Ming, for his height? Mariko would put a vote in for Grumpy Hardass if she had a say. It was probably a good thing that she didn't.

"Hell, Frodo, you look about as good as I do," he said. It had taken Mariko a while to figure out her own moniker. The hobbit part was easy—she was short—but the nickname really turned on Mariko's missing finger.

"Thank you, sir. You sure know how to make a gal feel good about herself."

"Don't get cute. In fact, turn around and go back where you came from. I know why you're here."

"Sir?"

"You've got a pet theory about who staged this attack. You're thinking it's only a matter of time before the boys in the bomb squad come back with chemical signatures for hexamine. When they do, it'll prove you were right all along. And for some reason you got it in your little hobbit head that if His Eminence hears all of this, he'll be oh so *very* proud of you and he'll give you your sergeant's tags back."

Mariko blinked. She tried to rebut but had some trouble opening her mouth. In fact, her reaction would have been exactly the same if she were a cartoon character and a stick of cartoon dynamite blew up in her face.

"Holy shit," Han said. "Mariko, you got demoted?"

"Uh, yeah," Mariko said, finding her voice again. "Lost my temper with Kusama."

Now Han was dumbstruck. She could see the wheels working in his head. He'd lost his detective's rank during a case they'd worked together, when she served not only as his partner but also his shift sergeant. This was Japan; guilt by association was the law. For Han, the only question was why she hadn't told him already that his own misconduct had damaged her career.

"Don't worry," she said. "It had nothing to do with you—"

"And it doesn't fucking matter, even if it did," Sakakibara said, as polite as ever. "Look around, both of you. You and I are standing in a bomb crater. That means everything has changed. *Everything.* So today is not the day I lose one of my sergeants because she's got a discipline problem."

He stabbed her in the shoulder with a long, callused finger. "Don't misunderstand me, Frodo. On any other day, you'd get what you had coming. But today the TMPD needs every detail sergeant it can find, and that means that if you keep your damn mouth shut, maybe I can save your career. Understand?"

Mariko nodded and bowed. "Thank you, sir."

"And you, Buzz, I'm going to shoot for getting you reassigned to detectives again. But listen to me: if you ever stray outside the lines again, I swear to you, I'll mount you as a ramming prow on my car."

Han nodded, chastened. Losing his assignment in Narcotics was a mistake he'd always regret, and one Mariko figured he'd never recover from. Then again, she supposed it was only fair that the TMPD reshuffle the deck in the light of a major terrorist attack.

A sudden shift in background noise drew Mariko's attention. A gaggle of voices all shouted at once, their tone insistent, not inquisitive. It could only be that last burst of reporters' questions as someone called a press conference to a close.

Sakakibara caught it too. "All right, here comes His Majesty," he said. "Both of you, just shut the hell up and let me do my job."

Captain Kusama became a different man as soon as he got out of sight of the cameras. His cheerfulness and vigor were just a masquerade for the press; once he joined Sakakibara behind the big, blocky Unimog, his shoulders slumped and he breathed as if he'd just come up for air. He didn't have a word to spare for anyone until he got a cigarette in his mouth.

"Detective Oshiro," he said, eyeing her up and down. Suddenly she was self-conscious about the state of her uniform. She couldn't even guess where she'd left her jacket and cap. "You've been hard at it, haven't you?"

"Yes, sir."

"Good for you. I'll see to it that a reporter gets to you for a couple of quotes. I know just the one, a very sympathetic woman from NHK. She'll make you look good."

Mariko didn't know how to take that. All the makeup in the world couldn't make her look pretty. Then she realized Kusama only had thoughts for repairing her smeared reputation. All she could think of to say was, "Thank you, sir."

"Think nothing of it. Listen, ladies and gentlemen, I've been giving press updates every half hour all night long. These ten-minute catnaps in between aren't doing the trick anymore; I've got to find a place to sleep. Lieutenant, you look like you mean business. Let's make this brief, shall we?"

"Absolutely," Sakakibara said. "Two things, sir. First, I want Buzz Lightyear and Woody here to be reinstated at their former rank."

Kusama studied Mariko and Han with a critical eye. "If I'm not mistaken, Officer Watanabe faced an internal review board and was lucky to come away with his skin. Got a covert informant killed, as I recall."

"I did, sir," said Han.

Kusama nodded, apparently appreciative of Han's forthright confession. "And I can't see how Detective Oshiro could be any less temperamental today than she was yesterday afternoon."

"Sir, I apologize—"

Sakakibara cut her off. "They're both smart cops. We're going to want every good head we've got assigned to this Haneda detail. We'll need detectives, and we need sergeants for them to report to. It streamlines everything if you reinstate these two; they already know the job."

Kusama sighed. "All right. If I weren't this tired, I'd fight you on it, but damn you, I *am* this tired." He fished in his pocket and produced a gold-and-silver pin. Mariko's sergeant's tag. Mariko hadn't realized he'd picked it up as they'd left his office. He looked at it, resting in his soft-skinned palm, then looked up at Sakakibara. "You do understand I'm doing this against my better judgment."

"Mine too, sir. These two are a royal pain in the ass."

"*You're* the one who's answerable for their mistakes, is that clear?"

Sakakibara fixed his eyes on Han and Mariko. His glare could have melted steel. "Crystal clear. Isn't it?"

"Yes, sir," Han and Mariko said in unison.

"Done," said Kusama, stifling a yawn. "Your second item?"

"I could use an update like the ones you're giving the press," Sakakibara said. "I wouldn't say we're all in the dark about what happened, but we sure as hell aren't in the light yet, either."

Kusama craned his head to peek through the crack between the Unimog's cab and its trailer. He didn't seem to like what he saw—too many microphones, perhaps— because he motioned for his three subordinates to follow him. He led them deeper into the airport, past where the security checkpoint used to be, back among the darkened storefronts.

"We have very little to go on," he said. "I've announced early reports that Jemaah Islamiyah has claimed responsibility, and that investigations are under way to verify those reports."

"Sir," Mariko said, "begging your pardon, but this isn't the work of Islamist extremists. This was the Divine Wind."

Kusama sighed, this time out of exasperation, not exhaustion. "I wasn't aware we had any women on the bomb squad."

"And I thought we agreed that you were going to shut the hell up," Sakakibara said.

Mariko bowed, and kept her gaze fixed on her captain's feet. "Yes, sir. Sorry, sir. It's just—well, I don't need to be on the bomb squad to know how Jōko Daishi thinks."

"Aha," Kusama said. "Do enlighten us."

"Jōko Daishi means 'Great Teacher of the Purging Fire,' *neh*? This guy sees society as being impure, and he wants to burn away all our sins. He thinks comfort and stability are obstacles to enlightenment."

"I remember the file."

"Well, that's why he detonated his bombs *outside* the security gates."

"Explain," said Kusama.

"He's telling us safety is an illusion. The security screens are supposed to make flying safer, *neh*? But they don't—at least not according to Jōko Daishi. They just create a bottleneck. They give him a target."

Kusama looked at her over the top of his smoking cigarette. "Then why not bomb the checkout line at a grocery store? Isn't that a bottleneck?"

"It is, sir. But the purpose of the cashier isn't to keep us safe. Look, back in the sixties, the bottleneck was right at the airplane's door. A crowd of hundreds turns into a single file, *neh*?"

"Sure."

"So with fifty years of hindsight, fifty years of new technology, all we've managed to do is move the bottleneck. Now it's the next stage after the ticketing counter. Thousands of people on dozens of flights, all lining up nice and neat."

Kusama puffed on his cigarette. "You're saying detonating the bomb outside the security gate sent a message. It says there's no security at all."

"That's right, sir."

"Mm-hm. And why couldn't Jemaah Islamiyah or al-Qaeda send the same message?"

"They could, but they didn't. You said that you've *announced* they claimed responsibility, not that they *did*. They haven't, have they, sir? You said that just to appease those reporters."

Sakakibara growled like a bear. "Frodo, do yourself a favor—"

"It's all right, Lieutenant." Kusama waved him off. "Sergeant Oshiro, you of all people ought to understand why I haven't mentioned Jōko Daishi to the press. Tell me, did you approve of it when I did the same thing with the Divine Wind's subway bombing?"

"Yes, sir." Mariko hoped all the dust caked to her face would keep him from seeing her blush.

"Yet you were the only one to suffer the consequences. Why approve of denying the Divine Wind's involvement in that case but disapprove of it here?"

"Because the subway story could be contained. This one can't. It's too big, sir, and when the truth leaks out, Jōko Daishi will say the people can't trust their police department. His goal is to erode the pillars of our society. We're one of those pillars, sir. If we compromise ourselves, we make ourselves an easy meal."

That got Kusama's hackles up. He stepped up in her face, and since he was a good fifteen centimeters taller than she was, when he locked eyes with her he was staring down at her. "You will *not* question my loyalty to the TMPD." He waved his hand in her face as he spoke, jabbing her sergeant's badge at her like an angry schoolmaster's ruler.

Mariko cast her gaze to the floor. "Terribly sorry, sir. That wasn't my intent. It's just—"

"Frodo, goddamn it, keep your mouth shut."

"I'll have her speak her mind, Lieutenant." Kusama didn't bother looking in Sakakibara's direction; he kept his eyes fixed on Mariko. She could feel him staring holes into her head. "Sergeant, I don't care for subordinates questioning my judgment, still less when they do it in front of other officers, and especially when they don't provide a single scrap of evidence to back up their claims. Why should I believe—no, why should I even entertain the *notion* that your beloved Jōko Daishi is responsible for this attack?"

"Occam's razor and sheer optimism, sir." Mariko swallowed. "We released a terrorist mastermind from prison this morning. A few hours later, the bombs went off. So either this is Jōko Daishi's work or else we've got two mad bombers running around Tokyo, and no leads on either one of them."

"It's a little too convenient, isn't it? You're obsessed with this man. You are by your own assessment our best expert on him."

"Not just me, sir. Me and Han. Um, Watanabe, sir."

"Just so. And lo and behold, you and Officer Watanabe come to me looking to get off my shit list by claiming it was your guy who orchestrated this attack. That doesn't sound contrived to you?"

"Sir, we let him go. Against my advisement. Because I knew something like this would happen. If it's contrived, it sure as hell wasn't contrived by me."

"That's enough!" Kusama's cigarette breath hit her in the face. "Is respect a foreign concept to you? Do you even listen to the words coming out of your mouth? I've got to hand it to you, Detective: I never thought I'd demote one of my sergeants twice in twenty-four hours."

He presented her sergeant's pin to her between his thumb and forefinger, gave her a good last look at it, then dropped it on the floor and mashed it with his shoe. "Lieutenant Sakakibara, you're authorized to restore Officer Watanabe to his status as a detective. Detective

Oshiro, on the other hand, will not retake the sergeant's exam for three years. Moreover, she's not to be reassigned from Narcotics."

He snorted at Mariko. "Have no doubt, Oshiro-san: Haneda will prove to be the most important case in the history of Tokyo law enforcement. You will have no part in it. Policemen will define their careers on this case, and you will stand off to the side, with nothing but the occasional petty pot bust to feed your massive ego."

He pulled an about-face and walked off in a huff. Mariko watched him go in shock. Three years. She'd graduated from police academy at the top of her class, and professionally speaking, she'd stayed there. That would never be true again. By the time she could take the sergeant's exam again, even the most incompetent candidates would have passed her by.

She couldn't care less about how prestigious the Haneda case would be. Not that Kusama was wrong. If anything, he'd understated the case. Haneda wouldn't define a career; it would define a generation. Ten years from now, twenty years, fifty, you could ask someone where they were when they heard about Haneda and they'd be able to tell you. It was one of those moments. And Mariko knew who had plotted it. She knew more about him than anyone else in the country, and she couldn't put that to use.

Sakakibara and Han had reached the same conclusion. Han tried to shrink into himself, to pretend he hadn't heard, to be anything other than a mirror of Mariko's shame. Their lieutenant looked like a disappointed father, more disgusted than angry. "I've got to hand it to you," he said. "You got his attention, all right. So congratulations, Frodo. I didn't think it was possible, but you're actually more annoying than terrorism."

6

Mariko borrowed Han's phone before she left. Lines were tied up all over the city, so it took her nine tries to get through to her mom and her sister. Mariko kept the call short, partly out of respect for all the others who were on their ninth or tenth attempt to complete a call, but mostly because she wasn't in the mood for conversation. Her demotion had crushed her like a freight train. Just thinking of it made it hard to breathe.

So she checked in, told her family she was all right, and arranged to meet them at her mother's apartment around lunchtime. Normally the subway could get her there in less than an hour, but Mariko had no way of guessing how many trains would be running on time in the wake of the bombing. The National Police Agency might well have shut down half the city.

But they hadn't. In fact, even the monorail to Haneda was still up and running; it just stopped at Terminal 1 instead of at the terminus underneath what was now Ground Zero. When Mariko got to the train, she found it was even departing on schedule, which, she was certain, could only have happened in Japan. Only Japan Railways was fastidious enough to guarantee on-time departures even in the wake of a terrorist attack.

The train roared as it barreled through the underground tunnels, then rose out of Tokyo Bay like a Bond villain's personal monorail. Its single track skimmed over the water on broad concrete trestles, their blocky silhouettes totally at odds with the sleek, streamlined angles of the train cars. The morning sun glittered on the bay, leaving dazzling spots in Mariko's eyes.

She caught a transfer to Tokyo Station, and almost rode right past it on her way to her mother's apartment. Then she remembered she was still carrying her service weapon, which she needed to check back in to post. Not for the first time, she envied the cops on all of those American police dramas who could just carry their weapons home with them. It wasn't that she felt unsafe without a firearm. This was Tokyo, not Detroit; her little stun gun was enough. That said, she felt an overwhelming need to crash on a couch and fall asleep. Stopping in to post was one more obstacle between her and that couch.

Tokyo Station was an anachronism. From the outside it looked like a large Victorian train depot, one that would have been more at home in Trafalgar Square in the 1800s. Surrounded by state-of-the art skyscrapers, the station seemed ill at ease, as if its modern neighbors had invaded its personal space. The grand lobby was also Victorian, capped with an enormous cupola ringed with windows. Their verdigris sashes were set into frames of white, which in turn were set into butter yellow walls and bracketed by arches and relief sculptures and other flourishes Mariko didn't know the names for. But buried underneath all of this was the most advanced mass transit technology in the world. It was the birthplace of the bullet train, and to this day it remained the hub of the fastest rail network on the planet. An underground mall provided every service a passenger could ask for, including cell phone technologies that would have drawn incredulous stares even in the 1990s, and in the 1800s might have gotten the seller burned at the stake for witchcraft.

Mariko had always thought of the station as being somehow dislocated in time, occupying three centuries at once, but yesterday's attack seemed to herald a new age. Tokyo Station served nearly four hundred thousand passengers a day, so Mariko, arriving at seven thirty in the

morning, should have faced crushing rush hour conges-
tion. Instead, she could actually see the stairs straight
ahead of her. It was weird to see so few children, weirder
still that so few were in uniform. All the schools must
have closed for the day.

Mariko's thighs burned in protest as she started climb-
ing the stairs to street level. At the top of the stairs she saw
a man putting his hands on a woman who clearly wanted
no part of it. Mariko would have noticed her even without
the obnoxious asshole drawing attention. The woman
was barefoot. She wore jeans that were obviously too long
for her, rolled up several times to make fat, heavy cuffs
around the ankles. She had a man's suit jacket clutched
around her skinny frame and she held a shoulder bag to
her chest. When the guy who was groping her pulled the
bag away, Mariko could see the woman's breasts. The
woman wore a diaphanous white blouse—no, a dress,
Mariko thought. It was bunched up around her hips, as if
she'd stuffed quite a bit of fabric into the jeans. Whatever
it was, it was see-through, and the asshole grabbing her
wanted a better look.

Exhausted as she was, Mariko had trouble summoning
the little hit of adrenaline she needed to charge up the
stairs. When she was halfway there she put her cop face
on, and in her cop voice she yelled, "Hey, shithead, keep
your hands to yourself."

The guy looked down at her and smirked. Clearly he
wasn't threatened by a woman of Mariko's size, especially not when that woman looked like she'd just crawled
out of a vacuum cleaner bag. Usually Mariko's uniform
earned her instant credibility, but after a whole night of
slinging rubble, her Class A's were hardly recognizable.
Not that it mattered; the fact that he wasn't running yet
meant Mariko had a good shot at catching him, and the
fact that she'd distracted him meant he wasn't hurting the
woman he'd accosted.

What was her story? A stripper, Mariko guessed, one
who had gotten herself into trouble somehow. Maybe
she'd worn that gossamer dress on stage, and maybe she'd
gone home with some guy who wanted her to wear it in

the bedroom. If things went sour, she could have stolen his jeans before making her escape, and since strippers weren't known for wearing practical shoes, maybe in her hurry she'd chosen to leave hers behind. Some chivalrous fellow could have lent her his jacket. Or maybe none of that was true. It was all conjecture, story-building, because detective's instinct automatically had Mariko looking for possible explanations.

Whatever her story was, a woman dressed like that would have drawn funny looks even without her tits hanging out. Now, embroiled in a tug-of-war over her shoulder bag, she drew looks from everyone. "Police!" Mariko shouted, and she unholstered her little stun gun.

Now she had the man's attention. The woman seized the opportunity, ripped the bag from his grasp, and swung it at him like a tennis racket. There was something damn heavy in there, because when it hit him in the knee it buckled his leg. Then Mariko was on him. She didn't need the stun gun to control him; he dropped of his own accord when Mariko reaped his leg out from under him.

She snapped a wristlock on him and used it to roll him facedown. He struggled, but her wristlock kept his arm as stiff as a crowbar. As long as she kept a little pressure on it, he was pinned to the floor as surely as if he'd been bolted down.

"Ma'am," Mariko said, turning to face the woman he'd assaulted, "are you—?"

She looked up just in time to see the shoulder bag flying at her head.

Fortunately, Mariko was used to people swinging weapons at her face. She trained in *kenjutsu* as many nights a week as she could manage, and her current sword master, Hosokawa-sensei, was a big believer in the most traditional aspects of the art. Most modern *kenjutsu* schools had relegated sparring to their sportier cousin, *kendō*, but Hosokawa kept the old ways alive. That was awfully handy at the moment, because sword sparring involved lots of strikes to the face mask.

Mariko didn't have a blade to parry with, so she bobbed her head backward, allowing the heavy bag to swing just past her nose. The woman in white began to run. That left Mariko with a choice: she could arrest the guy she was already holding or she could pursue the woman who had just attempted to deck her.

Back in her days as a beat cop, when an assault and battery case devolved into petty he-said, she-said stuff, Mariko tended to side with the woman. Maybe that was wrong in this case. Mariko hadn't seen the encounter between these two from the beginning. Maybe he wasn't trying to get a look at her tits; maybe she'd attacked him first. Maybe he'd grabbed her bag just to keep her from hitting him.

Mariko wanted to side with her anyway, but that was before the woman took a swing at her. Legally speaking, assaulting an officer was a far more serious charge than assaulting a civilian. And now the woman was running from the law. Mariko let go of her wristlock and headed after her.

The bitch was *fast*. Mariko was a triathlete, and a damn good one at that. Then again, she'd also been up for twenty-five hours straight, and spent more than half that time doing hard labor. She was running on fumes and her shoes weren't made for sprinting. Even so, it wasn't often that a perp could outrun her. A barefoot perp shouldn't have had a snowball's chance in hell.

But this woman bounded up the next flight of stairs like a gazelle. Mariko hurtled after her, ignoring the burning pain in her legs. The woman gave her the slip, vanishing from view at the top of the stairs.

Mariko ran up there anyway, and saw two people lying on the floor, maybe ten meters apart from each other. It was a sure bet that the woman with the shoulder bag had pushed them down, leaving a simple connect-the-dots problem in her wake. Mariko dashed past the two on the floor and kept on in that direction.

She heard a cry of protest somewhere ahead. Another dot. She made for the sound and saw her quarry barreling through a herd of high schoolers. The woman sprinted up the nearest flight of stairs and Mariko gave chase.

They were on the mall level now. None of the stores

were open yet, so the barefoot woman had nothing but wide-open space to increase her lead. But she was approaching the end of her endurance. Her pace was flagging. She looked over her shoulder, saw Mariko, and ducked around the nearest corner.

Mariko rounded the corner at top speed. The woman's shoulder bag hit her right in the face.

It laid Mariko out flat. The floor cracked her in the back of the head. Her stun gun skittered across the floor like an oversized cockroach. She saw stars, and through them she could just make out her assailant. Mariko curled into a ball, not out of fear but just to shield her vitals. She reached for her pistol with her left hand, and held her right in a kickboxer's high guard, hoping to ward off the next blow to the head.

The woman reared back for another swing. Mariko lashed out with her foot as hard as she could.

Her kick landed first, blasting the woman's leg out from under her. The shoulder bag missed its target, landing with a heavy metallic clang right next to Mariko's ear. She grabbed the bag with both hands and cradled it to her chest. This thing was not going to hit her again.

The woman stood over her, got a grip on the bag, and pulled like her life depended on it. Mariko let fly with a kick and hit her square in the crotch. It was a better target on a man, but not a bad shot on a woman either. Her assailant grunted and doubled over. Mariko had a shot at grabbing her hair, her clothes, anything to bring her down, but she knew she couldn't afford to let go of the bag. Another shot to the head would be the end of her.

Mariko rolled on top of the bag, pinning it with her bodyweight and freeing her left hand to reach for her sidearm. The woman let go of the bag and ran like hell. Mariko tried to get up and pursue, but made it only as far as her knees. Dizziness and nausea sat her right back down. Her vision was full of glowing squiggles. When she pressed her palms to her eyes to clear them, her right hand came away bloody. She probed her fingertips through her short, choppy hair and found a wide gash in her scalp.

Still nauseous, she crawled to the wall and pushed herself up to a seated position. Giving up wasn't her forte, but she was too dizzy to stand and she had no way to call for backup. She had to count herself lucky that her assailant had fled instead of fighting for the bag—or worse, for the pistol at Mariko's hip. Mariko was lucky to be alive.

Once she caught her breath, the squiggles started to subside. She found herself looking at the shoulder bag in her lap. One corner was stained with blood—Mariko's—with something pointy poking up from within the fabric. Mariko opened the bag to see what it was.

A familiar mask looked up at her. It had stubby horns and sharp teeth, and someone had sliced the tip off of one of the fangs. Its iron skin was pitted with rust and age. Whoever first crafted it had a gift, for it was astonishingly expressive, its scowl as livid as any human's.

Mariko had seen this mask before, most recently on the face of Jōko Daishi. The only difference was that it now had a ragged, gleaming, rust-free dent in its forehead, almost as if someone had ricocheted a bullet off the mask.

It was impossible—or if not impossible, then downright creepy at the very least. Not twenty-four hours ago, Mariko had asked Captain Kusama to seize the mask as evidence, to keep it out of Jōko Daishi's hands. Mariko had no doubt that Jōko Daishi had taken his inspiration from it in bombing the airport. And no sooner had it fallen into Jōko Daishi's possession than he lost it again. It could have gone to anyone, yet somehow it found its way to Mariko.

In her gut Mariko didn't believe in destiny, but intellectually, she had to acknowledge that this was more than coincidence. She didn't have a name for the forces that could have put the mask in her hands. She was certain the woman she'd taken it from hadn't intended for Mariko to steal it. Mariko had a grade two concussion to prove it. But she was equally certain that she couldn't have crossed paths with the woman by accident. There were thirty-five million people in greater Tokyo, and thirty-five-million-to-one odds against this woman losing the mask only to Mariko.

No, this was no coincidence. Someone had orchestrated their encounter. The only question was who, and why.

BOOK TWO

AZUCHI-MOMOYAMA PERIOD, THE YEAR 21

(1588 CE)

7

Shichio sat in the shade of the sedan chair, stroking his iron mask as if it were a cat.

Sedan chairs were supposed to be cool. That was why the upper classes hired them: to sit at ease, out of the sun. Or out of the rain, if the fickle dragon-god Kura-okami would visit a little rain on this forsaken land. Even a few clouds would be an improvement. Let them be as miserly as an old crone's teats; at least they would bring some shade.

But no. This was Izu, and that meant hot and miserable.

As if it were not bad enough to listen to his bearers' grunting, he could also smell them. Their sweat mingled with the dust of the road—and there was no shortage of dust, that was sure. Not a month past, a typhoon had lashed the entire eastern coast, from the Kansai all the way up to Totomi and Suruga, but it had stopped just shy of Izu. It was as if the clouds themselves had the good sense to avoid this place. The only water was the ocean, whose relentless droning filled Shichio's nose with a salty tang—which, sadly, did little to mitigate the stink of the bearers.

The mask's call distracted him from all of that. Though he would have thought any distraction would be welcome, in truth the mask frightened him. Its iron brow would never sweat, though hundreds of tiny pits suggested that salt and water had been at work over the years. Its features were so lifelike that sometimes Shichio thought it might well close its eyes to sleep. How many times had he wished it would? A little respite from the mask, just one peaceful night, was that so much to ask? Even an hour would bring him greater relief than the coolest monsoon.

But would it sleep? No. So long as he touched it, it haunted him with visions of bloodshed. As soon as he broke contact, it woke a need in him that was so similar to lust that Shichio sometimes felt himself stiffen inside his robes. More than once he'd slipped his hand in there to bring himself off, hoping to satisfy his need for the mask as well. But the mask would not be sated.

So there it was, the only other passenger of the sedan chair. It rested heavily on his thigh, cool to the touch. His thumb ran back and forth, back and forth across the tips of its pointed teeth. Usually it made him think of swords, of thrusting and stabbing, of blood oozing in its soupy, sickening way. Now, though, his thoughts ran to one sword in particular, longest and loveliest of them all. Glorious Victory Unsought, forged by Master Inazuma some four hundred years before, sullied of late by a bear cub's paws. The mask never relented, not even for the space of a breath, but now it tempted him with the respite he so desperately needed. He had only to claim that sword and the demon would release him.

Never before had it gripped him so firmly. Shichio could not stay in the sedan chair a moment longer. That sword was nearby. It had to be. He had only to get out and claim it. *Now.*

Then the mask bit him.

He cried out. Before he knew it, the mask was on the floorboard and his thumb was in his mouth. That all-consuming need for the sword vanished in the space of a heartbeat.

He looked at his own blood, which welled up nauseatingly from a long gash across the pad of his thumb. Shichio could not bear the sight of blood. And now his mask was bloody too. A single red pearl clung to the fang cut short by that damnable Bear Cub. The boy's Inazuma blade had marred the mask, shearing right through solid iron. All the other teeth ended in elegant points, but ironically the pointed ones could not bite. The square-tipped tooth was the sharpest. Not for the first time, it had stolen a taste of Shichio's flesh.

The sedan chair lurched as the bearers came to a halt. A voice outside said, "General Shichio?"

"Keep going! Mind your own affairs." Who did this lout think he was? Even if his lord cried out, that was for lesser ears to ignore.

"Sir, we've arrived."

Shichio sucked the blood from his thumb and pressed the cut tightly to the first knuckle of his forefinger. Then he pushed the shade aside. Sunlight raided the shelter of the palanquin. Holding a hand up to shield his eyes, Shichio saw his sergeant kneeling before him, his head bowed so low that Shichio could see the top of his lacquered red helmet. "House Inoue," the man said.

Beyond him, beyond the column of armored men that answered to him, beyond the gray dust kicked up by their boots, loomed the gatehouse of the Inoue compound. It stood five stories tall, which in Shichio's estimation was five times taller than it needed to be. These minor daimyo were always trying to outdo one another with embellishments like this, as if architecture alone could make them as lordly as the great houses of Kyoto and Nara. In truth this tower was an eyesore—or so Shichio thought, until he saw the arrow slits ended in small, round cannoniers.

The arrow slits themselves did not surprise him. If a lord saw fit to empty his coffers building such a monstrosity, he might as well give it some degree of defensive value. But Lord Inoue had refitted these ones, boring a round aperture at the bottom of each slit—a cannonier, to accommodate the southern barbarian arquebus. The gate itself was not so equipped, but above it, arquebusiers stacked four stories high would decimate any force approaching the castle. Shichio's agents had forewarned him that this Inoue was paranoid, but Shichio hadn't expected anything so excessive as this.

No matter, Shichio thought. A man this fearful could

well imagine the consequences if he were to gun down an advisor to Toyotomi Hideyoshi. In public, Hideyoshi was the most powerful daimyo the empire had ever seen. Behind closed doors, he and Shichio were lovers. Shichio called him Hashiba, a pet name no one else was allowed to use, and he earned that right with a tongue more talented than a Gion courtesan's. Inoue would know nothing of Shichio's illicit affair with Hashiba, but he had to know Toyotomi Hideyoshi would never stand for the assassination of one of his generals. Train as many arquebuses on me as you like, Shichio thought. Pretend they will protect you. I know the truth.

He had only to clear his throat and his sergeant sprang to his feet. As Shichio stepped out of the sedan chair, the sergeant dashed to the front of the column. In a voice that would shake rain from the clouds, he bellowed, "General Shichio, emissary of the Imperial Regent and Chief Minister, the great Lord General Toyotomi no Hideyoshi, demands to see Inoue Izu-no-kami Shigekazu!"

Immediately bars went into motion inside the gate, and soon enough the heavy gates began to open. How petty, Shichio thought. Inoue had manned the gates well before Shichio's company arrived. He'd left them barred just to show everyone that he could. Shichio marched with only twenty men—well, twenty armored samurai; the four palanquin bearers hardly counted as men, though they could serve as arrow shields in a pinch. But twenty men posed no threat to a fortified compound, and Lord Inoue wanted to remind him of that.

Shichio entered the compound with his troops in lockstep behind him. Two long rows of Inoue samurai awaited him. They wore black trimmed with silver. Each man wore a banner pole on his back, and each black banner displayed the white sparrow of House Inoue. The sparrows did no flying today; the banners hung limp in the dead air.

Inoue Shigekazu, Lord Protector of Izu, was a tiny man. Like his house colors, his hair was black with thin highlights of silver. If Shichio's agents heard it true, the eight personal bodyguards at his back were all his sons. But eight bodyguards and a host of samurai were not enough to put Lord Inoue at ease. Even from this distance Shichio could see his eyes darting this way and that, as jumpy as the little sparrows that his forefathers had taken as the symbol of their house.

The nine Inoues stood under the eaves of the largest building in the compound, a sprawling two-story great hall that still seemed like a squat, flat toad compared to the towering gatehouse. Shichio approached them with a swagger, the better to put the silly little lord on his heels. He knew the Inoues outnumbered his men at least three to one, but Shichio's were battle-hardened veterans, tested by fire and steel. Izu was untouched by the wars, so Inoue's samurai were stage actors by comparison. Shichio knew that Inoue knew that too.

"General Shichio," Lord Inoue said, "to what do we owe the honor of your visit?"

"The Bear Cub," Shichio said. "Daigoro. Formerly Okuma Daigoro. Formerly Lord Protector of Izu."

"Formerly my daughter's husband." Inoue's face soured. "What of him?"

"I want his head."

That brought a twinkle to Inoue's eye. "Then let us sit down to tea. I predict a fast friendship between us."

Soon enough Inoue had water boys attending to Shichio's troops and silk-clad maidservants pouring cold *mugi-cha* for the lords. "Such a pity that you want the young man's head," Inoue said, smoothing his thin mustache. "I had my heart set on the same prize."

"Keep it, then. I'll accept that magnificent sword of his as proof of his death."

Inoue smiled and raised his cup. "A fair compromise. I have no use for swords."

"Nor of heads, I hope."

He said it with the slightest hint of sexual innuendo, to see how Inoue would react. A petty lordling might take it as a jape at his own expense. A prude might take it as an accusation of deviant practices with the dead. Shichio wanted to know what sort of man he was dealing with.

Inoue just tittered. "For *that* head I would find a use. As a chamber pot, perhaps. But speaking of swords, I must warn you, I think you do not travel with enough of your own."

His eyes flicked toward Shichio's men, who kneeled in ordered rows on the shaded veranda. They had all received bamboo cups, and skinny boys in finespun cotton moved among them carrying ladles of water. The water was backlit by the westering sun, and it caught the light quite beautifully as it spilled from ladle to cup.

Shichio followed Inoue's gaze to the gatehouse, also backlit, with more arrow slits and cannoniers facing the courtyard. From this side he could see pinholes of sunlight through some of them—some, but not all. Shichio did not think that detail was important until he saw a shifting shadow blot out one of the pinholes.

"Not enough swords," he mused. "Shall I take that as a threat? Yes, perhaps I will. How many soldiers have you hidden in that grotesque tower of yours, lurking behind those cannoniers? Tell me, is there an arquebus trained on me as we speak? Do you think your good karma will outweigh the bad if you wait until my thirsty men have drunk of your water before you gun them down?"

Again he studied the little daimyo's reaction. If House Inoue still counted the Bear Cub among its allies, now might be the moment he ordered his arquebusiers to fire. If Lord Inoue was smart enough not to bring the wrath of Toyotomi Hideyoshi on his house, he might still be in league with the Bear Cub, in which case his face might betray some sign of his repressed desire to kill Shichio and his men. At a minimum, he should exhibit some small degree of shame in threatening his guests.

But Inoue was inscrutable. "My lord, you misunderstand me. Why should I threaten you?"

"Because the Bear Cub is your son-in-law."

"Was. Now he is a vagabond. But that is why I caution you. The boy has nothing to lose. He slew fifty at the

Green Cliff, my lord. Your twenty swords are not enough."

"Fifty!" Shichio clucked his tongue as if chiding a schoolboy who did not know his sums. "I have heard that rumor. And others. His sword fells three men in a single blow. He drinks poison as other men drink *sake*. He commandeered a frigate single-handed, and now he rides the waves as a pirate king. Shall I tell you stories of dragons and *tengu* next?"

"My lord, do you mean to tell me the fifty are a myth?"

Shichio gave him a tiny smile. Inoue was the very picture of befuddlement. He had more spies than any man in Izu. Not much of an accomplishment, but still, the Green Cliff was only a few dozen *ri* from where he sat. Surely his spies could not have bollixed the tale completely. And he was well aware that Shichio should have known every detail. After all, it was *his* fifty that fell.

"Not a myth," Shichio said, "but not the whole truth. Fifty men, the whole garrison, all slaughtered in the night. That much is true. But do you honestly believe the whelp acted alone? No. He hired *shinobi* from the Kansai. Hordes of them. Even assassins of the Wind. And his retainer was with him, a shabby *rōnin* but a fell hand with a blade."

Inoue nodded. "Katsushima Goemon. I know the man. Shabby, as you say, but quick as a snake. My eyes and ears tell me the two still travel together. All the more reason for you to travel in force, my lord. It would not do for a man of your station to be cut down on the road."

Shichio sipped from his teacup to conceal his dismay. I have no station, he thought, and you know that damn well. All of my wedding guests know it.

Everything had been arranged: Shichio would marry the Bear Cub's mother, Lady Okuma Yumiko. That would give him control of House Okuma's troops, who knew the Izu Peninsula better than any of Shichio's men. They would hunt down the Bear Cub. In the meantime, Shichio—now become Lord Okuma Izu-no-kami Shichio—would lay claim to name, rank, title, and station. He would leave his peasant blood behind him for good and all.

He had no love for the samurai. In truth, the prospect of becoming one of them chafed a little. As far as Shichio was concerned, the samurai were the source of every trouble in these islands, but as Hashiba's chief quartermaster he had no choice but to serve with them. He had no patience for their disrespect, and becoming samurai himself would bring an end to that.

Instead, what followed was the most embarrassing incident of Shichio's life. He'd known in advance that Lady Okuma was quite mad. As it happened, that suited his plans perfectly. He wanted to be a lord, not a husband, and he certainly had no intention of staying in Izu. His home was in Kyoto, at Hashiba's side. But little did he imagine how deep the woman's lunacy ran. She rebuffed him to marry an infant—an *infant!*—and Shichio was left empty-handed.

Now rumors crawled across the countryside like a plague of rats. Shichio, of such lowly stock that even a madwoman would not have him. Shichio, whose betrothed cast him out of the marriage bed when she saw his cock was smaller than a newborn's. Shichio, who challenged a half-dead cripple to single combat, then fled the field the moment the cripple set his hand on his sword.

The mere thought of it flushed Shichio's ears and cheeks and made them burn. *Of course* he'd backed away. What choice did he have? Crossing swords with the Bear Cub was suicide. This was the boy who bested Mio Yasumasa—Mount Mio, as some of the men used to call him. Mio was a titan. If even he could not stand before that Inazuma blade, Shichio had no chance.

Embarrassing as they were, the stories of his wedding paled in comparison to the one the whelp had yet to let off the chain. Daigoro knew Shichio's darkest secret, the one that took place at the Battle of Komaki. That story would cause Shichio not to lose face but to lose his head. And what vexed him most was that not a single word of that rumor had reached his ears. He had no doubt that this plague of wedding gossip was just cover, deliberately released by the Bear Cub in order to mask that fatal shot. Shichio had exhausted his resources deploying additional spies to track down the rumormongers. He would prefer to have had these agents riding at his side, armed and ready to take on the Bear Cub in the event of an ambush. But no. He'd deployed them all, not to quash the wedding stories but to keep that deadliest secret from reaching the wrong ears.

Yet no one had heard a single whisper of that rumor. There were only two explanations: either all of his spies were incompetent, or else the whelp had kept the story to himself. But why would he? He had nothing left to lose. Shichio had dispatched not just spies but also mercenaries—"bear hunters," as they had come to be called—and Daigoro's best defense against them was to see Shichio dead. So why hadn't he loosed the one arrow that would put Shichio in the grave? Or if he had, why had none of Shichio's agents caught wind of it?

That was a worry for a later time. At the moment, there was Inoue's comment about Shichio's "station" to deal with. It was ingratiating and insulting at once. Shichio had no surname, as Inoue well knew. His own daughter had been front and center during Shichio's wedding fiasco. Shichio remembered her all too well: her smile had been the biggest of all when Shichio backed down. Some day soon, Shichio meant to kill her, preferably with the Bear Cub as his captive audience. But it would not do to tell her father that. Instead Shichio said, "Tell me, why should you want this boy dead? You allowed him to marry your daughter, *neh*?"

"I did. A damned cripple, and I even gave him my blessing." Those beady black eyes finally stood still, matching Shichio's gaze and glowing with a murderous light. "He got her with child, then abandoned her. He even abandoned his own name. What sort of man does that, I ask you? Now my Akiko is an Okuma, not an Inoue. There is nothing I can do about it. And no sooner did she step from my ship onto that one than the Okuma ship started to sink."

"Oh?"

"Of course! Its lady is a lunatic and its lord needs a wet nurse."

Shichio hardly needed the reminder. He'd asked his question hoping for something juicier. He'd received a report that the Okumas faced some kind of financial difficulty, but he had yet to confirm it. "How poorly run is this ship? Do you have ears within their walls?"

"Of course."

"Then I think you know what I'll ask next. Is the Bear Cub hiding there or is he not?"

"No. But you know that already, General. Your garrison still stands outside the Okuma compound."

"Yes it does, doesn't it? But you see, Lord Inoue, this puts you in a difficult position. You *are* Izu's greatest spymaster, are you not?"

Inoue's beady eyes twinkled. "I am."

"Then you know I have searched Izu from top to bottom. I've lost count of how many bear-hunting parties I've sent into the wilds. Not one of my men has laid eyes on the whelp, and there is only one place we have not yet looked: your own home."

Inoue stiffened. His eyes flitted here and there as if an assassin might pop out from any corner. "General Shichio, why would I assist the boy I hate most in the world?"

"Why indeed?" He let the question hang in the air for a moment, and let the little man wonder if Shichio meant to have his answer by tearing the compound apart. "Well, of course you wouldn't, would you? Harboring a fugitive is a crime. But then where is the Bear Cub? I have agents on every road, in every port, at every checkpoint. They swear he has not slipped them by. Have they lied to me?"

"Lied? I think not. But there is more to Izu than ports and checkpoints."

"Obviously." Shichio was not stupid. He knew the difference between the fiction illustrated on a map and the truth laid out by the land.

Inoue paled at Shichio's tone. "A thousand apologies, my lord. Suffice it to say that I have eyes and ears everywhere, and all of them are out bear hunting. If Daigoro is in Izu, my people will find him."

"And if he attempts to leave, mine will find him." Shichio smiled thinly. "I shall send you his head, along with my compliments, if you give me your word as a samurai to reciprocate."

"I swear it," Inoue said, and Shichio knew he had him. These samurai were bullies and butchers, but deadly serious when it came to their honor. They would sooner die in a duel than suffer being called a liar. "Glorious Victory is yours, as soon as I take it from the boy's dead hands."

Shichio smirked and finished his tea. "Send me the hands too."

8

If you want these hands, you can have them, Daigoro
thought.

He knelt in the dark not three paces from where Shichio sipped his tea. Only a paper wall separated them. He
had only to step through it and he could wrap his fingers
around the peacock's throat. Shichio's samurai would
leap to their lord's defense, and no doubt Inoue would sit
back and let them, but Daigoro had no doubt he could
snap a skinny peacock neck before they could take him.

His hands had regained most of their former strength.
The left was healing well; none of the cuts had festered.
The right was still stiff, but the bones had mended well
enough that he would soon be able to wield a sword without pain. And how satisfying that would be, to return
Glorious Victory Unsought to his hands. From where he
sat, he could cut the wall in half with a single blow. With
a second he could separate the peacock's head from his
shoulders. It would hardly matter if Shichio's men attacked him after that. At least he would go down fighting.

Such an easy thing, to walk three strides and take an
enemy's life. An easy thing, as easy as grasping the moon.

Even if he could hold his *ōdachi*, he stood a better
chance against Shichio unarmed. His Inazuma blade
promised glorious victory, but only to those who did not
seek it. And what would be more glorious than to cut

down his most hated foe in the face of the father-in-law who would gladly sell him to the enemy? That would be a victory beyond price, and for that reason his sword would never let him claim it.

Yet the very thought of it made his heart race. He shifted silently where he knelt, rising from a *seiza* position to curl his toes under, pressing the balls of his feet to the floor. In *iaidō* this kneeling posture was a ready stance, and Daigoro started to invent scenarios in which he might be able to pounce. Lord Inoue knew he was hiding behind the *shoji*. In fact, he was the one to propose this dark little alcove as the perfect place to eavesdrop. What if he betrayed Daigoro's position? He'd promised he wouldn't—promised his daughter he wouldn't, which meant a great deal more than anything he could swear to Daigoro—but Inoue Shigekazu was no true samurai. By birthright he was entitled to the twin swords and topknot, but he did not live by the *bushidō* code. Neither had his father before him, and neither did his sons.

It was his daughter who stayed Daigoro's hand. He felt her feather-soft palm alight on his forearm, and when he turned to look at her, she pressed her other palm to her belly. She was the love of his life. As of six weeks ago they had been husband and wife, but Shichio's treachery forced Daigoro to surrender his love and lands. He'd signed a pact with Shichio, renouncing his name as an Okuma, and that meant the baby in Akiko's belly was now a bastard. Aki didn't see it that way; in fact, she'd put her fists on her hips and insisted that she wouldn't consider herself divorced until her husband cast her bodily out of the house. "That's what the law permits, and that's what I demand," she'd said. But Daigoro would stand by the pact; to do otherwise would be to break his word, and *bushidō* would not allow him that. He had every intention to wed her again, but he could not do that so long as Shichio lived.

Akiko put a finger to her lips and Daigoro realized he could hear his own breathing. The thought of avenging himself on Shichio had distracted him, but now he brought breath and heartbeat back under control. He listened as his erstwhile father-in-law exchanged final pleasantries with the peacock, and restrained his sigh of relief until he heard the Toyotomi company depart.

As soon as the great gate groaned shut behind them, Inoue Shigekazu ripped the *shoji* aside. Daigoro and Akiko blinked in the sudden sunlight. "There," Lord Inoue said. "I've lied to the crown. Does that satisfy you?"

"Not by half," Daigoro said. "It would satisfy me if you gave your arquebusiers the order to fire before the peacock gets out of range."

"I told you, boy, I will not invoke the wrath of the mightiest warlord in the land. Filling one of his generals with leaden balls would be the swiftest way to do that."

"His name is Daigoro, not 'boy,'" Aki said. "He made good on his promise to you, Father. He had his opportunity to kill his enemy and he let it pass. Now promise me again: you will not reach out to Shichio."

Inoue's beady black eyes darted from her to Daigoro and from Daigoro to the gate. "I won't."

"Swear it."

He glowered at Daigoro. "He is the father of my grandchild, Akiko. Kin of my kin, whether I like it or not. You need no oath from me."

Akiko's mouth became a flat, colorless line. She planted her fists on her hips and her eyes narrowed. Anger tended to raise little wrinkles on the bridge of her nose. Daigoro could never admit this to her, but he found it adorable.

Her father did not. He buckled physically, as if someone had dropped a yoke on his shoulders. With a long, exasperated intake of breath he said, "I swear to you, daughter of mine, I will not betray your faithless husband to General Shichio. Nor will I lend my aid to any of the countless hunters who seek to bring him to justice—which, I might add, they are right to do, since he is a known fugitive."

Daigoro gave him an anemic smile. Thank you for reminding me, he wanted to say. I'd almost forgotten the price on my head.

"Nor will I harbor him any longer," Inoue said. "Be-

lieve me, boy, I meant what I told the general. If not for
my promise to my daughter, I would sell your sword for a
song and keep your skull as a pot to shit in. If she should
miscarry my grandchild, or if any accident should befall
her, I will be the first to send messengers to General Shichio. Do we understand each other?"

"It's not a subtle point you're making."

"Then get my daughter to her home. Until I can talk
your lunatic mother into marrying my daughter to a better man, Akiko belongs behind Okuma walls."

She does, Daigoro thought; she belongs in the only
place on this earth where I am legally forbidden to stay.
That was the condition that allowed him to keep Shichio
from driving the entire Okuma compound into the sea.
The only way he could protect his family was to renounce
them, formally surrendering not just his title but his very
name. Okuma Daigoro was no more; only Daigoro remained, a *rōnin* and a wanted man.

But here he was unwanted. He gave Lord Inoue a curt
bow, then limped with Akiko onto the veranda. It was hot
in the sun, and Izu's drought showed no signs of relenting.
Aki had no tolerance for it—she overheated so easily now
that she was pregnant—but Daigoro took it as a gift. Wet
trails aided the hunter, not the hunted, and Daigoro's
hobbling gait left distinctive footprints. "My lord," he
called back, "may we stay until after sunset? Your daughter is not fond of riding in this heat."

The old bastard actually had to think about it. "Very
well," he said at last. "I suppose you'll be wanting something to eat too. Akiko may dine with me. You and your
man will eat at the servants' table."

Your man was Katsushima Goemon, who was just
emerging from the towering gatehouse. He was not yet
fifty, but his hair had grayed and long years of traveling
the countryside as a *rōnin* had wrinkled his sun-browned
face before its time. Sitting still, Katsushima might have
passed for sixty-some years, not forty-some. But those
who saw him move beheld a tiger in human form. Quiet,
surefooted, inhumanly fast, Katsushima was the victor of
more than fifty duels. He attributed his success to pa-

tience, a virtue he was forever trying to instill in Daigoro. Daigoro figured patience probably came much more easily to a man whose sword was quicker than thought.

Katsushima strode toward Daigoro with a stern look clouding his face. He carried a great bow and a single arrow in his hand. "I couldn't do it," he said.

"Couldn't do what?" Daigoro asked.

"It was that damned palanquin. Once he was inside, I never had a clean shot."

Aki gasped and rushed to Daigoro's side. Shocked as she was, she still managed to keep her voice at a whisper. "Buddhas have mercy! You didn't plan to shoot Shichio, did you?"

Katsushima frowned at her in exactly the same way he would regard a talking butterfly. "Why on earth not?"

"This is my father's land!"

"And your father prefers tiny leaden balls to arrows. Everyone knows that. No one would lay the blame at his doorstep."

"Your target was *on* his doorstep!"

Katsushima shrugged. "An errant shot. Loosed while pheasant hunting. Or peacock hunting, as the case may be."

He smiled at his own witticism. Aki did not reply in kind. Keeping her voice at a whisper only made her sound angrier. "Daigoro made a vow to my father—"

"And my name is not Daigoro, as you may have noticed. Nor is it Okuma. My quarrel with Shichio is my own."

Aki fumed like a volcano. She balled her fists as if she were actually going to strike him. That would have been a grievous mistake. Katsushima entertained her outbursts because he seemed to find them amusing. Being punched by a teenage girl would not amuse him. He was not above striking a woman—few men were—and he rode with Daigoro as a friend, not a retainer. Akiko may have been mother to the heir of House Okuma, but Katsushima had never sworn loyalty under an Okuma banner. He certainly had no fear of Aki's father, nor of any other man whose idea of battle was hiding in a tower and pouring black powder down a metal tube.

But Aki was highborn. Perhaps she should have feared a dusty itinerant *rōnin*, but she didn't have it in her nature. "You will take that look off your face."

"Aki, please," Daigoro said, taking both of her hands in his own. When she would not turn to face him, he stepped between her and Katsushima. "I have few friends left in this world. I would not have them fight. In any case, Goemon never loosed his arrow. No harm done, *neh*?"

"Neh," Katsushima grunted. "And we're not likely to see a better opportunity, Daigoro. He's getting wiser, hiding in that sedan chair instead of traveling ahorse. That troubles me."

"It troubles me more that my former father-in-law advised him to double his bodyguard." Daigoro ran his palm over his scalp. He had a field of short bristles where he once shaved his head in the manner of a samurai. He did not have the heart to snip off his topknot entirely, but he could not bring himself to shave his pate every morning. That was an Okuma's birthright, not Daigoro the *rōnin*'s. "But the peacock did bristle at that, didn't he?"

The anger seeped out of Akiko's face. She enjoyed seeing her husband being clever. "What are you thinking?"

"He has men enough," Daigoro said. "He told your father he's got eyes watching every port, every crossroads. That's a lot of eyes, *neh*? So he *could* double his bodyguard, or even triple it. Instead he protects himself from me by hiding in a sedan chair, and he sends his men out far and wide. Why?"

"Not to find you?"

"I don't think so, Aki. That sedan chair . . . it must be stifling in there, *neh*? He's a princess; he'd ride in comfort if he could."

"He'd lie on silken pillows sucking Hideyoshi's cock if he could."

Daigoro gaped, shocked at his wife's tongue. Katsushima barked a laugh. "Now I see why you like this woman."

"Well?" Aki's smile was at once gleeful and guilty, devilish and demure. "What's a girl to do if her father commands more spies than any clan in Izu? Is it so bad if I harvested a few for myself? Sometimes I hear things."

Daigoro still gaped. "Things about the regent's cock?"

"You take what fish swim into your net." It was almost an apology, almost a boast. She gave him that smile again.

"I suppose you do. . . ." Daigoro wiped a trickle of sweat from his stubbly scalp. It was hot in the sun, far too hot for a preening sophisticate to box himself in a sedan chair. Shichio would not travel that way unless he saw no other choice. So he feared Daigoro enough to shield himself from arrows, but something else scared him more—something greater than a physical attack. Whatever it was, it required dozens of men scattered all over Izu, men who could have served as bodyguards instead. "The wedding stories!" Daigoro said. "He's more worried about containing them than he is of a chance encounter with me."

Katsushima gave Aki an appraising look. "I take it back," he told Daigoro. "*Now* I see why you like this one. You were right to deploy those rumors, girl. That was well played."

Akiko answered with a self-satisfied squint and chose not to correct him for calling her *girl*. Turning to Daigoro, she said, "You see? Statesmanship, not swordsmanship. That's the only way to win this battle."

Statesmanship wasn't the word Daigoro would have chosen to describe Aki's tactics. *Ignoble* was the first that came to mind. The only path he understood was his father's path, the path of *bushidō*. Aki's father followed the path of skullduggery, and that way ran through unfamiliar territory. Daigoro would never have thought to order the men of his house to spread gossip in taverns and gambling halls. That was exactly what Aki had asked of her many brothers. Katsushima had been only too eager to help. He plotted a circuit from one pleasure house to the next, and in each one he dropped a few silver coins in the hands of the right whore. Through them, the tales of Shichio's wedding would swell from whispered rumor to common knowledge—and if Katsushima happened to engage in a little pillowing after his scandal-mongering, such were the rewards of a job well done.

Now Aki's strategy had paid off. It was already known that Shichio had deployed his *shinobi* far and wide. That much was clear even before Shichio set foot on Izu's shores. Their original purpose was simple: kill the Bear Cub. But of late they had changed tactics from hunting to trapping: where once they rode abroad, now they lay in wait. Bear traps on every road, in every port, at every checkpoint, if Shichio's boasts were true. Daigoro was not so foolish as to take him at his word, but this much was clear: the peacock used to ride in force, but now he took shelter in a wooden box and halved his personal guard. Once he dispatched hunting parties of his own, but now he sought to recruit Inoue Shigekazu to do his hunting for him. He was stretched thin.

There was one explanation: his *shinobi* had reported back to him with whispers of Akiko's wedding stories. The fact that he'd reacted so swiftly could mean only one thing: he saw them as a threat—a dire threat, one worth the loss of twenty personal guards, if that meant twenty more men stationed in Izu's taverns and common rooms. Anywhere men talked, Shichio needed ears.

"But why?" Daigoro said, thinking aloud. "What is he afraid of?"

"Losing face," said Aki. "No man wants his cock compared to an infant's."

"This one isn't a man," Katsushima said. "He tried to marry Daigoro's mother so he could take *her* name. And now you tell us he services Hideyoshi with his mouth? That's boy's work. Women's work. A man gives, he doesn't receive."

Akiko harrumphed. "And to think you haven't found a nice woman to settle down with."

"I've women enough. Even a nice one now and again. It's the settling down that bothers me."

Daigoro barely registered the exchange. His thoughts were still wrapped up in Shichio. Katsushima was right: if quashing these rumors were merely a matter of saving face, Shichio wouldn't bother. Shame might trouble him, but not dishonor. He had no honor to speak of. This was something else.

"He's competing with someone." Again he spoke aloud without meaning to. "He must be. He's lost his monopoly on Hideyoshi's attention. Now he worries who else Hideyoshi might listen to."

Aki and Katsushima stopped their squabbling. Daigoro let them watch him in silence while he took a moment to think things through. "Aki, you never saw him with General Mio—"

"Oh, he was that giant fellow, wasn't he?" She made a nauseated face. "Didn't you cut his ear off?"

"I did." In a fair fight, Daigoro thought. We shared a meal together afterward, and toasted each other with *sake* and whisky. Then Shichio tied him down and cut him to pieces. "You should have seen how the two of them spoke to Hideyoshi. They were yin and yang. Mio sat before him and spoke his mind. Shichio sat to one side and whispered in his ear. Mio spoke from the heart and never shied from the truth. But Shichio . . . I hardly know how to describe it. He doesn't say what Hideyoshi wants to hear; he makes Hideyoshi want to hear what he's saying."

"I remember," Katsushima said. "It verged on witchcraft."

"That's why he thinks nothing of besmirching his name," Daigoro said. "Whatever ill you say of him, he can twist it, so long as he can whisper into Hideyoshi's ear. But now there must be someone else whispering, someone whose witchery is strong enough to dispel Shichio's. He protects his name now because he must. This new advisor . . . I don't know who he is, but I think there must be *someone*, and I think he scares Shichio more than I do."

"Then let us make an ally," Akiko said. "We have held back our deadliest arrow. I say we let it fly."

A thrill rippled up Daigoro's spine. He could see Katsushima felt it too; the *rōnin's* fist closed tighter around his bow and arrow, as if seizing victory itself. Both of them were eager to loose this shot.

Daigoro knew the true story behind Hideyoshi's most ignominious defeat. The Battle of Komaki was four years gone, and Hideyoshi had won grand victories since then, but this one rout still loomed large in his memory. He had dared to test his might against Tokugawa Ieyasu, the only other warlord of his stature. Tokugawa had left Mikawa, his beloved homeland, undefended. At Shichio's urging, Hideyoshi made a bid for it. But a little-known samurai named Okuma Tetsurō anticipated the sally. Hideyoshi's vanguard thought to pounce on sleeping deer but found a pack of wolves instead. Routed, they sought another way around; it was Shichio's duty to find a vulnerability. He failed, not because Mikawa was impregnable but because Okuma predicted his movements, captured his scouts, replaced them with men of his own, and sent back false intelligence to Shichio. Shichio fell for the ruse and Hideyoshi ran home with his tail between his legs.

The tale had become one of Daigoro's favorite stories about his father. That battle was the last time Hideyoshi had taken the field against Tokugawa. Had he carried the day, there was no doubt that Hideyoshi would be not just the empire's mightiest warlord, but rather its uncontested ruler. If the general who cost him that victory had been samurai, he would have confessed his failure to his lord, then committed seppuku to erase his shame. But Shichio was a craven with no sense of honor. He lied to Hideyoshi from the beginning, and now, four years later, the regent still had not heard the truth. But Daigoro knew the true story, and he wanted nothing more than to write it in a message, tie it to an arrow, and sink that arrow right through Shichio's heart.

And for that reason, he was suddenly unsure. "Wait," he said. "Goemon, until now you've counseled patience. What changed?"

The bushy-haired *rōnin* nodded with approval. "A good question. You tell me: why did the old abbot on the mountain warn you against telling Hideyoshi the truth straightaway?"

Daigoro closed his eyes, trying to remember it word for word. He liked the abbot of Kattō-ji. His bald head and wizened face always made Daigoro think of a sea turtle—an ancient one, a great-grandfather of the ocean, possessed of a buddha's wisdom. The old man could be as aggravating as a pebble in a boot, but his advice was always sound. He was the one who first told Daigoro of his father and the Battle of Komaki. "'*Shichio manipulates men as deftly as a potter shapes clay,*'" Daigoro said. "As soon as I tell Hideyoshi the truth, I'll also have revealed that it was my father who bested him that day."

"Not bested," Katsushima said. "Duped. The difference between those two is the difference between having never heard of Shichio and having Shichio as your worst enemy."

"I am the last person you need to remind of that. So what changed? Why should I loose this arrow now, when before you advised me to stay my hand?"

"Have I changed my counsel? No. Your wife tells you to put this arrow to the string. I say that is good advice— *if* you are right about this new enemy in Hideyoshi's court. If Shichio has a rival there, someone who can wring the truth out of his lies, then arm this person with every weapon you can give him. Let him be the one to destroy Shichio."

Akiko gave Katsushima a startled look. "I thought you would tell my husband to claim his vengeance himself."

"Against a man, yes. Against a viper, no. Better to stand back and let someone else stomp the life out of it. Less chance of getting bitten that way."

Katsushima looked at the bow and arrow in his hand, then held them out to Daigoro. "She's right about this much: you have one shot. How certain are you that this new rival has come to call on Shichio?"

Daigoro only had to think about it for a moment. "It's the only explanation that makes sense."

"Then do not miss." He bowed as Daigoro took the bow from him, followed by the arrow. Then he headed for the stables.

That left Daigoro alone with his beloved. The sun was still hot, so Aki took him by the hand and drew him into the shadow of the gatehouse. For the thousandth time he wondered why she even consented to hold his hand. His fingers were calloused and scarred; hers were as soft as chrysanthemum petals. Her father had once hoped to marry her to one of the great lords of Kyoto. Instead she was the abandoned wife of a penniless cripple. Theirs was an arranged marriage, but they had quickly fallen in love. Daigoro had no idea what she saw in him.

"It does, doesn't it?" he asked her. "Make sense, I mean."

Akiko smiled sweetly. "It might. We could be certain if we knew the regent was expecting a new visitor. Someone of high station, of course. Better still if we knew this person had vested interests that were at odds with Shichio's."

"Aki, what haven't you told me?"

She pressed her lips together and refused to speak. Her eyes glittered giddily.

"Aki?"

"There's been a bird. I overheard my father talking with his pigeon keeper this afternoon."

"And?"

"Nene, Lady in the North. Hideyoshi's wife. She arrived yesterday. Rumor has it she's come to rid herself of Shichio once and for all."

9

The sun was setting much too fast for Shichio's liking. He had no love of traveling by night. Not in Izu, not so long as the Bear Cub was unaccounted for. His sedan chair was safe, but by the gods, it was *slow*.

He slid back one of the side panels and barked at the headman of the bearers. "Hurry, damn you! I'll have your skins if we don't make camp by nightfall."

Cool air and the scent of juniper washed over him. He could still taste the salt on the air, but at this altitude the tang of the sea wasn't so strong. The view from here was breathtaking. Far below him, where the northern slope of Mount Daruma ran down to the shore of Suruga Bay, the water had taken on a lavender hue. Beyond the bay loomed the ghost of Mount Fuji, purple like the sky beyond it, all but invisible. To the west, an orange sun fell swiftly toward the waves.

For that instant, Shichio regretted his grudge against Hashiba for setting camp in such an inconvenient spot. Shichio's company had reached the wharf ages ago, only to find the fleet at sea. Even now he could see the turtle ships. They seemed to be ablaze, their interlocking metal shields reflecting the sunset like a hundred bonfires. Beyond them lay the flagship, *Nippon Maru*, so huge that it looked like an island castle in the middle of the bay. When Shichio demanded a launch to be sent at once, the garrison sergeant in the harbor pointed up at Mount Daruma and told him the regent would receive him at camp. That sent Shichio into a rage, and the sergeant had a bloody mouth to show for it. But now, for a fleeting moment, he had to admit the landscape was quite beautiful.

Even so, he still wondered whether he ought to turn the procession around and march straight back down to the bay. It was safe by the water. Shichio could have commandeered the harbormaster's home and set a guard. For that matter, he could have boarded the flagship alone and waited for Hashiba to come to him. Hashiba wouldn't be pleased, but suffering his wrath was better than feeling the Bear Cub's sword biting through his flesh. Somehow the whelp still remained unseen. It followed that he could not be traveling by road or by sea, and that only left hiking overland—possibly on a darkening mountain slope just like the north face of Mount Daruma.

Three days earlier, when he'd sat down to tea with Inoue Shigekazu, Shichio had blown and blustered about the Bear Cub, insisting that all the tales of the boy's prowess were grossly exaggerated. The truth was that even the wildest exaggerations weren't far wrong. In the month since his wedding disaster, Shichio had steadily gathered all the facts. There had never been a creeping horde of ninja at the Green Cliff, as he'd told Inoue. Daigoro had no more than one *shinobi* in his employ. Together, the two of them had overpowered the night watch of a naval frigate—all armed men, trained well in their duties. There hadn't been any need for the fools to *defeat* the Bear Cub; they had only to live long enough to sound a horn. But the Bear Cub could move invisibly at will.

An entire warship, stolen. Not a word raised in warning. The same ship broke Shichio's blockade. Not a single spyglass saw it happen. From there the whelp and his *shinobi* went on to cut down fifty men at the Green Cliff. Some survivors said the boy's tattered, gray-haired *rōnin* fought as well. Others swore they watched arrows and musket balls shatter against the boy's skin. All agreed that "Bear Cub" was the most misleading epithet ever given. "Demon Spawn" was closer to the mark.

And now here was Shichio, surrounded by twenty samurai and whispering to himself, "Only twenty." When he finally spied Hashiba's encampment, the sight was like air to a drowning man. He wished he were sitting in a saddle, not a sedan chair. He'd have whipped his horse like a courser in the final stretch, galloping for the safety of camp.

The camp was a series of fabric walls suspended on taut lines from tall poles. Some were white, others red, others gold. All were emblazoned with the kiri blossom of Toyotomi Hideyoshi. The longest walls formed large, four-sided enclosures, and at this hour many of them glowed as if foxfires were trapped within. Shichio could smell wood smoke from the cook fires, and got a whiff now and then of succulent pork or sizzling fish. There were the other smells of camp too: horse dung, rice steam, sprays of tansy to ward off mosquitoes.

Hashiba's enclosure was the largest of them all, closest to the center. By their very nature the long fabric walls tended to form ad hoc roads, and that made the palanquin impractical. Corners were tight, and there would be no straight path to Hashiba's side. The camp always came into being organically, with no preordained design. Hashiba was in the center because he was always in the center. His high command staked out claims next to his. After that, the various platoons settled in more or less at random. There was no disarray; this was a military encampment, after all. Every corner was a precise right angle and every guy was tied with a perfect tent-line hitch. It was perfectly orderly; there just wasn't any logic to it. But there would be no Bear Cub here, so Shichio stepped out of his palanquin and into the cooler evening air.

He wended his way through the maze, greeting officers when he recognized them and paying the common men no mind. Hashiba's enclosure was at least ten *jō* on a side, large enough to practice mounted archery—which was precisely what Hashiba had been up to, judging by the wide rings of hoofprints and the target posts at their center. There wasn't a drop of warrior's blood in Hashiba's body, but ever since the emperor bestowed on him the right to wear the topknot and *daishō*, he did enjoy playing at being samurai.

He'd called for a high tower to be built along the back wall. That must have been a colossal task for the carpenters, given that there wasn't a tall, straight tree trunk anywhere on the mountain. Shichio guessed the uprights were spare masts plundered from the fleet in the bay. He could also guess at the tower's purpose. Hashiba always preferred to look at the world from high above, as much for the quiet as the feeling of lordship. This tower would afford him a majestic view of the sunset on the bay, and of the stars when they came out in their fullness.

Shichio brushed aside a fold of canvas and slipped into Hashiba's enclosure. Even as he entered, he heard Hashiba coming down from the viewing deck. He was speaking to someone, too softly for Shichio to make out the words. In the failing light he couldn't see Hashiba either; attendants had erected two bright fires on either end of the square, which left spots in Shichio's vision.

"Shichio-san," said a voice from above. "Your timing is most fortunate. We were just speaking of you."

Shichio's heart sank into his stomach. He knew that light, lilting voice. Now he had no choice but to kneel in the dust and bow. "Nene-dono. I wasn't told you had come."

"I have been away from my husband for long enough," said Nene, Lady in the North, first and foremost of Hashiba's wives. She wore orange and gold tonight, lavishly embroidered with crisscrossing cedar leaves. The train of her kimono was half as long as she was tall, and the cuffs of her sleeves hung down to her knees. Long black hair spilled down her back, with two neat tails draped over her collarbones and hanging down to the tips of her breasts. Her lips were painted black, her face white, with two black dots halfway up her forehead to symbolize the eyebrows she'd shaved away.

Nene walked with her hands tucked inside her voluminous sleeves, not arm in arm as Hashiba often walked with his wives and concubines. The regent had never been shy of physical contact, but he and Nene maintained quite a chaste relationship. She had provided him no sons—no children at all, in fact—but more than this, Hashiba seemed to think of her like an elder sister. She was ten years his junior, but from the beginning of their marriage, she had been his confidante and political advisor. It was absurd. No other warlord in the land would allow his wife to dictate policy.

In truth Nene *dictated* nothing. She had nothing to do with his military council, but in his political dealings she had been a central figure for as long as Shichio had known him. Even Oda Nobunaga had held her in great esteem. For that matter, Shichio had to admit that he himself gave her respect in his own way. She was his only worthy adversary. She was the reason he'd first seduced Hashiba into sailing to Izu instead of riding up the Tokaidō. Nene had no stomach for sea travel, and avoided ships at all costs.

"Come on, get up," Hashiba said. "Let's have a seat. We've got things to talk about."

As if by magic, attendants appeared out of the deepening shadows. They arrayed three folding stools near one of the fires, and Hashiba sat in the center. It did not slip by Shichio that Nene sat at Hashiba's right hand.

No, he thought, not Hashiba. That had been his name when Shichio first met him, and so Shichio had called him ever since. But in the company of others, Hashiba became the great Lord General Toyotomi no Hideyoshi, Chief Minister and Imperial Regent. Shichio must speak to him as his lord, not his equal. That too separated him from Nene. She had always spoken to him like a sister. He was still a powerful man, and she accorded him that respect, but she was allowed a degree of familiarity that Shichio could only express when he and Hashiba—no, Toyotomi-dono—were alone.

By the time Shichio sat, servants were already on their way with *sake* and tea and cold soba noodles to whet the appetite. "Shichio, tell me," the regent said, "did you see the sunset?"

"I did, Toyotomi-dono."

"Beautiful, *neh*?"

"It was, Toyotomi-dono."

"Good. Let it be the last one. We're going back to Kyoto."

Shichio bristled but could not let it show. It was true that Hashiba bored easily—bored as easily as a child, in fact—but this idea sounded like Nene's, not his.

"My lord, the Bear Cub—"

"Grew tiresome long ago. Don't mistake me: that wedding of yours was the best entertainment I've had all year. Oh, take that look off your face. You'd see the humor in it too, if only you didn't take that boy and his monk so damned seriously. We're going home, Shichio."

Shichio willed himself to stay calm. He would not walk away from the Bear Cub. He couldn't. Glorious Victory Unsought was the only thing that could sate the mask. Apart from that, Shichio was not one to forgive a grudge. The whelp had to die. As painfully as possible. That was all there was to it.

He looked at Nene, who gave him a friendly smile. "If this Daigoro is an enemy of the throne, then by all means, remain here," she said. "May I ask what sort of threat he presents?"

The whelp knows the truth, Shichio thought, and that truth will kill me as surely as a *kaishakunin*'s sword. It was a miracle that the story hadn't reached Hashiba's ears already. At long last Shichio's spies had captured a mail carrier, whose packet included a letter describing the Battle of Komaki in exacting detail. The trouble was, they'd only intercepted the one. If the Bear Cub had finally decided to circulate the story, Shichio's men should have run across it more than once by now. Something was very, very wrong.

But none of that would persuade Hashiba or Nene. "He embarrassed me publicly," Shichio said. "Is it not enough that I should defend my honor?"

"Oh, yes," Nene said. Her frown seemed to convey genuine sympathy. That was a sham, of course, but the woman had real talent. "My people passed word to me about that atrocious wedding. Believe me, Shichio-san, my husband may find it humorous, but I do not. I sympathize with your plight entirely. In fact, I've found a way to heal the wound. If you'll accept it, of course."

My people, Shichio thought. He knew she was well informed, but this was something else. The reference to her "people" meant she hadn't heard about the wedding from Hashiba, but that raised a new question: how did the woman have spies this far north? Had she brought them with her? Did they fly ahead of her, heralding her advance like a swarm of fireflies? If so, then why hadn't Shichio's agents warned him of her arrival?

He forced a sweet, submissive smile. "My lady, I am eager to hear your proposal."

"Kanagawa-juku. My old friend Oda Nobunaga had many allies there. I have found a suitable house for you, an old and respected clan with some ten thousand *koku.* House Urakami. Their fief includes one of the largest cities in the province."

The largest, and still a fishing village. Shichio knew of it. It was thirty-odd *ri* north and east of Izu, which was to say thirty-odd *ri* deeper into the barbarian hinterlands. Its remoteness was its tactical value. Shichio knew of it because the Odawara Hōjōs were one of the last holdouts in the north, and sooner or later Hashiba would have to fight them. As a coastal power, they would be difficult to attack by sea. By land, every approach from the south was utterly predictable. Shichio's plan was to sail past them by night, putting ashore at the sleepy little post town of Kanagawa-juku. From there the army could land in force and march on Odawara from the north.

"It is so far from Kyoto, my lady."

"But not so far from Izu. If this boy remains a threat, root him out. Then hold the north for us. Marry well and live well. As I said, House Urakami is a noble and venerated clan. Its lord died of the flux and now his dowager rules in his stead. I sent word to her and she has consented to accept your hand."

"Sent word?" Shichio was ashamed he'd uttered it aloud. Ordinarily he was the master of his own tongue, but this was outrageous news. Nene must have written weeks ago if she'd heard back from these Urakamis already. How long had she been simmering this little scheme?

"My lady, I appreciate your generosity. Let no man say I don't. But—"

"Excellent," said Hideyoshi. "It's settled, then." He clapped his hands and rubbed them together. When he smiled, he exposed teeth jumbled so haphazardly that they seemed to have been thrown into his mouth. They were sharp, and instead of standing like soldiers in an orderly line, they leaned against one another like so many drunks. "Steward!" he called. "Rice. Fish. Cook up some of that southern beef, too, the cut we had last night. Shichio, you've got to try this stuff. Nene's cooks brought it in her baggage train. It's the best damn thing you've ever tasted."

"My lady is most generous. But Toyotomi-dono, I have given much thought to what some of the officers have been saying. Is it proper for a man of my station to take on his wife's name in marriage? I am a general after all—"

"But willing to marry Lady Okuma," Nene said. "Is that not so?"

"It was," Shichio admitted. He hoped he'd said it without too much of a hiss.

"Aha," she said. "Is the problem that House Okuma is too small a name for one of my honored husband's favorite generals? The name Urakami is not so small. They are cousins to House Oda, who are cousins to my own house of Sugaihara. Their shadow stretches back over many hundreds of years."

Damn this woman, Shichio thought. She's foreseen my every move. He tried to keep his frustration off his face, with only moderate success. "My lady, I know this sort of concern seems trivial to you. You married a man of common descent despite your own samurai lineage. I daresay that was most foresightful of you, but also most unorthodox. And your husband did not take your name; he forged a name for himself, in the eyes of the emperor and all men."

"Then can you not do the same?"

That got Shichio's hackles up, but again he stifled that reaction before it reached his face. "I humbly serve in whatever capacity my lord general asks of me. I do not aspire to follow in his footsteps."

Nene inclined her head and smiled. It was a tiny movement, but it spoke volumes. Well played, she was telling him. "You have it right. The emperor will not raise you up. But honored husband, is it perhaps within your power . . . ?"

Hashiba turned to her, a quizzical frown crinkling his simian features. "What are you after, Nene?"

She bowed her head, the very picture of a submissive wife. "When Mio Yasumasa passed, you lost a long-serving *hatamoto*. Now I understand one who is not samurai can never be *hatamoto*, but perhaps in this case . . . well, General Shichio has been a most loyal servant, *neh*? Is there no way to reward his devotion?"

Hashiba smiled, revealing those sharp, jagged teeth again. It was little wonder that his enemies called him the Monkey King. Even the great Mio Yasumasa called him that, though only after he'd poured a bottle of whisky into that prodigious belly of his. Shichio still had nightmares about Mio's death. Those rubbery slabs of flesh flopping to the floor like fish . . . the thought alone was almost enough to make him retch. Shichio would never regret killing him, but he was horrified at the way he'd done it—or rather, at the way the mask made him do it.

Mio had been *hatamoto*, the highest-ranking banner-man in a daimyo's service. As Hashiba was the most powerful man in the empire, his *hatamoto* were the elite of the elite. It was an honor Shichio could not turn down, a fact Nene understood all too well. He could see every step plotted before him, like a condemned man walking to the execution ground. Nene had laid the path. *Is it perhaps within your power,* she'd said, directing Hashiba to wonder if there was anything he could not do. *Is there no way to reward his devotion,* she'd asked, making him think about the limits of his largesse. Shichio knew all of her tricks, because they were his tricks too.

Inevitably, Hashiba got to his feet, making himself feel larger. He flicked his hand as if swatting at a mosquito. "If only samurai can be *hatamoto*, then I will make him samurai. Shichio, kneel before me."

Dreading what was to come, Shichio did as he was told. Nene stood beside her husband, making it perfectly clear that she stood above Shichio as well. Hashiba removed his *wakizashi* from his belt, and with great ceremony he presented it to Shichio. Shichio had no choice but to accept it in both hands, and to push it through his own belt where a samurai would wear it. His katana came next. As they performed this exchange of arms, Hideyoshi gave his benediction. "Shichio, I hereby name you samurai, as shall be all your heirs forever more. I leave it to you to choose your surname and your crest, which all shall honor. I also name you *hatamoto*, and I bestow upon you mine own arms, as badges of your honored station. Now swear your fealty to me, to my house, and to the emperor, may Amaterasu protect and preserve him."

By the gods, Shichio thought, he can be quite officious when he sets his mind to it. He wondered whether this too was Nene's doing. She was of samurai blood, from House Sugaihara far to the south; ritualism ran in her veins. Shichio despised three things above all others: sweat, ugliness, and the samurai class. The emperor might have ruled in name, but it was the samurai who struck fear into the heart of every peasant. The whole point of Hashiba's rulership, the reason Shichio supported him in the first place, was that if one man could bring the empire to heel, that would spell the end of war. Without war, there would be no warrior caste. And now Shichio was to join that caste for good and all. He would have their respect, at the cost of his own self-respect.

Shichio pressed his forehead almost to the dust. Then he realized Nene would notice if he fell short of full submission when he accepted this great honor, and so he touched his sweating brow to the ground. He swore his oath, and Toyotomi no Hideyoshi, Imperial Regent and Chief Minister, bade him rise. Again Shichio could only do as he was told, mud-streaked forehead and all.

The pageantry was far from over. An adjutant vanished through a long slit in the fabric wall, returning soon afterward with Hashiba's barber. Shichio had given little thought to this aspect of his supposed promotion. As if wearing the twin swords was not ugly enough, now he had to part with his beautiful hair. Other men might feel their hearts race at the approach of a wrathful samurai; Shichio's heart quivered as the barber's razor robbed him of all the hair atop his head. Topknot be damned, and damn the honors that came with it too; Shichio was doomed to go the rest of his life as a man balding before his time.

But what choice did he have? More pointedly, what choice had Nene left him? He could not turn down land, rank, and station. Originally he'd sought it in order to stay by Hashiba's side. Now Nene had shackled him to this fishing village in the barbarian north. If he could swiftly get a son on this Urakami woman, would that be enough to free him? Was she even of childbearing years? Could he leave her to govern in his stead? The Bear Cub would be dead before the year was out. Once the whelp was gone, Shichio had no intention of spending the rest of his life languishing in obscurity. Somehow he had to find his way back to Kyoto. To Hashiba. And with any luck, to a *shinobi* who would take a bit of gold in exchange for putting a knife in Nene's ice-cold heart.

At least the barber was good enough to wash the mud from Shichio's brow. Then the highest-ranking officers came to call, and Shichio had to endure congratulations from all of them. They complimented the noble lineage of his swords and made the requisite jokes about the tan line left where his hairline once met his forehead. Shichio smiled and nodded and made many awkward bows, second-guessing himself about the level to which he ought to lower his head, given his new standing.

Dinner came as a welcome relief. The beef was exquisite, just as Hashiba had promised. Nene's chief cook also served fugu, which he'd somehow delivered all the way from the Ryukyu Islands. Its poison brought a pointed spice to the sashimi that nothing else could match. Hashiba joked that the fugu alone was a good enough reason to conquer Shikoku and Kyushu. These were among his most recent conquests, and the gathering drank many rounds of *sake* in toasts to their swift defeat.

After dinner and drinks came the *shamisen* and *shakuhachi*, and Hashiba's deplorable singing. Shichio, quite drunk, excused himself to have a piss and slipped outside. Then he found he really did have to piss, and after he'd relieved himself, he came back to find Nene outside the enclosure. She was waiting for him.

The long fabric wall luffed lazily in the breeze, but her cloth-of-gold kimono did not move at all. Even her hair remained undisturbed, which struck him as eerie; a ghost's hair was said not to move in the breeze either. On another level it made him miss his own thick, luxuriant hair.

Nene dipped her head in a tiny bow. "Shichio-san. You've conducted yourself with grace tonight."

"How could I not? You have bestowed such lofty honors on me." He made little effort to conceal his vitriol.

"I? Surely you mean my husband."

"I most surely do not."

"Then you've lost none of your cleverness." She bowed again, deeper than the last time. Shichio didn't miss the subtext: she respected the ability if not the man. "I was glad to see you accept the gift in the spirit in which it was given."

"Oh, quite. I will be the only *hatamoto* within a hundred *ri*. And a hundred and fifty *ri* away from anything that matters."

Nene allowed herself the faintest ghost of a smile. It put not a single wrinkle in her white face paint. "You do not yet know of my greatest gift to you," she said. With a pale and slender hand she removed a sheet of fine paper from her sleeve, ornately folded to make a perfect square. The wax seal was broken. In the dim light Shichio could not make out whose seal it was, but it hardly mattered. Regardless of who penned the letter, its content would spell Shichio's death.

"You intercepted one such letter," she said. "One and only one. What you do not know is that you received it only because I released it to you. My spies have intercepted the rest. I know all about your failure in the Battle of Komaki. I know you are responsible for my husband's most public shame. But more importantly for you, my honored husband knows not a word of it."

If the letter set his heart to racing, Nene nearly caused it to stop dead. "What? Why?"

"You will accept my gifts. Land. Lordship. Wealth. Esteem. And above all, quietude. Retire to your new estate and never return to the capital. If I see you there again, if I hear you have even pointed your horse in Kyoto's direction, my honored husband will hear of your treachery. You will die on that infamous table of yours, the same as my old friend General Mio."

Shichio seethed with rage. "No. I can beguile him, the same as you—"

"Not the same. Do not mistake me for his lover just because I am his wife. My concern is for my husband, and then for the good of the empire. I could not care less where he puts his cock."

"*He* cares. That's all I need."

Nene laughed out loud. She was so small, and her voice so high, that she sounded like twittering birds. "How long have you two known each other? Five years would be my guess. Hideyoshi and I have been married for twenty-seven. Do you have any idea how many playthings I've seen come and go in that time?"

She chirped again, as merrily as a flock of sparrows. "I'm told you are a special talent in the bedchamber," she said. "That's good. A whore ought to be talented; she has nothing else to recommend her. So by all means, find yourself a northern lord that wants to bugger you. Take as many lovers as you like. Just never let me hear from you again."

10

Nene could not help but laugh. Shichio looked so comical that he might just as well have been an actor on the stage. The man was cunning, to be sure, but when he lost control of his temper he raged like a little child.

"We will go back to the banquet now," she said, "and you will give me no more of these petulant looks. In exchange, I will not provoke you. In fact, I will say nothing to you unless I must. You will accept compliments and laugh at jokes and do everything else required of a noble lord. You will not be the first to leave, and you certainly will not spend your evening brooding in some dark hold of that monstrosity floating in the bay."

She'd heard far too much about his behavior after Lady Okuma's marriage to her infant groom. That was a shameful affair. Shichio might have been half child and half serpent, but he was one of Hideyoshi's generals, and the office warranted a high degree of respect. In shaming him, these Okumas had shamed her husband. The fact that her husband found it hilarious made no difference. Nor did the fact that Shichio had run off like a sulking toddler to hide under the covers and cry himself to sleep.

All the same, Nene was intrigued by this boy they called the Bear Cub. Okuma Daigoro, his name was—or at least it had been until he'd renounced it. Son of Okuma

Tetsurō, the Red Bear of Izu, who had sided with Tokugawa Ieyasu at the Battle of Mikatagahara and saved Ieyasu's hide at the Battle of Komaki. Both father and son were tied up in stories of the Inazuma blades, which drew whispers of fascination at court. Nene knew little more of these Okumas. Their house was a speck of foam on the smallest wave in the smallest corner of the sea. Yet somehow this boy commanded Hideyoshi's begrudging respect.

There was nothing begrudging from the men of the rank and file. They spoke of the Bear Cub as if he were Hachiman reborn. The god of war wandering the earth in human skin; that was what they were saying. Stranger still, many of the rumors were plainly true. All agreed he was a cripple, yet all agreed he'd bested General Mio—Mio, whom Takeda Shingen himself had once praised as the mightiest swordsman he'd ever known. True, that was years ago, but even if Mio was no longer the strongest, he was undoubtedly the biggest. By all accounts this Bear Cub was almost a waif. To hear the men tell it, the first blow knocked the boy so far across the dueling ground that Mio might just as well have delivered his next attack with a bow instead of his sword.

Little wonder, then, that the boy drove Shichio to madness. To be routed by a man with a host of banner poles instead of an army, and then to be outwitted by the same man's sickly teenage son! It was too much for anyone to bear.

But Shichio wasn't just anyone. He was her husband's confidant. And he was drawn to power like sharks to blood. He would insinuate himself back into Hideyoshi's inner circle given half a chance, and he certainly wouldn't balk at poisoning Nene to do it. Now that she'd exiled him from power, he might kill her just for spite. The man never forgot a grudge.

"Hm." She said it out loud without intending to. That was a small sign of how much he vexed her; Nene did not make a habit of losing her composure. But the thought of his many grudges inspired an idea in her.

"What?" Shichio snapped.

"Oh, I'm sorry. I'd quite forgotten you were there." She gave a little nod with her chin toward the tent. "Go on, then. Your guests will miss you."

He snorted, turned on his heel, and returned to the feast. She hoped he had enough self-control to keep the anger from his face. It wouldn't do for the assembled generals to start asking questions. That might require Nene to step back in and redirect the conversation, and she wanted a few moments alone with her thoughts.

Perhaps the Bear Cub could be of use. Shichio would never live down the shame of that wedding debacle, and even before the wedding, his grudge for the boy already burned as bright as the sun. Now that Shichio was samurai, it might even occur to him that he had honor to defend. For his part, the Bear Cub must have wisdom enough to know he could not rest until Shichio was dead. If Nene wanted to take the boy out of the game, she had only to rig a trap and offer Shichio as bait. The reverse was also true: to remove Shichio from play, she had only to set a trap with the Bear Cub as the lure.

Oh, yes, she thought, and what fun it would be to lay a double trap! Shichio was clever enough to sense a set-up, and he would never willingly expose himself as bait. But what if he believed he was not bait at all, but rather the trapper? If Nene could place the boy in a vulnerable position, Shichio would pounce on him, and if the boy was forewarned, he could counterstrike before Shichio landed the killing blow.

Now that was a clever notion. A bear trap, but in this case the bear *was* the trap. There was a witty haiku in there somewhere. Nene decided she'd write it after all was said and done.

In the meantime, she'd left herself a dangerous game to play, with a hunted bear and a spiteful cobra as her playmates. In the best of all worlds, the trap would result in a mutual slaying. But the worst case was very bad indeed. If she were caught in league with the boy, Hideyoshi's wrath would be swift and terrible. Shichio could not be allowed to escape her trap alive. But if she put the Bear Cub in the right position, how could she be certain he would strike true? Could she even trust him to strike at all? There was no telling. She didn't know his character. And there was only one way to rectify that; she would have to speak with him face-to-face.

She was like her husband that way: a keen judge of character, and loath to rely on hearsay when she could gather her information firsthand. But before she could arrange a meeting, she needed a plausible pretext for them to cross paths at all. It would not be enough for her to simply tell him she wanted Shichio dead. He would have no reason to believe her—and in fact no reason to believe she was not in league with Shichio. She had to *need* something from him, and then offer Shichio as payment.

But what? She would need some time to think about that. It was time to gather her spies, dozens of whom she'd sent to Izu before ever departing the capital. Nene was not one to act in ignorance; she had long maintained the habit of gathering as much intelligence as possible before making a decision. This evening's decision required special care. She needed the Bear Cub to believe the two of them were on the same side, and she needed him to believe that he was doing her a service, the payment for which would be Shichio's head. Only then could she lay the double trap she had in mind.

She mused on the problem over dinner, eating only lightly; her primary duty at table was to nod, smile, and issue the occasional word of praise as the assembled generals told their war stories. What could a rogue *rōnin* offer the Lady in the North? The obvious answer was Glorious Victory, but she knew he would never part with it. Nene had never fully understood men's fascination with their swords, though she supposed a genuine Inazuma was something special. But if not his sword, what could he offer?

A sudden shout from her husband broke her train of thought. "To General Shichio," Hideyoshi cried, rising drunkenly to his feet. He thrust a *sake* flask at the sky. "The best damned quartermaster anyone could ask for."

That raised a round of cheers. "And he'll damn well

need to be," Hideyoshi said. Suddenly he was deadly serious. "These islands are not enough for me, gentlemen. Within the year the whole empire will be mine—and what then? Eh? What then?"

His commanders looked at him, all of them sober-faced, some of them a little scared. Only Shichio knew the answer. "The world!" he shouted.

"The world!" Hideyoshi echoed, laughing maniacally. Up went the *sake* flask, like a sword thrust triumphantly at the moon. "Start learning Chinese, gentlemen, because by this time next year we'll be marching on the Forbidden City!"

The generals all laughed again, and some started shouting toasts and cheers. *"Banzai! Banzai!"*

Banzai indeed, Nene thought. The word meant "ten thousand years." She joined in the cheering, thinking, if only he had a hundred years, he could bring the whole world to heel.

In a flash she had the answer to her riddle: Streaming Dawn. If Glorious Victory was real, then why not Streaming Dawn? It too was said to be an Inazuma blade, and it was said to abide in these parts. How many spies had she sent in search of it over the years? Not one of them had so much as laid eyes on it. The best they could manage was to tell her it had been seen in Izu—not by one, but by many. Daigoro will have heard of it, she thought. That is what I can ask of him. If he does not believe in the blade, then let him think me naive, and be happy that I am selling Shichio's lifeblood for so small a price. If he believes, then he will understand why I want it for my honored husband—and by the buddhas, if the legends of Streaming Dawn are true, then that little *tantō* is far more powerful than the Bear Cub's great *ōdachi*.

Let the legends be true, Nene prayed silently, and give my husband his hundred years. Give me a path to the Bear Cub, and cloud his sight enough that he will not see the trap I mean to lay for him.

BOOK THREE

HEISEI ERA, THE YEAR 22

(2010 CE)

The man known as Sour Plum reached into his black leather jacket and pulled out his cell. He could have drawn the serrated Spyderco combat knife he kept in the same pocket, but as Mariko saw it, the phone was more dangerous than the knife.

She had a bright pink cast on her right forearm, a jagged line of stitches in her scalp, and bruises covering half of her face. The two bodyguards flanking her would make her look a lot worse if Sour Plum heard the wrong words come out of that phone. Thus far they'd been perfect gentlemen—or as gentlemanly as a black marketeer's heavies were ever likely to be. They hadn't broken her arm. In fact, no one had; the cast was a fake. They weren't the ones who bashed her face in, either. Those bruises were two days old, still lingering after the woman in the diaphanous white dress walloped Mariko right in the face during their foot chase through Tokyo Station. Mariko had lost track of the woman then and hadn't found her since.

She knew it was a million-to-one shot, but she had hoped to find the woman in a fancy second-story shot bar called the Sour Plum. The place was named for its owner, a big round man whose name in his Narcotics dossier was Lee Jin Bao. Since Japanese people couldn't pronounce the name Lee, he'd acquired the nickname Plum, the meaning of the kanji character for Lee. The Sour part was easy enough to understand: he wore a permanent Robert De Niro frown and he had a reputation for knifing people at the slightest provocation. Sour Plum was Chinese in a country that had no love for the Chinese, but being an enterprising sort, he'd used that fact to establish a niche for himself in the criminal ecosystem. Since no yakuza family would have him, he was the ultimate neutral party, the Switzerland of the Tokyo underworld. When rivals and enemies had no choice but to do business together, they met at the Plum.

As such, he was long overdue for a covert sting operation—or so Mariko had argued, anyway. It wasn't exactly a lie, but it certainly wasn't the whole truth. Sour Plum *was* on Narcotics Division's radar, but what Mariko really wanted was free rein to question him about his criminal associates. She was hoping a certain scantily clad, fleet-footed, shoulder-bag-swinging hellcat was on the list.

So that morning she'd talked her new shift sergeant into making a play. She went right out and arrested a mid-level dealer named Yuki Kisho who carried out most of his deals at the Plum. Yuki didn't always pay attention to the subtle details of the trade—nuances like not pissing off your girlfriend if she knows you sell meth for a living. Scorned girlfriends made for terrific covert informants, and in Yuki's case, he'd pissed off both his girlfriend and his mistress. Mariko's ex-partner, Han, already had contracts with both of Yuki's ladyloves; from there it was only a matter of waiting for the right time to burn down their cheating boyfriend.

Not long ago, Mariko and Han would have brought him down together. But that was before Han got himself busted back to general patrol. Since fate had a wicked sense of irony, it was his misconduct that freed him up to pursue Jōko Daishi. Mariko should have been working the same case, but instead she was stuck in Narcotics working penny-ante buy-busts. Given the choice between being ladylike and doing her damn job, Captain Kusama wanted Mariko to be a lady.

She wondered what Kusama would think of her now, working her first undercover job instead of sitting behind a desk with her pinky sticking out as she sipped her tea.

"Still ringing," Sour Plum told her.

"He'll pick up," Mariko said. "For you he'll pick up."

"He better."

Mariko winced at that. She could hardly tell him the truth: that she was only pretending to be Yuki's girlfriend, and that maybe Yuki hadn't answered the call because she'd tossed him into an interrogation room that got crappy reception.

Sour Plum narrowed his eyes at her, looking her up and down. Mariko wasn't sure if he was interested in her figure or in the plaster cast on her right forearm. Could he tell it was a fake? If so, then things were about to go south.

The only thing more conspicuous than her cast would have been the four-fingered hand it concealed. Losing that finger in a sword fight made her a media sensation for a week. She'd made the news again by fatally shooting a man on a populated subway platform. Captain Kusama had allowed the public to believe that Akahata Daisuke was unarmed when she shot him, and that made Mariko the most infamous cop in Tokyo. She was utterly useless for undercover work.

Until someone tried to bash her brains in with an iron mask. Now everyone would focus on the bruises, not the face that bore them. Truth to tell, she hardly looked like Oshiro Mariko anymore. The real giveaway was her missing trigger finger, which the cast concealed completely. The cast also went nicely with the bruises, and together they anchored Mariko's cover story—a story Lee was soon to confirm if Yuki would just pick up his goddamn phone.

"Don't make sense," Sour Plum said, his gaze roving from her cast to her tits. "What's a nice piece of ass like you want with a dumbshit like him?"

"Maybe I don't want anything from him anymore. Maybe you've got what I need." She pulled a thin stack of folded, sweat-slicked 10,000-yen bills from her bra. "Just sell me enough to pay off this yakuza asshole. Then maybe you and me can talk about what we want to do later."

"You got money. Why not pay him yourself?"

"Says he wants product, not cash."

Sour Plum took her money, held it up to his nose, and sniffed it like he was sniffing her panties. "Double," he said.

"Huh?"

He leered at her and smelled the money again. "You'll pay me double, 'cause most days you'd pay me in pussy. But I don't hit no woman, and I don't want nobody saying I do, neither. So double, or else walk your skinny ass out of here."

"Done." A thrill of adrenaline ran through Mariko's veins like bubbling champagne. Her first undercover job, and it was going off without a hitch.

And then Yuki answered his phone.

"It's me," Lee said. Mariko wanted to snatch the phone and toss it down the stairs. She already had Lee where she wanted him. There was nothing Yuki could say to make matters better, and ten thousand things he could say to make everything go right to hell.

"Shut up and listen," said the man called Sour Plum. "You tell some skinny bitch to come around here?"

Mariko hoped Yuki said, *Yes* and not, *Yes, but she's a cop*.

"How I'm supposed to know you ain't setting me up?" Lee grimaced as he listened. "Hey, you got yakuzas on your ass, that's your problem, not mine—and the next time you get in deep with one of those fuckers, you tell 'em to kick *your* ass instead of your woman's, you chickenshit. Now tell me where you're at."

Mariko's stomach fluttered like a bird trapped in a mason jar. Please, she thought, please don't tell him.

"I don't like surprises," Lee said. "You pull this crap again, you gonna look like your girlfriend."

He clicked off the phone, and when he returned it to his jacket pocket Mariko got another glimpse of the Spyderco. "Says he didn't rough you up. Says a yakuza did it."

"That's what I've been telling you," Mariko said.

"I know. I'm saying your bullshit matches his bullshit. So maybe it ain't bullshit."

"Then we have a deal?"

"We got a deal."

He took the money, Mariko left with a little baggie of meth, and half a minute later she took point on the raid. It went as smoothly as could be expected, given the tight quarters and the sheer mass of cops trying to make their way up the narrow staircase. Sour Plum's bodyguards let her by, thinking she was trying to flee from the police. That trapped Mariko upstairs with Lee Jin Bao while his heavies dealt with the rest of the squad.

Mariko had been entertaining a pet theory that a plaster cast could do lots of things a sword could do. Lee put that theory to the test. He was twice her size and damn quick with his knife. She parried the first slash with her cast, then snapped a *kote-uchi* strike to the wrist. His knife hit the floor. When he started throwing punches, she let him bloody his knuckles on the plaster for a while. Then a *shomenuchi* to the forehead dropped him right on his ass. Her cast was in tatters by the time she was done, but apart from that, she decided she'd logged some good *kenjutsu* practice tonight.

While the rest of the team searched the Plum for contraband, Mariko hopped onto a stool next to Lee Jin Bao. He sat at his own bar, looking profoundly uncomfortable with his thumbs zip-tied behind him. His breath came loud and angry through his nose. She pulled a couple of hastily folded pages from her back pocket and smoothed them on the spotless countertop. "You ever see this chick before?"

The first page was a grainy black-and-white image captured from a Japan Railways closed-circuit camera, centered on the woman who had kicked Mariko's ass with the demon mask.

"Couldn't say."

Mariko slid the next sheet in front of him: three more pictures of the woman in white, captured from three other security cameras. None of them were high quality, and none of them were head-on. Mariko had a sneaking suspicion that the woman had done that on purpose—that she'd deliberately faced this way or that so the cops couldn't get a good data set to run facial recognition software.

"How about now?" Mariko said. "Recognize her yet?"

"Couldn't say."

"Here, let's get some of this crap out of your eyes." She scrubbed Lee's face with one hand, and not as gently as she could have. Pink flecks of broken cast rained down on the counter. The trickle of blood snaking down from his hairline was now a smear across his forehead. It wasn't right, taking her frustration out on him, but she'd gone to a lot of work pulling these images and she wanted to see some results.

After getting her ass kicked by the woman in white, Mariko's first stop wasn't the ER, but rather the Tokyo Station security office. She knew the station would have dozens of cameras, and she planned to use them to track her assailant out of the building and into the streets. From there she'd hoped to track the woman via traffic camera feed, but by the time she'd climbed the stairs to the security office she felt woozy. After that, her next clear memory was coming to in the back of an ambulance.

No one would have blamed her for taking the rest of the day off. Even if she wasn't sporting a grade two concussion, the relief work at Haneda had driven her to the brink of exhaustion. But Mariko knew she couldn't afford to rest. Most security cameras recorded over their own feed, running a perpetual loop to save on data storage, and the length of the loop varied from one camera to the next. As far as she was concerned, the clock was ticking.

So the moment the ER doc had her stitched up, Mariko rushed straight back to the station security office. A flash of her badge gave her an all-access backstage pass. The Haneda bombing had people scared. They would give a cop anything she asked for, and the thought of a warrant never entered their minds.

The first thing she had to search for was the footage of

herself, turtling up while getting beaten half to death. Even watching it from the cold remove of recorded video was enough to make her heart race. From there, with the help of the security staff, she'd jumped from one monitor to the next, finally tracking her perpetrator out of the train station and into a taxicab. Then it was back home for Mariko, where a shower and a change of clothes made her look not quite so much like an exsanguinated corpse. From there she'd run off to post.

Tracking that taxi would have been easy enough for any cop with a smidgen of talent when it came to computers, which was to say anyone on the force except for Mariko. Accessing surveillance camera feed was a simple matter of logging in; she didn't even need a warrant. But after that Mariko was at sea. She could click through one camera at a time, but there were over a hundred surveillance cameras in greater Tokyo—and that was to say nothing of the traffic cams, weather cams, and privately owned Webcams whose owners streamed their feed online for all the world to see. Mariko's first instinct was to pull rank and order someone from Evidence Division to run the search for her. Then she remembered: she'd lost her sergeant's stripes. Pulling rank wasn't an option anymore.

So she'd spent two laborious days screening all the footage herself. Fortunately, she'd never had much patience for paperwork, which meant she had a perpetual backlog, which gave her an airtight excuse to ride a desk for two days straight. At last she'd tracked the woman in white to a blind spot between two cameras in Kabuki-chō, Tokyo's red-light district. A third camera was pointing right where she needed it, but karma must have been feeling pissy that morning, because a pigeon had made its nest right in front of the lens. Instead of a visual on where her target went to ground, Mariko had a close-up shot of twigs and molted feathers.

Not to be daunted, Mariko played the last trick in her book. Narcotics kept meticulous records: arrests, convictions, seizures, and—of particular importance for Mariko—addresses. Mariko had only to draw a half-kilometer radius around the blind spot, then check the files for violent crime busts or suspicious person calls within that circle. If the woman in white had priors, maybe she also had criminal friends she could hide out with after assaulting a cop.

The most promising hit had been the Sour Plum, and so here she was, sitting next to the proprietor and poking at the printed screen shots she'd pulled from the various camera feeds. "Does she come here often?" Mariko said. "Did she come here Wednesday morning?"

Lee shrugged. "Couldn't say."

Mariko sighed. "And suppose I were to ask you how many fingers and toes you have?"

"Couldn't say."

She got the idea. Lee would clam up until he saw a lawyer, and even then he wouldn't say much. But Mariko had a keen sense for lies. In her line of work, it was an indispensable skill. And that sense of hers said Lee wasn't lying. He honestly hadn't seen the woman before.

Mariko could feel her frustration mounting. It stiffened the muscles of her skull, like a giant hand clamping down on her head. She wanted nothing more than to jump behind the bar and pour herself a shot and a beer, but general orders prohibited drinking on duty. She considered violating orders anyway, but then the flat-panel TV mounted over the bar distracted her. Mariko went behind the bar, found the remote control, and turned up the volume.

She instantly wished she hadn't.

"—eighteen deaths and counting," the reporter was saying. "Police say the only common thread between them is that all eighteen were employed at St. Luke's or were patients there."

Behind him was a towering wall of blue glass that Mariko recognized immediately. The mere sight of it made her shiver like she'd seen a ghost. It was in the operating room of St. Luke's International Hospital that surgeons had removed a meter of razor-sharp Inazuma steel from her gut. She was almost pronounced dead after Fuchida Shūzō ran her through with Beautiful Singer. Her sole piece of good fortune that day was that he'd gutted her right across the street from a top-notch surgical unit.

Now there were eighteen more ghosts to associate with St. Luke's. "The cause of death is thought to be ricin poisoning," the reporter went on. "Because the poison can take as long as five days to kill once it enters a person's system, it is not known how many others have already been exposed. Hospital authorities and the National Police Agency urge everyone who is experiencing the following symptoms to go to the emergency room immediately—"

The reporter went on, but Mariko wasn't listening. She was wondering how she could show a connection between the ricin deaths and the Divine Wind. There was no doubt in her mind that Jōko Daishi was responsible. He didn't have his mask anymore, so in all likelihood he believed he'd lost his divine guidance, but he may well have ordered the attack before the mask was stolen. For that matter, he might have authorized high-ranking lackeys to execute such attacks independently. Only one thing was certain: attacking a hospital fit perfectly with Jōko Daishi's *modus operandi*.

His goal was to enlighten the people, and his method was to disrupt their faith in all of the things that kept life stable and harmonious. That included medical facilities. St. Luke's was supposed to be a place you went to get better; now going there could kill you. If ricin took days to kill, then everyone who had gone to St. Luke's this week had to wonder if they had also been poisoned. Everyone who felt even a hint of the symptoms would flood the nearest ER. Hundreds more would avoid going to *any* hospital, for fear that whoever had infiltrated St. Luke's would attack other facilities as well.

In short, Jōko Daishi had hobbled Tokyo's entire health care system.

Mariko's phone was in her hand before she knew it. She punched in Lieutenant Sakakibara's number and started rehearsing what she wanted to say.

"What do you want, Frodo?"

"Sir, have you seen—"

"St. Luke's. Yeah. What about it?"

"Sir, we know Jōko Daishi has expertise in chemistry. If he can cook meth and build high explosives, he can make ricin."

Sakakibara muttered something gruff, but Mariko didn't catch it. She muted the TV. "What's that, sir?"

"I said I don't care if the man knows how to make a nuclear bomb. It's got nothing to do with you."

"Sir, I know this man—"

"Yeah? Well, I know another man, and he outranks both of us. If His Eminence says you're stuck working bullshit buy-busts, then that's what you're doing."

"Isn't there someone else you could talk to? Someone higher up the chain of command?"

"I tried talking to *you*, to tell you to keep your damn mouth shut. How far did that get me?"

Mariko felt her face flush. She wasn't sure if it was out of shame or anger. "I know, sir. I'm really sorry—"

"I'll bet. Learn to live with what you've got, Frodo. Have you talked to that ex-partner of yours?"

"About what, sir?"

"About his case work. I got him assigned to Haneda."

Finally a piece of good news. Apart from improving Han's standing in the department, it also gave Mariko a personal contact inside the investigation she'd rather be working. "Thank you, sir."

"Don't thank me. Just don't call me again. Call Han next time."

"Sorry, sir. I only wanted to—"

"Just do your damn job, Frodo. Right now that means bullshit buy-busts, even if I could make better use of you elsewhere."

He hung up and Mariko had a dead phone in her hand.

Lee Jin Bao's perpetual frown curled into a smile. "Tough day at work?"

"Shut up."

12

The pounding in Makoto's head made it so hard to think.

He did not care for the way his concubines winced at him. It was in their nature, he supposed; they were trained to worship him. Nevertheless, their concern for their injured god strayed all too close to motherly despair. In *their* minds they would never infantilize him, but in their cringing faces he could see their need to reach out to him, to perform their ministrations on his body. If he could see it, others could see it too, and that threatened Jōko Daishi's godhood.

His fingertips ventured lightly, softly, painfully over the bruised flesh where his father had been. Even the slightest touch was a rasp on sunburned skin. His very skull felt as fragile as an eggshell. Contusions traced the bridge of his nose and the lines of his cheekbones. Small cuts ringed his eyes. His forehead was red fading into purple, darkest on the left side where the harlot's bullet had taken him. But for his father, Makoto would be dead. Not for the first time, Jōko Daishi had rescued Koji Makoto.

Makoto would happily submit to a thousand cuts and bruises such as these, a thousand times a thousand, if only they would restore his father to him. But his father was gone, stolen by the harlot whose name would never again be uttered in his presence. As soon as he'd regained consciousness, Makoto declared her dead to the church. Hamaya Jirō had already dispatched brothers and sisters to deliver the harlot to the afterlife. All men were in need of purification, but the divine flames would burn hungrily for that one.

Instead of his father's voice, Makoto heard a ringing, piercing pain. It lanced him through from temple to temple, when what he wanted most was clarity of mind to see his father's vision. "Thirteen-oh-four," he said. "One thousand. Three hundred. Four."

He ran the tip of his forefinger along a raised crease in the map unfolded before him. The map represented the city of Tokyo, and since it was very large, it showed the diseased metropolis in fine detail. With a blue pen he drew a long, straight line connecting a highway on-ramp to . . . to . . . to where? The closer he got to realizing his father's dream, the harder it became to remember the final details. A lesser man would see nothing but blinding white pain. But Makoto was not an ordinary man. His was a higher calling. He centered his concentration on his breath, then directed his *ki* to the acupressure points in his temples.

His father's dream became clear again. "Yes, I see," he said. "So beautiful." His blue line resumed its zigzagging course through the city.

His journal held down one corner of the map, filled with scribblings that only his father could help him decipher. Holding down the far side of the map was the L-shape of an automatic pistol fitted with a sound suppressor. It was not within reach, but it did not need to be. No one would harm him here. No one would find him here. He was constantly on the move, vanishing for hours at a time, resurfacing only in safe houses and never in the same one twice.

This one was a construction company whose storage building was large enough to serve as a sanctum of the Divine Wind. Makoto sat in the project manager's office, a cold, windowless space with only a small desk lamp for illumination. Brighter light would have sharpened Makoto's headaches. Hamaya Jirō stood in attendance, and eleven others as well, all of them nervously silent. Hamaya wore an arm sling and a pained expression. Both were due to the bullet he'd taken through the shoulder in defense of Jōkō Daishi. No god could ask for greater devotion.

Makoto studied the map, then connected one last path of green to the blue one he'd just drawn. Then he released a great sighing breath and set down his pen. At last the work was done.

Green signified the second phase, blue the third. The first phase was red, the most intricate, the most demanding. The green lines were few and the blue ones fewer, but slashes of red ink crisscrossed the entire city. From Makoto's perspective it looked like he'd sliced Tokyo's face with ten thousand razor blades. It pained him to think that Tokyo herself would feel that way before the end. But incisions were a part of surgery. A physician's hands sometimes had to harm before they healed.

"Behold," he told the twelve disciples gathered before him. "Behold the vision of Jōkō Daishi. This next teaching shall be my most profound. One thousand three hundred and four. It is a great number, and a heavy burden on our fold. Many hundreds of your brothers and sisters are called to action. We must be organized. We must strike without warning. And you, oh my brethren, you must do this without me."

That drew a gasp from the assembly. "Daishi-sama, no," said one of his disciples. The man was short but powerfully built, a foreman in the construction company Makoto now used as his sanctuary. "Do you still mean to go to the police?"

"I do."

The foreman came to Makoto's side and went to one knee. The muscles stood out in his forearms when he pressed his palms together in supplication. "Please, Daishi-sama, let me take your place. Once they have you, they'll never let you go."

Makoto smiled and clasped the man's hands in his own. "Do not doubt the vision of Jōkō Daishi. I am the light, and I will not have my children wander in darkness.

I have already illuminated your path. It is yours to walk, just as I must walk my own path. Alone."

"Please, Daishi-sama, *please* don't let them take you."

"How can they contain a being of light? I choose the hour of my coming and going. Their laws mean nothing. Their walls mean nothing. Their prisons are but shadows before me. Let them think their justice system makes them safer; I will show them the truth."

He released the foreman and stood to address the entire congregation. The act of standing sent splitting pain through his temples. He bore it stoically. "I go to reveal my wisdom to these defenders of delusion. Since they have misunderstood all that I taught at Terminal 2, I shall make them the subject of my next sermon. They call themselves 'law enforcement.' I will show them the true law, using their own bodies and minds as the vehicles for my revelation."

"But, Daishi-sama—"

Makoto fixed the foreman with a demonic glare. "Doubt deserves no place in your heart. Now which one would you have me cut out, your doubt or your heart?"

The foreman bowed to the floor and prostrated himself. "Forgive me, Daishi-sama."

Makoto looked down at him. With one stomp of his foot he could snap the man's neck. But Jōkō Daishi was a loving god. He was not here now—he could not return until Makoto was reunited with his father—but in his absence Makoto had to embody his virtues as best he could. He chose not to crush the life out of this man.

Instead, he held his arms wide as if to embrace everyone in the room. "I foresaw this trial long ago. But I shall return to you very soon. I have gone once before to these officers of the law. I go to them now a second time, and there shall not be a third. This I have seen. But while I am gone, my children, the Church of the Divine Wind has much to accomplish. Only four days remain until my greatest sermon, the sermon of the one thousand three hundred and four. You must do your part, as I will do mine."

All twelve of his disciples nodded, even the foreman who still prostrated himself on the floor. "Go, then, and prepare your brothers and sisters for what is to come. And may the Purging Fire burn away all that is impure in you. May you feel only the peace of those who have already given themselves up for dead."

13

It took three hours for Mariko and her team to close down the scene at the Sour Plum. At last her sergeant dismissed her, which still felt weird; she was used to being the one who dismissed people. Those days were gone. Now she needed permission just to step outside and get some fresh air.

The rain-slicked streets offered no relief. Kabuki-chō was supposed to be Tokyo on an ecstasy and nicotine binge, but now the whole city was on lithium. The neon still reflected in the puddles, the LEDs still flashed in their millions, but for whom? Hardly anyone was there.

If there was one thing Mariko had come to understand from her formative years in rural Illinois, it was that small-town people cooked at home and big-city people ate out. Her mom's love of cooking was very much the exception, while Mariko herself proved the rule: if she couldn't make it in a microwave, it was too much hassle. Let someone else do the cooking and cleanup. Tokyoites had places to be.

So Kabuki-chō's restaurants should have been filled to bursting. The streets should have been wall-to-wall *sarariman*, teetering drunkenly out of the bars on their way to penthouse hostess clubs or bargain basement blow job salons. There should have been teenagers with fake IDs, nervous and titillated as they ventured into the strip clubs.

It was Friday night, for God's sake. But instead those places had perhaps a tenth of their customary clientele.

Mariko noticed the same desolation in the Web cafés, the pachinko parlors, the boutique shops selling Pokémon smartphone cases. The city wasn't dead. It wasn't like some postapocalyptic movie where the remaining survivors were afraid to leave their homes. It was just that events like a terrorist attack made people reassess the importance of staying at home, and many of them found a new love for the comforts they'd rediscovered there. Mariko wondered how overworked the delivery rooms would be nine months from now, or whether New York and DC had seen a similar baby boom nine months after 9/11.

Mariko saw the city's desolation mirrored in her own life. Her demotion still weighed on her like a yoke, heavy enough to physically change her posture. Old aches and pains niggled at her. She felt a gaping hole where her sergeant's bars used to be, a mutilation just like her missing finger. She hadn't gotten used to that nothingness yet; when she looked at her right hand, she saw the hand of a cripple. Her American upbringing told her there was no disgrace in having a handicap, but Japanese tradition held otherwise. The potency of that tradition suffused every fiber of her being with shame. If losing the finger was disgraceful, losing her sergeant's rank was cause for seppuku. Police officers and samurai were alike: for them, honor was paramount, and Mariko's honor was indelibly marred. She had lost face and there was no getting it back.

If the empty streets were a mirror, then Mariko didn't care to look in it anymore. She had turned to head back up to the Sour Plum when she noticed a love hotel across the road. It rented rooms by the hour, with themed rooms catering to different fantasies and fetishes. In most neighborhoods, love hotels catered to ordinary civilians—trysts, one-night stands, spouses looking to spice things up—but in Kabuki-chō it would be johns and prostitutes more often than not. Usually such places prided themselves on secrecy and discretion, but here, where the typical client came for criminal activities, safety would be the greater concern.

Mariko hoped that might entail a security camera, preferably pointing straight out the door toward the blind spot.

She jogged across the street and into the lobby, where she was greeted by a loud and inevitable *"Irasshaimase!"* Ignoring the desk clerk who had just greeted her, Mariko scanned the perimeter of the ceiling, and indulged herself with a little fist-pump when she saw the lobby camera was facing the double glass doors that opened onto the sidewalk. She flashed her badge at the clerk—a skinny boy, easily intimidated—and said she'd like to review the security footage.

The kid didn't know how to operate the CCTV system, but by now Mariko had spent enough time around these things that this one wasn't too hard to figure out. She successfully cued up the morning of her assault, but her efforts were immediately rewarded with disappointment. The camera was aimed in the right direction, but it was mounted too high, angled too steeply. The little black-and-white screen showed her the lobby, the double doors, and even the legs and feet of a group of schoolgirls walking by. But the blind spot was still blinded.

Strange, she thought, to be able to identify high school girls solely by their legs. These girls had all decided on the same trendy shoes. They all wore scrunchy white socks, all of them pulled up to cover the calf. Mariko glanced at the time stamp again and wondered why these girls weren't in school at eight forty on a Wednesday morning. Then she remembered: this was the morning after the Haneda bombing. All the city schools were closed.

Then came the next question: why were any of these girls out of bed? They could have slept in, yet here they were, all dolled up at eight forty in the morning. As soon as Mariko asked herself the question, she intuited the answer: they weren't about to waste a day off of school by spending it with their parents. Better to stick to the routine, get out of the house, find the same group of friends they saw every day. Their city was under attack; they needed someone to talk to, and Mom and Dad wouldn't do the trick.

Mariko wondered whom she might have turned to if she were their age. By high school her sister, Saori, was already using; she'd have sought consolation in getting wasted. That had never been Mariko's style. In all likelihood she wouldn't have had a boyfriend either. Mariko had never been able to keep them very long. Maybe some of the girls on the track team?

She knew the man she wished she could have talked to: Yamada-sensei. He had been so much more than a teacher to her. In some ways he'd been a grandfather, in some ways even a father. He knew exactly what it was like to have your hometown destroyed. He'd been in Tokyo the day the first bombs fell; in fact, some of those bombs were direct hits on the building he was stationed in. He remembered the firebombing in 'forty-five and he'd seen the city rebuild itself from the ashes. He'd have known what to say in times like this.

But he was dead, and Mariko had never fully forgiven herself for her part in that. She should have been at his side and she wasn't, and maybe if she'd been there she could have stopped his killer. Maybe. That question would never be answered.

Now that whole drama was coming back around. She'd had her chance to put a bullet in Jōko Daishi's brain. Had she done so, a hundred and twelve people would have gone about their business on an ordinary Tuesday afternoon. Instead, all those people lay dead. A dark cloud of dread hung over her city, all because Mariko had frozen up when she could have pulled the trigger.

Tonight she had the opposite problem. Instead of having an obvious solution but not enough guts to follow through, she had the will to find this woman in white but she'd run out of options. She had half a mind to find herself a ladder and a drill; if she reset the angle of the camera, maybe next time it could do her some good. There was no solving her problem retroactively, but she wanted to busy herself doing *something*.

She shot the camera an irritated glare on her way out the door, and what she saw stopped her dead. Someone else had exactly the same idea about the ladder and the drill. Four empty holes described a rectangle in the wall, maybe ten or fifteen centimeters lower than the camera's current perch. Someone had elevated it.

Following a hunch, she went outside and looked around for her least favorite traffic camera, the one obstructed by the pigeon's nest. She spotted it, but not the nest. Only remnants of the nest remained, almost as if they'd been glued to the camera just to obstruct its view of the blind spot.

Just like that, the blind spot became the Blind Spot. It wasn't bad luck or poor timing or anything else. It was a creation, not an accident. Someone was hiding something here, someone connected to the woman in white. Whoever these people were, they'd taken extraordinary measures not to be found. Deliberately blinding a police surveillance cam was one thing, but it took a new level of paranoia to search the surrounding businesses for additional cameras to reposition.

Wait, Mariko thought. Paranoia? How far down that road had she gone herself?

What lengths would someone have to go to in order to move the hotel camera? Mariko's earlier fantasy was totally untenable; no business would allow a stranger to barge in toting a ladder and a drill. It would have to be the love hotel's handyman, or else a technician from the contractor that installed the security system in the first place. And contrary to the trope in so many movies, a person couldn't just show up with a toolbox and coveralls and expect to be given free rein to start drilling away. There would be bids, work orders, invoices, signatures, entries on the hotel manager's calendar. Faking all of that would take considerable resources. All so that just in case some bullheaded cop decided to look for one particular taxi stopping along one particular fifty-meter stretch of roadway, she wouldn't find anything.

That, or a manager decided the lobby would look nicer if the camera were fifteen centimeters higher.

Obviously the second theory was better. Obviously the first one was a textbook case of paranoia. So why was Mariko so sure the first one was correct?

She knew of just two people who might have been able to help her answer that question. One of them was dead. The other was too busy to return her calls. Right then and there, she decided the second one had kept her waiting long enough.

Her phone told her it was eleven o'clock, late enough that it was impolite to call. She called anyway.

"Let me guess," Han said. "There's a spider in your apartment and you want a big strong man to kill it."

"Yeah. You know any?"

"Ouch." There was a little rasp to his voice, as if she'd just roused him from bed. She knew him well enough to know the opposite was true: he never went to bed before midnight, which meant he was probably still on duty toward the end of a double-shift.

She said, "You heard about St. Luke's?"

"Mm-hm. You thinking what I'm thinking?"

"It's him. For sure."

An ambulance hissed by on rain-slicked tires, running neither lights nor siren. Mariko wondered who was in back, who was driving, whether anyone in there was going to test positive for ricin poisoning in the next day or two. But that was a rabbit hole she couldn't afford to go down at the moment. Instead she asked, "Did you have a chance to read any of those notebooks I loaned you?"

"Yeah. I've been meaning to call you about them, actually. I have some thoughts to bounce off you."

"Me too. Come down to Kabuki-chō and have a drink with me."

"Ooooh," Han said, "Kabuki-chō? I didn't think you were into nudie bars."

"Ah, what the hell. Maybe Kusama was right to demote me. Maybe I should explore new career opportunities."

Han chuckled. "Then allow me to be your guide, my lady. I know all the finest establishments. I can meet you down there in—oh, shit. Mariko, I have to go."

Mariko heard the squawk of a shoulder mic in the background. "What is it?" she said. "Are you at Terminal 2? What's going on?"

"I—I have to go. Let's do breakfast tomorrow. Eight o'clock?"

"Okay."

The line went dead, reminding Mariko all over again that bringing down Sour Plum and Yuki was child's play compared to the case she wished she was working. It wasn't a comforting thought to go to sleep by.

14

Mariko wasn't a morning person. She never had been. Her choice to be a makeup minimalist had nothing to do with fashion, nor was it a personal political statement about the double standard for men's and women's dress codes. It simply allowed her an extra five minutes of sleep in the morning. So it was a rare thing indeed for her to be *happy* to have somewhere to be at eight o'clock on a Saturday morning.

But this would be a good morning, because she got to spend it with the two men she trusted most in the world. Han met her at a high-top table for two at the window of a Mister Donut that overlooked the Blind Spot. Inevitably, he'd gotten there first—she'd slapped the snooze button once too often—and thanks to his near telepathic familiarity with Mariko's habits of mind, he'd ordered a steaming cup of coffee just as she liked it, timed so that the waitress delivered it to their table even as Mariko was walking up to the front door.

She saw Han already had a stack of yellowed notebooks on the table. Mariko had brought a few herself, tucked into the largest purse she owned. These slender booklets represented a tiny fraction of the reams of notes inscribed by Mariko's mentor and sword master, Yamada Yasuo. Yamada-sensei had been the one to open her mind to the possibility of the paranormal. Usually Mariko didn't go in for the X-Filesy stuff, but by now she'd accumulated too much evidence to ignore. She didn't go in for conspiracy theories either, but it was Yamada's notes on the Divine Wind that first put her onto Jōko Daishi, even before the attempted subway bombing. She couldn't help thinking that if only she'd read a little deeper, she could have prevented the Haneda attack.

She needed another pair of eyes roving over the notebooks, and that was why she'd drawn Han into this. She couldn't imagine letting any other cop see this deeply into her personal life. It was all too easy to dismiss these notebooks as the ravings of a demented old man. In fact, Yamada himself had predicted just that. He'd published volumes upon volumes as a history professor, yet he'd never submitted a single article on the cryptohistory that so fascinated him. Japan's top universities weren't ready for cursed swords and magical masks. Neither were Japan's police officers. Mariko was a detective; she believed only what the evidence allowed her to believe. If she ever let it slip that she'd witnessed swords that were something more than inanimate matter—swords capable of imposing their will, for lack of a better word—then funny looks at work would be the least of her worries. The boys already made stupid jokes about whether or not she should carry a gun while she was on her period. Sincere doubts about her sanity would spell the end of her career.

Han was different. He and Mariko were partners—not ex-partners but partners in spirit—and neither one of them gave a good goddamn where some camera-mugging captain decided to assign them. That was why Mariko felt she could reveal the notebooks. It was also why Han felt he could speak plainly with her, with none of the polite deflections that were the hallmark of the Japanese language. His jaw dropped the instant he saw her face, and the instant Mariko saw his reaction, she knew why he was gawking. She couldn't believe she'd forgotten: she and Han hadn't actually seen each other in the flesh since she got jumped. In Mariko's case, the flesh was bruised in umpteen different colors.

"Holy shit, Mariko, what the hell happened?"

Mariko cringed at the volume of his voice. "Keep it down, will you? I told you the other day. I got hit in a fight."

"Yeah, I saw your text, but . . . I mean, there's getting hit and then there's *getting hit*."

"I guess this would be the latter."

Han, still gaping at her, shook his head in disbelief. "I thought you said she hit you with her purse."

"Yeah, well, she had something really fucking heavy in her purse."

Mariko pulled out her phone, a newer model to replace the old flip phone she'd destroyed doing relief work at Haneda. It wasn't top of the line, but the camera function worked well enough. The photo she showed Han wasn't very clear, but it didn't need to be; Han knew the demon mask by sight. "This," Mariko said softly. "This is what she hit me with."

He gave the little screen a closer look, then studied Mariko's face, as if trying to replay how the mask must have struck her to leave the marks that it did. She could tell by his wince the moment he noticed the stitches in her scalp. "Please tell me you wrote 'head-butted by demon' on your injury report."

Mariko laughed, relieved that he was ready to joke about it. That meant they could put any further conversation about her injuries behind them. "How are things coming with Haneda?"

"Never ending. This one's going into extra innings for sure. That's why I dragged your ass out of bed so early; I have to be back out there by ten o'clock."

"It's okay. I just wanted to talk about Yamada-sensei's notes with you. I've been doing some reading—"

"Me too."

"I figured. I was hoping we could kick around some ideas together."

"Sure. Shoot."

Mariko sipped her coffee. "You remember the first time I had you come to my place to read these books with me?"

"Of course."

"Well, I think a lot of that stuff has to do with Haneda.

Remember the stuff Yamada-sensei wrote about the Divine Wind?"

"Are you kidding?" Han bounced in his seat like a little kid. "How could I forget? A five-hundred-year-old ninja clan in my own hometown? That's the coolest thing ever."

"Grow up, Han."

That wasn't going to happen. The best he could do was to slow the bouncing a bit. "See, I was rereading some of those notes too. I've got a theory about the woman who mugged you—"

"You think she's a ninja."

That stopped him short. "Uh . . . what?"

"You think she's a ninja, because that's what it would take to do what she did." Mariko said it as if she were reading instructions from a recipe.

"No way. You think she's a ninja too?"

"I think she received highly specialized training. As you're so fond of reminding me, she kicked my ass. Hell, Han, she made it look easy. Plus—and here's the part that really pisses me off—she outran me. I work harder at running than any other event in the tri. If you can out-swim me, fine. You out-ride me, fine. Even hit me in the face if you want, but do not fucking outrun me." Mariko found herself leaning toward him, punctuating the last few words by stabbing her finger at him like a weapon.

"Uh, okay."

"Sorry." Her face flushed and she backed off a bit. Other patrons were staring, and the waitress looked like she was trying to decide whether or not to call the police. Mariko gave them all a weak, embarrassed smile. To Han she whispered, "Sorry. Got a little heated there. It's kind of a sore spot for me."

"I gathered that, yeah."

Outside, a gaggle of teenage girls passed by wearing identical Burberry scarves and black Bulgari backpacks. Half of them chattered in rapid conversation while the other half walked head down, entranced by their phones. "Are you seeing this?" Han said. "I can't believe their parents allow them out of the house in skirts that short."

"Stop staring, Han."

"What are they doing up so early, anyway? When I was in high school, Saturdays were for sleeping in."

"Who knows? Giggling. Texting. Whatever teenagers do. Hell, these days they probably share tips on how to give a better blow job."

"Oh, how times have changed," Han said. "And oh, what I wouldn't give to be in high school today. Do you know how old I was when I got my first—?"

"We're not having that conversation."

Han laughed and scratched the back of his head. It called Mariko's attention to his short hair, which she still hadn't gotten used to. "Sorry," he said. "Back to your ninja chick. I think someone sent her after you, and I don't think it was Jōko Daishi."

"Seriously? You think this was a hit?"

"Maybe not a *hit* exactly, but maybe she was sending a message. The important part is that it wasn't from Jōko Daishi."

"How do you figure?"

"He went to great lengths to steal this mask, *neh*? Like, from the most bloodthirsty yakuza in Tokyo."

"Yeah." Mariko could picture his face: the Bulldog, Kamaguchi Hanzō, brutal even by the standards of organized crime.

"Okay," said Han, "so Jōko Daishi steals the mask, and a few days later we arrest him and he loses it again. A few days after that, we lose the mask to the Bulldog, and not long after that, the Bulldog sells it back to Jōko Daishi. Now he thinks he's got his hands on it for good, but then *bam*, some crazy chick in a nightie steals it."

"And then tries to take my head off with it. Thanks for reminding me."

Han winced. "Sorry. But here's my point: look at the timeline. Tuesday morning: Jōko Daishi makes bail and reclaims his mask. Tuesday afternoon: he commits the worst act of terrorism this city has ever seen. Wednesday morning: you've got his mask flying at your head because some whack-job ninja chick is trying to beat your brains out with it."

"Huh." Mariko was a little ashamed she hadn't thought of it that way before. "So either she found him within hours of the bombing—"

"Or else she had already insinuated herself next to him and she was just waiting for the right time."

"Or for the right orders. Han, I don't think she's operating alone."

Han blinked and shook his head as if a tiny flash-bang grenade just went off in his brain. He sat back in his chair and considered the implications of what Mariko had said. Mariko did the same. She hadn't consciously recognized the idea until she blurted it out. Now she had to wonder: if her assailant was being handled all along, who was the handler? Not Jōko Daishi, to be sure. The mask held holy power for him; he wouldn't give it up easily.

That meant someone stole it from him. That was a staggering thought. His Divine Wind cult had operated invisibly for years. They'd carried out murders, sold huge quantities of narcotics, amassed precursor chemicals to make bombs and drugs, all under the radar. In fact, the first time they'd drawn *any* attention from law enforcement, it was by wheeling fifty kilos of high explosives into the Tokyo subway system—a disaster Mariko managed to avert by a few tenths of a second. Yet this woman in white had not only found this invisible cult, but she'd stolen its holiest relic. How?

"All right," Han said. "What if we assume it takes a ninja to find a ninja?"

Mariko rolled her eyes. "Should I just go buy you some ninja action figures? Would that make you happy?"

"No, seriously. Hear me out." He counted off each point on his fingers. "One: Jōko Daishi was a ghost to us, but your friend the mask-swinger found him, like, instantaneously. Two: she's got higher-ups, people who can put her just where she needs to be. Three: in the notebooks, the old man refers to both—"

"He has a name, you know."

"Sorry. Professor Yamada. He doesn't always refer to the Divine Wind. Sometimes he just says the Wind."

Mariko remembered that. Before she'd ever met Jōko

Daishi, she had read Yamada-sensei's musings about the Wind and the Divine Wind. Mariko had been operating under the assumption that they were two names for one syndicate. If that syndicate was over five hundred years old, as Yamada surmised, it wouldn't be so strange to adopt a name change now and then.

But now Mariko questioned that assumption. She'd seen no evidence whatsoever of a second shadow group in Tokyo, but clearly *someone* was interfering with the Divine Wind's plans. Someone had put the mask in Mariko's hands—not Han's, not Sakakibara's, but hers alone. Why?

"Okay," she said, "let's say the Wind and the Divine Wind are separate organizations—"

"Separate ninja clans."

"Whatever. Suppose the Wind is fighting the Divine Wind. What's their end game? Why send the woman in white after me?"

Han threw up his hands. "That's the part I don't get. If she was supposed to kill you, she sure did a lousy job of it."

"Gee, thanks."

"You know what I mean. Of all the murder weapons she could have picked, a metal mask in a shoulder bag? Seriously?"

"Okay, good point."

Han looked pensively at the ceiling and scratched his cheek where his big, curly sideburn used to be. "Okay, let's rule out the possibility that this was an attempted homicide. What else would give her motive to jump you?"

"If I knew that, we'd have solved this a long time ago." She watched a pair of pigeons swoop in for a landing right in the middle of the Blind Spot. It would have been convenient for the woman in white to make an appearance just as suddenly. Mariko had plenty of questions for her.

Han followed her gaze. "What do you think is over there?" he asked. "In the Blind Spot. What's being hidden?"

"My best guess? A doorway, maybe to a safe house or something. Or maybe it's a dead drop. Or some way to leave secret messages in public, something no one would figure out if they saw it just once, but maybe they'd pick up on if they had some backlogged tape to study."

"Okay, back to the other thing. We've got an unknown assailant, attacking you for unknown reasons, with no perceptible motive, and disappearing to an unknown location, also for reasons unknown. Is that pretty much where we are?"

"You mean fucked? Yeah."

As they both gazed out the window, a pair of high school girls walked by their window, both of them wearing the ubiquitous tartan Burberry scarf that, by Mariko's estimation, must have been an obligatory purchase for every Japanese girl above the age of twelve. These two joined the small army of girls that had passed by a little earlier. They had encamped on a large flower planter not far from the front door of the love hotel whose camera Mariko wanted to reposition.

The sight of them suddenly wakened a memory in Mariko's subconscious: a black-and-white image of matching shoes and matching socks on matching skinny legs. Where had she seen it? On a CCTV feed. In fact, on the love hotel's CCTV feed; that was the only one pointed so low that it would capture just the legs. . . .

"That's it!" Mariko said. "Come on. I know how we're going to find where that bitch went to ground."

They quickly paid their bill, and Han had to hurry to keep up with Mariko. "Where are we going?" he said.

"To see the girls you wished you went to high school with. No asking for blow jobs."

She expected some witty repartee, but Han was too confused. "Do you mind telling me how a random group of girls suddenly became persons of interest?"

"I think they were here the morning after the bombing. At exactly the same time your favorite ninja chick was here."

"What?" Han thought about it for a second. "No way. That was a Wednesday. They would have been in school."

"Nope. All the schools were closed. Citywide."

"Huh." After a few strides, he added, "Good point. But so what?"

"So times have changed and all that. This generation is so different, blah blah blah."

"Still not following you."

They'd almost reached the girls, so Mariko slowed to a walk and lowered her voice. "When we were kids, you and I weren't tethered to a cell phone. We still talked to our friends instead of texting them. And we didn't have a camera in our pocket every second of every day."

Now the cartoon lightbulb lit up over Han's head. "Good call! Let's do this."

Mariko didn't need to fill in the rest. As they closed the last few meters, she wondered whether it was possible to boil down a teenager's incessant need to take frivolous pictures into some kind of mathematical formula. Oshiro's Postulate: for every student added to the group, the likelihood that one of them was taking a photo of another one multiplied exponentially, until at critical mass it was a metaphysical certainty that every one of them had been photographed by every other one of them from every possible angle. Mariko had no idea what they did with all the pictures, but she knew the sheer data storage required must have been driving up cell phone prices for years.

"Hello, ladies." Mariko flashed her badge as she reached the group. Han stood back and let her do the talking. "I wonder if you'd be willing to help us out," she said. "There was a crime committed in this area and I'm guessing one of you may have inadvertently caught the suspect in the act. Would it bother you if I clicked through some of your pictures?"

Had the girls been of Mariko's generation, one of them might have been savvy enough to know Mariko needed a warrant. But these girls were raised on Facebook and Twitter. They had no sense of privacy, nor even any sense that privacy was desirable. Their lives were open to the world. They were perfectly happy to let a couple of cops shuffle through their photo albums, and even to watch over Mariko's and Han's shoulders, giggling and reminiscing as the pictures flashed by.

In the end they captured three usable images. All three were pixelated and indistinct, mere slivers caught between the girls posing in the foreground. But there she was: the woman in white. In one image she stood in front of a storefront wall. In the next, captured on the same phone just a few seconds after the first one, the wall was there but she was gone. The third, taken by a different girl at almost the same time, was the mother lode: a gap in the wall, or rather a panel that looked like a wall but was actually a door, open just wide enough for the woman in white to slip through.

15

"So what now?" asked Han.

"Now I go kick the door down and get some answers."

Han winced. They'd hardly gotten out of earshot of those high school girls. Mariko managed two steps toward the secret door before Han clapped a hand on her shoulder and spun her back around. "Come on, Mariko. Anyone paranoid enough to create this Blind Spot of yours has got to be paranoid enough to monitor their own front door, *neh*? Don't you think there's going to be a security camera somewhere?"

"Fine by me," Mariko said with a shrug. "Let them come out and try to stop me. These people pissed me off, Han. Let one of them throw a punch and see what happens."

He steepled his hands plaintively in front of his chest, as if he were praying to her. "A quick reconnaissance run first, okay? Just for me? We'll pretend we're a couple shopping for sex toys."

"You're gross."

"Okay, chastity belts, then. Just walk with me, nice and slow like we're window-shopping. We'll get a good look at the door before you tear off and boot it down."

Mariko closed her eyes and sighed. It wasn't a bad idea. She wanted it to be, but it wasn't. "Fine. One pass.

Then I'm going in there, and goddamn it, I'm going to find someone to interrogate."

She offered her elbow to Han and he took it gently. Together they took a casual stroll, stopping occasionally to study the lewd posters plastered here and there. They pointedly took no interest in the secret door they'd discovered. The side streets of Kabuki-chō were so narrow that even though Mariko and Han tried to keep their distance, they still passed close enough to their target that she could see where the paint was peeling on the doorframe.

Smack in the middle of the Blind Spot was a strip club—one of dozens in this district. Strictly speaking, it only needed one sign out front, but it had fifteen or twenty instead, all of them in bright primary colors. Crammed amid all the Japanese were the few inevitable phrases of mangled English. WELCOME FOREIGNER BEST COMFORT CORNER was Mariko's favorite. Anywhere else in the city, this place would have stuck out like a mouse turd in a rice bowl, but in Kabuki-chō it was just another peacock displaying its plumage.

"Where is it?" Han whispered.

Mariko couldn't spot the secret door either. Or rather, she knew she was looking at it; she just couldn't see how it could be a door.

The front wall of the strip club was a series of painted white panels, each one the width of an average door but half again as tall. Photos of the club's dancers clung to the panels like wet leaves on a car hood. In most of the pictures the women wore little more than they wore on stage. In a few, the dancer wore nothing but little pink hearts digitally imposed over her bits. The middle panel, indistinguishable from the others, was the one that had swiveled open to admit the woman in white.

"No handle," Han said, just loud enough to be heard over the metallic clamor of the pachinko parlor across the road from their target.

"No hinges," said Mariko, and just like that they were past the target and continuing down the narrow street.

"I don't get it," Han said. "She must have hit that door at a pretty good clip. How did she open it?"

"Maybe an electronic key? Something that works automatically on proximity?"

"Yeah, maybe," said Han, "but you have to wonder where she's keeping it."

"Good point." Mariko had forgotten: the woman in white was wearing mostly stolen clothing when she'd fled. The only thing she was wearing that really seemed to belong to her was the see-through mini-dress. "So what, then? How did she open the door?"

"The bouncer, maybe? He could have a hidden switch."

Mariko risked one last glance at the undetectable door, and at the ordinary door a few meters away, where the club's bouncer would sit. Today it was closed; no one went to a strip club at eight thirty on a Saturday morning.

"I don't know," she said. "One thing is for sure: this is where you get off the bus."

"What? Why?"

"Because you're on duty and I'm not, and what I'm going to do next violates about a dozen general orders."

Han tightened his grip a little on her elbow. "You can't be serious. You're still thinking of going in there?"

"Hell, no. I'm done thinking about it. I'm going in there as soon as I can get rid of you."

"Mariko, you know there's no way in hell I'm letting you walk in there alone. We're partners."

"I know. But you just got your ass hauled in front of a review board for ethics infractions. It's a miracle that you still have a badge. If you think I'm going to let you commit *more* infractions by tagging along with me, you're nuts."

"Mariko—"

"No, Han. My career is fucked. Yours doesn't have to be."

Han stopped walking, and since he still had Mariko by the arm, he stopped her too. "Listen, I've been reading those old notebooks of yours and I've got this theory cooking. If I'm right about it, you're being set up."

"Hm." Usually Mariko and Han thought alike, but this time she couldn't see where he was heading. "Okay, you lost me. Explain."

Han bounced nervously on the balls of his feet, probably unaware that he was doing it. "All right, here we go. Remind me, how did you know the old guy who wrote all the notes?"

"'Old guy'? Really?"

"Sorry. Professor Yamada. How did you know him?"

"He was my *kenjutsu* sensei."

"Right. And you got that sword of yours from him, *neh*?"

"Yeah."

"Who'd he get it from?"

"Huh." Mariko frowned, biting softly on her lower lip. "You know, I don't think he ever told me."

"Is it possible he got it by chance?"

Mariko had to think about that one too. "Yes and no," she said at last. "With swords like these, you stop using the word 'coincidence.' But you may be onto something. I don't think Yamada-sensei could ever afford to *buy* an Inazuma. He was a college professor, and before that he was just an officer in the army. Not the kinds of jobs that pay well enough to buy historical artifacts."

"See, that's what I thought. I don't think that ninja woman was trying to beat you to death with that mask. I think she was trying to give it to you."

"You think?" She pointed at her bruises and stitches.

"Hear me out, okay? I've been studying your sensei's journals. He mentions another Inazuma sword called Beautiful Singer. Have you heard of it?"

"Yeah, you could say that." Just hearing the name was enough to make Mariko wince. She still had scars on her stomach and back where that sword ran her through.

"There's another called Streaming Dawn. Heard of that one?"

"No," she said, but suddenly she was all ears. A fourth Inazuma blade. She'd encountered three of them already—more than anyone else alive, in all probability—but she'd always wondered how many more were out there.

"Your sensei says he finds no record of either of these ever having been sold. They're named in a will here or there, or taken as trophies after combat, but in every case he says there were strange circumstances around the death of the previous owner. Guys losing duels they should have won. Master swordsmen suddenly going nuts on the battlefield. Stuff like that."

Mariko had no trouble believing that. Yamada-sensei had shared with her the grisly history of Beautiful Singer. Even if he hadn't, she'd witnessed firsthand how it could twist the mind of whoever was holding it. She wondered if this Streaming Dawn bore a similar curse. "Keep going," she said.

"All right, remember how you said that mask of yours is tuned to your sword? Well, it never gets sold either. Yamada makes a specific note of that. He says the Wind places it where it needs to be."

"Okay. So what's your point?"

Han was bouncing like a piston now, urgent and agitated. "I think there's a ninja Secret Santa out there, and I think he's setting you up."

Mariko wanted to grab him by the shoulders and plant him firmly on the pavement. She wanted to send him on his way and get down to business, but some nameless intuition stayed her hand. She'd only seen him this nervous when they were getting ready to raid a meth lab or close the deal on a yakuza sting. He was legitimately scared for her.

So she gave him the benefit of the doubt. "Let's say you're right. How is this setup supposed to work?"

"I don't know. All I know is that you're now the proud owner of a mask that's worth more than either of us is going to make this year, and a sword that's worth more money than we'll make in our entire career. So either they accidentally fell into your hands or that's exactly what the ninja Secret Santa wants you to think."

"I think you just like saying 'ninja Secret Santa.'"

"Okay, fine. Guilty as charged. But you know I'm right, *neh*? You weren't *lucky* that woman didn't kill you. That fight was choreographed."

Mariko was too stunned to speak. Han's logic was solid, but his conclusion hardly seemed possible. At the time, Mariko had been dead certain she was fighting for her life. Could the whole thing have been staged?

Yes. She had to admit it was possible. In fact, right from the beginning she'd had the sense that someone had arranged for her to cross paths with the ninja woman. But it had never occurred to her that her assailant had been the one to do the arranging. If so, then not only had she kicked Mariko's ass, but she'd chosen precisely how much to kick, and how much to let Mariko kick back. And she'd done it without Mariko ever noticing.

No. No one could be that skilled. Yet Mariko had no alternate explanation.

"See what I mean?" Han said it as if he'd read her mind. "Someone is setting you up, Mariko. I don't know why, but I know they might be waiting for you on the other side of that door if you decide to kick it down."

Then at least I'll get some answers, Mariko thought. But to Han she said, "You're right. Of course you're right. I need to think this through."

"Bullshit." Han jabbed a finger at her like an umpire calling a strike. "You're bullshitting me. You're going to wait until I turn my back, and then you're going to rush in there guns blazing."

"No, I'm—"

"No, you're not, are you? You don't have any guns to blaze with. Your service weapon is locked up at head-quarters."

Mariko had never seen him like this. All his witticisms were gone. What remained was a sense of urgency that bordered on anger. "Han, I can't get a warrant to go in there. I can only show probable cause if I reveal all the work I've done tracking that woman to this spot, and if I do that . . . well, this isn't a narco case, is it? As soon as Captain Kusama gets wind of it, he'll take a hatchet to whatever remains of my career."

"So what am I supposed to do? Sit back and watch you walk into a trap?"

"We don't know it's a trap. We don't know anything about it."

"And that's a *good* thing?" He peeled back his jacket

to reveal the Nambu M60 holstered under his left arm. "At least take a fucking gun with you."

"I can't. Not yours, anyway. If I have to use it, it's registered to you—"

"And that violates regs. Okay, so case closed, *neh*? You don't have a weapon and I'm not letting you go in there unarmed. I'm coming with you and that's that."

Mariko gave him a sad smile. "It's not. I've got the day off and you need to report for duty in about an hour and a half. So as much as I love you for wanting to join me on this career-ending caper, all I have to do is sit and have a cup of tea and wait for you to go to work."

Han fumed and steamed, muttering a litany of unintelligible curses. At last he said, "All right, then go do it. Right now, before I change my mind. At least this way I can stand outside and listen for enough reasonable suspicion to justify coming in after you. Do me a favor—hell, do both of us a favor: scream loud when they try to kill you."

•

16

Mariko took a deep breath to quell the butterflies in her stomach. Then she palmed her Pikachu and went back to the strip club.

For her first four years on the force she'd carried a Cheetah stun baton. It had never been ideal for plain-clothes work; it was too long, too hard to conceal under a jacket, and the 850,000 volts it boasted four years ago were downright anemic by today's standards. She'd made the compromise because of the baton's greater striking power. For her first four years on the job, she'd never felt strong enough to hit a perp and really make it sting. But thanks to her departed sensei, Yamada, she felt stronger now, more confident. The big guys didn't intimidate her as much anymore.

The first time Han saw her new stun gun, he joked that she'd traded a Cheetah for a Pikachu. He wasn't far wrong: two and a half million volts of whup-ass packed into a little black box the size of a pack of cigarettes. Un-fortunately, once Sakakibara overheard the joke, she was stuck carrying "the Pikachu" forever after. Somehow, somewhere along the way, someone had managed to stick shiny prismatic Pikachu stickers all over it when Mariko wasn't looking. She suspected Han.

On closer inspection, the invisible door wasn't quite invisible. Mariko still couldn't find hinges or handles, but she could see the tiny seam running the perimeter of the door. It looked like the wall panel had been painted over but the paint had cracked. Mariko guessed it was supposed to look like that.

Not surprisingly, pushing and prodding did nothing. She tried the front door instead, which was perfectly ordinary: a heavy pane of plate glass seated in a steel frame, with a little plastic box to slide a key card through to unlock the door. Mariko wondered what would happen if she zapped the lock with her Pikachu, and whether two and a half million volts would act as a master key or fuse the lock shut permanently.

In the end she didn't need to find out. The door opened at her touch. Weird, she thought. Tokyo wasn't exactly a den of thieves—the city saw as many burglaries in a year as New York saw in a day—but still, leaving the front door unlocked was asking for trouble. The whole thing felt wrong. In fact, it felt like she was being set up, just as Han suspected. But she went inside anyway.

On the outside the strip club was two stories of nothing but brightly colored signage. Inside it was just the opposite: a dark and cavernous expanse, lit only by the green glow of the emergency exit lights far off in the corners. The stink of stale cigarette smoke suffused the furniture, the carpeting, the very paint on the walls. A stage dominated the floor space, of course, dotted with stripper poles and surrounded by chairs. There was a bar in one corner, a flight of stairs in the other. The stairs led to a room overlooking the whole first floor and walled in by floor-to-ceiling one-way mirrors. The VIP lounge, Mariko guessed, but she didn't bother checking. The only detail she cared about was the secret door.

There was no trace of it. If it had led to this room, it would have opened up right under the stairs, but instead Mariko saw only a blank wall.

"No," she said to herself. She wouldn't allow the trail to go cold. Not here, not after she'd come so far.

It stood to reason that the door wouldn't open into this room. Secret doors were for secret places, not the decidedly un-secret main floor of a strip joint. So where did it go, then? There had to be a hidden space inside the wall. But how could she get to it?

She couldn't. Not from here. The whole point of that hidden space was to stay sequestered from the public areas of the club. So if there was no access on this floor, the only place left for it to go was up or down.

Let's try down, Mariko thought. She went cautiously to the bar, taking care not to stumble in the dark in this unfamiliar space. Behind the bar she spotted exactly what she'd hoped to find: a door to a staircase, which in turn led down to the stockroom. The door wasn't locked but the stockroom was. A good, hard kick ripped the hasp right out of the wood.

That was the moment she really wished she had her sidearm. Any bad guys on the other side of that door now knew exactly where she was. Unless they stepped within arm's reach, the Pikachu would be useless.

Mariko moved through the doorway fast and low, eager to find cover just in case bullets started flying her way. She needn't have bothered; the storeroom was empty.

Flickering fluorescent tubes automatically sputtered to life, triggered by the opening door. Mariko saw walls of heavy-duty shelving, stocked to the ceiling with cases of booze, boxes of napkins, giant bags of *arare*. No women in white, nor anyone else to tackle Mariko or put a slug in her.

A refrigerator's compressor purred contentedly, causing Mariko to look for the source. She found it quickly enough: a pair of tall, stainless steel, industrial-sized units, one a fridge and the other a freezer. Still no women in white, no ninja Secret Santas, no signs of any criminal activity.

Then she heard movement upstairs.

Heels thumped the floor hard and fast. They sped straight for the bar—straight for Mariko. She heard the door upstairs being knocked aside. Mariko dashed for the stockroom door, slipping behind it a fraction of a second before her intruder rushed into the room.

She jabbed him in the nape of the neck with the Pikachu and pulled the trigger.

"Fuck!" Han shouted. He jumped away from the contact studs like a bullet leaving a gun. At the same time, Mariko pulled the stun gun away. Han clutched his neck with one hand and brought his revolver around with the other.

"It's me! It's Mariko. Don't shoot!"

He blinked hard and shot a double take in her direction. His face was as red as a beet. An involuntary convulsion careened through his body. He could hardly stand up straight, but at least he lowered the gun. "What the hell, Mariko?"

"I'm sorry. I'm so, so sorry." Mariko managed that much without cracking up. Then she let out a guffaw. "You should see your face," she said, laughing so hard it was tough to get the words out. "I wish we could have filmed that. Best YouTube video ever. I swear, everyone in the department—"

"Ha-ha," Han said, not the least bit amused. "I come down here to save your life and this is the thanks I get?"

"What can I say? This cop thing is a dangerous profession."

"Damn right it is." He rubbed his neck and laughed. "You are *such* an asshole, you know that?"

Mariko almost forgot they were in enemy territory. "How did you know to look for me down here?"

"I heard a banging noise and I came in. I guess it was you kicking that door open. Anyway, I saw the light coming from downstairs behind the bar and I rushed to your aid. You know, like a superhero. And for that you tased me in the neck."

"I am so sorry—"

"Don't be. I'll just go buy a stun gun and get you back." He holstered his weapon and for the first time he looked around the storeroom. "What were you doing down here, anyway?"

"I was hoping to find where that ninja bitch's secret door lets out. Hey, what are you doing?"

Han was reaching for the handle on the refrigerator door. "Looking for something to drink. A little orange juice really hits the spot after getting electrocuted, you know?"

"Han, you can't."

"We're already guilty of breaking and entering; I don't think they're going to miss one little can of—"

At first it seemed like the door was a bit stubborn. Han tugged it a bit harder, and suddenly the whole refrigerator pulled away from the wall. It swung out as if one corner was connected by hinges to the wall—which, in fact, was precisely the case. The refrigerator doubled as another hidden door.

Han had the firearm, so he was the first one through. Mariko shadowed him, feeling useless with the Pikachu in her hand, but at least she could offer a second pair of eyes. As it happened, she was the first one to spot the light switch.

She flicked it and two long rows of fluorescent lights came to life. Below them stood at least a dozen desks, the pressboard kind with the thin faux-wood veneer. Each one was home to what looked like a little black octopus: a bundle of cables, zip-tied together and blossoming up through a plastic-rimmed cutout in the desktop. Power cords, Ethernet cables, USB something-or-others; Mariko wasn't great with computers, but she knew enough to understand there used to be a hell of a lot of them in this room.

Many of the cables ran to a large, blocky, important-looking metal armature on the back wall. Not long ago, this must have stored a number of smaller but equally important-looking gadgets, probably with lots of fans and LED lights. These would have something to do with servers and cloud computing and other networky things that might as well have been magic spells for all Mariko understood about them. Not that it mattered. Someone had absconded with everything a police detective might have used to figure out who had been down here and what they'd been up to.

There were no office chairs. No carpeting. No fabric at all, actually, which was a shame, because DNA evidence was especially clingy to fabric. The only things left behind had hard surfaces, and judging by the chlorinated smell that got stronger with each step into the room, they'd all been wiped down with bleach. Mariko and Han would find no useful evidence here.

"You wanted your ninja Secret Santa," Mariko said. "I think this is his workshop."

"And the ninja elves are all long gone." He whistled. "What the hell have you gotten yourself into?"

Mariko just shook her head. What was there to say? This place wasn't Jōko Daishi's style. She remembered his headquarters all too well. That place was just as sterile as this, but here she saw no place to worship. No private sanctum for the cult leader to fuck his acolytes either.

"Don't worry," Han said. "Whoever these people are, they'll have left trace evidence upstairs. We'll sweep the carpet, the bathrooms, the whole works. No one can keep track of every hair."

"They don't need to. Han, how many guys come to that strip club in a given weekend?"

Han shrugged. "I don't know. A couple hundred, maybe."

"See? Down here they leave no trace, while up there they leave too much. You want to send evidence techs into that club and tell them to catalog every last hair? You'll give them all heart attacks."

Mariko ambled around aimlessly, lost in her thoughts. Who was the woman in white? Who was pulling her strings? Why did they want Mariko to have the mask? Was it to weaken Jōko Daishi, to shatter his deluded belief in his own divine power? Or was it a ploy to draw him into attacking Mariko in order to reclaim the mask?

She had so many questions, and so far only one answer: she knew where the woman in white had gone once she'd disappeared through the secret door upstairs. A sturdy steel fire door on the right-hand wall concealed a ladder that climbed back up to street level. Solving that riddle brought her little solace; she had a hundred other questions she'd like to have answered first.

"Uh, Mariko? You're going to want to take a look at this."

She turned to see Han standing like a drunkard barely

able to keep his feet. A sheaf of paper sagged in one hand, and he could not have looked more flummoxed if he were holding a dead baby alien.

Dumbfounded, he passed the papers to Mariko—ordinary A4 paper, the same as she'd find in any photocopier in the city. Nothing remarkable there. The first line on the first page didn't knock her socks off either:

10-09-29 CEST 10:11:11 MX10-1-9-1 000807 UC VM PI

The time stamp was easy enough to understand, but the rest was gibberish. Almost gibberish, anyway. That MX number seemed vaguely familiar, but Mariko couldn't place it.

Thus, the rest of the page didn't do her much good. They were all slight variations on the first line. She could see each one had a different string of numbers, each time a little later in the day, but what were they? Stock trades? Print jobs? Train departures? There was no way to tell. Thirty lines per page, all of them useless.

Halfway down the next page, a line break and then a new list of alphanumerics, these dated *10-09-30*—September 30, 2010. Thursday. Apart from that difference, Thursday's gibberish was as unintelligible as Wednesday's.

"Han, what am I supposed to be reading here?"

"Skip to the end."

She shrugged and flipped to the last page. The very last line read,

10-10-02 CEST 08:00:00 LOC UNSPEC Meet Watanabe Masayori

Mariko dropped the paper like it was on fire. "What the hell?"

"My thoughts exactly," said Han.

No one in Narcotics called Han by his real name. In fact, most of the guys didn't even know his real name. Sakakibara had nicknamed him Han years ago and the name just stuck. Mariko might have been the only one who knew that his nickname before that was Masu, short for Masayori. Watanabe Masayori. Who met her at oh eight hundred hours this morning, October 2, just like it said on the page.

There it was, staring up at her. She picked it up again, and with each line she read, she felt her gut tighten. The penultimate entry: the previous night, twenty-one hundred hours, *commence sting operation against Lee Jin Bao*. The entry before that: same day, twelve thirty hours, *intake Yuki Kisho on suspicion of trafficking*. The entry before that: one day earlier, a string of numbers just like the ones that dominated the previous four pages. Except now she remembered why the MX number seemed familiar.

The city of Tokyo bought its traffic cameras from a company called Mobotix. TMPD sourced the same company for its surveillance cameras. MX10-4-137-29 was the location of one particular Mobotix traffic cam. What Mariko held in her hands was a complete list of every traffic cam and surveillance cam whose feed she'd pulled in tracking the woman in white from Tokyo Station all the way back to the Blind Spot.

This wasn't a pirated file. Mariko had never typed up a list of all the cameras she'd used. Half of them were duds, and even of the best hits, she'd just printed the clearest images and moved on. So no one had hacked her account back at HQ. Someone had been watching her the whole time. They had monitored all of her computer activity related to the woman in white, and they must have done it in real time. Not just Mariko's searches for camera feed, either; there were e-mails and memos about the Yuki collar too, and more about the raid on the Sour Plum. Hell, even her phone conversations; she and Han had spoken for all of thirty seconds in setting up this morning's meet. That was the last entry in the log.

"Han, these people were right here, in this room, less than ten hours ago. They listened to us, they packed up all their shit, and they vanished."

Han took half a step back, and Mariko realized she'd gotten a little animated with her gesticulations. "Sorry," she said, crossing her arms. "But you see what I'm saying. Ten hours flat, and they go from fully operational to ghost in the machine. Worse yet, they leave the front door unlocked, just to make sure I'd come down here to see what's left of their vanishing act."

"Hm." He looked at the pages in her hand. "So why'd they leave the log behind? Same reason? Like, just to fuck with your head?"

"Hold on. You don't think I'm being paranoid, do you? Please tell me you believe me."

"Are you kidding? Look around." He stretched his arms out wide, as if to take in the whole room. "Ninja Secret Santa's workshop. If this wasn't happening to a good friend of mine, this would be the coolest thing I've ever seen."

That was more than Mariko could take. She sat on the nearest desk and sagged in half. She thought her traffic camera trick was pretty good. She was especially proud of the trick with the high schoolers' cell phones. All along she'd thought she was flying under the radar, but this printout blew that illusion all to hell. Now, not only had she not found her quarry, but her quarry had only to send this cryptic list to Captain Kusama and that would be the end of Mariko's career. He'd given her a direct order to work nothing but narcotics cases, and here was a record of all the time she'd spent hunting her assailant instead.

Right from day one, she should have filed an injury report with the department. She should have passed the case to another detective. While she was at it, she could have passed along her idea with the traffic cams too. Cops didn't take this kind of thing lying down; the woman in white had attacked one of their own, and that meant they'd find her no matter how long it took. Instead she'd passed off her bruises as a *kenjutsu* injury, she'd disobeyed orders, and now she'd dragged Han into the whole mess. In the last five minutes she had committed breaking and entering, destruction of property, and official misconduct. It was enough to put her in prison.

All for nothing. And now she was out of leads. Her courage leaked out of her like water from a sieve. "Han, what the hell am I going to do?"

"Exactly what you've been doing. Look, Mariko, whoever these people are, you've got them running scared. That list? It's like a minefield sign on a field without any mines. They're trying to frighten you away."

"Yeah, well, it's working."

"No. I'm telling you, they're more afraid of you than you are of them. They thought they were invisible, but now they know they're not. Not to you. Not anymore."

Mariko wished she could find that encouraging. If there really was a Wind, and if they really had been lurking in the shadows for the last five hundred years, it would be quite an honor to be the first one to spot them. But how could she know she was the first one? There might have been a hundred by now but the Wind assassinated the other ninety-nine. For all Mariko knew, she could be next on their list.

BOOK FOUR

AZUCHI-MOMOYAMA PERIOD, THE YEAR 21

(1588 CE)

Daigoro cradled his stepfather in his arms. He decided he could get used to the feeling of holding a baby.

Lord Yasuda Gorobei was warm and soft and smelled like comfort. His tiny eyes clamped shut against the sunlight and he snuggled his face into Daigoro's kimono, bound and determined to sleep.

His father, Yasuda Kenkichi, had died just as he lived: drunk and disgraced. He met his end facedown in a puddle of muddy rainwater after a brutal tavern brawl. Kenkichi's father, Kenbei, had then taken custody of his grandchild, despite his many winters and his obvious disdain for fatherhood. His wife, Azami, was twenty years his junior but evinced the same indifference to motherhood. To judge by her stout arms and beetled brow, she would be more at home in a smithy than a nursery.

They had surrendered their custody when Gorobei married. Daigoro had arranged his mother's marriage to little Gorobei to protect her from Shichio, who had designs on her hand and then on House Okuma itself. Once Okuma Yumiko became Lady Yasuda Yumiko, she was out of Shichio's reach.

Now she was recovering from the many blows she'd suffered over the last year—first her husband's murder, then the death of her eldest son in a duel. As a younger woman she'd miscarried two pregnancies between Ichirō and Daigoro, and now her only remaining son could be executed simply for coming home to her. Her grief had visibly aged her. Crow's-feet stretched from the corners of her eyes, lengthening like cracks in ice, and her back had taken a slight but noticeable hunch. Now, after only a few weeks of caring for her newborn husband, she was standing taller. If she grew any new wrinkles, they would be laugh lines.

It helped that she was not alone in raising the child. Akiko was a tremendous help. Also, Yasuda Kenbei and his wife, Azami, had taken residence in the Okuma compound. They occupied the adjoining rooms that had once belonged to Daigoro and his brother, Ichirō. The brothers wouldn't be needing their rooms any time soon: one was dead and the other was a fugitive *rōnin*, legally banned from setting foot on House Okuma's lands. Shichio had roving patrols enforcing that ban, but they didn't know the footpaths crisscrossing the estate, while Daigoro had grown up playing hide-and-seek back there.

Thus Daigoro and Katsushima had slipped in unannounced and undetected, using a nigh-invisible postern gate in the orchard. Aki had long since arrived, since she traveled by horse and the main roads were still open to her. Her relief at seeing Daigoro alive was as palpable as the breeze. Daigoro's mother was delighted to see him too, though her husband was not, since all the fuss made it harder to sleep. The scent of unfamiliar women unsettled him, so he started to cry whenever Aki picked him up. Yet as soon as Daigoro took him, he pinched his eyes shut and nestled in to resume his nap.

"Daigoro, it is so good to have you back," his mother said. "How are you healing?"

"Better and better by the day." He curled and opened his fist to prove it. He didn't mention the stripe of pain in his right thigh. A sword had caught him there at the Green Cliff, and though the wound had healed over, three days of hiking through the backwoods had aggravated the muscle. Before bedding down for the night Daigoro would pay Old Yagyū a visit. His thigh was dreading it already:

Yagyū's massaging fingers would press deeply enough to bring tears to Daigoro's eyes, but in the morning the leg would feel like new.

"Daigoro-san," Yasuda Kenbei said. His tone was a little too informal, a little too insistent, almost like a parent chiding his adult child. "We must speak. Alone."

Kenbei was as grim-faced as his wife. His cold, steely eyes made Daigoro think of storm clouds. He was resplendent in Yasuda green, distinguished and lordly with his graying topknot. In time, perhaps his hair would go as white as his father's, Lord Yasuda Jinbei. Of all of House Okuma's allies, Lord Yasuda was Daigoro's favorite. In truth he was more like an uncle than an ally, though sadly he hadn't left his sickbed in months. When Daigoro had last seen him, Lord Yasuda's face seemed as hollow as a skull.

Daigoro did not expect the son of Yasuda Jinbei to speak to him so rudely, but he took it in stride. Bowing to his mother, he passed off the baby, kissed Aki's hand, and followed Kenbei to the tearoom. He was surprised to see Azami come along.

The three of them sat around a low table. Daigoro and Kenbei batted the necessary pleasantries back and forth: your grandson looks well, will this heat ever end, all the standard fare. Other women would have contributed the occasional *neh* to the conversation, or dropped a compliment here and there, but Azami remained silent. When she finally spoke, she just blurted, "House Okuma is in debt."

By the gods, Daigoro thought, you might at least have waited for the serving girl to bring some tea. "We are," he said, then realized he wasn't a part of that *we*. He had cast himself out. "That is to say, yes, my mother's house has taken on significant expenses of late. Skimping on a funeral brings bad karma to the deceased, and we buried two of our own. We also feasted the Imperial Regent—"

"With *our* coin," Azami pointed out.

"That was the wedding. We hosted him once before that, when he first paid us a visit. Food and *sake* for over a hundred men does not come cheaply."

Neither did poppy's tears, he chose not to add. His mother had been taking them nightly to help her sleep—and more often than not, a dose or two during the day as well. He'd speak to Old Yagyū later tonight about how she was holding up now that he'd weaned her off the treacherous stuff.

For now he had more pressing problems. "My lord and lady, may I ask what brings this on? If Lord Yasuda's medicines have become too expensive, it goes without saying that House Okuma's stores are open to you."

"No need," Kenbei said. His voice was deep and dour. "My father's care is expensive, yes, but it will not last much longer. After that, rule will pass to me."

"Oh?" Daigoro did not cloak his surprise. The Okumas and Yasudas had spoken openly with one another for many years. They had also maintained a unified front for that long, fending off all other comers, including Izu's other lords protector when they got too ambitious. "What of your elder brothers?"

"They maintain homesteads of their own, strategically placed for the defense of Izu."

"I know. It's just . . . well, I beg your pardon, Kenbei-san, but I would have thought *you* would assume one of those holds when a brother came home to rule."

"Home!" Kenbei's anger was sudden. Though he suppressed it just as quickly, it still lent a certain heat to his words. "*I* am the one who stayed home with Father. *I* am the one who manages House Yasuda—and also the one who must deal with Toyotomi Hideyoshi after you slaughtered so many of his men outside the Green Cliff."

"I am sorry for that, Kenbei-san. And I am eternally grateful for your family's support. Any number of soldiers and servants in your house could have betrayed me to my enemy, yet none have done so."

"We gain nothing by exposing you, and stand to lose much. You have been a useful ally. I do hope that will continue. When my father passes, I intend to make some changes."

"Oh?"

"House Yasuda has languished too long in the shadow

of the Red Bear. Your father was a mighty warrior and a shrewd diplomat. No Yasuda will say otherwise. But his time has come and gone."

"Speak plainly, sir."

"You renounced your name when you treated with General Shichio, *neh*? And with it, you renounced your marriage. Do you stand by your oath?"

"You know I do." And never mind that Aki won't hear a word of it, Daigoro thought. She insisted the law was on her side—he'd cast himself out of the house, not her—but in truth a woman had no say in matters of marriage. "Make your point, Kenbei-san."

Kenbei swallowed. He glanced briefly at Azami, then said, "You are no longer Okuma Daigoro. There is no man to speak for the Okumas now, and therefore no Okuma to speak for Izu. That duty passes to me now."

Daigoro bit his lip before he said anything rash. He could hardly believe his ears. And if he'd heard Kenbei correctly, the appropriate response was to beat him and his wife with a horsewhip.

That would have been Ichirō's approach. It was tempting, too. But their father would have taken the softer path. "Let me be sure I understand your meaning. When I approached you to arrange Gorobei's marriage to my mother, I did it to save my family from the depredations of a madman. But when you consented, you did it not to protect an ally, but to usurp my mother in her moment of weakness. Is that what I'm to understand?"

"She *is* weak, Daigoro-san. Would you honestly say she is in a fit state to rule?"

"We should question your fitness first. Need I remind you that your father is still alive?"

"For now."

"Then *for now* you ought to obey him. After that, obey your eldest brother, and when he passes, obey the next one. Have you no loyalty to your own kin?"

"My kin have lingered far too long. I expected more sympathy from you, Daigoro-san. You understand what it is to be the youngest son. Now imagine you were sixty years old and your father still clung to life. Imagine your brothers showed the same vitality. If I mean to rule before my hundredth birthday, I must take action."

Daigoro clenched a fist, wishing it was holding that horsewhip. "You ask me to imagine if my father and brother were still alive? I would give anything for that. Anything."

"And live only as a servant to your house?"

"Until my hundredth birthday. Or until tomorrow, if by giving my life I could grant them a hundred years."

Kenbei's face grew somber. "I am sorry. I should have thought of that."

"Yes, you should have. And think on this too: just what do you hope to become once you claim your father's seat? You will never be anything other than a servant to your house; you will only become the servant with the heaviest duties."

"So says the boy who abandoned his duties," said Azami.

"Not abandoned. Sacrificed. To save my house." And believe me, he thought, there are days when I am glad to be rid of them. The daimyo of Izu reminded him of nothing so much as squabbling hens. Impossible to silence, nearly impossible to govern, they presented the daily temptation to spit them, roast them, and eat them for dinner.

There was a time when Daigoro couldn't understand why a born samurai like Katsushima would live as a *rōnin*. Now he knew. Part of him wished he was like Katsushima, free as a wave. He would wash right over these two and roll back out to sea.

When the maidservant came with their tea, Daigoro dismissed her. His guests were not worth the price of a pinch of tea leaves. "So is that the way of it?" he asked. "We arranged the marriage of our houses for mutual protection against a common enemy. It served as our armor, but now you would reforge it into a dagger. Is that the message you would like me to deliver to Lord Yasuda? That you betrayed my house at the first opportunity?"

"Listen to you!" Azami snapped. "A tittle-tattle running to a grown-up."

"One party to a parley, treating with the other. Your husband is the one behaving childishly. Unless . . . well, perhaps he is not the cat, but only the paw. How much of this is your doing?"

"Leave my wife out of this," Kenbei growled.

"I'll thank you to show me the same courtesy."

Kenbei set his teeth on edge. Daigoro could see the veins swelling in his temples. His mouth was a thin, flat line. "You have no wife. By your own word, she is your ex-wife—or perhaps your widow, if Okuma Daigoro is truly dead. In any case, you have no authority to speak for her."

"Then why talk to me at all?"

As soon as he said it, Daigoro asked himself the same question. Did Kenbei have some ulterior motive for keeping Daigoro away from his family? Daigoro closed his eyes for a moment, the better to focus on what he could hear. Gorobei was crying and women were cooing at him. He heard Akiko's lilting tones in the chorus. That meant she was safe. Up until this moment, it hadn't even occurred to him to question her safety. But prior to this moment, his family's closest ally had never threatened a coup.

If she was safe, then something stayed Yasuda swords in their scabbards. Perhaps Aki was holding Gorobei. Perhaps Katsushima was too near and too feared. Or perhaps, Daigoro hoped most of all, Kenbei had no intention of hurting her. Before today, Daigoro would never have dreamt otherwise. Now he could not get it out of his mind that Aki's claim to power was stronger than Kenbei's, and the day she gave birth to Daigoro's son, the infant's claim would be ironclad.

If it was a son. If she lived long enough to see him born. If Yasuda samurai did not cut them both down.

"I speak to you because House Okuma still looks to you for guidance," Kenbei said, softening his tone considerably. "Support me. A man of my experience is better suited to govern than young Akiko will ever be."

"Lady Okuma," Daigoro corrected.

"She is no lady. She is a girl. Of what, sixteen years?"

"Who sits at the head of House Okuma." Daigoro delivered each word like a punch. In truth he was angry enough to escalate to swords.

Kenbei conceded the point with a bow. "You see what I mean. It is all too easy for the men of Izu to see her as a girl, not a landed samurai. They already look to me, for the same reason water looks for low-lying places: it is in their nature."

"No one looks to you, Kenbei. House Yasuda is the lowest and smallest of Izu's lords protector."

"And House Okuma is the highest of them. I will have that seat whether you like it or not, so why not come along willingly? Support me and I will see to it that Akiko and your mother live in comfort for the rest of their days."

"They already live in comfort. The only one who threatens to disturb that is you. Know your place, Kenbei."

Azami snorted like an angry dog. Daigoro would not have been surprised to see her bare her teeth. "You tell my husband to know his place? You're nothing more than a common criminal!"

"Not so common, or else you and your husband would not treat with me."

"I do not need to," Kenbei said. "I had hoped for your blessing, but if you will not give it freely, then I will take House Okuma by other means."

"Have you lost your wits? The Okumas and Yasudas have not gone to war for generations. Our alliance is the only reason the Soras and Inoues did not gobble us up years ago. The only reason Izu remains independent is that *we* force the lords protector to maintain a unified front. So why draw swords now?"

"I will not make war with steel when I can do it with gold. House Okuma's coffers are nearly empty, Daigoro-san. I will call in all of your debts. Since your family cannot pay in coin, I will force them to pay with their other holdings. I will take their home away shingle by shingle if I must, and leave them sleeping in the rain."

A derisive laugh escaped Daigoro's lips. "I would have thought to hear that strategy from your wife, not from you. Money is a woman's weapon."

The muscles stood out in Kenbei's cheeks. "My father speaks highly of you. I had not thought to encounter such stubbornness."

"You must not have listened to him very carefully. What you see in me is not stubbornness, it is honor."

"Where is the honor in allowing a sixteen-year-old girl to govern your house? Surely you can see the wisdom in what I propose. Let the younger Lady Okuma raise her child in peace. Together we can restore your mother's status as dowager. We will establish her as Lady Yasuda Okuma-no-kami, Protector of the Okumas. She will have sixteen years of peaceful rule before her husband comes of age."

"Peaceful rule, but in name only. No doubt you would be generous enough to step in and speak on your grandson's behalf."

"Only on the most important matters."

"And who would decide which matters are 'most important'?" Daigoro jeered, making no effort to conceal his scorn. This had gone on quite long enough. "You intend to unite our clans under one banner—a green banner, a Yasuda banner. You would make the Okumas your vassal."

"As is only just, if House Okuma cannot manage its own affairs."

Daigoro pushed himself to his feet. It took some effort; his withered right leg made everything more difficult than it should have been. In that regard it was just like Yasuda Kenbei. "We're through talking," he said. "Get out."

Kenbei's jaw muscles flexed again. He looked like a squirrel with nuts in its mouth. "I thought you would be more reasonable."

"I thought you would not forget your honor. How is it that a man as great as your father had so little influence on you?"

Kenbei looked at his wife. It was such a fleeting glance that Daigoro could hardly be sure he'd seen it, but there it was. Now everything began to make sense. Daigoro knew so little about money himself that it would never have occurred to him to wage a financial war. A man of *bushidō* was supposed to be above such venal concerns. He left such matters to his wife. No doubt Yasuda Jinbei had taught his sons just that.

But this son did not heed the lesson. He'd spent his entire life being passed up by his brothers. In a greater house perhaps that would not be so bad, but the Yasudas were the least of Izu's lords protector. That made Kenbei the smallest of the smallest.

Then he married a woman their father despised. Daigoro remembered the first time he and Lord Yasuda had spoken of Azami; Yasuda described her as a she-bear, and claimed she was at least as dangerous as Shichio. Together she and Kenbei had raised a pack of profligate sons— mountain monkeys, as their grandfather called them—and not one of them had made a name for himself. Now Kenbei was sixty, Azami forty, and they were without a legacy. Was it so surprising that they wanted to purchase one?

Yes, Daigoro decided. It *was* a surprise, or at least it should have been. Kenbei was samurai. His goal should have been to earn his legacy through deeds, and then to be completely dismissive of it. To value fame was to cling to selfishness and permanence. Both of those words should have been bitter in his mouth. Perhaps the aristocracy might develop a taste for them, but for samurai they were poisonous.

So this financial war was not his doing, and neither was it Azami's. Not solely. They had concocted this scheme together, with no regard for *bushidō's* demands. Once again, Daigoro found himself facing an opponent he could not understand. First his father-in-law, then Shichio, then Kenbei. Why could they not just draw swords and settle their differences like men?

Daigoro shook his head and sighed. "Have your war, then. Piss on what little honor you have left. But know this: I will send pigeons to your father and all your brothers. They will fly from this place before you do. I will tell your kinsmen exactly what you told me, and let them be the ones to judge you."

Kenbei and Azami shared a knowing glance. Azami smirked.

She didn't need to say any more. Daigoro shook his head again, chuckling ruefully. "Lord Yasuda's pigeon keeper is your man. Of course. What about your brothers? Have you bought their pigeon keepers too?"

"No," Kenbei said. "Not that it matters. You have no pigeons to send. It seems a fox broke into the Okuma coop a few nights past. There were no survivors."

Daigoro stormed out of the room. At the doorway he stopped himself. Without turning to look at them, he said, "Is this your idea of warfare? Coins as weapons, and innocent birds as the first casualties? And what did you gain by it? I can be at your father's side before sunrise."

"You could, if you were not a wanted man."

Daigoro gripped the doorframe as if he meant to strangle it to death. Mercifully it was his left hand that seized the wood; in his right, he might have rebroken some fingers. "You told me you valued our alliance," he said through gritted teeth.

"And you began this conversation by saying you were eternally grateful to me for not handing you over to your enemy. Yet when I ask a simple thing of you, how do you repay me? With scorn. Is that what you call eternal gratitude?"

Daigoro spun around and rushed them. Kenbei and Azami were still kneeling on the tatami; they could only shrink away as he drew close enough to strike. Azami raised her hands as if they would protect her. Her husband fumbled for his katana but seemed to have forgotten where he kept it.

Abruptly Daigoro drew himself short, out of Kenbei's range but well within Glorious Victory's considerable reach. "I can take both of your heads in one stroke. And I should. It pains me to see a good friend's son bring such shame upon himself. If I killed you now, would your brothers come for vengeance or would they come to thank me?"

Kenbei and Azami responded only with cringing silence. Their faces were red and sweating.

"I thank you for your service to House Okuma," Daigoro said. "Giving up your grandson was a noble sacrifice. Perhaps in time I will allow you to see him again."

Kenbei's mouth opened in a little O. Azami's bunched up as if she meant to spit venom. "And I sincerely thank you for your ideas about my mother's title," Daigoro went on. "I will arrange to have it passed on to her husband. But Yasuda Okuma-no-kami is too cumbersome, *neh*? Better to give a little lord a little name. I think he will enjoy the name Okuma-no-kami, Protector of the Okumas, and never miss the Yasuda. I cannot draw your blood from his veins, but I can ensure that he will never know he is descended from your twisted, sickly branch of the Yasuda tree."

At last Kenbei marshaled the courage to speak. "You're making a mistake. How long do you think you can escape these so-called 'bear hunters' if the clans of Izu turn against you?"

Daigoro took a step closer, looming over them. "There's another side to that coin. What happens after you betray me to the bear hunters? When I butcher every man Shichio sends after me, will he see you as an ally? Or will he think you conspired with me to set a trap?"

Kenbei worked his mouth but could not speak. He reminded Daigoro of a carp sucking at the surface of a pond. "Do not follow this path, Kenbei. Hideyoshi will snap up the whole of Izu and you will be crushed under his heel. So choose your father's path instead. Keep your faith. Stand fast with your neighbors. But make your choice somewhere else, Kenbei. You have worn out your welcome here."

Daigoro did not bother to see them out.

18

By sundown the next day, the Okuma coop was populated with pigeons again. They came one by one, nearly all of them from the north, since the Okuma compound lay on the southern reaches of the Izu Peninsula. They had all been raised here, trained carefully from their youth, then delivered in delicate cages to the coops of distant lords. They returned home unerringly, always with a tiny scroll case bound to one leg. Every time they came home, they were caged again and sent back to the coops of the distant daimyo. It never seemed to trouble them much, but this time their homecoming had them spooked. The lingering scent of fox still hung on the air.

"Here comes another," Aki said. They heard it before they saw it: a noisy fluttering on the ledge just outside the little octagonal window. Then came the bobbing gray head, daring a furtive glance inside before deciding in its tiny brain that there were no longer any foxes about. At last a full-breasted male came into view, big enough that he had to squeeze himself through the window into the coop.

Daigoro and Aki stood arm in arm watching the bird. The pigeon coop was in the dark and dingy attic of the Okuma stables. The horses and birds took shelter in the same structure, which made it a malodorous place, nowhere more so than in the attic right next to the coop. It was not a place the lord and lady of the house would ordinarily find themselves. But Daigoro was no longer a lord, and in any case he could not allow any gossip to escape this attic. Thus far the birds only brought bad news and worse news, and though the pigeon keeper had been hired specifically for his discretion, any man's tongue might waggle if the troubles on the horizon loomed large enough.

First came the news that Aki's father had no intention of bailing the Okumas out of their current predicament. He said a ship that could not right itself might well deserve to sink. It did not seem to trouble him that his daughter was aboard that ship. If he thought she would come swimming back to him after House Okuma foundered, he did not know his daughter very well.

It was a good thing Aki had built her own net of spies, because it was no easy thing to communicate without pigeons. The Inoues were easy enough to reach, as they were close neighbors; a swift rider could reach them in a day. The Green Cliff was just a half-day's ride, but no help would come from there. Lord Yasuda had been sick for months, and after his most recent turn for the worse, his healers kept him perpetually asleep. They said the aging lord needed all his strength to fight off the devil that beset his lungs; a steady diet of poppy's tears allowed his body to marshal its forces for its final battle. Daigoro could not wake him in good conscience.

Aki was not quite so scrupulous. "How do you know this isn't Kenbei's work?" she'd said. "It serves his best interests to keep his father asleep." When Daigoro had no response to that, she sent Old Yagyū and a handful of aides to the Green Cliff. Even Kenbei could not conscionably turn away the man who kept Daigoro's brother Ichirō alive even after he'd nearly lost his head. While Old Yagyū ministered to Lord Yasuda, one of the aides slipped into the pigeon coop and used Kenbei's own birds to deliver Daigoro's missives.

Old Yagyū would stay at Lord Yasuda's side, ostensibly to heal him, but his primary purpose was to defend the old daimyo from patricide. Kenbei could not be trusted. His brothers were of no greater help. Jinbei's elder sons had replied with birds of their own, conveying their regrets. Kenbei's behavior was disgraceful, they said, but as their father had formally given him charge of House Yasuda's day-to-day affairs, they had no say in how he managed the ledgers.

The next pigeon had come from Lord Mifune Izu-no-kami Hiroyuki, daimyo of House Mifune and Lord Protector of Izu. Lord Mifune's idea of help was simply not to call in his own debts. He thought it best to stand clear of this disagreement, lest he show favoritism—or so he said. It was almost true. No carrion feeder wanted a say in how other animals fought and died. His role was to wait on the sidelines and grow fat on the scraps of whatever was left.

The newest bird had come from Sora Izu-no-kami Nobushige. The scroll case lashed to its leg was lacquered blood red, which reminded Daigoro of Lord Sora's bright red cheeks. Sora's hands were perpetually red as well, some kind of skin condition in all likelihood, but he looked as if he'd just come from the smithy where he'd established his name. He talked that way too; all those years of hammering had left him half deaf, so he did not speak so much as shout. Between that, his arrogance, and his tendency to bluster on, Daigoro much preferred to converse with him via pigeon.

In a refreshing change from Lord Mifune and the Yasuda sons, Lord Sora was honest. Brutally so. In this case his message was simple: Kenbei had offered him the Green Cliff. In exchange, Sora would call in all his favors from House Okuma. Once Daigoro's wife and mother were penniless, Kenbei would cast them out, seize the Okuma compound for himself, and turn over ownership of the most formidable holdfast in Izu.

It was a tempting offer, and not because a clan's wealth was measured by its holdings. Sora Nobushige was obsessed with defense. Like Lord Inoue, he was cautious to a fault, but where Inoue relied on spies to keep him safe, Sora placed his faith in steel. His forge produced some of the finest armor in the empire. He tested his breastplates with a matchlock pistol at point-blank range. Daigoro could vouch for that; he'd put his own Sora *yoroi* to the test more times than he cared to count. Nothing could please Sora more than sleeping the rest of his nights behind the mighty moss-covered wall of the Green Cliff.

And yet there was that last line, the one that called the rest of the message into question. *Make me a better offer. I want Streaming Dawn.*

"Streaming Dawn?" Aki said. "I thought that was a myth."

"It's not. At least, I don't think so. But wherever it is, it's lost now."

Some said Streaming Dawn was an Inazuma blade. Others said Master Inazuma was never so wicked as to forge a weapon like that. Whatever the legends said—and there were many of them—all of them centered around a knife and a beautiful woman. In some of the stories she was Inazuma's daughter, or the daughter of whoever the true sword smith was. In others, she was wife, daughter, or sister to a great daimyo. In one version, she was a sword smith herself, the only woman ever to be ordained by the Shinto priest-smiths of Seki. Whoever she was, her fate was dark and cruel.

The details of her attack varied with the telling, but all agreed it was a samurai who killed her, and all agreed she suffered terribly before the end. Her killer was ordered to commit seppuku, and as the first rays of dawn streamed in, he plunged Streaming Dawn into his belly. He wailed long and loud, for there was no fate more gruesome than self-disembowelment. That was why a samurai nominated a second, a *kaishakunin*, to behead him if he should disgrace himself by crying out. But this man's *kaishakunin* refused to carry out his duty, and somehow the doomed man did not die. For three days he suffered, and for three days he did not bleed.

Still the *kaishakunin* would not end it. Because his appointment had been affirmed by the daimyo's court, he insisted that no one else had the right to take the killer's life. That duty was his and his alone.

Three days became thirty. Thirty became three hundred. With every breath the knife shifted in the killer's gut, so his every moment was sheer agony. He gnashed his teeth down to nubs. His fingernails gouged ruts in his palms, ghastly and bloodless. When he tried to remove Streaming Dawn, he found his own body defied him. His abdominal muscles clenched down tight on the blade. Even his viscera seemed to hold it fast.

The identity of the *kaishakunin* varied from story to story. Sometimes he was the murdered girl's husband, sometimes her father. In Daigoro's favorite version, the *kaishakunin* was her ghost, its ghastly white face hidden by helmet and *mempo*. That was the version that terrified Daigoro most as a child. In every telling, Streaming Dawn was said to be the cruelest blade of all, for it cut without killing. Daigoro's mother told the story as a cautionary tale, warning her sons that someday, when they had wives and daughters of their own, they should never be cruel. His father saw a different moral in the story: death is nothing to be feared, for to cling to life is to cling to suffering.

Sora Nobushige had taken quite a different lesson. He seemed to believe the blade could do what even the best armor could not. It promised eternal life. That wasn't a far cry from how the stories ended: when the *kaishakunin* was old and gray, still the doomed man lingered with Streaming Dawn in his belly. By then he was a quivering, withered husk. It was only after the *kaishakunin* died of old age that someone took mercy and beheaded the long-suffering murderer.

" 'Seventy-Seven Years of Seppuku,' " Aki said. "That was the name of the song a minstrel sang for us in my father's court."

"I think I know it. That's the one where the killer is twenty-two when he commits seppuku, *neh*? His *kaishakunin* was the same age, and they both lived to the ripe old age of ninety-nine."

"Yes. When I was little, it frightened me so much that

I couldn't sleep. But it's a ghost story, Daigoro. A fable. Lord Sora will not pass up the Green Cliff in favor of a knife from a fairy tale."

"My father always spoke of it as if it were real. He said he saw it once."

"Saw it. Once. Unless he took it home and left it in your armory, what use is that to you?"

Daigoro threw his hands up. "Aki, what choice do I have? Sora believes it exists. If I can find it, I take away Yasuda Kenbei's leverage. Your father isn't backing him; he's simply staying out of the fray. The same goes for Lord Mifune in the north, and even for Kenbei's own brothers. He's alone. Alone, you and Mother can deal with him. But united with the Soras? No. We're in no position to take on two at once."

"I don't like it. Your plan hinges on a mythical, magical knife, and on the goodwill of an arrogant windbag who is old enough to remember when our grandfathers were children. Suppose Sora keels over dead. Then where would you be?"

Even as she said it, an ill omen made its entrance. A jet-black bird alighted on the windowsill. It was the rarest of specimens, a black pigeon, and yet it was a near twin to the bird that arrived earlier that afternoon. Only Inoue Shigekazu was mistrustful enough to dye his carrier pigeons black. Only he would worry about enemy arrows finding them in the dark.

"Another message from my father?" Aki beguiled the new arrival with a sprig of millet, then untied the tiny leather thongs binding the slender cylinder to its foreleg. "What could he want?"

"Probably to tell you to find a better husband."

Aki's fingers were much more adroit than Daigoro's when it came to uncapping a scroll case as thin as a chopstick. When she unrolled the slip of paper inside, she said, "Oh."

"What?"

She didn't answer; she just handed it over. She looked like she might be sick.

Daigoro unfurled the scroll and squinted to read it in

the half-light of the attic. *Whispers spreading: Lady in the North seeks audience with Daigoro. Says Shichio is mutual enemy. Osezaki Shrine. Two nights hence, moonrise.*

"Tell me you won't go," Aki said.

"What? I . . . I haven't had time to give it any thought."

"I've had all the time I need. It's a trap, Daigoro."

"That doesn't make sense. You told me yourself: Lady Nene is Shichio's enemy. Now Nene confirms it."

"*If* Nene is the one responsible for these whispers. What if Shichio knows you're aware of his rivalry with Nene? What if this is one of his ploys?"

Daigoro had to grant her the possibility. "Maybe. But still—"

"Have you forgotten your Sun Tzu? '*To secure ourselves against defeat lies in our own hands, but the opportunity of defeating the enemy is provided by the enemy himself.*' Don't provide your enemy the means to defeat you, Daigoro. Don't walk into this trap."

"We don't know it's a trap. And Sun Tzu would tell me to gather intelligence before leaping to conclusions."

Aki's face grew dark. "Do you know Osezaki?"

"No. I've never been there."

"It is a long, thin spit stretching out into Suruga Bay. In the middle it's so narrow that I could throw a rock from the western shore to the eastern."

"And I have seen you throw," Daigoro said with a laugh. He tried to take her hand, but Aki snatched it away.

"The shrine is at the northern tip," she said, "totally exposed to attack by land or sea. Mount Daruma overlooks every road leading to Osezaki, down to the last goat path. There is nowhere to hide."

"Then an ambush will be easy enough to spot." Finally she allowed him to catch her hand. "Akiko-chan. Did you marry a fool?"

She made him wait while she thought about it. "I haven't decided yet."

"My adoring wife." He squeezed her fingers and she squeezed back. "My father raised me to be fearless, not suicidal. I love you. I love our child. I will not throw away my life for nothing. But you told me yourself: if I am to defeat Shichio, it will be through statesmanship, not swordsmanship. And in statecraft there are no better weapons than high-ranking allies. *Neh*?"

She nodded. They had discussed the matter many times—usually because Daigoro was too thickheaded to understand her the first time through.

"Well, who outranks Hideyoshi's wife?"

"Precisely. This is bait, Daigoro. It's too good to be true."

"And yet it makes sense. Imagine if Shichio was *my* advisor. As my wife, wouldn't you want him dead?"

"Yes. But Shichio knows that." She clutched his hand hard enough to make him grateful that she held his left hand, not the right with its still-mending fingers. "I am your wife. I don't care what pact you signed with the regent; I am still your wife."

"Aki—"

"Listen to me. So long as you are my husband, it is my duty to obey you. You tell me how you can be certain—*certain*—that this is Nene's work, not Shichio's, and you have my support."

She wasn't wrong. Daigoro knew that. For a woman raised by a spymaster, *certainty* took on a particular meaning. She allowed no room for doubt.

The daughter of a spymaster. That was it.

Daigoro held up the letter—more a curled paper ribbon than a letter, really—as if presenting her with a new piece of evidence. "This is your father's hand, *neh*?"

"Yes." It was well known within House Inoue that the lord was so paranoid that he wrote all his messages himself.

"And *he* says this is Nene's will, not Shichio's."

"Yes."

"Then the question is, can we trust him? Did he write this idly, without proof that this is not Shichio's doing? Or did he corroborate with his spies first, and confirm it was Nene before taking up his brush? If he holds true to his promise, then he cannot knowingly send me into enemy hands. If his promise is empty, then we can only speculate on who waits for me at Osezaki Shrine."

"Knowingly," Aki echoed. She looked not at Daigoro but at the black pigeon. Perhaps she hoped it would tell her something of her father's mood. "That's the riddle. If he *knows* Shichio has set a trap for you, then he breaks his faith by sending you there. But if he simply chooses not to find out . . ."

He clasped her shoulder with his right hand. The smooth, cold feel of silk felt good against his palm. He hugged her close and kissed her forehead. "Believe me, Aki, I want certainty as much as you do. But I have no time to visit your father and read him for myself. I must speak to Lord Sora immediately, before Kenbei hears anything of Streaming Dawn. From there, on a fast horse, with no Toyotomi patrols on the road, I *might* make it to Osezaki in time."

"All the more reason for doubt. Two days is not enough time. Your only option is to rush in headlong."

That is often what *bushidō* demands, Daigoro thought. He knew Katsushima would agree with him. But Katsushima would have another word for him too: *patience*.

To Aki he said, "That means everything hangs on this question: does your father mean to maintain his honor, or only a thin veneer of it?"

He was afraid he already knew the answer.

19

Osezaki Shrine was a little frightening in the middle of the night.

It was not quiet. The moon was a white sliver; behind its veil of clouds, it illuminated almost nothing, but there was still much to be heard. Low waves lapped invisibly on all sides. The first of the autumn crickets had come to sing. After Izu's extended drought, most of the leaves were dry and brittle; the wind made them sound like clacking teeth of the ghosts of a thousand children. The night before, sailors' voices would have been audible, but this morning Hideyoshi had sailed back to Kyoto with the fleet.

It was chilly this close to the water. Nene was surrounded by trees, but their foliage wasn't dense enough to serve as a windbreak. Nene nestled her hands deeper into their opposite sleeves, snugging her arms a little closer to her chest. Her long hair was heavy enough to keep the cold off the back of her neck, but the salt wind off the bay chilled her cheeks.

She would have preferred to wait in the shrine itself, out of the wind, but that was the only place where her bodyguards could remain completely invisible. Four would guard her directly and four more were hidden within the oratory, whose lattice windows afforded arcs of fire over the entire grounds. The tactical benefit was coincidental; the shrine was not built to shelter armed men. Nor were its pristine floors intended for filthy, booted feet, but Nene's bodyguards had not troubled themselves to remove their boots.

Nevertheless, Nene was not one to argue with experts about how to carry out their own duties. The captain of her guard positioned her just in front of the shrine, by a stone bench she found much too cold to sit on. Two foreboding lion-dogs looked down on the bench from their pedestals, their stone teeth bared to ward off evil spirits. Nene had a guard at each pedestal, a third directly by her side, and a fourth standing at the *torii* overarching the footpath leading up to the shrine. That was the captain. His station was the coldest, and the farthest from Nene's side, but it provided the best view of the path running from the peninsula to the shrine. He wanted to be the one to spot the Bear Cub first.

He didn't get his wish. A twig snapped right behind Nene, much too close for comfort. It gave her guards such a start that the closest one whacked her robe with his scabbard as he spun around. She would wait until her business with the Bear Cub was finished before she dismissed him from her service. For the moment, she forced herself not to whirl around, but to turn slowly, as if she'd known the intruder was there all along.

Even over such a short distance, the shade of the surrounding trees thoroughly occluded the meager moonlight, so that Nene could only make out the Bear Cub's silhouette. He had a tousled mop of a topknot, as if he'd just leaped off a galloping horse. She could tell he was armored, for there were lighter patches in his silhouette: the chest, the forearms, the thighs and shins. He wore large rectangular *sode* on his shoulders, and at this particular angle they made him appear to have wings like a *tengu*. Nene could see something in his left hand but she couldn't make out what it was. Not a sword, surely; it looked more like a fistful of spindly, twisted sticks.

"You're taller than I expected," she said.

"I hear that a lot."

"I asked you to meet me at moonrise. That was some time ago."

"You'll understand if I took precautions."

She approached the Bear Cub in the small, shuffling steps allowed to her by her kimono. A patch of moonlight caught the black tuft of his topknot, but she still could not see his face. That made him dangerous; if she could not read his eyes, she had no way of knowing what was on his mind. "We have a common enemy," she said. "I cannot kill him without raising my husband's ire, but you can. I can give him to you."

He backed deeper into the shadows. "Why should I trust you?"

"Because I am here. You are the most feared *rōnin* in these lands, and I am a lady whom the emperor himself sometimes invites to tea. Why would I leave myself so vulnerable if I thought there could be no trust between us?"

"Vulnerable? Yes, you'd like me to believe that."

With his left hand he tossed whatever he was holding at the feet of her nearest guardsman. Four short bows clattered against the flagstones. Their bowstrings were cut, dangling from the ends like so many fisherman's lines.

The guard who hit her over-robe with his katana scabbard spun again, looking back at the shrine. Nene did not bother. There would be nothing to see. The Bear Cub was as skilled as the rumors said he was. He'd disabled all four men in that shrine, stripped them of their weapons, and probably left them for dead, all without anyone hearing a peep.

"You spoke of trust, yet you came with assassins," he said.

"Bodyguards. Clever ones. There's a difference." She saw him incline his head as if to say, *as you like*. "But even if we call that a betrayal, let us say we are even. I brought archers; you eliminated them. Are you willing to call that a fair exchange?"

He thought about it for a moment, then nodded. Just then, serendipity gave her a glimpse of him. Even as a gust of wind parted a few branches, the clouds thinned just enough to cast a single fleeting moonbeam on the boy's face. His dark black hair was totally incongruous with his eyes, which were careworn and brooding, even wrinkled at the corners. . . .

"Taller than I thought, and now older than I thought," she said. "Much older. You're not the Bear Cub."

"That's right," a voice called out behind her. This time she did whirl around. Her guards drew steel. The pale, weatherworn door of the shrine slid aside, and out stepped a wisp of a boy dressed all in white. Even his armor was white, as if he intended to be buried in it—or, more forebodingly, as if he'd come to this meeting anticipating a funeral. He walked with a limp, just as the rumors said, and he carried the longest sword Nene had ever seen.

"Daigoro," Nene said. "At last we meet."

"We'll meet on better terms if you tell your guards to sheathe their weapons."

The captain of the guard came sprinting up the footpath, taken aback by the noise coming from the shrine. His armor plates clacked and clattered as he ran. "Hold," Nene said. She approached the Bear Cub as quickly as she could—not very quick at all, given the constraints of her kimono. But walking toward him at any speed was signal enough that she felt the boy posed no threat to her. The captain stopped, dropping to his knees so abruptly that Nene feared he might shatter his kneecaps inside his armor. Seeing him kneel, all the men in his command did likewise.

The man behind her came out into the light. He was a hand taller than the Bear Cub, and much older, even older than Nene. His hair was the same color as hers, a uniformly deep and glossy black, from which Nene deduced that he used hair dye. Was that normal for him, or did he do it just this once, to masquerade ever so briefly as the boy? Judging by his woolly sideburns and shabby cloth, Nene assumed this man was Katsushima Goemon, a known associate of the Bear Cub. If that was right, then he showed uncommon loyalty for a *rōnin*. By all accounts Katsushima cared nothing for his appearance. Dyeing his hair would be anathema to him. What must he have thought of dyeing it solely to complete an illusion that was only designed to last a few moments?

Katsushima circled around her to stand at Daigoro's side. Both of them were careful never to come within sword's reach of Nene, lest they spur her guards into action.

"I'm impressed," she said. "You've proven most resourceful. And not just with your little ambush. In truth I was not at all sure my invitation would reach you."

She hadn't sent birds, riders, or criers. She couldn't have. She didn't know where to send them; the Bear Cub was constantly on the move. Besides, Shichio's hunters combed the countryside in search of bear tracks. They would have intercepted any message she sent directly. The only option left to her was to put whispers in the right ears and hope that some of those ears belonged to friends of the Bear Cub—or at least friends of friends, or paid informants, or even enemies too weak to kill him but willing to gamble that this might be a trap. The boy showed remarkable foresight in establishing a net of spies. If Nene's intelligence was correct, he'd only been *rōnin* for a matter of weeks.

"You said you could give me Shichio. How?"

"I have already estranged him from my husband. I have given him everything he could ever ask for: land, lordship, even a samurai's birthright. Most importantly, I have given him a home far from here and even farther from the Kansai. But none of that will sate him. He will stay away for as long as he can, but sooner or later he will wheedle his way back to my husband's side."

"Let him. I know the truth of the Battle of Komaki. I have already sent missives to Hideyoshi—pardon me, to the regent, to General Toyotomi. Once he learns Shichio is responsible for his most public defeat—"

"I've intercepted your messages. All of them. My husband will hear nothing of them."

That got a surprised blink out of the boy. "Why?"

"Because Shichio is a snake, and it is in a snake's nature to wriggle out of tight spaces. He will find holes we cannot see." And I have ends of my own, she thought; it gains me nothing to shame my husband. "Your abbot's story is a deadly arrow to Shichio, but it is no mean feat to shoot a snake. . . . Have I said something to amuse you?"

The boy wiped the smile from his face. "No, my lady. It's just that you remind me of . . . of my beloved." That last word seemed carefully chosen. "May I speak candidly, my lady?"

"Please."

He bowed. "Begging your pardon, Nene-dono, but I do not think you need my help to kill Shichio. Nor will I believe that you crossed half the empire on the chance that I would accept an audience with you."

Nene granted him a nod and a little smile. "True."

"Then if I may ask, my lady, why are you here?"

He has uncommon grace for a *rōnin*, she thought. "Myths, some would say. In Kyoto, the nobility sometimes entertain themselves with ghost stories and the tall tales of farmers' wives. I happen to believe that some of these fables contain a kernel of truth. The legends of the Inazuma blades, for instance. Is it true that you carry Glorious Victory?"

"Glorious Victory Unsought."

Nene was not accustomed to being corrected, but she chose to let it pass. "And is it true that the man who wields this blade cannot be defeated?"

"No, my lady."

"Yet you bested fifty men in single combat."

"It is not *single* combat with fifty on the opposing side," said Katsushima.

The boy bowed, perhaps to conceal the hint of embarrassment in his face. Katsushima reacted quite differently; he swelled up like a rooster, filled with an almost fatherly pride. "Begging your pardon," the Bear Cub said, "but the truth of the Battle of the Green Cliff was . . . well, rather complicated."

"But you do not deny that Glorious Victory Unsought has uncanny power."

"No, my lady."

"What of the *tantō* known as Streaming Dawn? Do you know of it?"

That earned her a quizzical look. The boy exchanged

a glance with Katsushima, too quick for Nene to read it. Did one of them carry Streaming Dawn? It was plain to see that in addition to their twin swords, both *rōnin* wore curved knives in their belts. Could one of those have been the blade that promised eternal life?

Nene wanted to laugh at herself simply for having the thought. Ordinarily she was not one for such fantastic tales, but this case was different. She alone knew the lofty heights Hideyoshi's dreams could reach. Her husband had risen from the lowliest sandal bearer to the mightiest daimyo the world had ever known. Soon he would bring every last corner of the empire under his rule, and already he had his eyes on the mainland. Joseon would be the first to fall. From there he would march on China, or so he said after *sake* put a fire in his belly. And why not? If Kublai Khan could conquer half the world, why should Hideyoshi aspire to anything less? After all, the only people to repel Kublai Khan were the Japanese. Even the mighty Mongols were no match for the samurai spirit.

The only limit to Hideyoshi's ambition was time. He had accomplished more in his fifty-two years than any man alive, but he did not have another fifty-two years to complete his vision—not unless he had Streaming Dawn. The blade of eternal life was almost certainly a myth. Then again, so was the blade that guaranteed glory and victory. The Bear Cub was modest, but Nene could see the truth in Katsushima's paternal pride. One crippled boy stood no chance against fifty men. He didn't even stand a chance against General Mio, who was four times his size. Only the sword could explain his victories. If that one was real, then why not the other?

That furtive glance between Daigoro and Katsushima told her one thing: they knew of Streaming Dawn. They believed it existed. Whether they believed in its magic was of no consequence; that was up to Nene to prove. More important was for them to see that Nene believed in it. She needed them to see it as a worthy prize, one that Nene might buy with Shichio's blood.

"If you want Shichio's head, there are two paths you can take," she said. "You already know a direct assault will not avail you. Your only other option is to parley. My husband is a consummate tactician; offer him something more valuable than Shichio and he will not be so foolish as to let lust or friendship spoil the exchange."

"Why Streaming Dawn?"

It was impertinent for him to question his betters, but as she did with his earlier faux pas, Nene chose to let it pass. "When we married, an astrologer gave us a reading. She said that my husband would rule the world or die in the attempt. That was almost thirty years ago, but I have never forgotten it. Now my husband comes closer and closer to ruling the world—or to dying in the attempt. I would not see him fall before his time. If Streaming Dawn can prevent that, then I must have it."

The boy spent a long, mute moment thinking about what she'd said. During his silence, Nene became acutely aware of the cold. It made her feel vulnerable. She had risked much in coming here, and now everything hung on this young boy's next decision.

At last Daigoro said, "So who is it that wants the blade? You or your husband?"

Nene's captain of the guard sprang to his feet. His hands moved to his katana, ready to draw. "Who are you to question the Lady in the North? Know your place, *rōnin*."

"It's all right, Captain." Nene said it calmly, though in truth her captain wasn't wrong. It was not a samurai's lot in life to question nobility. How different these eastern provinces are from Kyoto, Nene thought. Had the boy asked the same question at court—or *any* question, for that matter—he might well have been crucified for it. But this wasn't Kyoto, and the wise swimmer aligned herself with the current. "Does it matter which one of us wants it?"

"I think it does, my lady." Nene was glad to hear the contrition in Daigoro's tone. "If your husband has forgotten your astrologer's soothsaying, then he is not the one who wants Streaming Dawn. And if you're the one who wants to exchange Shichio's life for the blade, then it's already in your power to deliver Shichio to me."

"Is it now?" He was bold, that was certain. Nene could

see what Hideyoshi liked about him, and also what Shichio hated about him.

"I believe so, my lady. If I am right, then . . . well, I must ask, Nene-dono: why have you not betrayed him to me already?"

Nene's captain drew his katana halfway out of its sheath before Nene raised a staying hand. Bold and then some, she thought. Daigoro's duty was to answer, not to inquire. "Is it so wrong for me to want payment in return? Or do you presume to tell me Shichio is a gift I should give you freely?"

"No, my lady. It's just . . ." She could almost see him choosing his words, as if he had to paint each one in his mind before speaking it. "I had not thought of Shichio as a prize or a gift. He is vermin. The fly is not a gift for the whisk; the whisk is made to destroy the fly. So my question was not, why does my lady not offer me this gift, but rather, why does my lady tolerate the fly any longer than she must? I can be your whisk, Nene-dono. Please, do me the honor of using me to kill this pest."

Much better, Nene thought. The poor boy had the wrong idea about his station, though. He was just another fly. Nene would trap them in the same jar. After that, it would be up to karma to decide which would die and which would escape the jar alive.

"I will do you that honor," she said, "but I will not do it for nothing. I told you already: my husband is a consummate tactician. We can take his plaything away from him, but only by offering him something of greater value in exchange. Kill Shichio without his blessing and my husband's wrath will be swift and terrible. Vermin he may be, but at the moment he is my husband's favorite vermin."

The Bear Cub did not like her answer, but he was wise enough to hold his tongue. "Find Streaming Dawn," she said. "Give it to me and I will deliver Shichio to you."

The boy nodded, deep in thought. At last he said, "May I ask one more question?"

He begins to learn his place, Nene thought. "You may."

"Why me? My lady must have countless men at her disposal. Why not send one of them to find Streaming Dawn? For that matter, why not send them to kill Shichio?"

Her captain bristled, but Nene stayed him with a look. "You have met my husband," she said. "He is fearsome when roused. Suffice it to say that there would be consequences if I were to deploy one of my own people against one of his. As for the blade, the simple truth is that you are expedient. My own agents have been unable to find this weapon; now I leave it to you to do better. But you must act quickly. Shichio is most vulnerable while he is here in the north. Once his plots and intrigues return him to my husband's side, he will cling to him like a tick. I will not be able to pry him free a second time."

Doubt played across the Bear Cub's face like the clouds scudding over the moon. Nene wondered whether he meant to play her false, or whether his honor code denied him that possibility. Hideyoshi would assure her it was the latter; he had marveled aloud at this boy's obsession with *bushidō*. Nene didn't know Daigoro well enough to make her own judgment, but she knew her husband was an exceptional judge of character. For now she would assume the boy would not double-cross her.

"I will find the blade if I can," Daigoro said at last, "and I will give it to you if I can."

"I am delighted to hear it," said Nene, though she did not fail to note the conditions he'd placed on his promise. Now that she thought about it, the fact that he'd phrased it so carefully made it all the more likely that he was being honest. If he meant to lie, he could have promised her anything in the world.

"How shall I send word to you once I have it?"

"My husband rules everything from Echigo in the north to Satsuma in the south. You're a clever young man. You will find someone who can get through to me."

"With all due respect to your husband, my lady, not all of his daimyo are true. How am I to know that the person I reach out to will not immediately reach out to Shichio?"

Nene chided him with a look. "Believe me, Shichio is not well loved among the generals."

"They need not love him; they need only know of him.

Shichio has placed quite a price on my head. Can you say all of them are immune to greed? Are all of them so well-heeled that Shichio's gold cannot tempt them?"

"Hm." That gave Nene pause. "There is something to what you say. So let us take another path. Prior to my husband, rule belonged to my friend Oda Nobunaga. His relations still hold power, and none of them is so destitute as to find Shichio's bounty worth pursuing. Through them, you can reach me. Will that suit you?"

"Yes," said the boy, though Nene had meant it as a rhetorical question. She did not much care what suited him. His boldness was wearing thin. But she had to admit he'd impressed her, and in any case she had few options left. None of her other spies had ever laid eyes on Streaming Dawn. If the blade existed, then Daigoro was the one to find it. If it did not, then she would find some other prize worthy of Shichio's head.

One way or the other, he was just the bait she needed to trap Shichio. One of these days she would have to sit down and write that haiku about the bear trap.

20

Daigoro watched as Nene took her leave. Her soldiers did not bother to collect the dead archers in the shrine. Daigoro supposed she meant to leave him to clean up the mess, since he and Katsushima were the ones who killed them.

He wished that hadn't been necessary, but even in hindsight he could see no way around it. In fairness, the only reason she'd hidden them there was to kill Daigoro if need be. Katsushima said he'd killed them out of prudence, even if he couldn't quite call it self-defense. How he'd known they would be there, and how he killed all four without raising the alarm, was beyond Daigoro's ken. Daigoro only knew that he himself had arrived just in the nick of time, with Nene and her bodyguard practically on his heels. Katsushima told him to hide in the shrine—among four dead men whose presence he hadn't bothered to explain—and then hid himself among the trees.

Now he and Daigoro sat outside the shrine, on a cold stone bench between statues of two lion-dogs, watching Lady Nene and her bodyguard take their leave. "How did you fare in your meeting with Lord Sora?" Katsushima asked.

"I survived. Which is to say I didn't grow tired of his ranting, run my sword through his bloated heart, and get cut down by his honor guard."

"You know what I'd have told you had I been there."

Patience, Daigoro thought. A thousand times patience. He didn't need to say it aloud.

"So tell me," Katsushima asked, "what did he have to say?"

"He thinks I have Streaming Dawn. He kept insisting that nothing else could have saved Ichirō's life after the duel with Ōda Yoshitomo."

That was an awful memory. First was the terror of watching Ōda's sword slice through Ichirō's neck. Ōda called it his "Diving Hawk" technique. He boasted that it had won him nearly forty duels, and slain just as many opponents. In fact, Ichirō was the only man to survive it, and just barely at that. Old Yagyū had stitched him shut with silk thread and a thick smear of pine resin, then buried him up to his neck in rice so he could not move. For three months Ichirō languished in that pit, flea-bitten and sunburned, mired in his own filth. No privy had ever smelled half so bad. In the end he survived, only to square off against Ōda Yoshitomo once more. Both of them died that night, Ichirō on Ōda's blade, Ōda on Glorious Victory Unsought. That was Daigoro's first duel and his first kill. Since then he'd seen far too many of both.

It was Yagyū, not Streaming Dawn, that had saved Ichirō's life. The old healer was as talented as they came; he'd trained with southern barbarian doctors in Nagasaki and Chinese masters in Nanyang. But Lord Sora had no way of knowing that. He'd heard what everyone else had heard: that young Lord Okuma had his head chopped halfway off and lived to tell the tale.

"He is a swollen, red-faced fool," Katsushima said. "But in this case the more foolish, the better. If he is willing to undermine Kenbei *and* give up the Green Cliff, all in exchange for this silly knife, then he'll serve our purposes perfectly."

"That's assuming we can find the knife. Sora insists I've loaned it to the Yasudas. He thinks that's why Lord Yasuda has held on this long."

Katsushima shook his head and rolled his eyes. Rising from the bench, he ambled slowly down the footpath to-

ward the shore. Daigoro joined him. When they reached
the beach, black crabs skittered away from them, vanishing into their holes or taking refuge in the surf. "You
don't believe in the power of the knife, do you, Goemon?"

"What does it matter?"

"It matters to me."

"No. The only thing that matters here is that very powerful, very gullible people are willing to give you what
you want."

Tiny orange pinpricks marked watch fires and paper
lanterns on the far side of the bay. The wind had calmed
a bit and the waves were flat enough to skip stones. Daigoro and Katsushima did just that. Daigoro absently wondered why such a childish pastime should still have the
power to entertain him as an adult. He wondered if he
would live long enough to see his child grow up to walk
on the beach and skip stones.

"Why should you care what I believe?" Katsushima
asked. "You're your own man; keep your own counsel."

"Well, you've got to earn your keep somehow. You
haven't taught me any *kenjutsu* in weeks. So if you're not
going to be my sword master, you may as well give me
some kind of advice. Otherwise, what are you good for?"

Katsushima laughed out loud and Daigoro joined in.
It felt good. There was too much gloom in his life these
days.

It was his own fault they hadn't done much *kenjutsu* of
late. Daigoro still did footwork drills on his own, but it
was hard to accomplish much in the way of swordsmanship if he couldn't hold a sword. Daigoro's hands had
been on the mend for the last month. And "what are you
good for?" was an unfair question to ask of a man who
had killed four men for him that very night.

Katsushima found a stone as large and flat as his palm,
and skipped it seven times before the darkness swallowed
it up. "I'll tell you why it doesn't matter what I think,
Daigoro: because sometimes you are only what you can
make yourself believe you are. No one else can do that for
you."

"I don't follow you."

"Hm. Have I ever told you about the dog on my family farm?"

"I didn't even know your family had a farm."

"Oh, yes. My father was a lowly *jizamurai*. Not even forty *koku* to his name. But that doesn't matter; what matters is the watchdog. His name was Kane, and he was a massive beast. I'd say he weighed as much as you do. Any time a neighbor would come by, he'd growl and bark like he'd lost his mind. But it was all bluster, *neh*? Kane was a friend to everyone. The only reason he was any good at chasing off rats or burglars was that they didn't understand he was running them down to play with them."

Daigoro collected a few more stones. "I don't see your point."

"Patience. One day a tiny brown tree squirrel came into the house. I suppose it must have smelled something good in the kitchen. I don't know. It comes in, it looks around, it makes sure the coast is clear. Then it goes rooting through my grandmother's vegetables, and it knocks a big, fat daikon to the floor. In comes Kane, barking like the world is ending. The squirrel bolts, but Kane cuts him off."

He laughed and skipped another stone. Daigoro had never heard Katsushima talk about his childhood before, and he'd never seen him so excited. "So there's the squirrel, cornered. Kane outweighs the poor bastard two hundred to one. He tries to catch it in his mouth and—*pop!*—the little thing bites him right through the nose."

Katsushima found this hilarious. He unleashed a laugh so loud that it echoed off the water. Daigoro looked over his shoulder, worried that Nene's soldiers might come back if they heard voices behind them. Keeping his voice rather lower than Katsushima's, he said, "I can't imagine your grandmother was happy to find a dead squirrel on her kitchen floor."

Katsushima laughed again. "Are you kidding? That dog ran for his life. He was a playmate, not a predator. No, it was the squirrel that showed the samurai spirit that day. Arrogance in the face of impossible odds. That's the way to win a fight."

Daigoro nodded and tried to smile. "So which am I? The watchdog or the squirrel?"

"That's my point, Daigoro: you're whichever one you believe you are."

"Oh."

Daigoro wasn't sure what to make of that. He knew he had the squirrel's spirit in him. Coming here was proof of that. But he felt the dog spirit in him too, and more than anything he wanted to indulge it. Spending his days in peace, protecting his home only when he had to, *that* was the life Daigoro wanted.

Was that cowardice? He opened his mouth to ask Katsushima's opinion, but then he thought better of it. For one thing, Katsushima had deliberately turned his back on domestic life. For another, he'd spoken the truth: his opinion was irrelevant. This was Daigoro's doubt. He alone could face it.

He crouched to pick up a stone when suddenly his knee buckled. Just like my hopes, he thought. At the last instant he stretched out his arm, avoiding an embarrassing face-first tumble into the surf.

"Daigoro, pick yourself up and tell me what you mean to do."

He did as he was told. "Look at me, Katsushima. I still haven't gotten used to the weight of this armor. Maybe I'm only cut out for the life of your friendly watchdog."

"Self-pity does not become you."

"All right." Daigoro threw his stone, but it sank immediately. Another ill omen. "What do I mean to do? A good start would be to turn myself invisible. That way I could sneak into Shichio's home and kill him in his sleep. After that, I'd like to make gold coins appear out of thin air. Let them appear directly over Kenbei's head. With luck they'd bludgeon him to death."

"More self-pity. Go cry to your wife; I have no ear for it."

"Goemon, I cannot walk the path before me. Even the first step is hopeless. I must find Streaming Dawn, though no one knows where it is. Then I have to give it to Lord Sora, to keep him from backing Kenbei. At the same time I have to give it to Lady Nene, or else break my word and lose my bid for Shichio's neck. Since I cannot give it to two people at once, I may as well give it to three people at once. If I give it to Lord Yasuda too, maybe its power will be enough to wake him, and then he can slap some sense into that greedy, shortsighted son of his."

"At last you're making sense. You said Sora claims to have seen this knife, *neh*?"

"Yes."

"And your father saw it too?"

"Yes."

"Then at least we know it exists. Finding it can't be harder than turning invisible, *neh*? It's surely easier than transmuting air into gold."

"I suppose so." One kind of impossible wasn't any harder than another kind of impossible, Daigoro thought. And Katsushima had it right—or his squirrel had, anyway: the only way to do the impossible was first to believe he could do it. He would probably fail, but if he believed that from the outset, he would fail before he even began.

And there was one more factor to consider: *Bushidō* asked the impossible of him every day. The way of the samurai was the way of honor, and if there was one thing Daigoro was sure of, it was that mortal men were *not* honorable creatures. By nature they were selfish, fearful, and petty, all of the vices *bushidō* stood against. If Daigoro could overcome his own human nature in living the warrior's code, then perhaps doing the impossible was within his grasp after all.

"All right, it's settled. We go to find Streaming Dawn."

The real trouble was figuring out where to begin.

BOOK FIVE

◆◆◆◆◆◆◆◆◆◆◆◆◆◆◆◆◆◆◆◆◆◆◆◆◆◆◆◆◆◆◆

HEISEI ERA, THE YEAR 22

(2010 CE)

2 1

Mariko envisioned Captain Kusama standing in front of her. Then she brought Glorious Victory Unsought crashing down on his head, chopping him in half.

It was the sixtieth time she'd done this. Her forearms and shoulders burned, but she had forty more to go.

This was her second *kenjutsu* drill of the morning. For the first hundred strikes, she'd imagined Jōko Daishi instead, leering at her from behind his demon mask. Those had been *kesagiri* strikes, slashing him open from his left shoulder to his right hip. Just like the *shomenuchi* she was using to bisect Kusama, the hardest part was stopping the enormous blade before it chopped the hardwood floor to bits.

She practiced on the top floor of her mother's apartment building, in a large studio with wheeled, folding Ping-Pong tables arrayed against one wall. On weekday afternoons, Mariko's mother came up here to beat the pants off of anyone who dared to face her in table tennis. Other residents used this space for morning tai chi classes and other group activities. A few days ago Mariko had invited herself over, in part because it was important to visit family in troubling times, and in part because she wanted more time for *kenjutsu* practice than Hosokawa-sensei would allow her at the dojo. She couldn't very well go to the nearest park; people tended to call the cops when they saw someone swinging a giant sword around in public. The penthouse studio in her mother's building was the only other place she could find to get some after-hours practice.

She noticed a rectangle of pink light on the wall. Sunrise, announcing its arrival. Mariko was usually dead to the world at this hour, but these days she found herself staring at the ceiling at four thirty in the morning, unable to go back to sleep. She'd tried cutting back on caffeine. She'd tried some stupid full-body relaxation thing she found online. She'd even tried one of her mom's sleeping pills, all to no effect. Usually she could read herself to sleep, but the only reading materials she'd brought with her were Yamada-sensei's notebooks, the ones Han had returned to her on the day she broke into the strip club. She'd learned some interesting details about Streaming Dawn—a wicked little thing—but still sleep would not come. Now here she was, doing *kenjutsu* and asking herself how things had gone so bad so quickly.

The latest attack from the Divine Wind had afflicted the whole city with post-traumatic stress disorder. Two days ago, at four o'clock in the afternoon, four drivers on four different roads suddenly jerked their cars across the centerline. The result was four head-on collisions with another vehicle. All four cars were white, the color of death, and four itself was the number of death. This was not lost on the general population. By coincidence, the crashes resulted in four fatalities. There were twenty serious injuries too, but the greater ripple effects were far more severe.

Yesterday's vehicular traffic had been a third of its normal volume. Deliveries were delayed or canceled all over the city. Grocery stores were devoid of fruit, vegetables, and seafood. In spite of the sparse traffic, collisions were up sixty percent as drivers panicked at the sight of a white car in the oncoming lane. That might not have been so destructive in other countries, but in Japan white was by far the most popular car color. More than half of Tokyo's cars were white.

The message was clear: *you are not safe*. It fit perfectly with Jōko Daishi's philosophy: take an ordinary thing and make it dangerous. In truth nothing had changed. Four fatalities and twenty injuries was a bad day, but in an urban area of thirty-five million people, there would never be a day with *no* traffic accidents. Jōko Daishi had only reminded people of a simple fact: a little stripe of paint was no protection. It was the illusion of protection. The only thing preventing thousands of head-on collisions was the goodness of total strangers. Everyone placed a mindless faith in it, a faith that was as fragile as an eggshell. Now Jōko Daishi had taken a hammer to it.

The terrible irony was that his teachings weren't a foreign philosophy to Japan. Buddhism held that all existence was fleeting, and *bushidō* embraced impermanence and condoned violence. Perhaps that was why Jōko Daishi had such success in recruiting members for his cult. Maybe something about his teaching spoke directly to the Japanese spirit, if only in a perverse way.

Whatever the reason, the media were having a field day with his latest attacks. They needed something to trump the ricin story, which had already run its course. Fatalities had topped out at twenty-three; once the medical examiner's office had identified ricin as the poisoning agent, hospitals worked swiftly to treat everyone who could have come into contact with the toxin. On the other hand, traffic accidents were the perfect fodder for fear-mongering websites and television talking heads. Now a simple hit-and-run could be read as a terrorist incident.

As the de facto mouthpiece for the TMPD, Captain Kusama had gone on record saying he hadn't ruled out Jemaah Islamiyah. When reporters asked him why the extremist group hadn't claimed responsibility for these attacks, he suddenly ran out of time and promised to answer more questions later. Mariko wished she could call him and tell him to stop saying stupid things that the department would burn for.

Out in the corridor, the elevator dinged, and as the doors slid apart there came a clucking of six or seven merry voices. The tai chi class. Mariko sheathed her Inazuma blade and quickly collected her things. As she did so, she saw she'd received a voice mail from an unknown caller.

She listened to the message as she rode the elevator back down to her mother's apartment. "Detective Oshiro, this is Captain Kusama," the little speaker said. "I want you at headquarters right this minute."

She checked the time stamp on the message. Twenty right-this-minutes ago.

Great, she thought. Yet another wonderful day in the life of Oshiro Mariko.

By the time she rolled in to post, Mariko's eyelids felt like they were made of sandpaper. Her most optimistic estimate said she'd logged three hours of sleep. She paused before her reflection in the door and tried to make something of her hair. That was when she noticed the tank.

She turned around and blinked hard, but the tank was still there. It rested on its massive treads in front of the entrance to the Imperial Palace, which stood just across from TMPD HQ. The tank's cannon pointed not straight ahead but angled benignly upward, as if to suggest that nothing was amiss, that perhaps the tank was parked there as a sort of curiosity, to give camera-happy tourists something other than the palace to shoot. But the truth was clear. There would be other tanks, one at each entrance to the palace, and maybe the National Diet Building too, or city hall, or the governor's mansion. Paranoia had gripped the highest halls of power.

Mariko was too tired to think about what that meant. She ambled into the elevator, thumbed the button for the eighteenth floor, and leaned in the back corner for the briefest of naps.

"Detective Oshiro to see Captain Kusama," she told the secretary.

"Go right in."

Uh-oh, Mariko thought. Having a captain lie in wait

for her could not be good. She felt like the goat in *Jurassic Park*, chained to a post and waiting for the T. Rex.

Kusama was on the phone, but he surprised her with a polite smile and motioned her toward one of the chairs in front of his desk. It was the same one she'd sat in when he'd held her maimed hand, the same one she'd fallen back into after he stripped her of her rank.

Mariko sat in the other chair and waited for him to finish his call. She'd forgotten how handsome he was. Of course, it wasn't easy to remember the good things about the man who had taken a hatchet to her career.

"Detective Oshiro," he said, nesting the phone back in its cradle. "You look tired, if you'll pardon me for saying so. Let me get you a drink. Coffee? Tea?"

"Thank you, sir, but no."

"Nonsense. Here, I'll have one myself." He rang his secretary, who materialized as if by magic with two coffees. Mariko's was black, one sugar, just how she liked it. She knew Kusama kept tabs on her, and even on her sister's progress in rehab, but she hadn't guessed his notes went all the way down to how she took her morning coffee.

"All right, Detective. Let's get down to business. I'd like to know which reporters you've been talking to, and why you thought it was a good idea to start doing my job as well as your own."

"Sir?"

"Forgive me. You look so tired; perhaps you didn't notice this on your way in." He slid a copy of the *Daily Yomiuri* across the broad, polished surface of his desk.

It was clear that he was trying to keep Mariko off-balance. Forcing her to accept the cup of coffee was old-school alpha male bullshit. Switching between the nice guy stuff and the personal attacks was a newer tactic, but it wasn't new to Mariko. She used it herself in questioning a suspect. She knew the right way to respond, too: don't get flustered. Pick a point on the table and stare at it. Talk to it, not to the person asking the questions. Stay distant.

She knew that was what she was supposed to do, but

even so, she blanched when she saw the headline. TMPD INSIDER: JEMAAH ISLAMIYAH CONNECTION "TOTALLY BASELESS."

"I seem to remember a certain conversation," Kusama said. He spoke in that tone parents took in public with their misbehaving kids: quiet, clipped, each word boiling over with anger. "A private conversation with a very small audience. Only four of us. Back in a dark, secluded corner of Terminal 2. Do you remember it?"

"Yes, sir." It was a hard one to forget; she'd regained her sergeant's bars, only to lose them again a few minutes later.

"We discussed Jemaah Islamiyah. I told you I had dropped that name to the reporters. Do you remember what you told me?"

Mariko swallowed. "I, uh . . ."

"Go ahead." His voice seethed with anger. "Say it."

"I . . . I told you that if you tried to pin this on Islamic extremists, Jōkō Daishi would use that to destroy our credibility. I said you should take everything else off the table and accuse the Divine Wind outright."

"So you did. Would you like to tell me 'I told you so'?"

"No, sir."

"But you did, *neh*? You did tell me so."

There was no safe way to answer that. Fortunately, if there was one thing she'd learned from him, it was that if she didn't say anything, she wouldn't have to wait long for him to fill the silence.

He stood up and walked to his enormous floor-to-ceiling windows. With his hands folded behind his back, posed against the dramatic backdrop of the cityscape, he looked more like a prime minister than a police captain. "It's not yet seven o'clock, and so far this morning I have spoken with the editors in chief of two newspapers and four television news programs. I know these men personally. I've been playing golf with one of them for over thirty years. All six of them called to give me fair warning that they would be running exposés on the police cover-up of the Haneda bombing and the false accusation against Islamic extremists. All because someone talked."

Mariko said nothing.

"There were four of us in that conversation," said Kusama. "Only four people could have leaked this information about Jemaah Islamiyah to the *Yomiuri*. Was it you?"

"No, sir."

"I remind you, these editors are friends of mine. If they press their reporters for sources, someone *will* talk. If I should find incontrovertible evidence that you were the one who spoke of Jemaah Islamiyah to the press, I will see to it that you'll never find a job as a policewoman ever again. Or you can tell me the truth right now and I won't fire you, because I'll be too busy carrying out my normal duties—namely, protecting the good name of the TMPD. So with that in mind, do you have anything to tell me?"

"No, sir."

"It was not you who spoke to the press about Jemaah Islamiyah? You're quite sure?"

"Absolutely, sir."

"Lieutenant Sakakibara, then."

"I doubt it, sir. I doubt that very much."

"As do I. That leaves me and your erstwhile partner—a man who is known for ethical improprieties, as I recall. Which one of us is the leak, Detective?"

There was no safe answer to that one, either. If she accused Han, Kusama would eat him alive. If she accused Kusama, she could expect the same fate herself.

But to Mariko's mind, he'd offered a false dilemma. "There's someone else who knows the Divine Wind carried out the attack."

"Oh? Who, pray tell?"

"Jōko Daishi, sir. He also knows what Akahata Daisuke was doing in Korakuen station with a giant barrel of high explosives. He could have leaked everything in these stories himself."

Kusama began to pace in front of the windows that afforded him his magnificent view of the city. "I see. Once again, the man you accuse is the one you happen to know more about than anyone else in the department. Convenient, isn't it?"

"Begging your pardon, sir, but I wouldn't describe four traffic fatalities, twenty-three ricin fatalities, and the hundred and twelve at Haneda as 'convenient.'"

"But you do want to work the Jōko Daishi case, *neh*?"

"Damn right, sir."

Kusama grunted and winced. "Perhaps it is your . . . oh, let's call it *enthusiasm* for this case that makes you speak to me this way, as if we are teammates on a softball team and not officers of the law. Look at my uniform, Detective Oshiro, and look at yours. You will note there are no jersey numbers."

Mariko quickly found a knot on his cherrywood desk and resolved to speak to it, not to Kusama. "Yes, sir. Sorry, sir."

"*Enthusiasm* is too forgiving a word to describe your antics. You ignored my orders and you have tied up valuable department resources that could have been used to aid in the Haneda investigation."

"Sir?"

"Do not be coy with me, Detective. I am well aware of your extracurricular activities. I know all about the hours you've wasted watching traffic camera footage."

Mariko was surprised to feel a great swell of relief. Only now did she realize that she had spent the last few days waiting for the hammer to fall. She knew exactly how Captain Kusama had come to learn of her efforts to track the woman in white. Someone had tipped him off. The same someone had been stalking her electronically for almost a week. Two days ago her stalker had tipped his hand. Deliberately. When she discovered the underground command center below the Blind Spot, she found a step-by-step report of her search for the woman in white. Dates, times, camera locations, informant files accessed, warrants requested, incident reports in various stages of completion. All of it.

Now her stalker must have delivered that report to Captain Kusama. Mariko had foreseen that possibility from the moment she and Han discovered the report. Since that day, she hadn't had a good night's sleep. But now the hammer was finally falling—right on her head, but at least the waiting was over. Kusama would do his worst, and then Mariko wouldn't have to imagine what the worst might look like.

"I assigned a few officers from Internal Affairs to study your traffic camera feed. They could find no connection to any of the narcotics cases you're supposed to be working."

"We nailed Lee Jin Bao on a buy-bust at the Sour Plum—"

"Unless you want to lose your detective assignment and spend the rest of your career as a meter maid, you will not interrupt me again. Is that clear?"

"Yes, sir," she told the knot of cherry wood.

"No connection. That's what they told me. And since I assigned you specifically to work only narcotics cases, I now have no choice but to reprimand you."

That was bullshit and Mariko knew it. A captain in the Tokyo Metropolitan Police Department had enormous power over the system. He could do more or less whatever he wanted. But Mariko chose to keep this to herself.

"As of this moment you are relieved of duty," Kusama said. "I think two weeks without pay is a good start. I may extend that if Internal Affairs requests more time to investigate your indiscretions. Any questions?"

Just one, Mariko thought. Who gave you that list? It was that person, not Kusama, who had forced the issue of her suspension. Kusama was jerking around at the end of someone else's string.

Ever since she got mugged, Mariko had been trying to figure out who the puppet master was. The woman in white had been her best lead—her only lead, in fact, and she'd already followed it as far as it would go. Getting suspended was almost a blessing; if she couldn't continue the investigation, she couldn't fail at it day after day.

"Good," the captain said, misinterpreting her silence. "You have one hour to make all the necessary arrangements. After that, you will have no further access to departmental resources."

Fine, Mariko thought. I haven't accomplished anything with them anyway.

She left Kusama's office as gracefully as she could. The "necessary arrangements" he'd spoken of were few. She had to check in her badge and she had to inform Lieutenant Sakakibara just how far the captain had kicked his boot up her ass. Her service weapon was already locked up, leaving Mariko to wonder what she'd do if she suddenly found she needed a gun. If her electronic stalker decided to do some physical stalking, she could only hope he preferred a sword fight to a drive-by.

Sakakibara wasn't in, which was the first stroke of luck she'd had all week. She'd send him the news via e-mail and avoid the verbal curb-stomping he'd have dished out if she'd told him face-to-face. Agonizing over just how to phrase it took about seven minutes. Aborting that plan and just blurting everything that needed to be said took less than two minutes. Kusama had given her an hour to leave the building, of which she had fifty-one minutes left to find the Wind.

But how? She had Google and her own two feet, and beyond that her search capabilities were limited. The department had many more tools at its disposal, but Mariko had exhausted them already. She'd identified the man who owned the strip club that sat atop the underground command center. He paid weekly protection money to the local *bōryokudan* strongman, but that was his only illegal activity. According to public records, the command center didn't even exist. Mariko had gone so far as to track down which electrical cables supplied the strip club and which supplied the command center, and followed up on who was paying the command center's bills. She learned that the bills were extraordinarily high, they were paid directly from an online checking account, and the bank of record had no idea who held the account. When Mariko tried the same trick with the Internet service, she found more or less the same thing: a big empty hole where its electronic footprint was supposed to be. The place had the bandwidth and computing power of the whole TMPD, yet somehow it was entirely off the books.

The worst part was that she'd done all of that legwork fully expecting it to fail. These people had created a blind spot in a citywide surveillance system; they weren't going to pay their electric bill by personal check. She'd dug up all the leads she could find, and she'd followed them as far as they would go. Every last one of them fizzled out.

Fifty-one minutes to do something meaningful, when the last five days hadn't been enough to make a single step forward.

"Fuck it," she said, and she opened her departmental e-mail one last time.

To Whom It May Concern:

If you found this message, then you are who I think you are. I know it was you who gave me the iron demon mask. I know it was you who tracked me tracking you. Your printout was a cute trick, but I don't believe you left it there in order to scare me off. I think you left it to tell me that you know I'm onto you. I hear your message loud and clear: you'll let me find you, but only on your own terms.

Now hear my message: I don't care about your terms. If you want to talk to me, you know where I live. Ring the doorbell. I'm not playing your stupid game anymore.

She saved the message in her Drafts folder without specifying a sender. Then she closed everything down and went to the pistol range. Forty-nine minutes. Plenty of time to unload a bunch of rounds and pretend the target was Captain Kusama's pretty office furniture.

22

Mariko didn't have to wait long for someone to ring her doorbell.

After the pistol range she went straight to the dojo, where Hosokawa-sensei begrudgingly admitted her into the morning class, which wasn't a part of her monthly membership and which she hadn't registered for in advance. He routinely allowed male students to drop in like this, but he was of the old-school belief that women had no place in *kenjutsu*. He didn't understand why Mariko, already twenty-seven years old, wasn't at home minding her children. A woman who was more interested in martial arts than marital arts made no more sense to him than a fish riding a bicycle.

Mariko was well aware of his views. He'd acquired them during the war years and showed no sign of surrendering them. On her first day he tried to persuade her to give up. On her second day he explained that the woman's weapon was the *naginata*, and that Tokyo was home to several excellent *naginata* dojos. But when Mariko proved too stubborn to quit, Hosokawa-sensei had no choice but to capitulate. He and Mariko had a sensei in common: Yamada Yasuo. Hosokawa was one of Yamada-sensei's first students and Mariko was his last. The fact that Yamada had spent his final days with Mariko, not with his more established students, made her important in a way that Hosokawa's seventh-degree black belt could not trump.

So Hosokawa-sensei had to put up with her, and if he wanted to persist in his bullheaded attempt to drum her out, Mariko would show him the meaning of bullheadedness. On this particular morning she needed someone to put her through her paces. She knew he'd work her twice as hard as everyone else, hoping she'd quit the art out of sheer physical misery. Today that was just what she needed.

By the end of class she felt her arms might fall out of their sockets. But at least her head was clear. All the nervous energy Captain Kusama had worked up in her was utterly spent. The only downside was that her fingers barely had the strength to button her blouse.

Her phone rumbled in her pocket. Fishing it out, she was surprised to see the caller ID said OSHIRO MARIKO.

"Huh," she said. She couldn't remember bumping the phone, and she didn't even know it was possible to call herself. She idly wondered which button she'd hit, then hung up on herself.

The phone buzzed again almost instantly. ANSWER YOUR PHONE, said the caller ID.

A chill ran down her spine. This couldn't get any weirder if it was Morpheus from *The Matrix* calling her. Then she remembered: she did have a Morpheus of sorts, an observer keeping tabs on her using methods she couldn't understand.

As if on cue, the caller ID changed to ANSWER YOUR PHONE NOW. Who the hell were these people?

There was only one way to find out.

"Hello?"

"Detective Oshiro," a man's voice said. "We should meet."

"Who are you?"

"I am To Whom It May Concern. You left a note for me to find."

Holy shit, Mariko thought, they found that thing already? Her e-mail draft wasn't three hours old. She managed not to say any of that aloud. "I want a name."

"I'll give you one: Yamada Yasuo. He was an old acquaintance of mine."

That was the last name she expected to hear. Yamada-sensei was never far from her thoughts, least of all when she was in the dojo. Her morning meeting with Captain Kusama had her wondering what advice her sensei might have given on coping with an obstinate commanding officer. She hardly imagined one of Yamada's old pals would ring her up.

"How do I know you're not conning me?"

"You're the one who invited me, Detective. Now, would you like a fresh change of clothes, or shall I pick you up from the dojo?"

She looked around furtively, then realized that was a forehead-smackingly stupid thing to do. She was holding a cell phone. A phone company tech on his first day could triangulate her location. These people could probably tell her which pocket she'd pulled the phone from and how much lint was in the pocket.

"I'll go home and change." After a moment's thought she added, "Do me a favor and don't watch me while I'm in the shower."

"Very droll, Detective Oshiro. When you are ready, go downstairs. A man will be waiting for you. You'll have no trouble recognizing him, as he'll be carrying a baseball bat."

"You're kidding. I figured you guys for the silenced Walther PPK types."

"Never in public, Detective Oshiro."

The line went dead. Mariko caught herself studying her phone as if it were a piece of alien technology she'd never seen before. On a hunch she checked her recent call history, and sure enough, there was no record of the call.

"Oh, what the hell," she said, and she took the next train home.

The order of events was eat; shower; change; find favorite purse for undercover work; find cigarette case used for undercover work; hide Pikachu in cigarette case; hide

Cheetah in purse's concealed pocket; toss cigarette case, cigarette lighter, tampons, gum, wallet, phone, keys, pepper spray, peppermints, compact, pack of tissues, second pack of tissues, little detective's notebook, pen, lipstick, lip balm, hand towel, hand lotion, hand sanitizer, and boot knife in the purse, all in plain sight; and go downstairs.

In an ideal world, when it came time for the guy with the baseball bat to search her for weapons, he'd find the boot knife and pepper spray, figure she was hiding something else, assume he'd found it when he found the Cheetah, conclude that he was smarter than she was, and overlook the Pikachu. That was the ideal world. In a less than ideal world, he'd disarm her completely, and to arm herself she'd have to kick the guy's ass and take his bat.

When she reached the sidewalk in front of her building, she was surprised to find a familiar face. His name was Endo Naomoto, and he was known in Narcotics circles. Endo was an ex-baseball player who still got to swing his bat now and again, but not at baseballs anymore. If it weren't for his choice of profession, Mariko would have found him kind of cute. He'd graduated from hero of the minor leagues to major-league disappointment, and after a much-too-early retirement he became a slugger on the black market. He didn't last long with the violent stuff, not because he couldn't hack it but because he quickly showed a knack for the financial end of the biz. Narcotics hadn't picked him up in several years, so either he was a hell of a lot smarter than most guys slinging dope—which was true—or else he'd gotten out of the business entirely— which was possible, given that he was currently serving as chauffeur and hired muscle for some very shady individuals.

As promised, he had the bat with him, and also a baseball, which he was idly bouncing on the end of the bat. When he saw her, he knocked the ball into his free hand. "Detective Oshiro?"

"Hi, Endo-san. You always walk around town with a baseball bat?"

He shot her a double take at the mention of his name.

She was glad to put him on his heels already, because that stunned look he was giving her was the same look she'd given her phone not half an hour ago.

He tried to play it off. "Hey, as far as you know, I'm just going to the batting cages."

"Uh-huh. Let's go see your boss."

He ushered her to a stately BMW sedan—white, she noted. She also noticed that the driver's seat was all the way back, and that if she'd been sitting in it, she'd need it all the way forward to be able to reach the pedals. It was the sort of detail Mariko collected routinely, apropos of nothing, but it was worth remembering his reach advantage if it came to blows. His bat would be longer than average too, and heavier to boot. She hadn't forgotten his baseball as a potential weapon, either.

He drove her to the Shinjuku Park Tower, a posh downtown icon that Mariko knew primarily as the sort of place her sister, Saori, would love to have her wedding in, if only the Oshiros were billionaires. (Or, as Saori would have been quick to point out, if she snagged a billionaire of her own.) When it was first designed, its three majestic white towers might have been likened to steps on the stairway to heaven, but today the first thing anyone would think of was three bars of cellular reception. At fifty-two stories, it was the tenth-tallest building in Japan, a distinction Mariko had always found utterly depressing. She remembered her grade school field trip to Chicago, and the jaw-dropping view from the observation deck of the Sears Tower. She also remembered her disappointment when she learned how tiny Japanese skyscrapers were in comparison. "They don't have typhoons in Chicago," she remembered her father saying. "No earthquakes, either."

Diminutive or not, Shinjuku high-rises were among the most expensive real estate on the planet. When Endo parked in the Park Tower's underground garage, Mariko felt underdressed just stepping out of the car.

It said something about Mariko's lifestyle that this wasn't the first time she'd been in a dimly lit parking garage with a known violent offender. Last time it was Kamaguchi Hanzō's enforcer, a bodybuilder named Bullet, leading her to an elevator not so different from the one Endo was approaching now. The difference was that last time the department knew where she was going—they even had a rolling tail on her—and Kamaguchi had every reason not to kill her. This time she was on her own.

As the elevator doors closed in front of her, Mariko tried to convince herself that Endo had no reason to hurt her. It didn't work. Endo was a lot nicer than Bullet, but Mariko's mind was too good at imagining possibilities, stories, worst-case scenarios. Cute, yes, but maybe he had a penchant for throwing women off of tall buildings. She'd seen weirder MOs in her career.

They emerged on the fiftieth floor, in a corridor of warm lighting and deep, soft carpet. A long, slender, marble-topped table faced the elevators, home to an *ikebana* arrangement whose flowers were real, not plastic. Apart from the elevator the hallway was perfectly silent.

"I have to search you now," Endo said.

"You'll be gentlemanly about it, won't you?"

"Yeah."

"Mind if I smoke?"

"Knock yourself out."

She set her purse on the table next to the flowers and stood with her arms outstretched. He did as he promised and didn't grope her. He was even polite enough to let her fish her cigarette case and lighter out of her purse before he searched it, which was exactly why she put the thought of being gentlemanly in his head in the first place.

He found the knife, the pepper spray, and the Cheetah. "No badge? No gun?"

"I'm off duty."

"Well, we're just going to leave your whole arsenal right here, okay?"

"Come on, my wallet's in there—"

"We'll send someone for it."

"Seriously? My phone, all my pictures—"

"Come on."

He steered her toward the end of the hall, where a floor-to-ceiling window opened onto a view of the city that rivaled Captain Kusama's. To the southeast she saw the sprawling forest surrounding the Meiji Shrine, highlighted here and there with the first hints of autumn gold. Everywhere else she saw urban sprawl. Even from this remove she could see her city was unusually quiet. The triathlete in her noted that it was a perfect day for biking; traffic was as light as she'd ever seen it. The cop in her saw the same evidence but reached a different conclusion: people were scared.

Just as they reached the last room, the door began to open. Mariko kicked it as hard as she could.

It flew away from her, hitting something almost instantly—something hard enough and heavy enough to bounce the door back toward her. A forehead, she guessed.

She didn't wait to find out. Endo had just enough time to look down at the Pikachu before Mariko jammed it in his armpit and squeezed the trigger. His teeth clamped shut. The tendons stood out in his neck like the cables of a suspension bridge. Mariko kept up the pressure, driving him toward the window. His whole body went stiff as a board, and finally he teetered backward over his heels.

The door opened behind her. Mariko was already in motion, Endo's bat in her hand. She turned to see a woman with a bleeding forehead coming straight at her. Mariko jabbed the Pikachu at her. The woman parried it expertly, knocking it to the floor. Mariko didn't care. She brought the bat around low and fast. It caught the woman in the shin with a meaty thunk.

The woman cried out but she didn't drop. Mariko got a good two-handed grip on the bat. The woman reached for a hip holster. Mariko timed a *kote* strike perfectly, smashing the pistol the instant it was visible. She probably broke some finger bones too, but she didn't hang around long enough to find out. She faked a chop to the temple, forcing the woman to duck and cover. That was all Mariko needed. She stepped inside the hotel room, slammed the door, and locked every lock it had.

She stood with her back pressed to the door, facing a small foyer. She'd never seen a feature like this in a hotel room before. Then again, she'd never paid the kind of money it took to stay in a luxury suite. A pair of cube-shaped chairs faced her from the corners of the foyer, upholstered in suede. To her right was a wall with a mirror, shoe rack, and coat hooks. To her left, an open doorway into the next room. Through the doorway she saw a shadow approaching.

She moved at once, but the man casting the shadow was too quick. He stood in the doorway, backlit. Mariko could see he had something in his right hand—a pistol, maybe. He held it the way Humphrey Bogart would hold it, parallel to the floor, his elbow tight against his ribs. He turned it toward Mariko.

She slapped it out of his hand. Whatever it was, it hit the carpet with a crystalline clink.

"Now *that*," the man said, "was an eighteen-year single malt."

He was a distinguished-looking gentleman, and if he found Mariko's baseball bat threatening he showed no sign of it. He wore wire-rimmed glasses, a charcoal gray suit from an expensive foreign clothier, and a most disdainful look, which he cast not at Mariko but at the wet spot on the carpet. "I'm quite sure it did not spend all those years in the cask so that *carpet fibers* could drink it up. Really, Detective Oshiro, you must be more careful."

"Uh, right . . ."

He looked up at her and blinked like a mole in the sun. He might have been Mariko's height once, but age had bent his back. As soon as she registered that observation, she realized his age was difficult to guess. The crow's-feet touching the corners of his eyes suggested mid-fifties, but judging by his liver spots he must have spent a hundred years in the sun. He was tan where he was not splotchy, with a high forehead and delicate hands. They were better suited for playing piano than assassinating wayward cops.

Behind her, Mariko heard a hollow sliding noise at the door, then the high-pitched grinding of an electric motor retracting the deadbolt. Either Endo or his lady friend had a key card—probably Endo, judging by the sheer mass that crashed into the door soon after. Mariko watched the door leap forward, only to slam to a halt when it reached the end of its chain. Endo dropped his shoulder into it again, and again the door only moved a few centimeters before it stopped dead.

"Oh, do keep it down," the ageless gentleman snapped. He could just as well have been fussing at a couple of pesky pigeons. "Need I remind you that ours is a *secret* society? You two are loud enough to wake the dead. Detective Oshiro, be a dear and unlock the door, won't you?"

"No, sir."

He reacted as if she'd poked him with a pin. "Excuse me?"

"I said no, sir." Mariko was surprised to hear herself speak so formally. Something about this man engendered respect. "I'd rather keep your hired muscle on the other side of the door, if it's all the same to you."

He pushed his glasses back up the ridge of his nose with one thin finger. "Oh, come now. They won't hurt you." Raising his voice, he said, "Do you hear that? You're not to hurt her."

"With all due respect," Mariko said, "the last time that woman tried to not hurt me, she damn near killed me. She *is* the one I chased through Tokyo Station, *neh*?"

He gave her a jolly but guilty shrug, as if she'd caught him stealing from the cookie jar. "Yes."

"And she was under orders to make sure I ended up with the mask?"

"Oh, very good, Detective."

Mariko pointed at the bruised half of her face. "This is what she calls restraint."

"And you? What do you call restraint? You may have noticed you've got a rather large club in hand."

Mariko aped his guilty shrug-and-grin. "Are you kidding? I'm the model of self-control."

It was true. Mariko could have shattered the woman's kneecap but chose to take her in the shin instead. She could have crushed every bone in her hand, but hit the pistol instead. She held back when she could have beaten the woman's brains out. And she could have taken the bat to Endo while he was down. But Mariko didn't feel like explaining any of that. Instead she just hollered, "Tell him, honey. Tell him how easy I went on you."

"You broke my fucking finger, bitch." The woman's voice was strained, squeaking like a rope under too much tension.

"See?" Mariko gave the ageless gentleman a broad smile. "A model citizen, that's me. Now if you want those two to come in and join us, you'll have to ask them to pass the pistol in here first."

He sighed. "I do think we got off on quite the wrong foot, Detective Oshiro."

"The pistol. Then my stun gun. Then their key cards. Oh, and tell them to go fetch my purse while you're at it."

"You are quite the intractable one, aren't you? Your file certainly wasn't wrong about that." He gave her an imploring look, and when that failed, another sigh. "Do as she says, Norika-san."

Mariko heard a catty harrumph in the corridor. Then came a heavy thump on the carpet, and the pointed toe of a patent leather pump pushed a Glock Model 27 through the narrow gap allowed by the door chain.

The Pikachu and two key cards followed. Squishing the purse through the gap was harder, but Endo made it happen. "There," the big ex-ballplayer said. "Happy now?"

"Almost," said Mariko. She bumped the door shut with her hip and relocked the deadbolt. Keeping her eye on the ageless man, she picked up the Glock. Her *kote* strike had knocked the weapon out-of-battery, which was to say the slide wasn't sitting right and the first round wasn't seated right in the chamber. It was a common malfunction that took all of five seconds to fix. She kept the Glock, returned the Pikachu to her pocket, and tossed the baseball bat in the corner.

"That's better. Now then, what did you say your name was?"

"Furukawa," he said. "Furukawa Ujio, at your service. I'll thank you not to point that pistol at me."

"No problem. I'll just need you to assume the position and let me pat you down."

"Oh, come now. Is that really necessary?"

"Afraid so."

He looked at her as if she'd just asked him to squat down and take a dump on the carpet. With great reluctance, he turned around and put his palms on the wall. "I must tell you, Detective, I've conducted a great many employment interviews in my day, but I daresay this is the worst yet."

"Employ . . . ? Huh? What do you mean, interview?"

"Well, of course. Why else did you think you were here? Detective Oshiro, I've arranged to see you today because I'd like to offer you a job."

23

Furukawa's suite was twenty times the size of Mariko's apartment. The dining table sat eight—or would have, if it weren't covered in computer equipment. Mariko didn't have a single room that would seat eight. The ceilings here were nearly three meters high. There was a parlor. A walk-in pantry in the kitchen. Two spare bathrooms. Mariko couldn't imagine why anyone would even *want* three bathrooms. It was just more to clean. Then again, if you had daily maid service, maybe that didn't matter.

Mariko couldn't tell what the computers in the dining room were up to; the monitors showed only a little text box for entering a username and password. An old-school landline phone sat on the table, hooked up to a boxy gray gadget she'd never seen before. Cables ran down from the gadget onto the floor, then to a hasty stapling job along the baseboard, then to all the other phones in the suite. There were no folders, no papers, no pens—nothing analog.

There was, however, a pool table. It dominated an open space just beyond the dining room, and its mere existence was a staggering display of affluence. If you put them side by side on a floor plan, Mariko's entire bathroom would have a smaller footprint than the pool table. The same was true of her kitchen. Then there was all the space *around* the table; it had a boundary as deep as the length of a pool cue. In Shinjuku, that much floor space could easily cost half a million dollars.

Mariko got to see every last feature of the suite, not because her host gave her the grand tour but because she insisted the two of them wouldn't sit down and talk until after she'd cleared every room. No matter the thread count of the sheets, this was enemy territory.

"There," Furukawa said, "are you quite satisfied? No, wait, don't answer that. Allow me to pour you a drink first. We ought to share a toast."

"A toast? What for?"

"A momentous meeting. It was decided some time ago that our paths would cross. Now, at long last, here we are." He wrapped one of his slender hands around the neck of a broad-shouldered crystal decanter. Mariko assumed the smoky amber liquid within was the eighteen-year-old whisky she'd spilled earlier. "Shall I pour two?"

"A little early for the hard stuff, isn't it?"

"Oh, how very gauche of me. I do apologize. In my line of work a man keeps odd hours."

"And what line of work would that be?"

He pondered the question for a moment. His free hand circled subconsciously as he thought. "Let us say 'middle management.' That strikes close enough to the mark."

"I didn't know ninja clans had middle managers."

That got a good, deep laugh out of Furukawa. "My dear, we all but coined the term. If you and I were to be having this conversation five hundred years ago, I would be the *chūnin*, quite literally the 'middleman.' I would be answerable to some high-ranking *shōnin*, just as my *genin* would answer to me."

Just like *kenjutsu*, Mariko thought. She practiced many techniques from a *chūdan* stance, a middle position below *jōdan* and above *gedan*. "That Norika," she said. "She's one of your *genin*?"

"She is."

"And that's what you want me to do? Be your *genin*? Run around train stations in my nightie?"

"Oh, no. You would serve in quite a different capacity."

Furukawa filled a tumbler with three fingers of whisky and settled the crystal stopper back into the decanter. "You're sure you won't have one? Or perhaps something more fitting for the brunch hour—say, a mimosa? We've got some very fine fresh-squeezed orange juice on hand, though I must tell you, the champagne in this hotel is best described as potable."

Mariko didn't know what to make of this man. He was alone and unarmed, and when faced with the fact that Mariko had trounced both of his bodyguards single-handedly, his only concern was waking the neighbors. Had she been on duty, he would have had no cause for worry; between the law, general orders, and standard operating procedure, there was very little Mariko could do to threaten him. But she was under suspension. General orders and SOP had no bearing on her, and Furukawa knew that. As far as the law was concerned, all she had to do was say she was trapped in his room against her will and she could shoot him on the spot. Yet his biggest worry was that the champagne wasn't up to snuff.

"Maybe we can skip the toast and get down to business," she said. "On the phone you said you were a friend of Dr. Yamada's."

"Friend? No. Ours was . . ." His free hand gestured in its idle way, tracing circles in the air. "Well, a *complex* relationship, shall we say. But we had each other's respect. And he certainly had a great deal of respect for you."

"You talked to him? About me?" Mariko had to take a step back to steady herself. She knew so little of Yamada-sensei's private life. They'd only known each other a few weeks before he was murdered. If he had spoken to Furukawa about his newest student . . .

"You must have studied *kenjutsu* with him, *neh*?"

"Oh, heavens no. My interest in swords was . . . well, their interest. I appreciate their appreciation." He snickered; clearly he found this to be the height of wit.

"I don't follow you."

"I'm a collector, Detective Oshiro. Antiquities. Fine

art. And good whisky, of course." He raised his glass to her.

"Then what did the two of you say about me? I don't know anything about art."

"Nor about whisky, I daresay. No, my dear, we spoke about your role in the Wind."

There it was. The one word Mariko had been waiting to hear. She'd noticed earlier when she dropped the word "ninja" that Furukawa didn't balk. All his *shōnin-chūnin-genin* stuff was related to the ninja too, but that didn't mean it was related to the Wind; it could have been just a history lesson. But now Mariko had it right from Furukawa's mouth. The Wind was more than Yamada's notes or Han's half-baked theories. It was real.

Not so fast, her detective's instincts warned. Sometimes hearsay was good enough, but sometimes people just told you what you wanted to hear. Furukawa wasn't above braggadocio. The suite alone was testament to that. "The Wind," she said, deliberately sounding more skeptical than she felt. "The same Wind that was around five or six hundred years ago?"

"Even older than that. Yes."

"And you're telling me Yamada-sensei knew of it? I don't mean historically, I mean now. He knew you still exist?"

"Oh, quite. He was one of us."

The words struck her like a bucket of ice water in the face. She shook her head. "No. No way. No way in hell."

"You knew him as a historian," Furukawa said. "We knew him as our archivist."

It wasn't true. It couldn't be. Her sensei was a good man. She remembered talking with him about his protégé, Fuchida, the one who would ultimately come back to murder him. Fuchida was born a yakuza, but Yamada had earnestly believed he could turn the young man away from that path. Mariko had never seen Yamada-sensei so ashamed as when he confessed that his erstwhile student had returned to his criminal roots. Yamada sincerely believed martial training was *moral* training, that self-discipline and self-control made one not just a better fighter but a better human being.

Mariko remembered that conversation well. She remembered another one, too, when Yamada discovered that Mariko had contacts within the *bōryokudan*. In his mind, police officers did not fraternize with the enemy. Cops and yakuzas were only supposed to interact when the former slapped handcuffs on the latter. Yet to take Furukawa at his word, Yamada had been affiliated with the Wind, a criminal syndicate. "No," she said again. "No way in hell."

"The lady doth protest too much, methinks. So young, so naive."

"So full of shit."

He winced a little, as if her discourtesy physically pained him. "As it happens, it's of little consequence whether you believe me or not. It only matters that you believe we exist, and that you listen to my offer."

"Oh, right. The job offer. Getting me suspended from the force so I can become your ninja."

"In so many words, yes."

"Gee, thanks. Why am I the lucky girl?"

He pushed himself up from his chair and gestured vaguely toward her with his tumbler. "You are . . . well, uniquely positioned, shall we say. And uniquely talented. You may not realize it, Detective Oshiro, but you are already an accomplished ninja."

Mariko could only wrinkle her face in puzzlement. "It's true," Furukawa said. "Consider your recent stealth operation in the Sour Plum. You entered in disguise, you gathered intelligence, and based on that intelligence you carried out a raid."

"Hmph." Mariko hated to admit it, but the old man had a point. She wouldn't have described a buy-bust as an intelligence-gathering operation, but when it came right down to it, evidence was just another form of information.

Even so, it wasn't as if she snuck in there in a black mask to assassinate Lee Jin Bao. When she told that to

Furukawa, he said, "Quite right. But neither did the ninja of old. Better to think of them as spies than assassins. The same is true of the undercover Narcotics officer, is it not? Perhaps there was the possibility that you would kill your target, but that was never your goal."

Mariko had to grant him that point too. She didn't know what to do with this eccentric, genteel, criminal, ageless man. His words varied from fanciful to insightful, from outright lies to undeniable truths. Stranger still, he reminded her of someone. But who? What gave him insights into police work that she'd never considered herself? Could he have been a cop? No. He was too effete; he'd never survive academy. But then how did he know Mariko's job better than she knew it herself?

An easy explanation lay in plain sight. The Wind was real. Furukawa was a member. He knew the ins and outs of the TMPD because he knew the ins and outs of *everything*. That was his job as middle management in an invisible criminal syndicate. There was only one problem with that explanation: a centuries-old, all-powerful, supposedly nonexistent ninja clan was pretty hard to swallow.

"Prove it," she said.

Furukawa's carefully groomed eyebrows shot up. "I beg your pardon?"

"The Wind. Prove it exists."

A hint of a smile touched his dry lips. He regarded her with a sparkle in his eyes, as if she were a little child who had inadvertently asked a deep philosophical question. "And how would you have me do that?"

"Well, what the hell is it that you people do?"

He thought about that for a moment. "I suppose you could say we're in the king-making business."

"Then make one."

"Hm." He thought it over as he returned to the liquor cabinet, to refresh his tumbler of whisky. After some consideration he said, "We do not make a habit of tugging the puppet strings just to illustrate a point. But in this case . . . well, your reputation precedes you. You're not likely to change your mind without evidence."

"Nope."

"Very well. Now let me see. If I recall your address correctly, your district's member of the House of Councillors is . . . oh, who is it? Takanuki Hayato?"

"That's right. A little creepy that you know where I live, though. I mean, at least pretend you need to look it up. Otherwise . . . eww."

Furukawa smiled ungraciously. "Don't flatter yourself, Detective. I know your address because I ordered a watch placed on it."

"Huh?"

"You have a very expensive mask in your apartment and a sword that is beyond price. Koji-san—pardon me, you think of him as Jōko Daishi—well, he wants both of them, *neh*? He's already stolen the sword from you once before. Do you think he hasn't tried again?"

Mariko didn't like the sound of that at all. "Do you mean *won't* or *hasn't*?"

"He has tried on four separate occasions since you reclaimed the sword. Always through his acolytes, you understand. He seems to have suspended his efforts; we're not sure why."

Four? Jesus, Mariko thought. She didn't like being talked to this way, as if she should already know everything he was telling her. It was familiar somehow, but Mariko couldn't think of who Furukawa reminded her of.

"I don't suppose you want to tell me what happened to the acolytes," she said.

"You'd rather not know." Furukawa raised his whisky in a little toast—*to eliminated enemies,* he seemed to say—and savored a mouthful of whisky. "But let's get back to Councillor Takanuki. What do you think of him?"

"I think it's a damn shame we're stuck with him for another six years. He's a cheap prick who keeps trying to cut federal support for local law enforcement budgets. That's pretty much the only issue I vote on."

"Then let's not make a king of him. Shall I unmake him?"

"I don't see how you could. He was just reelected."

Furukawa picked up the phone that hung on the wall next to the liquor cabinet. He pressed one button, said,

"Takanuki Hayato," and hung up. "Let's continue our conversation in the other room, shall we?"

He walked with short steps that made him seem considerably older than he appeared. Mariko followed him into the enormous room with the pool table. A massive flat-screen TV hung on one wall like à painting. Below it lay a dormant fireplace, home to a realistic ceramic reproduction of stacked, burnt logs. The pool table dominated the opposite half of the room, its ten balls packed tightly in their triangular rack. A universal remote sat nearby. Furukawa thumbed a button and the TV sprang silently to life.

"Do you play billiards, Detective?"

"Not really."

"Pity."

Furukawa fiddled with the remote, powering up the room's top-of-the-line surround-sound system. Opulence upon opulence, Mariko thought.

"Oh, look at this," Furukawa said. "The Hyatt does like its toys." He pressed another button and with a whoosh the fireplace sprang to life too.

"Actually, that's pretty cool."

"Isn't it? Ah, here we go."

He got the sound system synched with the television, which was tuned to JNN, one of the all-news channels that Mariko never bothered to watch. She wasn't alone; many detectives found the daily news too depressing. At work they stood eye-to-eye with the worst aspects of human nature; for them the purpose of watching TV was to wind down, not to take a closer look at just how awful people could be.

Sure enough, the anchorman was just wrapping up a story on yet another sex abuse scandal in the Catholic Church. He turned to face a different camera and the image behind him changed. An annotated bar graph vanished in a flash of computer-generated lens flare, replaced by a close-up of a well-dressed man wearing a scowl. Mariko recognized him.

"How much is enough?" the anchorman asked. "That

is the question for Councillor Takanuki Hayato. JNN has breaking news on a campaign finance scandal that may have netted Takanuki as much as ten million yen in the last year alone."

Mariko's heart stopped. She couldn't have been more surprised if the anchorman had stepped out of the TV screen and walked into the room. Furukawa, on the other hand, only had eyes for Mariko. For her part, Mariko belatedly noticed that she was gaping at the television with a wide-eyed, openmouthed stare. It shamed her to be caught like that, with no more than a *gaijin*'s control over her facial expressions.

"How did you—?"

"You asked for proof of the Wind's existence. Now you have it."

Mariko shook her head. "That's the why. I'm interested in how."

"Quite simple. We were the ones to teach him how to siphon the money without being caught."

He said it as if anyone could do it. Mariko gaped at him—again, to her embarrassment—but Furukawa just ambled toward the pool table. With one hand he held his whisky. With the other he lifted the triangular rack from the pool balls and set it aside. An idle swipe with his long pianist's fingers sent one of the balls rolling lazily across the table.

"No." Mariko could not make herself believe it. "Even if that were true, you . . . no, it's impossible. You make a phone call and thirty seconds later it's on the news? How?"

"I suspect you can answer that yourself."

Mariko looked at the phone, then the anchorman, then the phone again. "You have someone in JNN. Like, right there in the studio, right this minute."

Furukawa nodded. "Go on."

"It's got to be, what, an executive producer? Someone like that, anyway. Someone who has the power to . . ." The thought went careening through her brain, setting off sparks of other ideas. "It's not one producer, is it? You have someone in there twenty-four hours a day. And it's not just JNN. You could have done this through the papers, the nightly news. . . ."

"I could have, if I thought you could wait a few hours to see your evidence. Patience isn't your strong suit, though, is it?"

Mariko scarcely heard him. "Wait. What if I'd said someone other than Takanuki? You can't have dirt on *everyone*."

Furukawa sipped his whisky. "Not everyone. Just everyone that matters."

"Come on. You can't tell me every single person takes the bait when you offer them a payoff."

"Oh, no. But they don't need to. In the court of public opinion, guilt by association carries a death sentence." He ran his fingertips over the pool balls, scattering them. "We never act to achieve only one goal, Detective. It's much like billiards. It's not enough to sink your shot; you must always set up the next shot. You required me to expend Takanuki to prove a point. He was a ball that can only be sunk once, so now we will choose who will fall with him."

"How?"

Furukawa gave her a devilish grin. "Once you prove a man is corrupt, all of his closest allies are subject to scrutiny. Their alliance need not even be real; in a matter of minutes we can fabricate a relationship of many, many years. Oh, is it a wonderful thing to be in the espionage business these days. Your targets always set themselves up for a fall."

"You're talking about electronic records."

"Quite right. Financial transactions in this case. Can you imagine what the ninja of old must think of our targets today? The poor fools save every aspect of their lives in digital form. *Voluntarily.*" Furukawa let out a laugh and slapped his belly, a masculine gesture for such a feminine hand. "It's like leading lambs to the slaughter, but these lambs operate their own slaughterhouse."

Mariko wasn't laughing. "That's what we are to you? Livestock?"

"Oh, do have a sense of humor, Detective."

She gave him a paper-thin smile. Furukawa put her ill at ease, but she hadn't quite figured out why. She also hadn't put her finger on why he seemed familiar to her. He was almost like a *bunraku* puppet: human enough, but existing in the uncanny valley where the more lifelike the puppet was, the more unsettling it became. But if he reminded her of someone, who was it?

Since she couldn't put her finger on it, she had no choice but to set it aside and let it percolate through her mind. Mariko crossed the room, swiped up the TV remote, and zapped the anchorman into oblivion. The Takanuki story had rubbed her raw. "Okay," Mariko said, "let's say I believe you. You belong to the Wind, and the Wind has puppet strings everywhere. *Neh?*"

Furukawa nodded. "There is no place the Wind cannot reach."

"Then what do you need me for?"

"That is the question of the hour, isn't it?" He took his hand away from the table, focusing entirely on Mariko. "We believe you are the one who can put an end to this reign of terror. Koji-san's ambitions have grown far too grand for our liking. As a cult leader he was no trouble, but now? Now things are different."

"So let me at him. Tell me where he is. If I get the credit for arresting him, maybe I can get myself off Kusama's shit list."

"Would that I could," Furukawa said. "There was a time when we might do just that, but no longer. Koji-san is too good at staying hidden."

"Hidden? From the guy who can pick up the phone and end the career of any politician he wants? I don't think so."

Furukawa could not respond. He looked like a man at a funeral, not sad but drained. Empty. He picked up the black eight ball, tested its weight in his willowy fingers, and sent it on a collision course with its kin. Balls clicked and clacked, rolling in every direction. Not one of them found a pocket. Mariko got the distinct sense that Furukawa felt like one of those billiard balls: powerless, ruled only by the heartless forces of inevitability.

She had seen that same fatalistic detachment before. Not often, but she'd seen it. The first time was with Yamada-sensei, who had first opened Mariko's mind to the possibility that fate was something other than defeatist thinking. The second was Shoji Hayano, a blind woman and Yamada's friend of over sixty years. She was a *goze*, a seer, exactly the sort of thing Mariko never would have believed in until she saw it herself. But she *had* seen it. Shoji foretold Mariko's encounter with Fuchida. She even foretold Mariko's death, and did nothing to stop it. She'd given up trying to defy fate.

The third person was Jōko Daishi. He had spoken of his heavenly calling with the same overtones of inevitability. He believed in the supernatural too. And, come to think of it, he was the first person who had ever spoken to Mariko of the Wind. *Born of the Wind, yet not of the Wind.* That was how he described his Divine Wind cult. At the time she had no idea what to make of that. Now Furukawa had given her a little more to work with.

"Jōko Daishi was one of yours, wasn't he? A *genin* of the Wind?"

"At first, yes. He rose to become *chūnin*, like me. Middle management."

"The Wind trained him?"

"I am ashamed to admit we did."

Mariko jerked the Glock from her waistband. "Then as far as I'm concerned, the Wind sent four drivers straight into oncoming traffic. You killed four and injured twenty."

She racked the slide and put her front sight right on Furukawa's breastbone. The suddenness of her anger surprised her; she found herself blinking back tears. "You killed twenty-three more with ricin at St. Luke's International," she said. "You killed a hundred and twelve at Haneda, and you damn near killed me too."

"Detective Oshiro, I assure you—"

"Shut up. I was *there* when the second bomb went off. I saw the people you murdered. Some of them . . ."

She clenched her jaw and blinked hard against the tears. She'd never experienced grief so violently as this.

But she'd be damned if she would let this bastard see her cry. "There was so little left of them that you couldn't tell where one body ended and the next began. Their families didn't even have enough to cremate. A hundred and twelve people, all dead, all because of you."

"That was Koji-san's doing."

"No." In two strides she crossed the room to an antique rolltop writing desk with an old-fashioned rotary landline phone. Her pistol sights never left center body mass. "Not Jōko Daishi. Not the Divine Wind. *You*. You trained him. You set him loose. So the only question left to me is, which one do I pick?"

She swept up the phone in her right hand. "I can call for backup or I can shoot you where you stand. One way or the other, you're middle management in a terrorist organization and I *will* see you burn."

24

"What do you mean?" Captain Kusama Shuichi asked his secretary. "He just walked through the front door?"

"Yessir." Junko, his secretary, was a joyless golem who nonetheless took great care in doing her job, and was therefore extremely good at it. She was the only person in the Tokyo Metropolitan Police Department who outshone Kusama in personal grooming. He'd never seen a fleck of lint on her uniform, nor the smallest smudge on her shoes. But whereas Captain Kusama took pleasure in looking his best, with Junko it was as if her operating system didn't support messiness software.

"When?" said Kusama.

"Thirteen minutes ago, sir." This was one of the longest sentences she'd ever spoken to him. She did not need to consult her watch.

"Thirteen minutes? Why didn't you tell me immediately?"

She blinked at him.

Damn it all, he thought. Junko was nothing if not punctilious. If he told her to hold his calls, then that was what she would do, even if the cause for the interruption was capturing the most wanted man in the country.

"All right, Junko-san. That will do. Thank you for alerting me so . . . scrupulously. Oh, what floor—?"

"Eleven."

Narcotics Division. That was strange. Given the nature of the Divine Wind cult, Organized Crime was the more natural fit. Not that it mattered. In the end, Kusama would put the man wherever he damn well pleased—at the end of a rope, soon enough, but this morning he'd allow Sakakibara's boys to handle him.

Captain Kusama donned his jacket and cap, then gave himself a quick inspection in the mirror on the backside of his office door. He knew what the rank and file would have whispered about him if they saw him straightening his tie. Vain. Hungry for the spotlight. Gunning for elected office. Sometimes the rumors stung—Kusama wasn't immune to the judgment of others—but he found he could take comfort in being so thoroughly misunderstood. His obsession with public image had not the slightest thing to do with vanity.

Too many cops never grasped the simple truth: effective policing was first and foremost a matter of public perception. If the average man on the street believed the police were corrupt, he would live in fear. If he believed they were incompetent, he would live in fear. And the surest way to inspire belief in a department's integrity and dependability was consummate professionalism. That was why the squad cars were waxed and the helmets were polished. That was why an officer in a dirty uniform was sent home without pay. Most cops in the rank and file thought all of this had to do with discipline. If they had been soldiers, they would have been right. But this was a police force, not a military unit, and everything they did was done in the name of public safety.

It was true that being in the spotlight had its perks. Kusama couldn't deny that. There were days—maybe even most days—when he enjoyed being the department's point man with the press. When a Tokyo cop did something heroic, something to warrant his picture in the paper, Kusama was happy to be in the background of the photo. But when he spoke at a commendation ceremony, it was because honoring officers with medals and awards reinforced that all-important public perception that the police were an omnipresent force for good. It had nothing to do with one man's public image. The pictures in the papers were incidental; what mattered was what they symbolized.

Meeting grounds were symbolic too. Thirteen minutes was enough time for every last cop in the building to hear who was in the interrogation room on the eleventh floor. It would be a madhouse down there. Kusama didn't like to raise his voice and he certainly didn't care to elbow his way through a boisterous mob. There would be a lot of high-fiving going on down there; this was a major coup. So instead of joining the circus, he called Junko and ordered the suspect to be brought upstairs.

"In your *office*?"

"He's a lone man, not an elephant stampede. I'm sure we'll survive the experience. Oh, and call the press corps next. I'll issue a statement in thirty minutes."

Half an hour wasn't a lot of time, but Captain Kusama was eager to announce the capture of the nation's most dangerous felon. Two hours later he would give an update. Every two hours after that, either he or one of his delegates would return to the pressroom. It was de rigueur; Kusama had groomed the reporters to expect this pattern, and through it he controlled the headlines.

In fact it was not a stampede of elephants who entered his office, but neither was it a lone man. First came Lieutenant Sakakibara, striding in on long legs and looking as stern as ever. Then came the suspect's lawyer, Hamaya Jirō, whose right arm was in a sling for some reason. Next came two SWAT officers. One had his M4 rifle in hand; the other had his pistol in one hand and the suspect's handcuff chain in the other. And of course there was the man of the hour, Japan's Osama bin Laden.

Koji Makoto, Kusama recalled. Dredging that name up from his memory took some doing. He and everyone else had taken to calling the suspect only by his self-appointed religious appellation, Jōkō Daishi. Great Teacher of the Purging Fire. Now that was an ominous title if ever there was one.

Great Teacher or not, someone had beaten the hell out

of him. A bruise as dark as an eggplant dominated the left side of his forehead, fading progressively to blood red as it spread across his face. Kusama had seen tire irons leave less dramatic marks. The perp's clothes were blood-stained, too—only a little bit, but it was fresh blood, as if he'd torn some scabs loose on his chest and the wounds were slowly saturating the fabric. He wore white pants and an airy shirt of simple white linen. Over these he wore a long, sleeveless white robe in a style Captain Kusama wouldn't have found out of place if this was a 1970s chop-socky movie instead of his office.

"You've got a limp," Kusama said. "I'd heard that about you."

"I was marked from childhood." There was a hint of pride in his voice. "My mother is the future and my father is the past. The child of destiny comes into this world marked, so that others might know his coming."

Kusama shot a startled glance in Sakakibara's direction. The lieutenant only responded by rolling his eyes. Kusama could appreciate the sarcasm, but he didn't share it. This Jōko Daishi was more unbalanced than anyone had led him to believe. He'd assumed Detective Oshiro's reports were fanciful—premenstrual hysterics at best—but now he saw she hadn't exaggerated one bit.

"Well, do have a seat, Koji-san."

The SWAT cop forcibly compressed the cult leader into one of the leather chairs facing Kusama's polished teak desk. "Officer, have a care," Kusama told him. "If not for your suspect, then at least for my office furniture. I'll thank you not to bloody it."

The cop mumbled his apologies. For his part, Jōko Daishi looked down at his own chest. It was hard to notice, given the sheer volume of his wiry black beard and mustache, but Kusama could just make out that the man was smiling. He seemed pleasantly surprised, as if he hadn't even noticed he was bleeding. "My newest stigmata," he said. "They weep for you."

"Oh? How very compassionate of you."

"Compassionate. Yes. Even in your cynicism you unwittingly speak the truth. I came here to speak to the woman, and when I came, my wounds were not weeping. I did not come for you, but here we are. I have seen you on the television, spouting false prophecies and distracting the people from my revelation."

"Your revelation. Right."

Jōko Daishi gave him a sad, pitying smile. "You understand nothing of the Haneda sermon. You understand nothing of the sermon at the hospital. And so yes, Kusama Shuichi, I weep for you. My very body weeps for you. You are a drowning man swimming ever deeper into darkness. Come back to the light."

Kusama found himself looking to Lieutenant Sakakibara again. Jōko Daishi snickered to see it. It was not often that Captain Kusama found himself speechless. He was keenly aware of his silence now. Despite all the talk of sermons and prophecies, he found he'd fixated on only one thing. "Woman? Which woman?"

Jōko Daishi giggled. "The swordswoman. Who else?"

"Oshiro?" Kusama didn't mean to sound so offended. With half a second's hindsight he knew it wasn't Jōko Daishi who had given offense. There was no derision to his laughter; it was childlike, even innocent, if that was something one could say of a mass murderer. No, what offended Kusama was that somehow Detective Oshiro managed to wheedle her way right into the middle of this again. She wasn't in the room. She wasn't even in the building. So how the hell had she inserted herself into the conversation?

He couldn't help but notice a self-satisfied gleam in Sakakibara's eye. Oshiro was his pet. They weren't fucking, so far as Kusama knew; that was the kind of thing he'd have heard about. Closer to say she was his circus dog. It wasn't natural, making a woman behave like a man, but Oshiro had a gift for it. Clearly Sakakibara enjoyed showing off how well he'd trained her to prance around on her hind legs.

There was a time when Kusama himself had hoped to use the performing dog to the department's advantage, but that was before he learned that no one had ever trained her not to bark. Sakakibara must have found her misbehavior endearing, or else he'd have whipped it out of her. His greater offense was that he'd been there when Kusama tried to discipline the bitch himself. The first time Kusama demoted Oshiro, it had been for good cause. The second time—well, he remembered that one only too clearly. He had been at his wit's end. Exhausted, angry, more than a little scared. The smoke in Terminal 2 was literally rising from the ashes even as he and Oshiro spoke. And then she barked one time too many.

Captain Kusama knew his reaction was petty. Even in the moment he knew it. If he and Oshiro had been alone, he might have found some way to lift his punishment and still save face. But with Sakakibara there, Kusama had no room to backpedal. Oshiro was popular with the rank and file—more so than she even understood herself—and Kusama had punished her unjustly. If he was honest with himself, he hadn't stopped punishing her. He still blamed her for putting him in the position to do what he did. It was unfair and he damn well knew it, and so now whenever he thought of that woman, he tasted the bile boiling up in the back of his throat.

So it sure as hell didn't help her case when the most dangerous criminal in the whole damn country came knocking on the front door, looking for a disgraced and uppity ex-sergeant and having to content himself with a highly decorated captain instead. The son of a bitch never even noticed the view.

"Detective Oshiro isn't here right now," Kusama said. He managed not to growl. "Not that it matters. Wanted men don't get to choose which detective interrogates them."

"My client hasn't been accused of anything," Hamaya said.

Kusama snapped his head around so fast he could have given himself whiplash. In truth he'd forgotten the lawyer was there. Hamaya stood in the far corner of the room, gazing down at the city, the traffic, the first yellow tinges of autumn. He'd chosen a black pinstriped suit to match the sling of fine black mesh that cradled his right arm. Kusama couldn't help but admire the fashion choice.

Sakakibara felt otherwise. He stalked up to stand chest to chest with Hamaya. "You want to say that again?"

The lawyer shrank away from him, having nowhere to go except to lean against the thick windowpane. The glass was engineered to withstand the shear forces of an earthquake, but even so, Hamaya must have been wondering whether it could support his weight. "You held my client on every charge you could," he peeped. His mousy, frightened eyes flicked like Ping-Pong balls between Sakakibara and the precipitous drop. "Then you let him go, because you had insufficient evidence to hold him. So unless you have further evidence . . ."

Sakakibara leaned in a few centimeters closer. Hamaya shrank back. Kusama imagined he could hear the window flexing under the man's weight. "Further evidence?" Sakakibara snorted at him like a bull preparing to charge. "How about boasting about his goddamned 'sermons'? Your client just admitted to twenty-three counts of murder at St. Luke's alone."

"No. He spoke of *the* sermons, not *his* sermons."

"Says you. Maybe I remember something different."

"Then the digital record will prove you wrong." Hamaya smiled feebly. "I took the precaution of wiring myself for sound."

A rumbling like distant thunder welled up from somewhere in Sakakibara's chest. He looked the cringing man up and down like a K-9 dog sniffing for drugs. His right hand rose high as if to deliver a backhanded slap, but instead of striking Hamaya he brushed his necktie aside to reveal a tiny microphone from one of those spyware/surveillance shops, clipped through one of the buttonholes in his shirt. Kusama immediately shifted his attention to Jōko Daishi. If the madman was wired, there was no hope of spotting it in that thicket of a beard.

"You need a better attorney," Kusama told the terrorist sitting in front of him. "Any breach of the peace that alarms and disturbs the citizenry constitutes disorderly conduct. I'd say Lieutenant Sakakibara looks alarmed and disturbed, wouldn't you?"

Jōko Daishi replied with one of his childlike smiles. Hamaya wasn't quite so cheerful. "He looks that way," the lawyer said, still cringing. "But legally, police officers cannot be 'alarmed and disturbed.' It's an important check on your abuse of authority, as I'm sure your lieutenant understands. I can quote the case law if you like."

"No need," Kusama said. He knew the law as well as anyone. "At ease, Lieutenant."

Sakakibara growled and fumed, but in the end he stood down. He left his feet planted right where they were, though, so Hamaya had to squirm awkwardly around him to find a less compromising place to stand.

"If you didn't come to confess," Kusama asked, "why are you here?"

"To bring you to the light." Jōko Daishi leaned forward a little in his chair, as if sharing a secret. The truth was that he couldn't lean back—not with his hands cuffed behind his back—but even so, his posture suggested intimacy, even across the vast expanse of Kusama's desk.

"You think you protect your city with your lies," the lunatic said. "Instead you only help to fan the flames of the Purging Fire. Today those flames illuminate the truth. Today the people will learn the Haneda sermon was not the false teaching of some foreign terrorist. They will see your forked tongue for what it is. When they learn you have deceived them from the beginning, you will lose their trust. I will expose you all as the defenders of delusion—"

And there's not a goddamn thing I can do about it, Kusama thought. Not legally, anyway. The son of a bitch was right. Worse yet, Oshiro was right. She'd warned him against implicating Jemaah Islamiyah. She told him this day would come. When the public learned the full truth about Jōko Daishi, it would be the most scathing scandal the TMPD had ever seen. As soon as it came out that Kusama had a Japanese suspect for Terminal 2, the media would ask how he'd known. That would expose the cover-up of the attempted Korakuen station bombing. Then it would come out that Jōko Daishi was released from custody just hours before the first bomb went off at

Haneda. Now the prime suspect would walk again, even as reporters flooded through the front door to attend Kusama's press conference. Some of them might literally bump into Jōko Daishi as he left the building.

And then, goddamn her, Oshiro would regain her celebrity. The woman didn't have the patience to fend off a lengthy siege. The reporters would hound her day in and day out, demanding to know why her superiors dragged her name through the mud after Korakuen. Sooner or later she would lose her composure and mention Kusama by name. That would spell the end of his career. He had willingly besmirched the name of a hero. What did it matter that he outranked her? What did it matter that she was legitimately a pain in the ass? Insubordination paled in comparison to a deliberate assault on her honor.

Kusama wished he believed in the seven gods of good fortune. If he started praying now, maybe they would bring him a miracle.

Jōko Daishi kept bleating his sanctimonious bullshit, but Kusama wasn't listening. He needed a solution, starting with some excuse—*any* excuse—to hold Jōko Daishi. He would not go down as the police captain who let a terrorist mastermind escape twice.

Then it came to him: what he really needed was for Jōko Daishi to implicate himself. Interrupting the lecture, he said, "I think you're a psychopath."

"No doubt the carcinoma thinks the same of the oncologist," said Jōko Daishi.

Not close enough, Kusama thought. He didn't quite threaten to cut me with a scalpel, did he? This would have to be perfect; those little microphones were listening. "Was that the point of the ricin? Chemotherapy? Poisoning all the cancers in our society?"

"That is impossible. In this patient there are more tumors than healthy tissue. Very difficult to remove."

"I see. Better to let this case go, then, *neh*? Burn everything to ashes in your Purging Fire and start again?"

"I hope not. This is a most unusual cancer; it is one you deluded ones can cure yourselves. The host can reject the tumor. He has only to see the path."

Damn it, Kusama thought. Jōko Daishi may have been out of his mind, but he was disciplined enough never to mention himself or his own goals. Hamaya had coached him well.

"What about me?" asked Kusama. "What if I said the Tokyo Metropolitan Police Department is the only oncologist this patient needs? Suppose I told you to get the hell out of my operating room?"

Jōko Daishi giggled. "You are the most talented physician of a thousand years ago. You know nothing, even at the height of your craft. You see chemotherapy and you mistake it for torture. But I say unto you: you will learn better medicine, whether you will it or not."

Close and getting closer, Kusama thought. But just like that, Hamaya stepped in. "My client and I must be going. Unless . . . well, do you intend to detain us, Captain?"

Kusama wanted to smack that smarmy grin off his face. In the old days he could have done just that. Disciplined or not, Jōko Daishi would probably react to getting hit by striking back. He was violent enough, that was certain. As soon as he threw his first head butt, every cop in the room could pile onto him. No matter what the perp said after that, the cops could refute it. Officer safety first.

Back in the seventies that was business as usual. Strike first, get the story straight later. But today perps could wear tiny fucking microphones. For all Kusama knew, this entire meeting was already streaming live online. There were probably countries out there where that was illegal; too bad Japan wasn't one of them.

He looked up at Hamaya, whose grin was smeared across his face like two tapeworms laid side by side. Kusama could throw him in a cell, and his client with him. Not legally, not without probable cause, but nothing could stop him from doing it illegally.

He thought about Detective Oshiro and her disregard for authority. For all her flaws, when she had the chance to stand by her partner she'd chosen to stand by the law instead. What would she say if her captain broke the law to do the right thing?

Kusama caught Sakakibara's eye. The Narcotics LT must have been entertaining the same thoughts, and darker ones too. The heel of his palm rested on the butt of his pistol, as if he were debating whether it was worth his freedom to shoot both of these men in the back of the head. For Captain Kusama, that wasn't a hard question: of course it was worth it. Jōko Daishi was responsible for over a hundred murders. But probable cause was probable cause, and Kusama didn't have it.

Fuck it, he thought. "Lieutenant Sakakibara, I want you to—"

"Get these men out of your office? Right away, sir."

That wasn't at all what Kusama had in mind, and Sakakibara knew that damn well. But he was good police, and this morning that meant he'd obey the law even when his captain lost his nerve and wanted to break it. "I'm giving you shitheads ten seconds to get out of here," Sakakibara said. "After that I'm going to arrest you for loitering and tresp—"

Kusama never saw the SWAT cop reach for his sidearm. The weapon just appeared in his hand. He reached out with the barrel, intending to press it right to Jōko Daishi's skull before he pulled the trigger.

The world went into slow motion. Kusama sprang up from his chair. He sprawled across his desk, pawing for the pistol, for Jōko Daishi, for *anything*. But the desk was too wide. He couldn't reach.

Thunder and gun smoke filled the room. Something sharp and hot lacerated Kusama's cheekbone. He expected blood spatter, not bullet fragments. Then he saw the truth: it was Sakakibara, not the SWAT operator, who had fired. Now the SWAT cop twisted and fell, almost as if through water.

Everything happened so slowly. Kusama saw him level his pistol as he fell, training it on Jōko Daishi. Kusama couldn't help but admire him for that; he wouldn't give up, not even after Sakakibara put a round in his flak vest. Even now, Sakakibara's pistol followed the man. Why wasn't he still shooting?

Now Kusama saw it. The other SWAT operator

loomed over his buddy, intent on smothering the weapon, but he seemed to hang in the air. The world still moved in slow motion. Kusama leaned farther across the desk, reaching for Jōko Daishi. Even as he did it, he wasn't sure if he meant to pull the man out of the line of fire or push him into it. It didn't matter. He was too slow. He couldn't reach.

Sakakibara shifted his aim a couple of millimeters. Somehow he snaked in a shot right between the two SWAT cops. Two pistols roared almost in unison. Their reports stabbed Kusama in the eardrums. He watched as the bullet meant for Jōko Daishi splattered bits of Hamaya Jirō all over the windows.

Then the world zoomed back to normal speed. "Down, down, down!" the second SWAT cop bellowed. He flattened his partner and wrapped both hands around his gun arm. The man on the bottom howled in pain. Kusama, flat on his desk like roadkill, saw no blood down there. He assumed Sakakibara's second round also hit the bulletproof vest. If so, that was one hell of a shot.

On the other side of the room, the wind whistled through a little bloody hole in the window. Gray matter containing Hamaya's law degree oozed slowly down the glass. The attorney himself lay on the carpet, gaping at the ceiling. He seemed to have grown a second mouth in the side of his head; the hollow-point left a hideous crater in its wake.

Sakakibara paid the body no mind; his weapon was trained on Jōko Daishi's center body mass. For his part, the cult leader just looked around, much like a little boy trying to decide which animal to watch at the zoo. That more than anything told Kusama the man was out of his mind. He'd narrowly survived an assassination attempt, his friend took a bullet to the head, and the look on his face never changed. He didn't even seem to notice the ringing in his ears, a ringing Kusama was damn sure he heard, because his own ears blared with a steady blast like a distant car horn.

Captain Kusama finally managed to haul himself off his desk. He scrambled around and helped the SWAT operator disarm and handcuff his one-time comrade. "You were thinking the same thing," the shooter said as the cuffs clicked shut around his wrists. "I know you were."

You're right, Kusama thought. Damn you, you're right. That was why he'd started to tell Sakakibara to arrest Jōko Daishi: because it was a better plan than gunning him down.

His office door flew open. Junko kicked it aside, a little .32 revolver in her hands. Behind her, so many voices were shouting that Kusama couldn't keep count. By now every cop on the floor had heard the shots and come running. Faces and the muzzles of pistols appeared in the doorway, one after another. Jōko Daishi watched them with an air of expectant joy, like a child watching the carp come flocking to the surface after the first chunks of bread hit the pond.

When he stood up, Sakakibara clamped a hand on his shoulder and slam-dunked him back into his chair. "Hey, Bullet Magnet, sit the fuck down."

"Why?" cried the handcuffed cop on the floor. "Why save him?"

Because the law demands it, Kusama thought. Sakakibara answered differently: "Because I'm standing next to him, dumbass. When people get jumpy, sometimes their shots wander a bit. Which, you know, you might have noticed already."

He fixed his furious glare on the gun-toting crowd clustered in the doorway. "What are you, a firing squad? Holster your weapons. Now."

They did as they were told. Kusama and the other SWAT operator helped the handcuffed cop to his feet, and together they ushered him into the room outside. Kusama ordered an escort for him, first to the emergency room, then to a holding cell. He told everyone else to disperse, and all but one of them did. Junko, strangely territorial all of a sudden, refused to turn her back on Jōko Daishi. "You're my boss" was the only explanation she offered.

Kusama lacked the energy to fight her, so he just shut

the huge office door in her face. He needed time to think. "Fucking hell, Sakakibara, what are we going to do?"

"Down the freight elevator, straight to the motor pool. We stick him in the back of an SUV and we drop him off anywhere he wants to go. And you, Bullet Magnet, you're going to comply, because otherwise I can't vouch for your safety."

Jōko Daishi craned his neck to look back at him. "Oh, but I can. I have foreseen the hour of my death. My time has not yet arrived."

Sakakibara snorted. "How nice for you."

The lunatic turned back to Captain Kusama. "May I ask a favor of you?"

Kusama almost choked on his breath. "You have to be kidding."

"No." He glanced at his fallen attorney. "Hamaya-san has escaped the fetters of this deluded world. I rejoice for him, but I do not know your laws as he did. Tell me, can you legally force me to leave this building only on your terms?"

Kusama and Sakakibara exchanged a glance. Sakakibara closed his eyes and shook his head. "No," Kusama confessed.

"Then I believe I shall leave through the front door."

Kusama strangled the air. The opportunity for a disorderly conduct charge dangled right in front of him. The mere sight of Jōko Daishi was sure to get civilians alarmed and disturbed. But that meant the only way to arrest him was to wait until he got into the public view, and today wasn't the day to raise questions about whether the TMPD was trampling civil rights. Could they rearrest him every time another human being laid eyes on him? If not, then why arrest him this time? Was it just because they could get away with it? Was it because he didn't have legal counsel anymore? Kusama was sure he could spin Hamaya's death as the accidental discharge of a firearm, but that would get sticky if the TMPD used this as an opportunity to hold Jōko Daishi without representation.

The terrorist stood up from his chair, and none of the cops in the room did a damn thing to stop him. He presented his back to Sakakibara, who had no choice but to uncuff him. "I have one more favor to ask," he said. "Would you pass a message to the swordswoman for me?"

Kusama huffed angrily. "One of your sermons?"

"A benediction. Tell her she must forgive herself for what is to come."

25

"Please, Detective Oshiro." Furukawa pressed his long-fingered hands together as if he were praying to her. Maybe he was doing just that. "Shoot me or arrest me as you will; I am powerless to stop you. But allow me to observe that neither one will advance your interests."

"Justice," Mariko said. "That's my interest. You're a murderer."

"So you say. But you are not so naive as to think I will go to prison."

Mariko didn't need to think about that for long. This was a man who could change the face of government with a single phone call. He had the kind of money it took to rent a Shinjuku penthouse large enough to have a pool table. That, or else he was backed by that kind of money, which meant there was a hell of a lot more where that came from. Middle management, he'd said. How powerful would the upper management be, if a middleman was capable of all this?

That realization only made Mariko tighten her grip on her pistol. "Oh, come now," Furukawa said. "You won't shoot me. Not if you want to leave this suite alive."

"Are you threatening me?"

"I don't need to. It is a simple truth: the Wind will not abide the assassination of one of its *chūnin*. But that is irrelevant, since you have no intention of pulling that trigger. You want Jōko Daishi, and I am the one who can give him to you."

Mariko focused on the Glock's sights, then on Furukawa's skinny, sunken chest. She wasn't going to pull the trigger. He was right.

"You see, Detective Oshiro, this is how the Wind operates. What need is there for coercion? We put people in a position where their interests align with our own. They only need to do what they always do. What they inevitably do. Then they do our work for us."

"What if I'm stubborn? What if I refuse?"

"You won't, or else you and I would never have met. Do you think I would allow you to see my face if there were any possibility that you could arrest me? Do you think I would put myself in a room with you if I thought you could actually kill me? No. I placed your captain in a position to suspend you. I placed you in a position to indulge your own impetuous curiosity. It is no different than playing billiards. Apply the right impetus from the right angle and the balls will do exactly as you bid them."

Mariko glowered at him. She hated that he'd read her mind so easily, that she'd allowed herself to be so easily read. She never would have shot him unless he presented a lethal threat, but *he* didn't have to know that.

A glint of triumph glimmered in his eyes when he saw he'd struck the bull's-eye. Mariko recognized that look, and all at once she understood that ineffable similarity she'd seen in him all along. She'd known one other person who had that maddening knowledge of her own affairs, someone who was always a step ahead of her, who stood in judgment over her like a stern grandfather. Not many people could make her feel like she was always catching up, but Furukawa did, and one other man did too: Yamada Yasuo.

"You *did* know him," Mariko said. She'd harbored a healthy skepticism about that before, but now there was no doubt. "You two are so alike. So why was he a good man, and why are you such a corrupt son of a bitch?"

There was that wince again, as if her words stuck him

like a needle. The attack on his character didn't seem to bother him at all; it was her discourtesy that rankled. "We both know you're not going to shoot me, Detective. Would you be so good as to lower your pistol?"

She did as she was told. Her thumb automatically groped for the safety, but there wasn't one. Glocks weren't built that way. But Mariko's brain was running on autopilot, coasting on its default position that this was her favored SIG P230. The sight of the Glock in her hand made her realize something she should have registered already: she was now illegally in possession of a firearm. If this were a legitimate police operation, she'd call in the cavalry, turn over the weapon in the course of processing the crime scene, and that would be that. But now she was on suspension and trapped by a criminal syndicate. She didn't have to think long about whether she planned to turn the Glock over to Investigative Division. She spent more time thinking about how much she didn't like the prospect of stuffing an unsafetied weapon into her waistband, and what a hassle it would be to run Norika down and steal the holster the crafty bitch must have had on her.

Since she didn't have anywhere safe to put the weapon, Mariko just held the damn thing. Her trigger finger tapped irritably on the outside of the trigger guard. "So? What now?"

"Now you accept my offer. Join the Wind. Bring an end to the reign of Jōko Daishi."

"Bring an end to—?" Mariko didn't like the sound of that at all. "You can't be serious. You want me to kill him?"

"It's the only way to stop him."

"Okay, first of all, no, it isn't. Prison works just fine. Second, do you understand what happens when I follow you down this road? Do you have any idea how often I run across a perp who I *know* is guilty, but I can't prove it yet? It happens every week. If cops start taking the law into their own hands, *there is no law.* I'm not crossing that line. Not for you, not for anyone. Go sell your ninja suits someplace else."

Furukawa deflated with a sigh. He had the air of a

disappointed schoolmaster. "Ninja suits! I suppose you'd like that. I could wear the black *shōzoku* and you could wear a white cowboy hat. Quite the appropriate garb for your movie theater moralizing. The world is not black and white, Detective."

"If you don't like how I see it, find someone else. Don't you have assassins of your own? Send that bitch Norika after him."

"We tried. For years she posed as one of Jōko Daishi's concubines—originally to serve as a bodyguard, you understand. That was when we thought we could control him. Terminal 2 changed all of that. Norika was given the order. She tried to kill him but failed; the man is too well protected. It was all she could do to recapture the mask and escape. I sent her straight to you."

"Why me?"

"Because we believe you are the only person who can kill him."

"Then you're an idiot." When he gave her a quizzical frown, she aped it right back at him. "Seriously? What do you not get about this? I'm not doing it."

"It is the only way to stop his reign of terror."

"It's first-degree murder!"

Mariko thought that was pretty self-explanatory. When she saw it didn't move him, she turned and headed for the door. "I'm a cop. You want a vigilante. We're done, Furukawa-san. Have a nice day."

"Detective Oshiro, I haven't given you permission to leave."

Mariko press-checked the Glock, confirming she had a round chambered. Waving good-bye with the gun, she said, "I've got my permission slip right here, thanks."

"You've killed before."

That stopped Mariko in her tracks. "Excuse me?"

"Akahata Daisuke. You shot him right through the head."

Mariko didn't need a reminder. She had replayed that nightmare in her mind a thousand times. "That's none of your damn business," she said coldly. "And it was in self-defense, by the way."

"Oh, you don't believe that's relevant, do you? There were fifty-two people on that subway platform. You saved them all. If you hadn't been there—if you had been a sniper far out of harm's way—you'd still have taken the shot, wouldn't you?"

Damn right, I would, Mariko thought. But she wouldn't give him the satisfaction of hearing her say it.

"Do you know what I think? I think you'd have shot him even if he were innocent."

A hot tear rolled down Mariko's cheek. "You don't know what the fuck you're talking about."

"Oh, but I do. What do guilt and innocence matter in the face of arithmetic?" Furukawa laughed as much as spoke. "Suppose I put you there again. Suppose this time Akahata's only crime is bad luck. I have wired a bomb to him. In ten seconds it will explode, but only if he is alive. Shoot him and you disarm the bomb. Hold your fire and he will innocently blow himself to pieces, and fifty-two others besides. Can you tell me the *law* matters?"

It does matter, Mariko thought. It has to. That was the oath she swore when they gave her the badge. The law was supposed to matter, even when morals and logic and everything else said it shouldn't.

Suppose I put you there again, he'd said, but he didn't have to. She'd placed herself on that platform as soon as he started comparing numbers. That's what got the tears flowing.

The vision stood out in her mind as clearly as if Akahata were in the same room. Her left hand squeezed smoothly; a black circle appeared in Akahata's forehead. The kick of the gun seemed to come much later. Its deafening thunderclap too. Even in the moment, Akahata seemed to stand on his feet for an eternity, clutching that high school boy he'd grabbed as a human shield. When they finally fell together, Mariko was dead sure she'd shot the kid.

What would that mean, shooting the hostage instead of the bomber? Mariko didn't believe in karma, but if there were such a thing, would it matter that Mariko was the one who killed the kid, and Akahata who blew up everyone else? Did it matter that the kid would have died anyway?

It *did* matter. It *had to* matter. Didn't it?

Furukawa gave her no time to ponder the question. "The proposition before you is simple, Detective Oshiro. Join us, kill Koji Makoto, and make your city safe again. Or do not, and live with the guilt of doing nothing."

Mariko looked down at the gun in her hand. A teardrop fell from her eye. She watched it fall all the way down until it splashed against the front sight of the pistol.

She rubbed her eyes with the nub of her right forefinger. It came away wet and glistening. Shaking her head, she told herself, "I can't believe I'm going to do this."

"You must," Furukawa said. His voice was gentle now, almost grandfatherly.

"No." Mariko looked him right in the eye. "I'm not a pool ball. You want to knock me around, you better be ready for me to knock back. I'm going to walk out that door, and I don't want to see you again. Ever. Find someone else to do your dirty work."

Furukawa had no idea what to do with that. He watched, dumbstruck, as Mariko slammed the door behind her.

BOOK SIX

◆◆◆◆◆◆◆◆◆◆◆◆◆◆◆◆◆◆◆◆◆◆◆◆◆◆◆◆◆◆◆◆

AZUCHI-MOMOYAMA PERIOD, THE YEAR 21

(1588 CE)

26

"You're a little one, aren't you?"

The man who asked the question was anything but little. He had shoulders like an ox and a belly like a whale. He carried a long *naginata* with a blade as broad as a butcher's cleaver. It was rusty, ill kept but well used. There was no mistaking the notches taken out of its edge; this one had seen plenty of fighting.

The big man—already named Whalebelly in Daigoro's mind—had two accomplices. On his left stood a flat-faced man wielding two short *kama*. The sickles were intended for farming, but they were increasingly used in hand-to-hand combat now that the Sword Hunt had disarmed most of the population. On Whalebelly's right stood a lean, haggard, foul-smelling woman who looked tougher than the other two put together. Her yellow nails were broken but her knives weren't. She had one in each hand and half a dozen more tucked into her belt.

For his part, Daigoro was armed primarily with a huge bundle of dried wattle. It was his best disguise to date. The sheaf was large enough, and bowed his back enough, that bystanders had trouble making eye contact with him. It was light but it didn't look that way, so no one would question a boy of his size limping under the load. Better yet, it was long enough that he could hide his father's *ōdachi* in the center of it. So disguised, Daigoro found he could pass unnoticed within an arm's reach of Shichio's patrols.

On the other hand, his hunched posture restricted his peripheral vision, which made it easy for *yamabushi* like Whalebelly to take him unawares. His disguise also made it impossible to draw Glorious Victory, so if it came to blows, he would have no choice but to face these bandits with his *wakizashi*. Even that was tucked up into the bundle, frightfully slow on the draw.

"Wattle don't sell for much," he said, affecting a low born vernacular. "Not much use to folk like you, neither."

"What do you mean, 'folk like you'?" Whalebelly demanded. "You think you're better than us, farmer boy?"

"No, sir. Figured you're not fond of building fences is all."

A sudden gale brought the surrounding bamboo forest to life. Leaves rustled. Long, green stalks clacked and clattered. The wind carried the smells of the *yamabushi* too: old sweat, oily hair, clothes so dirty they would never be worth washing again. And yes, alcohol. Whalebelly was drunk and spoiling for a fight.

Daigoro looked past them, down the natural tunnel formed by the overarching bamboo. It ran straight downhill to the road. Once he reached the road, he knew he'd see the moss green banners of House Yasuda. No more than a hundred paces, he guessed. A hundred paces and he would have peace. Damn you, he thought, damn all you gods and devils. Why could you not give me just a hundred paces more?

A lone boy versus three armed bandits. A one-sided fight to say the least. "I'll give you one chance to retreat," Daigoro said.

"Hah!" Whalebelly whacked his *naginata* against the ground, just like a bull pawing the earth before a charge.

"So that's the way of it," Daigoro said.

A one-sided fight, if the lone boy was samurai. Daigoro predicted the woman for a thrower—no reason to carry eight knives if she wasn't—and he made sure her first shot went into the wattle. Flipping his sheaf the other way, he intercepted Whalebelly's charge. The oversized *naginata* entangled itself irretrievably in the tangle of bundled sticks.

Daigoro ducked the next knife. Then he pulled the first one from the wattle and rammed it into Whalebelly's diaphragm. It sank all the way to the hilt. That was enough to send the other man running.

The woman stood her ground, but only for the moment. Whalebelly clutched his weapon, trying desperately to keep his feet, so between the dying giant and the huge sheaf of sticks, Daigoro had adequate cover against her knives. Every missed throw would arm her quarry with another blade. "I'll go," she said, "but only if you let me take his wineskin."

"It's all yours."

She crept up cautiously, expecting a double cross. Then, quick as a cat, she sliced it free of her dying leader's body and fled along the nearest game trail. In moments she vanished into the bamboo. Just like that, Daigoro was alone again.

Not for the first time, he wondered what the gods of good fortune meant for him. He was unlucky to encounter these *yamabushi*, but lucky that Whalebelly hadn't bled much. Daigoro's disguise would be useless if it were doused in human blood. He was lucky to have survived the battle, short though it was. On the other hand, was it lucky to send two survivors into the back hills? Sooner or later, tales would spread of the skinny little boy who killed Whalebelly in a single blow. Once Shichio's hunters heard the stories, they would know Daigoro had been here.

Luck and unluck. He was lucky that Whalebelly's lot didn't answer to Shichio, lucky that there were three of them and not six, but supremely unlucky to have to run into them at all. He was sure to run across more *yamabushi* so long as he traveled the back country, but he could not ride the roads so long as Shichio's patrols were abroad. Life would have been so much easier if that damned peacock could just choke to death on a piece of sushi. "Give me that," Daigoro said, looking up to the gods. "Give me bad fortune too if you must, but give me this one good thing."

He looked himself over once more. Then, satisfied that he wasn't a bloody mess, he shouldered his burden once again and headed downhill.

When he reached the road, he found himself on the outskirts of the growing city of Yoshiwara. Rice paddies sprawled to his left and right, and before him the little lane sloped down to the checkpoint he and Katsushima had been trying to avoid. They'd met with success, because Daigoro was now west of the checkpoint; to get back to Izu, he'd have to go back through and follow the Tōkaidō east. That was good. The Yoshiwara checkpoint was the safest one for him to cross, for it lay firmly within Yasuda territory, but that did not mean it was unwatched. Shichio was sure to have spies there. If they were smart, they would be looking east, not west.

Daigoro took shelter under his bulky load and limped for the little castle bearing the white-on-green centipede banners of House Yasuda.

Fuji-no-tenka was no Green Cliff. It did not have to be. The Green Cliff was the last bastion of House Yasuda, while Fuji-no-tenka was its forwardmost observation tower. The Yasuda forefathers knew their Sun Tzu as well as Daigoro did: the linchpin of a strong defense was knowledge of the enemy's disposition. House Yasuda's stables were renowned for their fast, hardy, intelligent horses. That reputation was founded in Fuji-no-tenka, where swift-footed messenger mounts were bred for rapid relays. The castle was built as much for horses as for men; its donjon was modest, its keep vast.

Daigoro had come to think of it as a relay station of his own. It was his first safe haven on the way to Kiyosu, which was where he decided to start his hunt for Streaming Dawn. The town of Kiyosu held the only advantage Daigoro had over Nene, whose resources vastly outstripped Daigoro's in every conceivable respect. He could only assume she'd already gone to great lengths to find Streaming Dawn; beseeching Daigoro for help smacked of desperation. But Nene lacked one thing: the bedtime stories Daigoro had grown up with. How well he remembered his father's tale of the *tantō* that cursed the bearer with a ghoulish, twisted form of eternal life. That tale always began in Kiyosu.

But Fuji-no-tenka came first, because with any luck, it would be in Fuji-no-tenka that Daigoro would solve the conundrum of giving Streaming Dawn to two people at once. Yasuda Jinichi, eldest son of Lord Yasuda Jinbei, was lord of Fuji-no-tenka and eldest brother of the miserly, petty-minded Yasuda Kenbei. If Jinichi commanded it, Kenbei would have to end this ridiculous war of coins. There would be no more murdered pigeons, nor any reason for Kenbei to seek Sora Nobushige's backing. Sora would lose his bargaining position, and Daigoro could give Streaming Dawn to Lady Nene with no fear of jeopardizing his family.

Everything depended on whether Jinichi was more like his father, a noble and honorable man, or more like his brother Kenbei, a spark that had flown a long way from the fire.

Despite the fact that Daigoro had spent his whole life with the Yasudas almost on his doorstep, he'd never met Jinichi in the flesh before. Jinichi was old enough to be Daigoro's grandfather, and he'd served as lord of Fuji-no-tenka for forty years. He reminded Daigoro of nothing so much as a well-used walking stick. He was scrawny, almost knobbly, with skin like knotted, polished wood. Careworn but strong.

Though they'd never met, he recognized Daigoro on sight—not an especially difficult feat, once Daigoro cast off the farmer's guise. Glorious Victory Unsought was unmistakable, and as close allies to House Okuma, the high-ranking Yasudas knew all about Daigoro's weakling leg.

"So it's true," Jinichi said. His voice was thin and reedy, just like his father's. "You no longer wear the Okuma bear paw."

Daigoro bowed and tried not to blush. "I suppose you've heard why."

"Oh, what haven't we heard of you? If I believed all of it, I wouldn't know whether you're alive or dead. That's what some folk are saying of you now: you're a vengeful ghost. Have you heard that one?"

Daigoro felt his cheeks flush despite his best efforts. When Jinichi saw it, he reached out with a gnarled brown finger and gave Daigoro a poke, as if to be sure he was there. "There, you see? Not a ghost. Not a traitor either, I think. Or a pirate. Or a ninja lord. Or a bear *kami* that can take human form. Now that's something I'd like to see before I die. Tell me, can you turn into a bear?"

"I'm afraid not."

"Too bad." He gave Daigoro a yellow-toothed smile. "Tell me, son, why are you here? And why on earth did you *walk* all this way? Judging by the state of your *hakama*, you must have been wading through mud."

That, or I've been wearing the same *hakama* for four days, Daigoro thought. The same everything else too. By the gods, what I wouldn't give for a bath.

But he said none of that. "I come to discuss House Okuma's debts to House Yasuda."

"Then send a pigeon next time. By the Buddha! You must have worn your feet down to nubs."

Daigoro explained why he couldn't do that, and why his family's debts to the Yasudas had become a concern in the first place. With each new detail, Jinichi's mood grew darker. At last he could take no more. "Stop. I hear you trying to speak gracefully of my brother, trying to avoid offense, but let me nip that in the bud. Kenbei was always the runt of the litter. That was his karma, and he should have learned to make peace with it a long time ago. How to cope with a grown man who acts like a child, I don't know. If I were back home, I would bend him over my knee and spank him."

Daigoro's whole body sagged, and he realized that prior to that moment his every muscle had been tight with anticipation. He'd never been sure whether Jinichi would take his side or Kenbei's. Now relief washed over him like cool rain on a hot summer's day. "I'm relieved to hear you say that. I have the feeling your father might beat you to that spanking when he wakes up."

"If he wakes up. And that's the trouble, isn't it? Father named Kenbei steward. It is not my place to countermand him. If it were up to me, we would handle House Okuma's debts the way we always have: as neighbors. As friends. As men of honor. But it is not up to me, Daigoro-san. My hands are tied."

Daigoro deflated like a sail in a dead wind. He'd come to the conversation braced for disappointment, but Jinichi's scorn for his brother had broken the braces down. Now that cool rain of relief became cloying and clammy. It chilled him to the bone.

"It's not what you wanted to hear," Jinichi said.

"No." Daigoro could not think of a softer way to say it.

"Let me grant you a loan, at least. From my personal coffers, not from House Yasuda's. Will that keep Kenbei's claws away from your family's purse strings?"

"For a while." Daigoro should have softened that too, but he lacked the energy to come up with something more appropriate to say. They negotiated terms, but it was clear from the outset that Jinichi could not meet even a third of what Kenbei demanded. Daigoro could hardly turn down the coin, but even as he accepted it, he wondered how he would give Streaming Dawn to Lord Sora and Lady Nene at once.

As that thought struck him, he asked, "What do you know of Streaming Dawn?"

"The knife?" Jinichi's lips pursed and his eyes widened. "Now that's a name I haven't heard in a long while."

"Did you ever talk to my father about it?"

"How could I not? That was quite a story."

"Would you tell me what you remember?"

"Of course, of course. Come, let's have some tea."

They had more than tea. Jinichi called servants to prepare a formal dinner, then sent a messenger into the foothills to fetch Katsushima. Daigoro had left his traveling companion with the horses in an abandoned logging camp. On the back roads they could ride together, but never in the public eye; Shichio's mercenaries knew to look for a traveling pair, a crippled boy and his *rōnin* companion. Daigoro's mount was a giveaway too. With one leg heavier than the other, staying in an ordinary saddle was a constant struggle, so Daigoro rode with the special saddle Old Yagyū had constructed for him. It was one of a kind, all too easy to spot.

When Katsushima reached Fuji-no-tenka after dark, he came with what looked like a packhorse in tow. From a distance, Daigoro didn't recognize his own mount; Jinichi's messenger had brought a pack harness with him, and crammed Daigoro's unique saddle into one of the panniers. For that Daigoro was supremely grateful; it was a clever ruse, and it had allowed Katsushima and their horses to reach Fuji-no-tenka unnoticed.

Jinichi and Daigoro talked over dinner while Katsushima remained characteristically quiet. Afterward, Daigoro had expected Katsushima to go out and find himself a sporting woman, but evidently his friend had taken an interest in the dinner conversation. "Forgive me," he said as a maidservant poured *sake*, "but I've not heard the entire story; I've only heard the two of you comparing memories. Let me be sure I understand: do you honestly believe Okuma Tetsurō fought a demon?"

"I do," said Jinichi. *And I can turn into a bear,* thought Daigoro.

"You don't mean this poetically? You mean an actual creature from hell?"

Jinichi nodded. "A horned fiend with skin like polished steel. They say it could travel in human form, in the guise of an old crone. Lord Okuma told me its barest touch could kill the body while trapping the living mind inside. In those days people called it the demon assassin."

"'Those days' weren't so long ago," Daigoro said. "I think I was nine or ten when my father came home to tell us about it."

"You're missing the point, my boy. This creature was hundreds of years old. The first time it visited Izu, I wasn't even your age. Scared me half to death, it did. They say *shinobi* spellcraft summoned the creature. No one knows what dark bargain its masters struck with it, but somehow they commanded it to serve them. For hundreds of years it reigned as the deadliest killer in the realm."

Daigoro held his tongue and drank his *sake*. The version Okuma Tetsurō told his sons was quite different. The demon was a disguise, not a creature. The wearer was indeed an assassin, and while it was true that some said the assassin was immortal, Daigoro's father put the point rather differently: so long as the assassin goes masked, who can say whether it's the same man? If ten men wore it over the span of a hundred years, did that make the assassin a hundred years old?

Of all his stories, this was the one Daigoro never asked him to repeat. It was the only one in which his father lost a fight. "But for an assassin's mercy, I would be dead," he'd said. Daigoro remembered little more than that; at the age of ten he had no interest in hearing about his valiant father's vulnerability.

"So Lord Okuma fought this . . . *demon*," Katsushima said. "Where?"

"In the shadow of Kiyosu Castle," Jinichi said.

"And that's how he got Streaming Dawn?"

"In a manner of speaking. He never kept it."

Daigoro leaned forward, all ears now. "Did he tell you what he did with it?"

"He did what any wise man would do: he went straight to the nearest shrine that could wash its evil from him."

Katsushima could not have said that sentence with a straight face. Yasuda Jinichi was gravely earnest. "I tell you, that blade was forged in the fires of hell," Jinichi said. "I wouldn't be surprised if every demon carries one. It may well be the key to their immortality."

"Ah." Katsushima drained his *sake* cup. He refilled Jinichi's and Daigoro's before topping off his own. In his most patient tone, he said, "Forgive me, Lord Yasuda, but I don't believe in evil swords. They're all made for killing. A *tantō* isn't a whittling knife or a kitchen knife; it's for spilling human blood and that's that. Call it evil if you like—"

"Answer me this," Jinichi said. "Was Okuma Tetsurō a superstitious man?"

"I regret that I never had the honor of meeting him."

Jinichi turned to Daigoro. "Well?"

"No," Daigoro said. "I never knew him to be superstitious."

The old man nodded emphatically. "Nor did I. A most practical fellow. Yet after he took Streaming Dawn from that demon, he went straight to Atsuta Shrine to have the evil *kami* purged from him. *Atsuta*, mind you. There were plenty of neighborhood shrines along the way. Buddhist temples too, but no, he went to the holiest site he could find. Now you tell me why a man like him does something like that. Hm?"

He drove the point home with a confident jut of his chin. The wattles stood out in his wrinkled neck. Daigoro could only bow, signaling his agreement. There might have been other explanations, but none of them mattered. At last he could see the next step on his path.

2 7

"Tip up," Wada-sensei said. "Shoulders back. Weight forward—not so much. Keep your center. And what did I just tell you? Keep your tip *up*."

Shichio raised the tip of his sword, training it on Wada's neck. "Not so high," Wada told him. "You want the throat, not the chin. Here." He tapped the hollow where the tips of his collarbones met. Then, without warning, he tried to smack Shichio's sword out of the way. Shichio anticipated the move, tightened his grip, and shoved Wada's deflection aside.

"Tip up, Shichio-sama. When you parry, you come back here. Every time." He tapped the hollow at the base of his throat again.

Shichio wanted to gut him. He wanted to stamp his feet, to scream, to throw his sword across the dojo—but more than anything, he wanted to get this *right*.

Wada-sensei was a mailed fist in a silken glove. He was a handsome man, with arms of sculpted bronze and eyes like tigereye gemstones. He was genteel in speech, but he pressed Shichio almost to the point of breaking. Wada was the only man who could promise that Shichio would never again risk the embarrassment he'd suffered in the Bear Cub's courtyard. The next time I'm called upon to hold a sword, Shichio thought, I'll damn well know how to use it.

He found *kenjutsu* to be odious and exhilarating in equal measure. The pain in his thighs and forearms he could live with. His blistered hands could be salved. Far worse was the constant badgering, the thousand niggling corrections and rebukes. But worst of all was the sweat. It began in the small of his back, and soon enough it soaked through his *kosode*, making the silk cling to his ribs.

On the other hand, the mask relished sword combat. It sent thrills surging through his veins with every cut.

His first sword master had laughed when he heard Shichio meant to train while masked, and japed that only women wore silk into battle. Shichio asked him to show a little sympathy, and to help him along that path, he had the man gelded and then bound head to toe in silk. When asked, Shichio's second sword master voiced no objection to silk robes or iron masks.

In fact, it was the second sword master, Wada, who observed how effective the mask was in combat. He even asked to wear it himself, and Shichio briefly obliged him. Wada called three other samurai to spar with him, and Shichio watched as the mask transformed his sensei from a master into a living hurricane. He trounced all three opponents with ease, then four, then six. "I don't even need to see them to fight them," he said afterward, drained but elated. "It's as if the mask sees their weapons on its own."

Yes, Shichio thought. It's just like that. Without the mask, he was an indifferent student at best. With the mask, his form was still weak, his strikes too slow, his counterstrikes too late—but oh, did he fight with spirit! That was half the battle, Wada-sensei said. If he could only get Shichio to keep the tip of his sword pointed at the opponent's throat, he would be nine-tenths of the way there, because the mask gave Shichio one more advantage: the ability to parry. That was no easy skill, Wada-sensei insisted. It was so hard to tell the difference between a feint and a genuine attack, and trying to block a feint was exactly what the opponent wanted. Wada preferred to teach counterstriking instead, but the mask gave Shichio preternatural awareness of what his enemy's sword would do.

Wada chopped lazily at Shichio's shoulder with his *bokken*. Steel rang against white oak. Shichio brought his katana back to center. Another chop, faster this time, and again Shichio recovered. A third strike and a fourth, strong enough to rattle Shichio's shoulders in their sockets, and again he brought his katana back to the sword master's throat. "Better!" said Wada. "Did you feel it that time? Strong spirit and strong form. They'll carry you through against anyone who isn't trained."

But the whelp *is* trained, Shichio thought. And he comes for me; I must be ready.

He lowered his weapon and stepped away. "Let's take a rest."

"Shichio-sama, we've only just begun—"

"I said we'll rest. Oh, and call me Lord Kumanai henceforth. I've finally settled on a surname."

"Yes, Kumanai-dono."

Wada kneeled, bowed, and stayed low until his lord and master left the dojo. Shichio stepped out onto the veranda, away from the smells of tatami fiber and sweat, into the cool predawn air. His new estate sprawled before him. House Urakami was every bit as wealthy as Nene had promised, if wealth could be measured in mosquitoes. The village of Kanagawa-juku was a festering swamp. At least the Urakamis had the presence of mind to build on a hill, but that protected the manor from flooding, not from the heat. The only respite came early in the morning and late at night, hence Shichio's training sessions at this ungodly hour.

House Urakami no longer, he thought. This was House Kumanai now. He was quite pleased with the name he'd chosen for himself. *Kuma*, meaning "bear," was the second character in the name Okuma. *Nai* was the ancient reading of *mu*, the Buddhist doctrine of absolute negation. Thus *kuma-nai* meant "no bears," and with just a touch of poetic license, "no Okumas." Shichio meant to make good on his name and hunt House Okuma to extinction.

It was a pleasant meditation to begin the day, but now his sweat began to distract him. Beads of it gathered on his scalp and trickled into his eye. Once again he missed his hair. Damn that woman, he thought. Damn this topknot, damn these swords, damn Hashiba for giving them to me—but above all, damn that woman for making him do it.

He wondered if there was some way he could talk Hashiba into fucking his wife. It was a ridiculous thought. No man ought to need convincing. Nene was comely enough—past her prime, to be sure, but Hashiba was too. Not that he'd lost his libido. His taste for women was a match for any teenager's. So why not bed this one?

How many of Shichio's woes would disappear if only Nene behaved like a proper wife? If her only problem with Shichio was jealousy, Hashiba could have laughed it off. I'm the regent, he could say; I'll stick my cock wherever I like. It would be so easy to convince him of that. Just saying it aloud would make him feel powerful. But Nene didn't care where he spent his nights. Her love for him was a sisterly concern for his well-being, not a catty, possessive need. Hashiba *had* to take her seriously.

"General Shichio?"

It wasn't Wada-sensei's voice. Shichio turned around to see his adjutant, Jun, the only one of his original servants he'd been allowed to keep when he took up residence in House Urakami's compound. All the rest of his attendants were still in Kyoto, absorbed into the Jurakudai's staff. Jun was as meek as a feather on the wind and weighed little more. The man was so skinny he threatened to slip between the floorboards. He huddled over his knees, a portrait of obsequiousness, his forehead and palms pressed to the veranda.

"It's Lord Kumanai now. Or General Kumanai, if that's easier for you to remember."

"Very good, sir. General Kumanai?"

"Yes, Jun?"

"You have a visitor."

"Oh?"

"Yes, sir. Waiting for you."

"Yes, I gathered that, since as you can see"—he stretched his empty palms at the equally empty surroundings—"there is no visitor standing next to me. Perhaps you'd like to tell me where this person is?"

"In your study, sir." Jun bowed so low he seemed to shrink.

"You might also consider telling me his name, Jun."

"He . . . he says he hasn't got one."

"Yet you admit him into my house? Into my study? Do you have any idea how many scrolls I have in there, how many secrets—?"

Shichio cut himself off. There was one visitor he was willing to see at this hour, the only one who would arrive unnamed and unannounced. A week from now, he would have been anxious *not* to hear from this man, but Shichio hardly expected him to appear so soon. Leave it to Nene to vex him so sorely that he could forget his quarrel with the Bear Cub.

He strode past Jun, faintly aware that he owed the young man an apology, but it was not for a general to apologize. Not a samurai's place to apologize, either, he realized. It was the first time today, but assuredly not the only time, that he had to remind himself of his new station.

The thought made him reach for his topknot, wondering just how unkempt it had become. In touching his hair he felt the leather thongs binding the mask in place. He'd entirely forgotten he was wearing it. Quickly changing course from the study, Shichio ducked into his residence and found a mirror, comb, and face powder in his dressing room. Then he remembered the sodden state of his *kosode*. He slipped into a curry yellow kimono and lordly black *hitatare*, and in that very moment he decided the colors of House Kumanai would be black and gold. They would be a fetching complement to Hashiba's red and black.

The mask went into a little sleeve of Chinese brocade, which in turn went under his pillow. He remembered his swords, and then had to don a heavier *obi* to support their weight. Then he went to his study, adopting the measured pace befitting the lord of the clan.

There he found the most bestial human being he had ever laid eyes on. The *shinobi*'s face was as flat as a mountain monkey's, and looked like it had been punched and kicked into those contours. His hair, mustache, beard, and single long eyebrow were all of uniform length. The backs of his hands were crawling with wiry black hair, which crept down even to the first digits of his fingers. Shichio would not have been surprised to see claws instead of fingernails.

"Lord Kumanai," the *shinobi* growled.

"What? How did you know I—?"

"The Wind hears all."

And so do you, even with all that hair sprouting out of your ears. Shichio was disappointed in himself; he shouldn't have allowed this man to set him on his heels so quickly. He reclaimed his composure and folded himself into his customary seat behind his knee-high writing table. "I would offer you a drink, but I know you would refuse. What shall I call you?"

"I am of the Wind. The Wind is without name."

"So you told my man Jun. Now you are speaking to me. I am your employer; I will have your name."

"I am of the Wind. The Wind is without name."

Shichio imagined his katana pointed at the *shinobi*. Then he imagined taking a step forward and splitting him right through the throat. "The Wind is also without number. I only have interest in one particular man. How am I to know you're the *shinobi* who accompanied the Bear Cub to the Green Cliff?"

"Ask what you will. I can answer."

Shichio bottled up his frustration and began to test him. The man proved as good as his word; he knew every detail, including the precise phrasing of the false missive Shichio had received, proclaiming Daigoro's death. BEAR STRIPPED OF PELT TONIGHT. THERE IS NO MAN THE WIND CANNOT REACH. Shichio would never forget the elation he'd felt at reading it, or the crushing frustration when he learned it was false.

"The note was your handiwork, was it?"

"Yes."

Shichio fumed. "Do you have any idea how much I'd like to kill you for sending that?"

"Stupid. Hopeless."

It was clearly a threat—*try it and you die*—yet the *shinobi* showed not the slightest emotion. He was deadly, but like an earthquake, not a dragon. Both could swallow you up, but this one had no feelings about it, not even a conqueror's glee.

Once again Shichio had no choice but to choke down his irritation and press forward. "Do you know why I've summoned you here? There are only two men alive who have worked closely with the Bear Cub since he became a fugitive. That ragged *rōnin* of his is one. You are the other."

The *shinobi* looked at him as if he'd just explained that water was wet.

"I want to know your impression of him."

"Short. Frail. Slow."

"Hm. I have the sneaking suspicion that you're being less than honest. It's almost as if you feel *loyalty* to the boy. But that couldn't possibly be true, could it? You're a mercenary—a *shinobi* of the Wind, no less. Your only loyalty is to clan and coin. Isn't it?"

"Obvious."

Shichio found it creepy that the man never seemed to blink. Rather than lock stares with him, the lord of House Kumanai smoothed his robe, reached for an ornately carved box of genuine Ming jade, and withdrew a golden *ryō*. The oblong coin held the oil lamp's reflection, producing the illusion that it radiated orange heat from within. "Clan and coin," he repeated. "So if you knew just how the whelp commandeered my ketch, or how he managed to run my blockade, or how he vanquished two full platoons, you'd be obligated to tell me—at least so long as I keep doling out the coins, *neh*?" With that he flicked the coin directly into the *shinobi's* hirsute chest.

It struck with a padded thump and fell impotently to the tatami. His guest paid his antics no mind. I'll throw the next one at your eye, Shichio thought. Maybe that will make you blink.

Summoning the last of his patience, he said, "You will tell me everything you know of the Bear Cub. I want to know how he thinks. Where does he go when he vanishes from the highways? How does he pass through towns and checkpoints unseen? Has he been stealing food or paying for it? Where does he sleep? How does he hide that limp of his, or that remarkable sword? You know his tricks; I would have you betray every one of them."

By the time the *shinobi* was finished, the sun had long since risen and Shichio had twice waved away the maids bringing breakfast. Wada-sensei had gone, so Shichio would learn no more *kenjutsu* today. But that was of no concern; he'd discovered so much about the Bear Cub that his mind could scarcely hold anything else.

The whelp could no longer hide from him. Shichio knew his every secret. He would pass them along to his bear hunters, and from there it was just a matter of waiting. "Tell me one more thing," he said. "Do you know what the boy has in store for me?"

"He means to kill you."

"How? When?"

"Unknown."

Shichio snorted and huffed. "You don't know, or the Wind doesn't know?"

"There is no place the Wind cannot reach."

"That's not—" He cut himself short. "So your masters *do* know. Why will you not tell me? Is it a matter of payment?" He seized the heavy jade box and slid it over to the *shinobi* with a mighty shove. "Tell me, damn you. Tell me what you know of the whelp's plans to kill me."

His guest pushed the box back toward him with a single iron-hard finger. "I know nothing."

"Who, then? Who must I pay?"

Was that pity in the *shinobi*'s eyes, or merely contempt? Neither, Shichio thought; this one is incapable of human emotion. "Suit yourself," he said. "Tell me this, at least: does the Wind track his movements?"

"There is no place—"

"Yes, yes, enough of that. Do *you* know where he is?"

"No."

"But you could find out?"

"Stupid question."

Shichio shoved the coin chest back toward him. "I want his head. Name your price."

"I cannot kill him."

"What? Why not?"

"Reasons are irrelevant. Concern yourself with facts."

Shichio tossed the desk aside, scooted forward, and slid the chest far enough that it struck the *shinobi* in the knees. "Is he paying you? I'll double it."

"No."

"Triple, then."

A grumbling, growling sound welled up from deep within the *shinobi*'s chest. "You are worse than the boy. You do not hear. You do not think. You have the patience of a squalling infant."

Furious, Shichio backhanded the man—or tried to. An instant later Shichio was on the floor, tasting the tatami. His wrist was a ball of stabbing, ice-cold pain. The bones in his hand ground against each other like teeth gnawing on rocks. Some abstract part of his mind understood the *shinobi* had him in a wristlock, but what Shichio felt in the moment was an angry bear chewing on his hand.

Release me, he attempted to say, but what came out was, "Reeesssssssssss—"

"No," said the *shinobi*.

"I am the master of this house," Shichio whispered through gritted teeth. It all gushed out as a single sibilant word. "I can have you killed for this."

"No."

Shichio tried to cry for help. A hundred flaming arrows shot through his arm, silencing him instantly. The *shinobi* had total control; Shichio could not even express pain except in the way his tormentor allowed him.

For Shichio this was not a wholly alien experience. He had introduced many lovers to the delights of domination and surrender. But this was a perverse corruption of that.

Taken with a certain sense of play, there was pleasure to be found even in the sharpest pain. But not in this. This was sheer coercion, brutal in its simplicity.

"Let me go," he whimpered. "Pl-please."

Just like that, his arm was his own again. As hellish as the pain had been, he was surprised to see no outward signs of injury. He'd half expected to find bloody tendons dangling out, finger bones jutting randomly like thorns from a bramble. The *shinobi*, on the other hand, seemed to have taken no notice of the entire exchange. He sat just where he was before, stone-faced, unblinking.

Shichio scrambled away from him, groped for his up-ended writing desk, and placed it back between the two of them. Too late he realized he'd left the coin chest on the opposite side of the desk. Then he decided he'd rather let the *shinobi* walk away with the money than get close enough to take it back. "So," he said, holding his wrist. "Your masters have forbidden you from killing the whelp. Was that your meaning earlier?"

"No."

"But something restrains you. Something personal."

"At last you begin to think clearly."

Yes, pain is so wonderfully clarifying, Shichio thought. He would not dream of saying it aloud. It scared him a little just to have thought it in the *shinobi*'s presence. Hastily, as if to drown out his own thoughts, he said, "Something personal, but not loyalty. Not allegiance. You're entirely too mercenary for that. . . . Ah! He paid you. *Neh?* He foresaw this conversation. He paid you in advance not to kill him."

The *shinobi* dipped his chin in a tiny bow.

"Damn that boy." And damn me too, Shichio thought; have I become so transparent? "Damn, damn, damn."

Just this once, he wished he had his mask. It tended to focus his thoughts when it came to plotting a murder. Now, with the benefit of hindsight, he had to admit this latest move *was* predictable. No one was better suited for a successful bear hunt than the beast who sat in Shichio's study. He had studied Daigoro, traveled with him, fought with him. It was not so hard for Daigoro to foresee the threat he posed.

"There must be another who can kill him," Shichio said. "Of all the Wind's assassins, one of them must be the best. Who is your canniest, deadliest fighter?"

"The warrior eternal."

The man spent no time at all thinking about it. That was encouraging. "Who is that?"

"Not who. What. An ancient title, held only by a few."

More encouraging yet, but Shichio was still unconvinced. "A title is little defense against Glorious Victory. You've seen the Bear Cub fight. He is a force of nature. What makes you think this warrior can stand against him?"

"The warrior eternal is protected. Relics. Weapons. Protective magics. The innermost secrets of the Wind."

Now that's just what I'm in the market for, Shichio thought. But he might get a better price if he didn't mention that aloud. "It's not enough. The mightiest warrior alive is harmless if he has no one to fight. He needs an opponent. Tell me where the Bear Cub is and I will hire this warrior eternal."

"Stupid question."

Shichio felt his anger spike, and he doused it just as quickly. His wrist had not forgotten its pain. "Pray tell," he said as sweetly as he could, "what makes that a stupid question?"

"Meaningless. Ask the question that matters."

How long must I endure you sitting here? That was the question he wanted to ask. Or, how long would you survive in a cauldron of boiling water? How many cuts would it take to kill you on my table? But those questions would not get this woolly brute out of his sight, nor would they locate the Bear Cub any sooner—

Oh, very clever, he thought. The question that matters. "You don't know where the Bear Cub is. Even if you could tell me, he'd be gone by the time I got there. But you know where he's going, don't you?"

The *shinobi* slid the chest away, and at first Shichio

thought this was a signal that the man was beyond brib-
ery. Then he understood: pushing the box toward Shichio
was a silent demand for payment. Shichio obliged him.
He drew the carven chest closer, opened it, and clacked
golden *ryō* on the tatami one by one until he reached the
Wind's price for that all-important question.

In that guttural, ursine voice, the *shinobi* said, "Atsuta
Shrine."

28

A brash and unusually ambitious rooster trumpeted its morning call from just outside Daigoro's window. Its crow was loud enough to break pottery. Daigoro woke as suddenly as if the damned beast had pecked him in the forehead.

If only he'd had his bow ready to hand, he would have shot it through the heart and carried it down to the kitchens. Nothing could be a better memoriam for his murdered sleep than eating its killer for breakfast. Why the bird had flown all the way up to a third-story windowsill was a mystery. There was no feed to scratch, no hens to pester, no other cocks to challenge. It wasn't even daybreak yet.

Daigoro wormed back between the futon and closed his eyes. Again the wretched monster blared its defiance. "Be gone!" he shouted, and still half in a daze he fumbled for something to throw. His hand found something knife-shaped, and before he knew it he flung it right out the window. It wheeled end over end, and had it been a knife it would have pierced the creature right through its evil black heart. Sadly, he'd only thrown his hairpin. The rooster squawked, flapped noisily to the next window, and resumed its harangue from just out of throwing range.

Daigoro was not yet ready to bear the indignity of

limping downstairs with his hair drooping to his shoulders, so he retreated to the dwindling warmth of his futon and thought about his brother. Ichirō would have marched down to the yard to fetch a longbow. Even in the dark, he would only need one shot. He was the finest archer in the northlands. Everyone said so.

Daigoro often woke to thoughts of the family members he'd lost. Ichirō, lying in red slush. His blood stained the snow and made it steam. Their father, cold and pale, staring up at the cold, pale sky. Were Okuma men doomed to die on the road? Would this journey claim Daigoro's life before the end? Was there any way to know his fate other than to ride forth and meet it?

The damnable bird crowed again. Sleep had become a priceless luxury in Daigoro's life, but this morning it was lost to him. Of all the wondrous inventions created by mortal man, he'd never imagined that a soft, clean, warm, dry bed was foremost among them. Life as a samurai could never have taught him that; he could learn it only as a fugitive.

At last he dragged himself from his rooms, bleary-eyed and annoyed. His hair was undone, but at least he could don his swords. He would feel naked without them, especially since he also had to carry what Jinichi had given him: two big sacks of brass coins. It was more money than Daigoro had ever seen in his life. He slung a bag over each shoulder and limped ponderously down the stairs, making his way toward the stables. He had to step very carefully with his right foot, lest he buckle his knee; he was carrying half his own body weight in coin.

As he neared the horse barn he found his mare snorting and shaking her head. She wore a pack harness, and it seemed to rub at her the wrong way. Katsushima tugged at it here and there, making adjustments. "Look at this," he said when he saw Daigoro. As little as he cared for decorum, he didn't even notice the state of Daigoro's hair. "Remember that clever fellow who brought in your horse last night? It seems he's been up to no good."

"Oh, no." Daigoro limped closer to stroke his mare's

neck. She settled down a bit, and he unlimbered his heavy bags, which hit the ground with chittering, clinking sounds. "What's wrong?"

"Wrong? Nothing. You're *rōnin*, Daigoro; being up to no good is what you do now."

Katsushima had a mischievous gleam in his eye. He'd always enjoyed ruffling Daigoro's feathers. Usually Daigoro was a good sport about it, but this morning had already been a trial.

"See here," Katsushima said, tugging again on the horse's tack. "Looks like a pack harness, *neh*? Fill these crates and you'd say she can't bear any more."

Daigoro had to agree. A pair of boxes hung on either side of her, four in all, and the largest ones were big enough for Daigoro to sit in. They were slung across a quilted moss-green blanket that totally concealed Daigoro's unique saddle. His mare was still upset by Katsushima's pulling and prodding, so Daigoro ran his hand down her neck in long, slow strokes.

"Now watch this," Katsushima said. He unbuckled a couple of straps and folded back the two smaller boxes, which slipped right into the two larger ones. The pack blanket rolled back just as easily, uncovering the saddle. Just like that, Daigoro's mare was ready to ride. Switching over from the pack harness to riding tack should have been a hassle; this took only a few moments.

"Suppose you filled all four crates with straw," Katsushima said. "Overstuff them. Do you think you could hide Glorious Victory in one of the big ones?"

Daigoro eyed it carefully. "Barely. It would be close."

"We'll test it before we leave. You'll hide your armor in the other crate. Between towns we can ride the highways, and as soon as we get within sight of other people, we can buy . . . well, whatever there is for sale. Rushes. Thatching. Anything cheap. I'll ride on, you'll walk your horse through town, and we'll meet on the other side."

Daigoro imagined it and smiled. "In the eyes of the world, we're not two outlaws riding together. I'm a tired farmer—"

"And I'm a dashing, dangerous-looking *rōnin* with a little time to spare if there happen to be any whores about."

Daigoro couldn't help but laugh. Katsushima was certainly in fine fettle. The old rogue enjoyed a good caper. It was too bad they wouldn't be riding together any longer. Daigoro did not look forward to telling his friend they had to part ways.

"What did you make of Jinichi's tale last night?" asked Katsushima.

"Most of it matched what my father told me."

"But not the nonsense about Atsuta Shrine. You don't think *the* Okuma Tetsurō would go running there to escape evil *kami*, do you?"

"No. I think he wanted to show honor to a worthy opponent. A priest of Atsuta praying over her ashes would be respect enough, I think."

"Wait. *Her?*"

"Yes. He said the assassin was an old woman. I remember laughing at him at the time. Ichirō told him little old grannies couldn't fight. Father said this one taught him otherwise."

Katsushima mulled it over for a moment. "The stories say demons disguise themselves as old crones. Maybe it's true. In any case, I can't imagine your father losing to a wizened grandmother any more than I can imagine him losing to a demon, so it's all the same to me."

Daigoro frowned. "I know what he told me."

"All right. A demoness, then. She defeated your father, yet she was the one who died. Was that the way of it?"

"That's what he said." Seeing Katsushima wrinkle his brow, Daigoro added, "I was only a boy. I didn't ask many questions."

"Mm. Did he bury this 'evil knife' with her?"

"No," Daigoro said. "He tried to, but he was set upon by thieves."

"And?"

"He stabbed the first one in the heart with Streaming Dawn. The others went running after that."

Katsushima nodded stoically. "That usually works."

"He said their friend fled with them."

"The one with the dagger in his heart."

"Yes."

Katsushima paused to consider that for a moment. "All right, that's something I'd like to see. Are we off to Atsuta Shrine?"

"I am. You're not." He dropped his voice to a whisper. "I need you to take these back home for me."

He hefted the two heavy sacks off the ground again and lugged them a little closer to Katsushima. Their weight threatened to collapse his bad knee. Katsushima eyed them over, and when curiosity got the better of him, he crouched over one of them and untied the top. What he saw inside made him gasp, a totally uncharacteristic expression from him. "That's . . . that's a lot of money."

"Keep your voice down." Daigoro looked over his shoulder, then scolded himself for it. Everyone in the compound was loyal to Jinichi. Even so, he could only bring himself to speak in a whisper. "It's barely a quarter of Kenbei's demand. Not nearly enough, but it's a start. You're the only one I can trust to get it where it needs to go."

"Trust Jinichi. It's his, *neh*?"

"It's mine now. He loaned it to me."

"Then he should protect his investment. Ask him to send riders with it, all the way back to your mother's doorstep."

"I can't do that, Goemon. He's already emptied his vault for me; I can't ask him to go to the expense of—"

Katsushima stood up and took a step back, as if physically separating himself from the money would also distance him from any responsibility for it. "Daigoro, he's willing to help you. He may even be willing to saddle Kenbei with the expense of boarding his people and feeding their horses once they get where they're going."

"I can't ask him to do that."

"Then leave it here and we can take it to your family compound after we return from Atsuta. Either way, I go where you go."

"Goemon, please—"

"Daigoro, when I announce myself at your front door and I present your wife and mother with all this coin, they're going to ask where you are and whether you're well. What would you have me tell them? That I turned my back on you? That I have no idea where you've gone or whether you're still alive?"

It was a good point, and it stung. Indignant, Daigoro said, "You don't owe me anything."

"True. A *rōnin* swears oaths to no one and no one swears oaths to him. He's alone in this world except for his friends. I don't *owe* you friendship, but you have it from me anyway."

"I know, Goemon. But the money—"

"Isn't any safer with me than it is with a fully armed platoon. Though I appreciate your esteem for my sword arm."

Daigoro tried to object, but Katsushima silenced him with a look. "How many towns lie between here and your family's doorstep? And in those towns, how many taverns? How many whores? Do you mean to send *me* along that road, with two sacks of brass and no one looking over my shoulder? Find a better way to spend your money, Daigoro."

That was the finishing blow. Daigoro knew he'd lost the fight well before then, but that was what made him surrender. His head sagged, and a noise escaped him that was part laugh and part sigh, partly dejected and partly relieved. "Have it your way. But do one thing for me before we depart. Lend me a hairpin."

29

Daigoro had heard of Atsuta Shrine because everyone had heard of it. Legend had it that Emperor Keikō founded it to house the Kusanagi no Tsurugi, the fabled Grass-Cutting Sword. At fifteen hundred years old, it was known simply as "the Shrine," and it was without doubt one of the holiest places on the face of the earth.

Having heard of the Shrine did not prepare him in the slightest for the sheer size of it. In Izu, Shinto shrines were rarely more than a single sanctuary to enshrine the *kami*, connected by a short path to the obligatory *torii*. Osezaki, where he'd conducted his midnight rendezvous with Lady Nene, was uncommonly large; the smallest sites were little more than two upright posts connected by a braid of sacred rope. By contrast, the word "shrine"—even *the* Shrine—did not begin to describe Atsuta. Better to say it was a village of shrines, scattered throughout a sprawling forest under the protection of spirits, gods, and men.

A thick green canopy held in the cool humidity of recent rain, which condensed to form scores of tiny pearls on Daigoro's forehead. The cool air came as joyous relief from the harried, hurried, breathless voyage from Yoshiwara. Back at Fuji-no-tenka, Jinichi had insisted that Daigoro should make all possible speed. He knew all about Shichio's many eyes and ears, and about the roving packs of bear hunters. He also knew of a swift ship, *Pride of Suruga*, said to be able to make the run from Izu to Ayuchi in two days flat.

The *Pride* was as fast as Jinichi promised, but the weather was against her, so it was not until morning on the third day that Daigoro and Katsushima guided their mounts onto the boardwalk in the port city of Ayuchi. From there they rode straight to Atsuta, not stopping to break their fast. Daigoro was feeling pressed for time; the lost half day weighed on him as heavily as his Sora breastplate. But now, enveloped by cool air and history, he did not know what to do with himself.

The Shrine was a sight to behold. Narrow canals babbled here and there, their walls equal parts hand-laid rock and moss laid down by the *tao*. A bridge arching over the water formed a perfect wheel with its reflection. Decorative stone lanterns were home not to evanescent candles but to lichens a thousand years old. No two lanterns were alike, and there would be hundreds of them in this forest, standing sentinel like the trees.

Daigoro had no idea how he would ever find his father here.

He'd spent his entire life trying to follow in his father's footsteps. Here, from the moment he crossed under the first towering *torii*, he knew he was doing precisely that. His father had walked these very paths. His boots had trodden the same rain-slicked stones. But this place was so vast. There was no way of knowing which way to go.

"He came here to honor a worthy foe," Daigoro mused aloud.

"But not to bury her," Katsushima said. "These Shinto priests are notoriously prickly about contaminating their gods."

Daigoro wasn't sure *notorious* was the right word. Here of all places, the *kami* were at their most pure. A dead body was the ultimate pollution. But Katsushima was right: gods were entombed here, not assassins.

"He must have had her cremated somewhere else," Daigoro said. "A Buddhist temple, probably. Then he came here to have a priest say prayers over the ashes."

"Why?"

"*'A worthy foe deserves a worthy funeral.'* It was one of his maxims." Daigoro continued to live by it. His brother Ichirō shared a tomb and a death poem with his murderer, Ōda Yoshitomo.

"There's wisdom in that," Katsushima said. "It seems to me the cremation would have been enough, though. I've never known a dead man to fuss over his funeral rites."

Daigoro shrugged. "Maybe demons are different. I don't know. Truth to tell, I'm not even certain my father ever came here. We got that from Jinichi, and that man is far too credulous for my liking. By the Buddha, Goemon, he asked me if I could change into a bear."

Katsushima shook his head and laughed. "You should have said yes. Maybe he'd actually set Kenbei straight if he thought he had a bear at his heels."

Daigoro forced a laugh too. It sounded desperate even to his own ears. "You see my point, *neh*? This whole voyage might be for nothing."

"That's the dog talking. Defeated by the squirrel before the fight even began. You remember the story?"

"Yes."

"Then show a little spirit, will you? I didn't come all this way just to hear you whine."

Daigoro willed himself not to blush. Katsushima was right: bellyaching would get him nowhere. He led his mare to the nearest fountain, then dismounted so he could purify himself. The water chilled the bones in his right hand, reminding him of the old pain there. He held the reins of both horses as Katsushima performed the purification rite, then stepped up into the saddle again. "Let's suppose Jinichi had it right," he said. "There's no use supposing otherwise. If Father was here, if this really was the place where he cut down that thief . . . well, a fellow running off with a *tantō* stuck in his heart isn't the sort of thing that's easily forgotten. Someone must have seen something, or heard something, or overheard it secondhand. If we ask enough questions, we'll get to the truth."

Katsushima gave him a satisfied nod, and together they ventured deeper along the wooded paths. Their horses' hooves clipped and clopped on the flagstones. Now and then a cold droplet from an overhanging branch would slip right down the back of Daigoro's collar, making him shiver. Katsushima seemed undisturbed by such surprises. Then again, at thrice Daigoro's age he'd had a few extra decades to bring his body's unconscious responses to heel.

As they came across each shrine, one of them would dismount and step inside to make a few discreet inquiries. Usually it fell to Daigoro to do the asking; despite his lame leg dragging at him each time he stepped in and out of the saddle, he was not as heavily encumbered as Katsushima, who found the questioning quite embarrassing. Talk of demon assassins and magical knives was all too provincial for a *rōnin* who had spent most of his days in sprawling cities like Ayuchi and Kyoto.

Late in the afternoon, in a beautiful broad-roofed shrine surrounded by ironwoods, Daigoro found an acolyte scrubbing the ancient floorboards. He was middle-aged, and therefore much too old to be charged with such trivial chores. Daigoro guessed the man must have been born into some other occupation at first, taking the cloth only later in life. He regarded Daigoro with an inquisitive, somewhat surprised look in his eyes, as if he were unaccustomed to seeing armed and armored men in this peaceful place.

"What is your business here?" he asked.

Daigoro didn't often hear such brusque tones from a member of the priesthood. Then he remembered: the world did not see him as samurai anymore. He was an undersized, overproud boy armed not with *daishō* but with two grossly mismatched swords. His cloth was finely spun but in dire need of washing, which called into question any right he might have to dispense haughty looks.

"I come seeking rumors," Daigoro said, adopting the soft manner of a peasant. "Perhaps you've overheard them, or know of someone who has. There was once a battle in these woods, or so I'm told, one samurai against a pack of thieves."

"And one of the thieves was struck through the heart," said the acolyte.

"Ah! So you've heard the story."

"No, but I've heard of the two riders asking around about it. Word travels quickly here, even among those who oughtn't gossip." The acolyte gave him a sheepish grin.

Daigoro returned it with a little bow and a kind smile of his own. "Can you tell me where I might turn to find my answers?"

"My uncle may know. He is the head priest at Daimatsu Shrine, and has been for some time. He would have been here when your story took place. It's not half a *ri* from here; I'll lead you if you like. Only . . . well, you'll have to wait for me to finish scrubbing my floors."

Daigoro was in no mood to dawdle. "I wouldn't think to trouble you. If you'd be so kind as to point me in the right direction. . . ."

"But of course."

The acolyte ushered Daigoro outside, where Katsushima minded the horses. He pointed them in the right direction, then vanished back inside. "A very helpful fellow," Daigoro said. Then they were off.

"Helpful?" Katsushima asked a little while later. "The fool doesn't know his left from his right." In fact he and Daigoro had to double back more than once; the acolyte was hopeless when it came to giving directions. In the end they finally stumbled across Daimatsu, an imposing two-story shrine whose sweeping roofs were twice as wide as the sanctuary itself. Its stout timbers had grayed with age and its roof tiles were heavy with lichen.

Walking along the veranda was a senior priest who bore a strong resemblance to the acolyte. They shared the same lean body, the same high cheekbones and strong chin. They might have passed for twins, if only twins could be born fifteen years apart. The priest's back was bent, his steps shuffling. He strained his neck forward when he saw Daigoro and Katsushima ride up to his shrine, squinting to make the most of the failing light.

"Good evening," he said in a reedy voice. He wore long white robes, bright purple *hakama*, and a ceremonial black hat that made Daigoro think of a shark's fin. His sleeves were so long that they almost touched the floor. "If you've come for the wedding, I'm afraid you've just missed it."

"Wedding?" Daigoro said.

"They've all gone into the city." The priest gestured vaguely toward the south. "If you hurry, you may yet catch them."

Katsushima frowned and turned in his saddle, seeming to study the empty space where the priest had pointed. Daigoro's attention remained with the priest. "As it happens, I believe you're the one we've come to see. Are you the high priest of Daimatsu?"

"I am."

"Your nephew sent us. He says you've heard tell of a thief who survived after taking a knife through the heart."

The priest's eyebrows popped halfway up his forehead. "Well, now. I know the tale, yes, but we don't talk about it here."

"I'm not looking to stir up any old ghosts; I only want to sort out a few of the details. I promise it won't take long."

The priest weighed it over for a moment, then welcomed them inside. Even before they entered, he apologized for the rather empty feeling of the temple. The groom was one of Daimatsu's priests, he explained, and very popular with the rest of the staff. As such, they'd all gone to the wedding reception, leaving the high priest in sole custody of the shrine. "Come, sit," he said, ushering them into a little room for private worship. "I'll come back with some tea."

It was impossible to sit down while wearing Glorious Victory Unsought, so Daigoro unlimbered the great sword and laid it along the back wall of the little room. He couldn't help but notice that Katsushima kept both of his blades. Out of old habit the *rōnin* flicked his katana back and forth in its scabbard with his thumb.

"What troubles you?" Daigoro asked.

Consternation wrinkled Katsushima's brow. "Hoof-prints," he said.

"Hm?"

"There weren't any. The priest said we'd have to hurry to catch the wedding party, but there's no evidence that they were on horseback. So why should we *hurry* to catch up with them? They're on foot; we're mounted."

"Maybe they left a while ago."

"No. He said they'd just left. And did you see the altar?"

Daigoro shook his head. "No."

"No sakaki branch. You and Aki laid a branch on the altar when you married, *neh*? This couple didn't."

"Come now, Goemon. Couldn't the priest have—?"

Daigoro cut himself short. He had been about to say "disposed of it already," but that couldn't be right. The sakaki branch was a sacred symbol of matrimony. It would be burned with all the rest in a *dondoyaki* ceremony at the turn of the New Year, not tossed aside like an old chicken bone. Perhaps Daimatsu Shrine had a cupboard set aside for such ritual objects, but even so, it would have been indecorous to take it from the altar so soon. Atsuta was not the place for such impropriety.

"Now you've got me worried," Daigoro said. "Probably over nothing, but still . . ."

"You see?" Katsushima kept his voice low. "Something's amiss."

Daigoro thought about the strong resemblance between the high priest of Daimatsu and the acolyte from the previous shrine. They could pass for twins—or even for the same man, if he were sufficiently skilled at feigning old age. And, of course, if he could fly like a falcon between one temple and the next.

"The botched directions," Daigoro whispered, thinking aloud. "What if he deliberately steered us awry, to give himself time to race over here? Then . . . then nothing. This is silly, Goemon. We could just as well suspect our horses of playing us false."

"Did our horses arrange for an entire temple to be empty but for one man? Or did one man beat us here, and then—"

"Then what? Kill every last priest? Leaving no sign of struggle?" Katsushima nodded, apparently quite satisfied. Daigoro scoffed in reply. "Oh go on, Goemon. Think of what you're saying. Is it so strange for a man to look like his own nephew?"

"Is it so strange for one of Shichio's bear hunters to dress as a priest instead of an assassin?"

"Only if he wants to dress himself to lose a sword fight. Even if he were armed, how could he draw a blade with those dangling sleeves? He's more likely to fly away on them."

"Maybe. Maybe not." Katsushima kept his voice to a conspiratorial whisper. "This much we know for certain: he was quick to explain why this shrine is empty, even though we did not ask. He was quick to rush us in here, behind closed doors, rather than let us roam around. You said 'no sign of struggle.' I say it's better to look around and see what we can find."

He started to stand, but then they heard the priest returning to the door. "Drink nothing he offers you," Katsushima whispered, barely audible. "Let us see how he reacts."

The priest knocked gently, then slid open the *shoji*. The smell of hot green tea preceded him into the room. Daigoro studied him closely, trying to convince himself that this couldn't possibly be the acolyte from the other temple. He failed. Daigoro's experience with *shinobi* was limited, but he could not help but remember a certain agent of the Wind, one who had saved his life many times over. That one could pass for a corpse at will, or even pass for Daigoro himself when the need arose. Daigoro had seen him do both, in full view of Toyotomi archers, and not one of them saw through the ruse.

"Please, enjoy," said the priest, kneeling before them and filling their cups. His black shark-fin hat was so tall that Daigoro had to move his head aside when the priest bowed toward him to offer the tea. "Now then, you had a mind to discuss that old tall tale. The fellow who survived a blade through the heart."

"Yes." Daigoro picked up his teacup but did not drink. "But this tale's not so tall. Many people here have told me it's true. What do you know of it?"

The priest shrugged. "Not much. But more than most, I suppose."

"Tell me about the thief. Where did he go after he was stabbed?"

"Sounds to me like you're more interested in the knife than the thief. Do you mind if I ask why?"

No harm in asking, Daigoro thought, if only Katsushima didn't have me on edge. But now that his hackles were up, he realized the priest hadn't answered any of his questions. Daigoro didn't know what to make of that. The abbot of Kattō-ji was just as inscrutable. Was it a clergyman's duty to ask enigmatic questions? Or was this priest concealing something, as Katsushima suspected?

Only one thing was sure: Katsushima distrusted the man. Daigoro had never known his friend to be wrong in such matters. He raised the cup to his lips to judge the priest's reaction. There was none. "Still too hot for my liking," he said, lowering the cup once more. "If you don't care to discuss the knife or the thief, we can talk about something else."

"Such as?"

"A different tall tale," Daigoro said. "In this one, you and I don't meet by chance. You're told a story about a boy whose sword is too big for him, a boy with a keen interest in the blade known as Streaming Dawn. You were told to wait for him at the Shrine. But you never expected him to appear so quickly. You thought to look for him some days from now, but this afternoon you spy a young man fitting his description. He wears no house insignia, so you have to ask him about the blade. It's the only way to be sure you'll strike the right target."

"Target? I am no arrow, sir."

"No? Perhaps your role was simply to mark me out for hidden archers."

The priest's face soured. "No doubt my young lord is

tired from his long journey, and that is why he speaks to a high priest of the Shrine in such a rude, suspicious tone. Perhaps a little tea might refresh his body and temper his spirit. . . ."

"You see, that's just it. We never mentioned any journey to you."

"Nor did you need to." The priest maintained his stern, paternal facade. He was a masterful liar, or else a wronged and innocent man. "It's your accents. You don't sound like you're from around here."

"Oh, but I do," said Katsushima. "I was born not ten *ri* from where we sit."

"I don't care for your tone either," said the priest. "A man your age should have more sense. What do you make of your friend's story? Do you think the hallowed ground of Atsuta is crawling with archers? Was I to paint a red circle on the young man's chest when he entered the Shrine?"

Katsushima's only answer was to loosen his katana with a flick of the thumb.

The priest stood in a huff and made for the door. "Insult me if you will, sir, but I will not stand for being threatened. I'll leave you two to enjoy your tea—and to speak spitefully about me behind my back, I have no doubt."

It was the fact that he was pretending to leave that made Daigoro drop his guard.

It was only for the blink of an eye. Daigoro had been watchful from the moment he voiced his suspicions. So long as the priest continued to feign innocence, he remained a threat. It was only in that brief instant when the priest turned to remove himself from the room that Daigoro relaxed.

The blade of the priest's foot struck him in the throat.

Daigoro went flat on his back. He could hardly breathe.

Katsushima was already in motion, his katana snapping out like a whip. Somehow the priest was faster. He spun in a low whirl; his long sleeves flew like wings. One white sleeve caught Katsushima's sword. With a quick twist, the priest wrapped up both the katana and the arm holding it.

Daigoro rolled to his knees. The priest's heel caught him in the temple. Daigoro blacked out. He came to an instant later when his face struck the floor. He saw Katsushima struggling to pull his sword free. The priest jammed his thumb into Katsushima's eye socket, and Katsushima had no choice but to retreat or be blinded.

He reeled away and drew his *wakizashi* and *tantō*. Daigoro had never seen his friend fight two-bladed before. No one had ever taken his katana before.

Katsushima sprang to the attack, a hurricane of flashing steel. The priest was a typhoon of swirling white. The two storms collided. Blood flew; Daigoro could not tell whose.

He knew he needed to join the fight, but his head was foggy and his body was slow to respond. He snatched up Glorious Victory Unsought, then realized her great length was only a liability in such close quarters. That was too bad; now more than ever, Daigoro needed her power. He drew his *wakizashi* and crept around to flank the priest.

Suddenly Katsushima was airborne. Daigoro had to fall flat or be impaled. He dropped to his back. His friend sailed over him trailing blood, and stove in a wall when he landed. An instant later his katana flew after him, straight as an arrow. Daigoro managed to knock it spinning. It careened through a *shoji* window and disappeared.

Daigoro scrambled to all fours, keeping his *wakizashi* between him and his opponent. The priest's white robes were striped with blood, none of it his own. Daigoro meant to change that.

The priest stood back and allowed him to stand. It was an act of the highest contempt; he feared Daigoro so little that he was willing to give him the advantage of fighting on his own two feet. A tiger would not have been so gracious, but Daigoro was not facing a tiger; he was facing a veritable god of war.

The priest hadn't even troubled to arm himself. Daigoro was an even match for any two men, Katsushima for any four, yet this one treated them like paper dolls. "You were right not to drink the tea," he said. "You were right about the other question too: I had not thought to see you here so soon. I salute you. Not many victims force me to rush."

He bent low to pick up the teapot. It was a moment of vulnerability, but Daigoro was too intimidated to make good on it. "I hurried in playing my hand because your reputation preceded you." The priest—no, the *assassin* gave him a regretful wince. "I'm sorry to say the stories vastly outstrip your actual prowess. You're not your father's equal. The story is true, by the way. He stabbed me right through the heart. His only mistake lay in not withdrawing the blade. But you? You've made nothing but mistakes from the moment we met."

They circled each other, Daigoro with a sword, his foe with no more than a steaming teapot. Somehow it was Daigoro who was too scared to speak. "No, you're not worthy of a warrior's death. I think I'll resort to the weapon I originally intended to kill you with: the tea. Are you ready?"

Daigoro tightened his sweating fingers around his *wakizashi*. Behind the *shinobi*-priest, Katsushima rose silently to his feet. His face was a dripping red mask. He blinked hard, as if he was seeing stars and trying to clear them. But his blades were steady enough.

There was only one way to prevent the assassin from noticing him. It was suicidal, but Daigoro pressed the attack.

A white sleeve whipped toward his eyes. He sliced it off. His blade found cloth, not flesh. The priest-assassin stepped in. His free hand clamped down on Daigoro's wrist. He twisted it around, driving the *wakizashi* toward Daigoro's own body. Gracefully, almost lackadaisically, he poured scalding hot tea over Daigoro's face.

It burned like dragon breath. Daigoro shut his mouth tight against it, but still he feared the poison would leak in. The more he strained to keep his face out of the downpour, the less he could concentrate on his sword. Already he felt the blade brushing the inside of his thigh. The artery there was huge. He would bleed to death in a matter of heartbeats.

Katsushima pounced. The assassin sidestepped. With

a backward swipe he shattered the teapot on Katsushima's cheek. Katsushima grunted and lashed out. He missed with his short sword, but he drove his *tantō* deep into the assassin's lung.

The assassin collapsed around the blade, but instead of dying on the spot he rolled backward, somersaulting to his feet on the far end of the room. Katsushima's knife protruded from his rib cage dripping blood. Daigoro and Katsushima stood shoulder to shoulder and advanced, swords at the ready. The assassin drew a blade of his own, a chisel-pointed *tantō*. Then he drove it right into the side of his neck.

Daigoro waited for the man to fall. Surely he meant to take his own life before his enemy could question him. But no. He pushed the *tantō* all the way through his throat. Then, with agonizing slowness, he slid Katsushima's knife out of his chest. Impossibly, there was no blood—not from Katsushima's knife, nor even from the dagger in his neck. If anything, the assassin seemed to have greater resolve.

Katsushima retreated a step. The sword sagged in his grip. Daigoro sympathized; what use was swordsmanship against an enemy who could not bleed? The astounded look on their faces could only bolster the assassin's morale.

Daigoro moved away from his friend. If Katsushima could not rally and charge, at least he could stay put while Daigoro outflanked the enemy.

The *shinobi*-priest lunged, but not for Katsushima. With snakelike flicks of the knife, he drove Daigoro all the way to the wall. Daigoro took a cut to the wrist, another to the thigh. Then the assassin was gone, rolling across the floor. He came up in a low slash, aiming for Katsushima's hamstring.

Instead he got a *wakizashi* in the arm. Katsushima cut deep but somehow the wound was bloodless. The assassin responded, raking his knife across Katsushima's belly. Katsushima responded in kind. Both cuts were superficial. Katsushima staggered back, pressing a hand to his stomach as if to keep his guts from spilling out. Still the priest would not bleed.

Daigoro attacked but his target proved too elusive. Katsushima slashed weakly but the assassin danced away. Daigoro anticipated the dodge and rammed his *wakizashi* home. The sword entered the assassin's kidney and punched out through his navel.

He should have been dead. Instead he stabbed Daigoro in the leg. Daigoro crashed to the floor.

Now Katsushima was on him. He deflected a slash to the eyes by hacking at the assassin's knife hand. Fingers went flying. So did the knife, but the assassin snatched it right out of the air with his other hand—too late. Katsushima ran him through. His *wakizashi* punctured both lungs and stayed there.

Still the assassin would not fall. He would not even show pain. And now Katsushima was unarmed.

Daigoro drew his own *tantō*—his last weapon—and rammed it all the way through the assassin's calf. It bought Katsushima a precious instant, just enough to dodge the savage chop meant for his throat. Still on all fours, Daigoro groped for the assassin's foot, his pant leg, anything to keep him from advancing on Katsushima. He missed.

The assassin had four blades stuck in his body and a fifth in his hand. Katsushima would die on that dagger and Daigoro would be next. The only other weapon in the room was Glorious Victory Unsought, resting on the floor in her sheath. She was so heavy, and Daigoro was so weak, but she was his last hope.

Channeling all his desperation into his right hand, he drew the massive blade and swung it for all he was worth. In a blow worthy of his father, it sliced through the *shoji* wall, then through both of the assassin's knees.

The assassin might not bleed, but neither could he stand. When he fell, the wall fell with him. The butchered *shoji* toppled out of its frame, crashing down on the *shinobi*-priest. Daigoro scrambled to him, found Streaming Dawn, and pulled it out of the assassin's neck.

This knife could only be Streaming Dawn. Nothing else had the power to keep a man alive through all that punishment. The assassin should have been dead six times over. As soon as the Inazuma blade left his body, the blood flowed from him like a groundswell. He would be dead in moments.

But not yet. His hand punched up through the rice-paper window of the *shoji*. Still clutching Katsushima's bloody *tantō*, he drove it into Daigoro's back.

It was his last act, but it was enough. Daigoro fell beside him.

Daigoro saw the room go dark. Only two pinpoints of light remained, directly ahead of him. He could no longer feel his wounds. The worst was that he had no fear of dying. He had already accepted it.

Such a terrible fate, to come so far only to fail. Daigoro held Streaming Dawn in his hand. He had only to ride home. Even if he would not live long enough to kill Shichio, at least he could have delivered the blade to Lord Sora. He could have saved his family.

Streaming Dawn. In his hand. He had seen its power. The knife could save him.

He tightened his grip on its haft, turned its tip toward his body . . . and found he could go no further. He'd lost too much blood. The fear of death had left him, but so had his strength. Even a knife was too heavy for him now.

Such a pitiful fate. He wished he could see Katsushima, to know how badly his friend was hurt. It would have been enough to hold his hand. But now there was only darkness. "Goemon?"

"I'm here." Daigoro could hardly hear him. Was his hearing fading like his sight, or was Katsushima that weak?

"Take . . . take them the . . ."

Those were Daigoro's last words. Then the darkness consumed him.

BOOK SEVEN

HEISEI ERA, THE YEAR 22

(2010 CE)

30

Mariko hadn't been to Machida in a long time. She'd forgotten how green it was out here. It was quiet, too. First she left the rattletrap drumming of the train behind her, then the traffic lights with their little droning melody. As she turned away from the larger streets and into the residential area, even the sounds of passing cars faded, until at last she was left with the rustle of leaves and the occasional barking dog.

Her own mind was far from quiet. Every aspect of her life had gone from bad to worse, all in one day. This morning she got suspended from her job. Then she was all but kidnapped by the Wind, who presumably let her go only because they knew they could take her again whenever they liked. Then came the blow that shook her down to the very core of her being. Jōko Daishi attacked the Tokyo Metropolitan Police Department.

In the wake of Haneda and St. Luke's, perhaps "attack" was too hyperbolic a word to describe an impromptu press conference. No one in the press was calling it that, but of course that was the point: it was designed to look like an implosion, not an outright assault.

The terrible irony was that Kusama must have invited all the reporters himself, to announce a major break in the Haneda case. Jōko Daishi met the first of them right at the door where Mariko went to work every day. He declared himself the prophet of the Divine Wind, and when they asked him what he was doing at police headquarters, he said, "I do here what I am called to do everywhere: to shine a light on the truth." He told them that the police knew a great deal more about Haneda than they were willing to share, that Captain Kusama had a devotee of the Divine Wind in his office who was intimately familiar with all of the details about the attacks, and that the reporters could interview the devotee themselves if only a police officer hadn't shot him in the head.

The media had a field day with it. Only the stragglers thought to press Jōko Daishi for answers about Haneda; all the go-getters had rushed inside, slavering to be the first to publish photos of the dead body leaking brain matter onto a decorated police captain's carpeting. Jōko Daishi just disappeared in the shuffle, leaving a few cryptic quotations behind. Somewhere along the line, some conspiracy theorist leaped to the conclusion that it was Hamaya, not Jōko Daishi, who was the lead suspect on Haneda and St. Luke's, and that his capture was to be Captain Kusama's big announcement. Those with more journalistic integrity took the trouble to look up who Hamaya was, who his clients were, and what he'd been up to recently. That led to a screen shot from some Correctional Bureau computer—maybe hacked, maybe leaked—that quickly became the most viewed image in the country: Koji Makoto's release forms, complete with date, time, and mug shot.

The headline of the *Daily Yomiuri*'s morning edition—TMPD INSIDER: JEMAAH ISLAMIYAH CONNECTION "TOTALLY BASELESS"—had been enough to get Mariko suspended. The evening edition's headline was enough to make her sick: TOKYO'S FINEST COVER-UP: POLICE RELEASED TOP HANEDA SUSPECT HOURS BEFORE BOMBING. Mariko had advised against letting him go, then advised against withholding his name—not just advised but pleaded, forcefully enough that it cost her her rank. Now everything had gone just as Mariko said it would. Jōko Daishi got exactly what he wanted: Tokyo's top law enforcement agency was now one of the bad guys.

Mariko wished she could take comfort in having been right all along, or at least some smug satisfaction in watching Kusama get his ass kicked in front of the microphones. But when the shit hit the fan, it didn't just splatter back on him; it smeared the whole department. She'd worked her whole career to make it into Tokyo's most elite police unit, and now that unit was being dragged through the sewer.

It would have been healthier not to ground so much of her self-esteem in her career. She knew that. When work went to shit, so did everything else in her head. Usually *kenjutsu* cleared her mind. Not tonight. Before she'd taken up the sword, forty or fifty kilometers on her bike would have done the trick. Not tonight. So she'd come here, to the only place that might make her feel at ease.

Yamada-sensei's house was just as she remembered it. A high slat fence the color of milk tea surrounded the backyard. A wooden lattice arched behind it, densely embroidered with wisteria vines. The blossoms were gone, and with them their creamy scent, but the chrysanthemums in the front yard were in full bloom. The heavy door resonated deeply when she knocked on it. It was a relic of an earlier time, solid oak, not composite with a wood veneer.

She thought of the whole house as an island in time. There was no cable modem, no Wi-Fi connection. Yamada never even owned a microwave. He used to boil water for tea the old-fashioned way: in an iron *tetsubin* teapot heated on a gas range.

The door creaked open to reveal an old woman wearing big black Coco Chanel sunglasses. She wore a black Chanel jacket with fat white buttons, black Chanel slacks, and a white Chanel blouse. Her outfit cost more than Mariko's dress uniform, which was by far the most expensive outfit Mariko had ever owned. Shoji Hayano had always enjoyed looking good.

"Mariko-chan!" Shoji said. "Come in, dear. Oh, how good it is to see a friendly face."

It was a figure of speech; Shoji didn't *see* her at all. She'd lost her sight during the war, when she was still a little girl.

It was around that time that she'd first met Yamada-sensei, before his name was even Yamada. She had always called him Keiji-san, his given name before he was dishonorably discharged from Army Intelligence. He'd been forced to abandon the name Kiyama Keiji in order to escape his war record, adopting the alias Yamada Yasuo in graduate school and founding a storied career on it: a doctorate in medieval history, a professorship at Tōdai, thirty degrees of black belt spread across five or six different sword arts, and enough published books to bow the shelves in Shoji-san's sitting room. The finishing touch was a star of the Supreme Order of the Chrysanthemum, bestowed posthumously by the Emperor himself—who, apart from Shoji and the Empress, was the only other person to refer to Yamada-sensei as Kiyama Keiji.

Yet Mariko was supposed to believe this man—her hero—was a criminal.

That was what that sun-blotched bastard Furukawa Ujio would have her believe. If Yamada was the Wind's archivist, as Furukawa claimed, then her beloved sensei had been a member of a criminal organization. Mariko didn't buy it for a second. Nevertheless, she couldn't get Furukawa out of her head. She had a keen sense for when people were lying, one she'd first developed as the sister of a meth addict, then sharpened as a beat cop and honed to a razor edge as a detective and a narc. That sense had saved her ass many times over, and she'd learned to trust it without question—until today. Today it insisted that Furukawa was telling the truth.

Mariko hoped Shoji-san might help her solve the paradox. If anyone could do it, it was the blind woman who knew it was Mariko on her porch even before she opened the door.

Mariko took the old woman's hand and placed a little box of cookies in it. "Bisuko," she said. "Your favorites."

"You remembered," said Shoji. "Aren't you a dear?"

Something was wrong. Shoji's voice was thick, as if she'd been crying. On a second look, Mariko noticed she *had* been crying; her nostrils were rimmed in red and her cheeks were flushed. "Shoji-san, are you all right?"

Shoji sniffled. She tried to force a smile, but it just made her seem sadder. "It's this awful business about the . . . the airport, the hospital . . . just all of it. It's all so horrible."

Mariko took her by the arms and gave her an awkward hug. She wasn't any good at this kind of thing. She'd never known Shoji to be the type to take such events so personally, either. Growing up with earthquakes, typhoons, and tsunamis, Japanese people tended to be fairly stoic about national calamities. But in the very moment she had the thought, Mariko realized that she herself was unwilling to include terrorism in the same category as all the natural disasters. This *was* different. There was someone to blame.

Including you, Mariko told herself. Furukawa's math was perfectly clear: one living cult leader equals dozens of dead civilians. Mariko was no assassin, but she had to accept the consequences that came with that decision.

"Come on, let's go inside," she said. "Let me fix you some tea."

Once they were in the house, Shoji's domestic instincts kicked back in. Under her roof, she would be the one to make the tea. She was most insistent, so Mariko wandered into the sitting room.

She loved this room. This was where she'd had her most important conversations with Yamada-sensei. It was where he became a grandfather to her. It even still smelled like him—or rather, it was redolent of old books, a smell she would forever associate with him. Bookshelves lined the walls, and technically every last volume belonged to Mariko. Yamada-sensei had left everything to Shoji in his will, but since none of the books were in Braille, she'd given them all to her old friend's protégé. Shoji insisted on keeping them here since she knew Mariko's apartment was far too small to house them all. "I'll be your library," she'd said at the time. "That way you'll be sure to come visit."

Mariko didn't visit as often as she'd like. Shoji-san had been a friend to Mariko when no one else was there. They'd met soon after Yamada-sensei's murder, right in the morgue. She had invited Mariko to tea and Mariko said yes. That had evolved into an invitation to come home with her and catch a nap and a shower. Again Mariko had agreed. It ran totally against Mariko's nature to leave herself vulnerable in a strange place, but she'd done it anyway. Somehow it felt as if she and Shoji had known each other for decades.

In fact, there was a sense in which they had—a very weird sense, but then everything was weird when it came to Shoji's senses. She was a *goze*, a seer, possibly the only one alive. There was a time when Mariko put as much stock in *goze* as she had in space aliens, but as a detective, she had to accept whatever the evidence told her. If little green men beamed down and bowed to her, Mariko would have bowed back, and if a little blind lady foretold her future, then Mariko would listen.

"Shoji-san," Mariko said, drifting toward the kitchen, "does the name Furukawa Ujio mean anything to you?"

"Hm. That's not a name I expected to hear from you."

"So you know him?"

"I used to. He was . . . well, you could say he was my son's doctor."

Mariko's brain did a stutter step. "I didn't know you had a son."

"No? I guess not. We don't talk much about family, do we, dear?"

"No . . ." Mariko trailed off; most of her attention was dedicated to catching up with her own thoughts. Shoji knew Furukawa. Furukawa was—how did she put it? Her son's doctor. Not *our family doctor*, which would have suggested a general practitioner. A specialist, then. Was he a pediatrician? Or did her son have special medical needs? How rude was it to ask? More to the point, Mariko asked herself, how rude am I willing to be?

Shoji came into the sitting room carrying a platter with a steaming *tetsubin* pot, two matching teacups, two tea bags, and a little plate of sandwich cookies. She walked slowly but surely, without the aid of her cane. Carrying out domestic duties seemed to have bolstered her spirits; she was totally unlike Mariko in that respect.

"There," she said, "let's sit. Now why should you have run across the name Furukawa Ujio? Is he in trouble?"

That sounded alarm bells in Mariko's mind. "Why do you ask?"

"Because you're a police detective. Don't sound so suspicious. If you must know, I've been quite glad not to hear from Furukawa-san. It's about time he ran afoul of the law."

San, not *sensei*, Mariko thought. Doctors always received the honorific *sensei*, even the ones who deserved to go to prison. Well-mannered women of Shoji's generation would never make that slip. The only reason she didn't refer to Yamada as *sensei* was that she thought of him as her old friend Keiji, not the PhD from Tōdai. So what did that mean about Furukawa? A doctor without a doctorate?

"He's not dead, is he?"

"What?" Mariko said.

"Furukawa-san. He wasn't killed in one of those automobile accidents, was he? Or in that horrible business at St. Luke's?"

"No."

"It's been a long time since I've been grateful to be blind, Mariko-san. I was glad not to see the firebombing in 'forty-five, and I'm glad not to see these awful, awful pictures coming out of Terminal 2. It's bad enough just to hear about it—"

Just like that she was crying again. Mariko hurried out of the room, mostly to give Shoji a moment of privacy but also to fetch a tissue box. When she returned, her old friend had composed herself. "I'm so sorry, dear."

Mariko didn't know what to say. Handling emotional stuff came about as naturally to her as handling snakes.

Shoji folded the tissue into a neat triangle and raised her sunglasses just enough to dab at her eyes. "I have a guess," she said. "Furukawa-san is not dead, and neither is he in trouble with the law. Does that mean he made contact with you?"

"Wow, Shoji-san, you must be psychic."

"Don't mock what you don't understand, dear."

"Sorry." Mariko gave a little bow, as was customary with an apology. As soon as she did it, it occurred to her that with someone who couldn't see, the bow was probably moot. "Um, yes, he called me. We talked."

"About my son?"

"No. I told you, I didn't know you had a son."

"About Keiji-san, then."

"Yes."

"And he told you some things you didn't want to hear."

"Yes. How do you—?"

"My son is a schizophrenic," Shoji said.

Mariko didn't see how that was relevant, but she didn't want to interrupt. Shoji took a deep breath before she went on—to steel her nerves, by the sound of it, so now she even had Mariko bracing herself for what was to come. "It is a terrifying disease. Terrifyingly powerful. Visions, voices, delusions, these were my son's bullies in childhood. They toyed with him, Mariko-san. Without medication, he had no chance for a normal life."

Shoji's every word dripped with humiliation. Mariko had a good guess as to why. Most people in her culture saw mental illness as a cause for shame. Mariko was more sympathetic—Saori's meth addiction had opened her eyes to a few things—but people of Shoji's generation would be much less so. "That must have been awful," Mariko said. "This was, what, the sixties?"

"Yes."

"So when it came to treating something like schizophrenia, pretty much everyone had their heads up their asses."

Shoji tsked her. "Language, Mariko-san."

"Sorry."

"The truth was worse than you imagine. It's easy for young people to forget, but as a country we were a very long time convalescing from the war. We rebuilt ourselves on manufacturing—Honda, Toyota, Sony, all the worldwide names. But who did we have developing new medicines? We were decades behind. I would hear outlandish stories in the news—first a heart transplant, then the artificial heart, and none of it happening *here*. Even the Germans made medical advances we would not see for years. And the British? The Americans? They were like sorcerers. Every day I wished one of them would whisk me away. I know I'm not supposed to think that way, but what else was I to do? I had a very sick boy; I needed help."

Mariko nodded sympathetically, and realized belatedly that Shoji couldn't see her. "Of course you did," she said. "But Shoji-san, there's no need to be ashamed. Any mother wants what's best for her child."

"Yes, but I . . . I made compromises. I talked to Furukawa Ujio. He told me of an organization that . . . well, there was no place they could not reach."

A cold wave washed over Mariko's skin, raising goose bumps up and down her arms. "You? No. You couldn't have."

"My son was sick. He needed better medicine. Furukawa's was state-of-the-art."

Mariko's heart sank. "But he didn't give it away for free, did he? And he didn't help just any schizophrenic kid, either. How did he know you were a *goze*?"

Shoji sniffed and dabbed the tissue to her eye. "I don't know. But what was I to do? The best antipsychotic drugs in the world, and all I had to do was tell him what I saw. I was going to see it anyway. All I had to do was tell him. . . ."

She broke down crying again. "I never knew," she said. "I swear to you, I never knew what would happen."

"Shoji-san, I don't understand what you mean."

"I had a vision. When Furukawa-san came into our lives, when I accepted his help, I saw the future. The day would come when I had to make a choice: save my child or save all the others. I had no idea what it meant. But any mother would choose her child, wouldn't she?"

Mariko took her by her soft little hand. "I'm sorry, Shoji-san. I still don't understand."

"My child or the others. That was what I saw. But I thought it meant the medicine. I thought . . . I don't know what I thought. Maybe Furukawa stole his drugs from a laboratory. Maybe one more experiment there would have helped more children. But you must understand, my son was hurting himself. It happens with schizophrenics. He climbed out a window once, trying to escape whatever he was hallucinating. When he fell—can you imagine, Mariko-san? Finding your son lying there unconscious, his leg broken in five places, and being *thankful*? We lived on the third floor. It could have been so much worse. . . ."

An ice-cold dread settled in Mariko's stomach, malignant as a tumor. "Shoji-san, what's your son's name?"

Shoji gave her a sweet, sad smile. "Makoto. Makoto-kun. It means 'truth.'"

Shoji Makoto. But the kanji for *sho* could also be read *ko*. Koji Makoto. Shoji's son was Jōko Daishi.

As soon as the thought struck her, Mariko knew it was true. The weight of it crushed the breath out of her. There was a saying in English, one that had always stuck with Mariko because it seemed so Japanese: *the child is the father of the man*. In Jōko Daishi's case, the child with a badly broken leg became the man with a rolling limp. The child suffering from schizophrenia became the delusional man with a god complex. The *goze*'s child became the man who claimed to foresee the future—a man who was utterly fearless because he believed he'd already seen the hour of his death.

Mariko was a little ashamed that she hadn't seen the connection between Shoji and Jōko Daishi before— though if she was honest with herself, there was no reason she should have caught it. Shoji and Koji were both common surnames. Since they shared the same kanji, on a police report they'd look identical. It was unusual for a son to change his surname, but perfectly ordinary among Japanese religions for a person to take a new name when taking on the cloth. Japan's most famous monks and nuns were all known by their Buddhist names, not their given names. The *daishi* of Jōko Daishi was clearly meant to evoke this tradition; it meant Great Teacher, just as in Kōbō Daishi, one of the greatest figures in Japanese Buddhism. Perhaps Koji Makoto would have changed his name more dramatically, but his mother had already given him the perfect name for a religious leader: read literally, the kanji for Koji Makoto meant Short Path to the Truth.

Why change from Shoji to Koji? Maybe to save his mother from a shameful association, once his name finally became public? Even if he saw himself as bringing enlightenment to the masses, he had to know everyone else would see him as a monster. In his warped mind, changing his name was probably an act of compassion.

Mariko remembered the one time she talked with him. It was hard to forget; she'd never encountered anyone who spoke of mass murder with such childlike delight. *My mother is the future and my father is the past.* Gibberish at the time, but now Mariko understood at least the first half: his mother, a *goze*, could see the future. So who was his father? Shoji made no mention of any husband. In fact, the conspicuous absence of a husband in her story suggested that she had raised her son alone. What a scandal that must have been, to be a single mother in the sixties. Compound that with being blind in an era when there was no social tolerance for disability, then add schizophrenia to the picture. Was it any wonder she turned to someone for help? Even if it came from the Wind?

Little wonder, too, that the Wind would be interested in a seer. They were an intelligence agency first and foremost; all the political scheming was founded on having more information than anyone else. And Shoji had the ear of the Imperial house. She was the Emperor's personal seer. Not that heads of state used fortune-tellers and soothsayers anymore, but Furukawa would surely find some use for a woman who could get herself an invitation to tea at the Imperial palace.

Shoji was crying again, and now it made sense. Her son's name was all over the news. *Goze* or not, Shoji had probably been telling herself what any mother would tell herself: it wasn't him; it can't be him; my son has his troubles, but he'd never do something like that. That was what you told yourself if your son murdered somebody. You didn't automatically believe the worst of him; you gave him the benefit of the doubt.

Until he was the leading news story in the country.

Denial had its limits. That was especially true in Shoji's case, for she was burdened by the power of prophecy. *Your child or all the others.* That's what she saw in her vision. From the beginning, she'd said the meaning wasn't clear. Now it was coming into focus.

"Shoji-san," Mariko said, "you can't blame yourself."

"Oh yes, I can. I turned to criminals to find medicine for my son. What if I hadn't? What if he'd spent his childhood in a psychiatric ward, with no help from me or Furukawa-san? This awful Divine Wind would never exist. A hundred and thirty-nine people, Mariko-san. He's killed a hundred and thirty-nine so far. All of them had mothers. I chose my child over theirs—"

"No, Shoji-san. *He* did this. You did everything a mother is supposed to do: you took care of your sick child. But I hold adults responsible for their own actions. He's not dangerous because he's ill. He's dangerous because he's willing to murder innocent people to prove a point."

"You don't understand," Shoji said. "A hundred and thirty-nine dead, and still my vision has not yet come to pass. I see a number, Mariko-san. 1304. I don't know what it means, but I know it's awful. A hundred and thirty-nine dead already, and I can only think, it's not so bad yet. It's going to get so much worse."

31

There was no consoling Shoji after that. Mariko coaxed an invitation out of her to spend the night, just so Shoji wouldn't be alone. Mariko needed the company too; she was wrestling with her own fair share of guilt. She once had the chance to shoot Jōko Daishi in self-defense but she'd chickened out. Furukawa offered her a second shot at him and she turned him down. There would not be a third, because Jōko Daishi wasn't just a lunatic, cultist, or terrorist anymore; he was a good friend's son. Regardless of whether he deserved to die, killing him was out of the question.

She knew she couldn't blame herself for another person's behavior. Saori had taught her that. The only sane way to deal with addiction was to hold the addict accountable. Even so, there was no escaping that niggling thought that maybe, just maybe, if Mariko had somehow figured out the right thing to say, she could have kept her sister from using. It was pure self-abuse. Mariko knew that. She could beat herself up all night and it wouldn't change the fact that Saori had damn near killed herself using meth. By the same token, Jōko Daishi wasn't finished with his killing spree. It wasn't Mariko's fault, but she couldn't help blaming herself.

She hadn't brought anything out to Machida except her purse, so to stay the night she had to run out and pick

up a couple of necessities. On her way to the stores, she
took care of some phone calls. First was Saori, to invite
her to come out to Machida the next day. Shoji enjoyed
her company too, and it had been a while since the fabu-
lous Oshiro sisters had gotten together. Then a call to her
mom, to break the news about her suspension. Her mom
was a lousy liar; she feigned sympathy but Mariko could
hear the relief in her voice. A suspended cop was unlikely
to get shot or stabbed or any of the other things that happened on the syndicated American police dramas her
mother followed so masochistically.

The next call was to Han, who didn't pick up, so
Mariko left a message asking for a Terminal 2 update.
She knew she'd have to tell him about her suspension
too—preferably over a couple of beers, so she invited him
to go out the following night. Then, finally, came the call
she didn't want to make.

"I wondered when I might hear from you," said Furukawa Ujio. "Did you have a pleasant visit with your friend
Shoji-san?"

"How did you—?"

"Please. I know where your phone is. Even if I didn't,
our earlier conversation raised questions in your mind
about Professor Yamada. There was only one place you
could go."

Mariko didn't know which pissed her off more, the fact
that he was right or the fact that he was so damn smug
about it. Yamada-sensei had a similar ability to read her
mind, and Mariko had always found it maddening in him
too. She hated that Furukawa reminded her so much of
Yamada.

"Thirteen oh four," she said—too loudly. There were
other pedestrians in earshot. She'd reached the narrow
street where she planned to do her shopping, an urban
box canyon and an all-out assault on the senses. All of
the stores were brightly lit, and most had English names:
FamilyMart, ABC-Mart, Mode Off. A pachinko parlor
chimed and dinged and chattered, loud as a Vegas casino.
Its signs were in English too, and though they were supposed to advertise slot machines, the placards read

PACHINKO AND SLUTS. Cigarette smoke gave way to the syrupy, succulent smells of a *yakitori* restaurant. Between the sensory overload and the cramped quarters, it was enough to drive anyone into a full-blown panic attack.

Lowering her voice and covering her mouth, Mariko said, "Does that number mean anything to you?"

"No. Why?"

"Look into it. It has something to do with Jōko Daishi's next attack."

"I see. His mother told you this?"

"Yes—and by the way, threatening to withhold a sick kid's medication is pretty low even for you."

"Withhold?" Furukawa seemed surprised. "Far from it. We went to great lengths to treat young Makoto."

"Of course you did. Out of the goodness of your heart."

"That's quite enough," said Furukawa. "I have no further appetite for your moralizing, Detective Oshiro. Either hang up the phone or come upstairs so we can speak like well-mannered adults."

At that very moment someone tapped her on the shoulder. She whirled around, her elbow flying high, only to see Endo Naomoto backpedaling with a startled look on his face. "Whoa," he said. "Totally sorry about that."

The other shoppers flinched away like a skittish school of fish. Sudden violence out of small women was not a part of their daily routine. Endo was just as rattled. "What the hell?" Mariko said. "What are you doing here?"

"Playing billiards," Furukawa said through the phone. At the same time, Endo nodded up at a fourth-floor window behind him. "The boss shoots pool here," he said.

Mariko huffed and got her heart rate under control. She looked up at the long row of windows on the fourth floor, with a sign running under them reading BILLIARDS BAGUS. "You have to be kidding me," she said, looking Endo in the eye while speaking into the phone.

"Come upstairs," Furukawa said. "Let's talk."

"We already talked."

"You have more questions now. You *have* been speaking with Shoji-san, *neh*? About her son?"

Mariko hated that this man knew so much about her—not just her private conversations but even which store she was heading to. He got in her head in a way only Han and Yamada-sensei were allowed to. "Good night, Furukawa-san."

"Whatever Shoji shared with you, it's not the whole truth."

"She has no reason to lie to me."

"Oh no? Did she explain Professor Yamada's role in her son's life? Did she explain the assignment Yamada was supposed to give to you? Or why he gave you his sword?"

Mariko laughed—not too dismissively, she hoped. She didn't want to oversell it. The truth was that she knew precious little about her sensei and she was always eager to learn more. One of the great mysteries in her life was why he'd taken her under his wing and entrusted her with Glorious Victory Unsought. Yet one more secret that Furukawa knew about her. How did he pull this stuff out of her head?

He had the good graces not to make her ask. "Please, do an old man a favor. Spare my knees and come upstairs so I don't have to come down to you. We can speak in private here. Endo-san will show you the way."

"Nope. Endo-san will do my shopping for me."

Endo seemed earnestly offended. "What? No way."

Mariko took out the little notebook she carried everywhere—standard detective equipment, as she thought of it—and tore out a page. "Here. The stores are closing in twenty minutes. If I have to talk to your boss, you have to run my errands."

"Boss, come on—"

"Do it," said Furukawa, and Mariko passed on the message. It wasn't quite fair to say Endo's head sagged like Charlie Brown's, but Mariko thought sad piano music would have been appropriate. He pulled the shopping list out of her hand and read it dejectedly. "You have to be kidding me. Underwear?"

"What? I didn't bring any with me."

He gave her an imploring look, striking the impression

that at least as professional criminals went, he really was a nice guy and he didn't deserve this kind of punishment. In truth Mariko had forgotten she'd put panties on the list. On any other night with any other man, she would have been mortified. But Endo was twice as embarrassed as she would have been, equal parts awkward teenager and sad puppy. Mariko found it hilarious.

"You know what?" she said. "On second thought, just get me a pair of sweatpants. I don't want you thinking about me in my unmentionables."

His spirits only slightly lifted, the big ex-ballplayer moseyed toward the FamilyMart. "That was indelicate," Furukawa said.

"Boo-hoo." Mariko hung up on him and, despising herself for doing it, trotted up the stairs.

Billiards Bagus was a dark place with low ceilings. Electronic dartboards lined two long walls, their round faces illuminated with a bluish glow. A rank of pool tables stretched toward the back wall, each one lit by a long, boxy light hovering over it like a UFO. There were no dart players or pool sharks; the tavern was empty but for the bartender and the old man with ageless eyes and pianist's hands.

Furukawa hunched over the nearest table, cue stick in hand. He had a drink already waiting for her; whisky, she guessed, probably an expensive pour. She ignored it, not because he struck her as a James Bond bad guy who would poison her drink—which, in point of fact, was exactly how he struck her—but because she wouldn't be beholden to him any more than she had to be. "So what's thirteen oh four?" she said.

"We have people working on it. I can tell you more, but only if you join us."

"Thanks but no thanks."

Furukawa bent over with a grunt and began retrieving sunken balls, setting each one on the table with a heavy *thwack*. "What if Professor Yamada had asked you?"

"Asked me what? To be your assassin? He'd never do that."

"I'm afraid you're quite wrong about that. His last assignment for us was to recruit you. I'm sorry to say he died before he could complete it."

Mariko scoffed. Furukawa narrowed his eyes at her and said, "Have I said something to amuse you?"

"For a secret clan that's supposed to know everything, you guys can be pretty dense. You know how to make the whole damn country sit and beg and roll over at your command. How can you know so little about *people*?"

Mariko could see she'd startled the bartender with her sudden rudeness, but she didn't pay him any mind. For his part, he desperately pretended not to have heard her. "Yamada-sensei was a good man," she said. "He wasn't about to try to sell a cop on becoming a killer for hire."

Furukawa gave her a disapproving look over the edge of the pool table. "One would have thought a police detective would gather more information before leaping to conclusions. If you'll forgive me for saying so, you haven't the slightest idea what you're talking about."

"Then enlighten me."

He retrieved the last of the balls and began to rack them. "Your sensei was the most highly trained swordsman in Japan—which, if I may be so bold, made him the deadliest in the world. I believe you saw that firsthand."

Mariko wished he were wrong, but he wasn't. She'd seen Yamada square off against four armed *bōryokudan* enforcers. Outnumbered and outflanked, not many could have survived that altercation. Yamada was eighty-seven years old and blind, and still those yakuzas never stood a chance.

"He did not join the Wind as an assassin," Furukawa went on. "He had no love for killing, and in any case we don't dabble much in the assassination game anymore. It's much too crude for our purposes. No, it was his obsession for the Inazuma blades that brought him to our attention. The Wind has been using these relics for centuries, never revealing their exceptional powers. Needless to say, we were astonished to learn a historian had somehow discovered their existence."

Mariko smiled at that. She could read between the lines easily enough: the Wind had been actively trying to conceal the existence of these weapons, yet Yamada discovered them anyway.

"Imagine our surprise when we learned he was also a close friend of our very own Shoji Hayano. We suspected her of espionage, of course; it was a little too convenient that after all those years of secrecy the Inazuma blades should suddenly be rediscovered. When we found all parties were innocent, we invited Professor Yamada to work for us."

"Why would he do that?"

"For the library, of course. Our records of his beloved relics were far more complete than he could have imagined. And I confess that they were in a dreadful state. We cannot maintain a permanent archive, you understand. We must remain mobile. We had documents scattered hither and yon, and so he had a lifelong project: to bring order to the collection."

He must have been like a kid in a candy store, Mariko thought. "I get it. He's another pool ball to you. You put him in front of the pocket and you give him a little nudge, right?"

"Just so. But Yamada proved most recalcitrant. He refused."

Mariko refrained from doing a fist-pump. Score one for the good guys, she thought.

"In a way, it was Jōko Daishi that changed his mind," Furukawa said. He'd racked the balls; now he took up a cue and lined up a break. "Or rather, Koji Makoto, formerly Shoji Makoto. His mother told you about his maladies, I think. Did she tell you he was raised under my care?"

"She said she got his meds through you."

"Quite right." The cue ball struck with a loud crack, sending the other balls hurtling in every direction. "He required constant monitoring. You understand, psychiatric pharmacology was still in its infancy. Many of his medications were still in testing. In effect, the Wind raised him as one of its own. This was a common practice for us in ages past, but it has been many generations since we trained our *genin* from childhood."

"Sure. Those pesky child labor laws must be a real pain in the ass in the ninja racket."

"Very droll, Detective. The point, if I may ask you not to interrupt me any further, is that young Makoto was our very best. Even as a boy he was possessed of a scintillating intellect. He showed a particular knack for chemistry—the evidence of which you have already seen, I think."

Mariko nodded emphatically. His "knack" blew her right off her feet at Haneda, and would have torn her limb from limb if Akahata had managed to detonate his bomb in Korakuen Station.

"It may interest you to know his passion for chemistry started from entirely peaceful motives," Furukawa went on, casually sinking one ball after the other. "His interest was in pharmaceuticals, not weaponry. He aspired to exorcise his own demons. But I ask you, Detective, how could he study psychotropic drugs and not learn the secrets of amphetamines or high explosives? It is all one science. Unlock it and you unlock all of it."

And now he uses all his tricks, Mariko thought. His terrorist recipe book went beyond high explosives and ricin. He cooked MDA too, a psychedelic amphetamine he distributed widely to his Divine Wind cultists. It heightened his godlike status—or demonlike, if that was how they thought of him. Mariko didn't understand all the ins and outs of the cult. She didn't feel the need. He was recruiting cultists and bending them to criminal purposes; that was enough for her to do her job.

"We believe he inherited his mother's gift of foresight," Furukawa said. "Imagine what that power would do in a mind already given to hallucinations. Many schizophrenics suffer from delusions of grandeur, even delusions of their own immortality. The difference for Koji-san is that some of his hallucinations occasionally come true. Is it any wonder he thinks of himself as a god? Would you or I not come to the same conclusion?"

"So you used him," Mariko said. "You had a very sick man and you propped him up as a phony cult leader. You guys keep getting better and better."

"The cult of the Divine Wind was entirely his idea. And your moral pronouncements are wearing thin."

"Hey, you're the one who called me, asshole. If you want someone who doesn't give a shit about right and wrong, maybe law enforcement isn't the best place to go looking for new recruits."

"Thin and getting thinner, Detective. And fraying at the edges too. Can you hear your own hypocrisy? I seem to remember an intelligence asset of yours. Shino, I believe, though you called him LeBron. Did your partner have him killed on purpose? No. He sent the boy into harm's way, and all the while he lulled himself into thinking he was doing the right thing."

Mariko didn't need the reminder. She could still picture Shino's body, sprawled facedown in the basement of Jōko Daishi's covert headquarters. His face was as red as the worst sunburn, the result of cyanide poisoning.

"And what did your lieutenant do, noble man that he is? He kept your partner in the field as long as possible. Then he promoted him to detective again at the first opportunity. And your captain? He was complicit in that promotion. He demoted you without cause. And lest we forget, he has been deliberately deceiving this city for a week straight. Jemaah Islamiyah!" He scoffed. "There isn't a journalist in the country who could make that story stand—not without evidence, and of course there isn't any. Only a policeman could get away with such a lie."

"Look, I told him not to say that stuff—"

"Oh, yes? You and how many others? Where are the legions of officers coming forward to speak the truth? Hundreds could do it, and how many have we seen? Not one. To a man, they stand behind your captain's lie. And you preach to me about the *ethics* of your profession."

Mariko's cheeks burned. He was right. She could have gone straight to the press with what she knew, but she'd chosen silence instead. This was not the first time Furukawa had showed her an ugly truth about her profession that Mariko hadn't seen herself. Maybe she'd suspected its existence, but she'd always chosen to look away rather than stare it in the face. She asked herself—not for the first time—how this man could know her own job better than she knew it herself.

"I'll thank you to listen," Furukawa said, "and to think carefully before you speak. We did *not* have a deranged cult leader to abuse as we saw fit. We had a brilliant young man who appeared to have his schizophrenia fully under control. He cultivated that appearance very carefully over the years. You must understand, Detective, Koji-san is a master manipulator. In his presence, you believe what he wants you to believe."

"Bullshit. I've seen him. I've talked to him. He's out of his mind."

"You saw what he wanted you to see. You underestimated him, you let him loose, and he made you pay the price for that. I do not say this as an insult, Detective Oshiro. He duped me just as he duped you."

"Then you're not half as smart as you think you are. I only talked to him once. You worked with him for decades. How did he fool everyone in your organization?"

"By getting results." As if to accentuate the point, Furukawa sank the eight ball with a hard, stabbing shot. "You must understand, Detective, the border between genius and lunacy is a hazy line at best. True, Koji-san's methods were unorthodox, but so long as he delivered everything we asked of him, what need was there to question his motives?"

"Come on. The guy founded a cult. That didn't make you a little curious?"

"Oh, quite the contrary: we marveled at it. It was a ploy so ingenious that it never occurred to any of the *shōnin*. Koji-san's principal task in recent years was to upset the balance of power in the drug trade—a regular occurrence, you understand. Routine maintenance."

"Sure. Like an oil change."

Furukawa ignored her cynicism. "The black market is like any other market: supply and demand reign supreme. Tinker with one or the other and everything changes. Koji-san adopted a radical new approach: the Divine Wind. So long as the cult's allegiance was to him and not to profit, it could act in unprecedented ways. You saw one instance of that: by flooding the streets with the drug known as Daishi, he flipped the entire amphetamine trade on its head. Ordinarily such gross actions draw scrutiny, and that is something the Wind prefers to avoid. But this new cult leader was not a hidden power to be rooted out; he was an easy mark. If an underboss like Kamaguchi Hanzō took advantage of him, no one would question it."

"But he didn't just play Kamaguchi. He played you."

"It shames me to admit he did. Such is the force of his personality. When he looks you in the eye, you have the distinct sense that he can see into your soul."

Mariko rolled her eyes. She didn't believe in souls. She knew all about that zealous look, though. She remembered standing nose to nose with Jōko Daishi, gripping two fistfuls of his wiry black beard, looking him in the eye behind that eerie mask of his. Furukawa was right: Jōko Daishi's eyes were different. Darker. Deeper. Like bottomless wells. But Mariko didn't see genius in there. She just saw a whole lot of crazy.

"Imagine it, Detective. Imagine how he must seem to those already of a malleable mind—the sort of people who seek the comfort and camaraderie of a cult. Unmedicated, this is a man who believes he is a god. With his hallucinations under control he is a virtuoso of deception, master of the Wind's innermost secrets. We believed that Koji Makoto was the actor, and Jōko Daishi the mask. He convinced us that his growing power was no threat to us."

"But?"

"The truth was quite the opposite. It was not Jōko Daishi who taught Koji-san how to imitate a god, but Koji who taught Jōko Daishi how to imitate a man. He learned just what to say and how to say it. Koji Makoto became the mask."

A wry laugh escaped Furukawa's thin lips. He shook his head, scornful of himself. "It's so obvious now. That was the language he used: actors and masks. I should have seen it coming. Even as a boy, he was obsessed with ancient relics—no thanks to your sensei Yamada, I might add. It was Dr. Yamada's love for the past that made him the ideal archivist, but it led to the rediscovery of artifacts that even the Wind had long since forgotten. Better for us all if that demon mask had remained hidden. But no. Yamada found it, Koji-san fell in love with it, and now look· at what it's done."

"It? Hell no. You. You did this."

Furukawa picked up the cue ball. His eyes grew so cold that she thought he might throw it at her. "*I* argued for its destruction. *I* saw to it that it would stay far away from Koji-san forever. And then . . ." He dropped the ball back on the empty table with a loud, sullen crack. "Then I allowed other things to become more important. I forgot the mask. We all did—everyone but Koji-san."

"But it came back. You must have known. When we arrested Jōko Daishi, we impounded the mask. That went in the computer, and I know you guys can hack our records."

"We can," he said dejectedly. "We did."

"Then why didn't you steal it from us? Or let it get lost in the system, or—I don't know, whatever the hell you people do. Make the damn thing disappear."

"We tried. But the Divine Wind was far more resourceful than we anticipated. They have people within your system."

"So do you, *neh*?"

"Of course. But Koji-san knows ours and we don't know his. I told you: we thought he *was* ours. We gave him access to everything he needed to betray us."

"Which you didn't figure out until he tried to blow up that subway station," Mariko said.

Furukawa nodded. His head and neck seemed to sag under the weight of his remorse. "All of the balls were in place. We never saw it. We just handed him the cue and he ran the table. There is one thing left for you to understand, something you've misunderstood from the beginning: not even the *shōnin* could have prevented the Haneda bombing. That responsibility falls to Professor Yamada."

"Don't you dare!" Mariko wanted to snatch his pool

cue and break it over his head. "Don't you dare blame that on him."

"How can I not? I told you earlier that Yamada denied us when we courted him. It was his friend Shoji-san that convinced him to join our ranks. She foresaw that only the person who wields Glorious Victory Unsought could kill her son. Yamada agreed to become our archivist, and named Glorious Victory Unsought as his price."

"So what? That doesn't set off any bombs in an airport."

"When I learned of Shoji's prophecy, I assumed Dr. Yamada was being noble. He would see to it that his friend's son died painlessly. If he were a samurai, *bushidō* would demand nothing less. It was my mistake: I saw his fascination with the sword and his strong moral stance, and I assumed the two went hand in hand."

"They *did*," said Mariko. "I don't have to listen to this."

"You do if you want to understand the truth. Right after the Haneda bombing, we sent six assassins after Jōko Daishi. He killed five of them. The sixth escaped with her life, and with his mask. She says he took three bullets that night, including one to the head that the demon mask deflected. Any one of those three rounds should have killed him. Why does he still live?"

Because ballistics is a weird science, Mariko thought. Because the human body can be pretty damn stubborn when it wants to be. But she knew where Furukawa was headed. "You think it's fate. You think only my sword can kill him."

"I think that is one part of the truth. There are deeper secrets about Koji-san's remarkable resilience, secrets I can share with you only if you join us. But what matters for the present is what *Yamada* believed. He trusted Shoji. That's why he claimed the sword for his own: so none of our people would kill his friend's only son."

"Come on. Aren't you supposed to be a ninja master? Why didn't you do some ninja stuff? You could have stolen the sword, killed Jōko Daishi, and returned the sword before anyone knew it was gone. Hell, you wouldn't even have to be a ninja for that. You'd just have to be in a good heist movie."

"Don't think it didn't occur to us." Furukawa re-racked the balls as he spoke. "But Professor Yamada assured us that your heist movie antics weren't necessary. He said he had a new protégé. He said *you* would do what he could not."

"What? That's the stupidest thing I've ever heard."

"Is it? He was a deadly swordsman. You are a deadly marksman. Both of you have had occasion to prove it. And both of you accept that killing one to save ten is undoubtedly the right thing to do."

"It's not—"

Mariko didn't even know how to complete that sentence. She killed Fuchida to save her sister; that was one for one. Why not one for ten? It seemed simple. She killed Akahata to save herself and fifty-two others. Given the chance to do it again, the only thing she'd do differently would be to shoot sooner. It seemed simple, and yet it wasn't. It was the hardest thing she'd ever done. She still had nightmares about it. So killing one to save ten? Maybe it was the right thing to do, but it wasn't *undoubtedly* so. It was still a hard choice.

There was one choice before her that wasn't hard. "Why are you telling me this?" she asked. "So I'll kill Jōko Daishi for you? Well, guess what? I'm not doing it. Shoji's my friend. Even if she weren't . . ." Mariko threw up her hands. "I don't even know how to get this through your head. I took an oath to uphold the constitution. You're asking me to commit premeditated murder. Those two things don't go together. End of story."

"And yet you will kill him. Shoji-san has already seen it. The only question is how many must die between now and then."

"No. You trained him. You deal with him. If you're so convinced that I'm the only one who can kill him, here's an idea: maybe you could try *not assassinating him*. Tase him, cuff him, and give him to us."

"Oh? And then what? Watch your people let him slip away again?"

"I don't know." This conversation was giving her a headache. "What happened to your stupid magic phone calls? There is no evidence the Wind cannot fabricate, *neh*? Give us something solid enough to hold him without bail."

"To what end, Detective Oshiro? So he can find another lawyer? Tie up the system in endless appeals? The Divine Wind will live on. You are the only one who can behead it."

"No." Mariko wanted to wring his scrawny neck. "You're looking for a hit man. I'm a cop. That's all there is to it."

Furukawa sighed. "You're worse than Dr. Yamada. I hadn't expected such intransigence from you."

"I'll take that as a compliment."

She left without another word. Her headache lingered, but a surge of self-confidence put a spring in her step. She'd never been so proud to be Yamada-sensei's student.

32

As she went to sleep in Shoji's spare bedroom, wearing the camouflage Bape sweatpants Endo Naomoto had purchased for her, Mariko thought the best thing about being suspended was that she'd be able to sleep in as late as she wanted.

She awoke to a living nightmare.

A lance of sunlight poked through the gingko tree outside. It angled between the leaves to stab Mariko right in the eyes. This woke her up just enough to hear the low, soft sobs coming from the next room. It could only be Shoji. Mariko rousted herself out of bed, rubbed the sleep from her eyes, and shuffled down the hall to knock on Shoji's bedroom door.

The door was open. Shoji sat on the end of her big, Western-style bed. She wore a long, frumpy, comfortable-looking nightgown and her face was streaked with tears. Mariko had never seen her eyes before—had never seen her without her big black sunglasses, in fact—and was surprised by the scars she saw there. She knew Shoji had lost her sight as a child, and she knew Shoji was a little girl during the war, but somehow it had never occurred to Mariko that Shoji might have been blinded by violence.

"Are you okay, Shoji-san?"

Shoji shook her head mutely and pointed at the radio.

"—confirms thirteen kidnapped from Sumida ward

elementary schools," the news anchor was saying. "That's thirteen from thirteen different schools. We're told all of them are from the first grade—"

Mariko sank to the floor. She felt like she'd been punched out cold. The radio kept going, but she hardly heard it. "Thirteen oh four," she whispered. "Is this the thirteen?"

"It's worse," Shoji said. "So much worse."

Mariko focused on the announcer's voice. "—one child each from all sixteen schools in Chuo ward, and seventeen more abductees from the nineteen schools in Minato ward. The two remaining Minato schools have not yet confirmed—"

Another knockout punch. Mariko needed him to read the whole list again before she could make sense of it. Finally the awful truth sunk in: one first-grade child from each school in Tokyo. That was the plan. Not dozens of children but hundreds. In fact, even that was an understatement. If the kidnappers wanted a hundred kids, they only needed to hijack a couple of buses at the aquarium. This wasn't two or three guys with pistols; this was a citywide effort. But most terrifying of all was its surgical precision. Precisely one child per school. If the kidnappers could do that, they could take anyone, anywhere, at any time.

Only Jōko Daishi would think to attempt it. His mission was to unsettle people, to rip them out of their comfortable, complacent lives. To him, feeling secure was a spiritual crutch. He intended to kick it away, to show society that it could stand on its own two feet. That was the message in bombing Terminal 2: what you think of as security does not make you secure. Family was another crutch, and now he'd kicked that one out as well. He wasn't just threatening children; he threatened all hope for the future.

And he was doing a damn good job of it too. The radio anchor's voice cracked, and a producer somewhere switched over to a station identification before the anchor could break down crying.

"My child or all the others," Shoji said. "I see it now.

This is what it meant—what it was always destined to mean, all those years ago. My child or all the others." She broke down sobbing.

Mariko couldn't blame her. Hundreds of kidnappings—1,304 of them, to be precise. That was what the radio would say soon enough, when they finally got a call through to some shell-shocked spokesman from the Ministry of Education. Mariko couldn't claim to know how many elementary schools there were in Tokyo, but she was sure of the number all the same. Shoji was sure. She'd seen it.

One thousand three hundred and four first graders kidnapped, and every parent in the city more frightened than they'd ever been in their lives. Mariko couldn't even imagine their fear. She *could* imagine what today would have been like if she hadn't lost her badge. She'd only hear about one abduction at first—maybe a request from another detective, to run down a plate or something, because a missing kid was more important than Mariko's pissant buy-bust. Then she'd run across a weird coincidence. Maybe Han would tell her he got pulled onto a kidnapping case too. It would be three or four coincidences before any one person could see a pattern—maybe twenty cases citywide, with more than a hundred cops roped in. Detectives. Patrol response. Air support. Maybe even SWAT, if anyone had a decent lead on a location.

Only then would someone see the horror for what it was. It would be someone up top, someone in a position to start drafting an official statement. Rumors would trickle down from cop to cop before the announcement went public. One child per school. The largest mass kidnapping in history. Had Mariko been on duty, she'd have witnessed the story evolve minute by minute, one awful blow at a time. But today—the one time she'd ever slept in on a workday—she woke up to a full-blown terrorist attack.

She could have prevented it. With a single bullet. Or maybe by thinking of something smarter than a temper tantrum to persuade Captain Kusama. Or by signing on with Furukawa. There was no telling what might have happened if she'd joined the Wind. With their resources, maybe she could have—

No. There was no point in thinking that way. This was Jōko Daishi's fault. Not Mariko's, though in theory she could have changed what happened. Not Shoji's either, though she could have changed it too. Mariko understood that as an intellectual principle. But in her gut the guilt had such a crushing grip that she could hardly speak.

It was an hour before she could pull herself together—or if not *together* together, then at least together enough to manage a phone call. Furukawa picked up on the first ring.

"Here's how this works," Mariko said. "I team up with you long enough to bring down Jōko Daishi. Not *kill*; I said *bring down*. As in arrest and arraign. Once he's behind bars, we're through. Understand?"

"I do," he said.

"Then let's start with you telling me how this goes. I've never worked in organized crime before."

BOOK EIGHT

◆◆◆◆◆◆◆◆◆◆◆◆◆◆◆◆◆◆◆◆◆◆◆◆◆◆◆◆◆

AZUCHI-MOMOYAMA PERIOD, THE YEAR 21

(1588 CE)

33

Fat, cold raindrops assaulted Katsushima Goemon like a thousand tiny arrows. The whistling wind gave them speed enough to sting.

They rattled against the oilcloth tarpaulin that he had draped over the top of his stolen wheelbarrow. It had been some time since he'd looked underneath, into the belly of the barrow. It was too dark, and even if it were not, he could not bear the sight of his friend's sleeping face. He knew Daigoro wasn't asleep.

Lightning flashed, illuminating his path. It was not much farther now. That was good; Goemon had lost so much blood that he was hardly able to stand. The barrow seemed to push back against him. When he left Daimatsu shrine, he'd headed first for the horses, but the mere sight of them was enough to dissuade him from riding. He was in no state to properly tack up a horse, much less to hoist himself into the saddle. Nor was he willing to simply heave Daigoro's limp body over the back as if it were nothing more than a sack of rice. At least he could pretend his friend was a little more comfortable in the barrow, sheltered from the pelting rain.

Horseshoes clopped behind him, splashing in the puddles. He could not ride, but neither would he abandon his mount to be stolen. The horse deserved better than that, and so did Daigoro's mare. He'd hitched one to the other, and he'd walk them all the way back to Izu if it came down to that. In truth Goemon's horse didn't even belong to him; he'd borrowed it from the Okuma stable, and he would see it returned home. If he lived that long.

At last he reached the gate of Ōda Tomonosuke, who could hardly be called a friend. Closer to say Lord Ōda owed a debt, one so deep that it was not wrong for Goemon to rouse the man from sleep on such a foul night.

He smashed his fist on the gate. It left trickles of blood in its wake. Goemon was no healer. He'd bound his many wounds as best he could, but the knots had loosened on his long walk, and now his bandages wept with red-tinged rainwater. That was why he'd come to call on the Ōdas. Their *kenjutsu* was the best in Ayuchi, and of necessity the best martial schools always employed skilled healers.

Goemon pounded the gate again and heard an irritated shout on the other side. The rain drowned out the words, but it was clear that someone was coming. When the gate opened, Goemon was surprised to see not a door warden, not a servant, but Ōda Tomonosuke himself. He was not much older than Goemon, with stern, sunken eyes and the scraggly beginnings of a beard. His hair was a matted mess and his clothes were soaked through.

A quizzical frown wrinkled his face as he laid eyes on his visitor. "Do I know you?"

"You do, though it's been a while," Goemon said. "Twenty and thirty years ago we used to face each other in duels. Right over there, in your own dojo."

"I fought many men in those days."

"Your students will remember if you do not. I bested you every time. And three or four years ago, I fought your son to a standstill on the same ground."

Ōda's owlish eyebrows drew together as he searched his memory. "Katsushima Goemon."

"Yes."

Ōda's face grew as dark and sullen as the storm clouds. "Why have you come? My son is gone. There is no one else here to fight you."

"I have not come to duel. I come to heal."

"I'm in no need of healing—"

Ōda cut himself short. For the first time he noticed Goemon's seeping bandages. Then, aided by a flash of lightning, he saw the mix of blood and rain dribbling out of a leaky corner of the wheelbarrow.

He took hold of the tarpaulin, pulled it aside, and looked in horror at the bloody form it sheltered. He would have no reason to recognize Daigoro in his current state, but the massive Inazuma blade was familiar enough. He had seen it before, about a year ago, when he and his son Yoshitomo rode all the way to Izu. They had come to test House Okuma's *kenjutsu* against their own. Since then, Ōda must have seen the blade ten thousand times in his mind. Yoshitomo had died on its edge.

Goemon had not been there to see the duels, but by all accounts they were shameful, childish affairs. Daigoro's brother Ichirō was as obnoxious and belligerent as only an eighteen-year-old can be. He provoked Yoshitomo so sorely that he'd forced an escalation from *bokken* to live steel. It very nearly cost him his head. A few months after that they fought again, a loud, ugly affair in the middle of the Tokaidō. Ichirō died at Yoshitomo's hand, but then Yoshitomo made his fatal mistake. Like Ichirō, he was a braggart, and when he sang his own praises and insulted his fallen foe, Daigoro had no choice but to avenge his elder brother.

Now Lord Ōda looked down at his son's killer awash in blood. The weapon that took Yoshitomo's life lay across his lifeless form. "Have you come looking for a bounty?" asked Ōda. "I never put a price on this boy's head. Even if I had, I could not pay it. You can see for yourself: mine is a ruined house."

Goemon peered past him and was shocked by what he saw. The Ōda compound was overrun with its own detritus. Creeping vines threatened to pull down the walls. Dead leaves mounded in every corner. Where there was paint, it was peeling. There was standing water everywhere.

"What . . . ? What happened?"

"This boy. These Okumas. They are 'what happened.'"

Ōda sneered, and for a moment he looked like he might spit in the wheelbarrow. If he did that, Goemon would have to kill him.

But the father showed more restraint than his loud-mouthed son. "You're a swordsman," he said. "You should understand. My Yoshitomo was our clan's champion. His Hawk and Phoenix style was indomitable. Had he lost a duel here, out of the public eye, we might someday have recovered. Not in my lifetime, but someday."

Goemon nodded. He would not make a bereaved father say the rest. His son's arrogance not only cost him his life; it ensured that everyone would remember the Hawk and Phoenix of House Ōda—and remember how they'd failed, to fatal effect. Yoshitomo had nailed the doors shut on the Ōda dojo for ever after.

But his father blamed the wrong man. "This boy cost me everything," Lord Ōda said. "*Everything.* Go bury him somewhere else. I won't do him the honor of a decent funeral."

"He did as much for your son," Goemon said. "And you will do more for him. He is not dead. Not yet. You will muster your healers, and you will do everything you can to keep him alive."

Ōda backed away from the wheelbarrow as if he saw a ghost in it. "No. Never. This boy is the ruin of me."

No, that honor goes to your idiotic son, Goemon thought. It was so tempting to say it. But he needed this man to step aside. "You owe House Okuma a blood debt."

"No! An Okuma died. An Ōda died. The ledgers are balanced."

"Wrong. They were balanced when your son won his duel and walked away. Then he provoked a defeated foe, murdered him, and boasted about it to anyone who would listen."

There was much more to be said. Because Ichirō died, Daigoro's mother lost her wits. She'd lost a husband and a son in less than a year, and in her madness she nearly lost everything else. She'd spoiled delicate negotiations, which then forced Daigoro's hand in marriage. That had distracted Daigoro from dealing with his beloved abbot, whose bald head Goemon should have put in a box ages ago. Then came all the trouble with Shichio, another son of a pox-riddled bitch whose head Goemon should have separated from his shoulders. And now came all the trouble with that money-grubbing lout Yasuda Kenbei. All because of one woman. It was as if some evil spirit possessed her—and if so, Goemon should have cut it out of her. He knew that now. Honor and friendship had stayed his hand, but if he'd ever wanted to be a true friend to Daigoro, he should have put that madwoman out of her misery.

No. If he'd done that, he and Daigoro would have come to blows. Goemon could not abide that thought. Better to ride with him and help him weather his many storms than to draw steel against him. But how many more storms would come? In Daigoro's life they seemed to be endless.

"The Okumas have fared little better than the Ōdas," Goemon said, omitting the rest. "All because your son could not be satisfied with a decisive victory in a fair duel. Now you will stand aside and we will enter. Do I make myself clear?"

Ōda looked angry enough to draw his sword. He studied Daigoro, whose only sign of life was the blood trickling from his many wounds. Then he shook his head in disbelief. Reluctantly he stepped aside. His derision had not subsided in the least, but now he directed it at himself.

Goemon rolled Daigoro through the open doorway before Ōda had a chance to change his mind. "Show me to the cleanest room you have," he said, pushing the wheelbarrow over a carpet of wet brown leaves. "And summon your healers, if you did not dismiss them along with your gardeners."

Daigoro awoke to the nauseating sensation of a knife sliding out of his body.

"Hold him, hold him, he's awake," someone said. Daigoro did not recognize the voice. Through blurred eyes he saw an old grandmother hunched over him, gnawing her lower lip with crooked yellow teeth. He could not see her hands, but it felt like she was stabbing his shoulder with needles. Whatever she was doing, it demanded all of her concentration.

He tried to flinch away, but iron-hard hands held him tight. The feeling of being trapped automatically made him struggle. The frowning woman tsked him and jabbed him with something sharp. The knife slid farther out of him. Blood spilled down his back in a hot cascade. He twitched and wriggled but the hands held fast. "Daigoro, lie still," said a deep voice. "You'll tear your stitches loose."

The voice was familiar. "Go-Goemon?"

"I'm here. Now show a little patience and stop your squirming."

It was another day before Daigoro could keep himself awake for as long as an hour, a day after that before he began to feel like a human being again. He had a splitting headache, the kind he got when he went too long without water. He'd spilled too much of his lifeblood on the floor of that shrine. The only remedy was to drink enough to drown a whale. That gave him an hourly need to make water, but getting out of bed made the walls spin. And when his head and his bladder were not pestering him, Katsushima continuously forced food on him. The healers insisted the best medicine for drastic blood loss was chicken livers and ginseng root—bowlful by heaping bowlful, enough to suffocate him.

At least he would choke to death in comfort. He lay on a soft futon on clean bedclothes. Daigoro gathered that Katsushima had ordered the lord of the house to lodge his guests in the cleanest room in the compound. The lord's steward was none too pleased, for it was his quarters that became the hospital. Daigoro never got the man's proper name—he went only by Karei, which meant "steward"—but he gleaned quite a bit about his displaced host just from how he kept his rooms. Karei was tidy to a fault. His bedroll, scroll cupboards, and writing tools were all here, suggesting that he spent the great majority of his life in these spare, orderly rooms. Daigoro had no doubt that Karei's quarters did not usually stink of blood and chicken livers.

"I have a confession to make," Daigoro told Katsushima, pitying Karei every bit as much as himself. The livers had coated the roof of his mouth like thick, wet fur. "I'm giving serious thought to killing the cook."

"Don't. Lord Ōda's serving staff all abandoned him when he stopped paying them. The healing woman who stitched up your wounds is serving double duty in the kitchen."

"It shows. Her cooking tastes like medicine . . ." He trailed off, because his sluggish, staggering mind had finally latched on to the most important thing Katsushima had said. "Did you say Ōda? You can't mean Ōda Tomonosuke."

Katsushima only answered with a mute nod.

Daigoro's thoughts stumbled over each other like rocks falling downhill. They all tried to hurry out of his mouth at once, and the result was a mishmash of quasi-words. At last he managed to say, "Why? Why would he save me? I slew his son."

"He felt he was duty-bound to help."

Daigoro did not miss the smugness in Katsushima's tone. "Oh no. What did you do?"

"I told him if it were not for his idiotic son killing your idiotic brother, both of your houses would have escaped their evil karma. Well, I managed to put it a little more politely than that. Have a care when you speak to him, Daigoro. His family has suffered as much as yours."

"I find that difficult to believe."

"Believe what you like. Just be delicate in handling him."

Daigoro choked down another pasty mouthful of liver. "If I live long enough to speak with him. This vile mash may kill me yet."

"Keep eating." Katsushima spoke like a father to a child—or rather, like a mostly sober friend to a reckless drunk. For the first time Daigoro noticed Katsushima was almost as poorly off as he was. He seemed older than his years, hollowed out somehow, like a sloughed-off snakeskin. Black silk stitches traced thin, weeping lines on each cheek, and Daigoro suspected he'd find many more stitches under the cotton fabric binding both of Katsushima's forearms. Clearly the old rogue was holding himself together for Daigoro's benefit. Equally clear was that he'd prefer to push Daigoro out of bed and go to sleep himself.

"You're a good friend, Goemon."

"You're talking like a drunkard. Here, flush it out." He pressed a stout Bizen water cup into Daigoro's hands.

Daigoro did as he was told. He knew Katsushima would not tolerate rebellion. The rough clay of the cup pricked him when he touched it to his lips. Exploring with a cautious, delicate fingertip, Daigoro found the lower half of his face was burned and blistered. The tea. He remembered now: that priest-assassin had tried to pour scalding-hot poison down his throat.

That thought spawned visions of the assassin's awful

wounds. Every one of them should have been fatal, yet somehow that mysterious *tantō* staved off death. Thinking of it made Daigoro recall his first waking memory after the fight: that very dagger, sliding sickeningly out of his body. That sparked off a new realization about his friend Katsushima. "You believe in enchanted swords now."

"Hm?"

"You stabbed me. With Streaming Dawn. That's the first thing I felt when I came to: that knife, stuck in my back. Let me tell you, it hurts a lot more coming out than going in."

"The sharp ones always do."

"Yes, well, my point . . ." It took him a moment to remember what he meant to say. His thoughts were swimming through muddy water; it was easy to lose track of them. "My point is that you stabbed me with it. You wouldn't have done that unless you thought it would save me. You had to believe in the power of Streaming Dawn."

"Ehh." Katsushima grunted and shrugged. "What other options did I have? If I did nothing, you were sure to bleed to death. I tried the knife because there was nothing else left to try."

"No. You believe now. I can tell."

"You still sound like a drunkard."

Katsushima gave a didactic look at Daigoro's water cup. Daigoro obliged him and drank. "Thank you, Goemon."

"Shut up."

"I suppose I ought to thank Ōda-sama too, sooner or later."

"Let it be later. Gather your strength."

"No, it may as well be now." Daigoro shot a foul glare at his livers and ginseng. "I've already got a bitter taste in my mouth."

35

He found Lord Ōda Tomonosuke praying at the small shrine erected by one of his forebears in a remote corner of the compound. The shrine was as neglected as everything else Daigoro had seen here. Its proud *torii*, once a brilliant orange, had faded to the color of peach flesh. Its paint had chipped and cracked in a hundred places. The surrounding gravel seemed dirty somehow, as if the rain had deliberately neglected this place. Clearly no groundskeeper's rake had been here in ages. Fresh sticks of incense burned in a bronze censer so pitted and rotten that it threatened to fall apart at any moment. If this was how Ōda kept up the holiest of possessions, Daigoro could scarcely imagine what his kitchens must look like, or his bedchamber.

Ōda himself was in little better shape than his shrine. His face was puffy, his eyes bloodshot. He'd put on weight since Daigoro saw him last. He'd given up care for his clothing and made only desultory efforts at grooming. A mole on his cheek had grown hairs as long as Daigoro's little finger.

"My lord," Daigoro said, "may I join you in prayer?"

Ōda studied him with red-rimmed eyes. Only his eyes moved, not his head. At last he muttered, "Why not?"

This was not the genteel man Daigoro once knew. When Lord Ōda's son Yoshitomo had come to challenge the Okumas, Ichirō insulted him and Yoshitomo was only too glad to begin the bloodletting. Only Daigoro and Lord Ōda showed self-restraint. They sat down to tea, shared polite conversation, then established the terms of the duel. *That* Lord Ōda would never have given such cruel looks out of the corner of his eye. This one was little more than a shadow.

Even so, Daigoro was certain the two of them could find common ground. They had lost so much. According to Katsushima, there was a time when House Ōda was renowned for its swordsmanship. It once enjoyed wealth and prestige, but clearly that was lost to them. Daigoro couldn't understand how they'd fallen this far—it was less than a year ago that Ichirō and Yoshitomo were killed— but if he could tease that story out of Lord Ōda, he might find something they shared in common, some foundation on which he could start building sympathy.

To put himself on a level with Ōda, he kneeled beside the older man. His bad knee buckled, so Daigoro fell as much as kneeled. The rapid movement made him light-headed. To keep his head from spinning, he fixed his eyes on the grave markers arrayed before the shrine. The newest was a tall wooden stele, painted with the name Mutsu no Mikoto. Daigoro remembered the name; Lady Mutsu was Ōda's wife. "My lord," he said, "I am sorry for your loss. I remember you speaking of your wife when we first sat down to tea. May I ask when she passed on?"

"She died the day she learned you killed her son."

Daigoro was stunned. Well-bred people did not speak so bluntly. "I . . . I don't understand."

"I suppose I ought to thank you," Ōda said scornfully. "You must have been the one to send a rider, informing us of Yoshitomo's death."

"I was."

"When my wife read your letter, it shattered her spirit. Yoshitomo was more than our dojo's champion; he was her favorite son. She never admitted as much, but I always knew it."

"I'm so sorry."

"Are you? Then be sorry for this too. My house is

ruined. My dojo had been losing money for years. When word reached us of this braggart in the north, Okuma Ichirō, we knew silencing him might earn us the fame we needed to stay afloat. And indeed it did. But then rumors reached us that the braggart would not die. Why could he not shut his mouth?"

I might ask the same of your son, Daigoro thought. But he could not say that. Neither could he think of any words of comfort.

"I married above my station," Ōda said. "My wife's family was far wealthier than mine. When the Ōda dojo began to crumble, she became despondent. Poverty did not become her. Once Yoshitomo died, our financial fate was sealed. It was more than she could bear. That letter of yours, that's what broke her."

Buddhas have mercy, Daigoro thought. He knew what came next, and it made his heart sink.

"She took her own life," said Ōda. "To her credit, she did it properly, the way a samurai's daughter ought to. Right here. Right in front of this shrine."

Daigoro looked in horror at the gravel he knelt upon. Had Ōda bothered to cart it off and replace it after his wife's suicide? Or had that been the moment he decided to abandon decorum? Had the last of his servants washed this holy site of her blood, or had he left the rain to perform that task? Was Daigoro kneeling in her lifeblood even now?

"I hope I can die with as much dignity," Ōda said. He spoke with scorn and sorrow in equal measure. "It is the only hope remaining to me: to die as a samurai. As did my wife. As did my son. I suppose I ought to thank you for that too."

"You need thank me for nothing," said Daigoro. "Tell me, is there anything I can do for you?"

Ōda's eyes widened in surprise. Perhaps he had not looked for such generosity from the Bear Cub of Izu. He studied Daigoro for a long moment, pensive and silent. At last he said, "Yes. There is one thing you can do. Kill me."

"My lord, please—"

"You asked, so I've answered. Let a line of warriors

end as warriors. What hope do I have of dying with a sword in my hand? My warring days are long past me. I cannot even teach *kenjutsu* anymore. No one will come. When I die, my family's dojo dies with me, and I must go to my forefathers to tell them I failed them. Give me this one thing at least: let me tell them I died on an Inazuma blade."

Daigoro was horrified at the thought. Even so, he knew it was not his place to question a samurai's wishes. Like it or not, Daigoro wasn't samurai anymore. Though it pained him even to think it, he said, "If my lord were to challenge me to a duel, I suppose I could—"

"No!" Ōda sprang to his feet, overflowing with rage. "My last act in this life will not be to suffer defeat. I did not say duel with me. I said kill me. In cold blood. Draw your sword if you have the courage, or else be gone."

Daigoro struggled to his feet. "Lord Ōda, we must find a middle path. There is still something I must ask of you."

Ōda coughed and staggered back, just as if Daigoro had kicked him in the chest. "You dare to ask a favor? Of *me*? After all you've done?"

"Begging your pardon, my lord, but in the eyes of the law and in the eyes of men, I have done your family no wrong. I did only what *bushidō* requires of me. I think you know this, Lord Ōda. I think you understand *bushidō* better than most, or else you would not rue the prospect of dying as less than a samurai."

Ōda's face grew red. The tendons and veins in his neck stood out. The way he pursed his mouth, he looked angry enough to spit. "Ask, then."

"Are you any relation to Oda Nobunaga?"

"Of course. The Ōdas and Odas are cousins. Our branch is the more storied lineage, I'll have you know—or at least it was, until that sadist Nobunaga chopped his way into power."

"There is a woman I must reach out to. She was a friend to . . . to the sadist Nobunaga. She said I could make contact with her through her allies with House Oda."

"Ah. And you believe I am one of these allies?"

"I don't know. But I think you must know someone who is. He was powerful here. So were you."

Ōda wiped his hand over his mouth. Daigoro could hear his whiskers scraping against the pads of his fingers. "This woman you want to reach, is she called Nene by any chance?"

"Yes."

"Then you are a fool. What business could the Lady in the North possibly have with a half-dead, homeless, crippled, bloodthirsty *rōnin*?"

Daigoro did not rise to the bait. Clearly Lord Ōda still wanted to die. There was no other reason to insult an armed man so brashly. "Our business is our own," he said flatly.

"*Our* business? Talk to her often, do you?"

"These days more often than usual." That much was not a lie. Clearly it impressed Ōda; it wiped the smirk off his face.

"I see," Ōda said gravely. "So this is the favor you would ask of me? To send word to Lady Nene?"

"Yes. Most importantly, I want your sworn word that no one else will intercept the message."

Now the smirk came back. "Don't be an ass. These are troubled times. War is afoot. Who can guarantee that a messenger should find his way through unmolested?"

"You can and you will. Carry the message yourself if you must."

Drawing himself up to his full height, Ōda sneered. Daigoro could see where Yoshitomo's swagger had come from. "So now I've become your pageboy, eh? But you've told me too much, Daigoro. Someone wants to read your letters. Perhaps this someone wants to know where you are. Are you a hunted man, Daigoro?"

"You are enjoying yourself entirely too much, sir. I can only hope you will do your duty just as gladly."

Another sneer. "And what duty would that be?"

"I will hand you a letter. You will deliver it or die in the attempt. *Bushidō* asks no less of you."

"Bah! Are you my liege lord? No. You came here in a wheelbarrow. That brigand Katsushima could have delivered a load of manure the same way. Why should I give a moment's thought to you and your oh-so-important message?"

In an act of surpassing generosity, Daigoro did not cut him in half. Instead, in a low, measured voice, he said, "If I were to set fire to your house, it would be my duty to put it out, *neh*?"

"Do you threaten me, boy?"

Daigoro ignored the question. "Suppose the house burned down. Would you agree that it is my duty to build you a new one?"

"Yes. What of it?"

"Suppose it were not me, but rather my son who burned your house down. Whose duty is it to rebuild it for you?"

Ōda grumbled and steamed. "Whatever your point is, please make it soon."

"You cannot begin to imagine all of the things your son cost my family when he killed Ichirō. If he had simply burned our house to the ground, he would have done less damage. And if that were all he had done, my lord, you would not have to be samurai to recognize your duty to set matters right. Even merchants and yakuzas teach their sons as much: if the child will not atone for his wrongs, then his parents must do it for him. Without that bond of shame, our society would fall apart."

"So what if it would?"

"Your son owes my family a devastating debt. In repayment I ask you the simplest favor. I could demand that you beggar your own clan to build a new house for mine. Instead I only ask you to carry a letter to someone, and to let no one read it but her. If you will not do that, are you even worthy of the name 'samurai'? Or are you just a coward with a topknot?"

Daigoro's words stung Ōda like wasps. Daigoro could see him flinch. Lord Ōda did not care to hear about his son's offenses, nor of the debt he'd incurred. He certainly didn't care to suffer an assault to his honor as a samurai. But the reason he felt the words sting was that they were envenomed with truth.

"Your letter," Ōda said, his eyes vacant. He seemed to be speaking to a ghost. "Your letter . . ."

He returned to the shrine and uprooted a weather-beaten stele that stood next to his wife's. Watching him tug at it reminded Daigoro of pulling a sword out of a dying man's belly. The ground seemed to cling to the wooden stele, just as a body clutched jealously to the weapon that pierced it. At last he pulled it free and handed it to Daigoro.

Daigoro could barely make out the writing on its dried, grayed face. Yoshitomo no Mikoto, it read. It was his son's grave marker. Below his name ran a haiku:

> *Stones cannot climb up;*
> *A boar will never back down.*
> *Some can only fall.*

"Do you recognize the poem?" said Ōda.

"Of course." Daigoro hadn't thought about those lines for a long time. Reading them now made him blink back tears. "I . . . I wrote it for your son and my brother. It was their death poem."

Ōda closed his eyes and swallowed. "You wrote it in a letter too, the one that accompanied Yoshitomo when you sent him home with his swords. Is it true that you engraved it on a stupa to hallow where they fell?"

"I did."

"Do you remember how you closed that letter?" Daigoro thought about it a moment and had to confess he did not. "You invited us to send a portion of Yoshitomo's ashes to you, and promised to bury them at the stupa. That was the sentence that made my wife rip your letter to shreds. My scribe had to piece the scraps back together to copy the death poem just as you'd written it."

Ōda's words fluttered in his throat. "I told my wife I would send you a bottle of my own piss before I sent you a single speck of her beloved son's ashes. Now I break my vow to her. I refuse to recognize this debt you say my son incurred against your house. If he ruined your clan, you ruined mine. We are even. But I would not have Yoshitomo's spirit wandering the earth in search of his final resting place. If I give you a vial of his ashes, will you bury it where he fell?"

"I swear it."

"Then in exchange I will carry this letter of yours to the Lady in the North. Unopened and unread, upon my word. I ask only one thing of you: write it quickly, then be gone from my house."

Daigoro was not as quick in writing his letter as his host might have liked. Katsushima readied their horses and still Daigoro hadn't finished. Then Katsushima cajoled the healing woman in the kitchen into providing them with a little food for the ride. Daigoro only made negative progress: he set a candle flame to his first draft, scattered the ashes in the courtyard, and started afresh with a blank page.

It was hard to know what to write. He hadn't forgotten what Aki had told him: *don't provide your enemy the means to defeat you.* If Ōda was as good as his word, then Daigoro could tell Nene anything he liked. If he was false, then Ōda would betray him to Shichio at the first opportunity. It hardly mattered that Ōda had never heard of Shichio. He'd already guessed Daigoro was a wanted man; he had only to announce Daigoro's name and Shichio's bear hunters would come straight to his door.

Thus if Daigoro set terms in his letter for how he and Nene should meet, he might as well write his own death poem. But if he did not set terms for meeting her, then how could they complete their pact? He needed a second audience with her, but it was too dangerous to nominate a place or a time.

"It's dangerous to write *anything*," Katsushima insisted. He knew the classics as well as Aki did. Sun Tzu's famous maxim was at the core of Katsushima's fighting style: *He wins his battles by making no mistakes. The good fighters of old first put themselves beyond the possibility of defeat, and then waited for an opportunity to defeat the enemy.* "This letter opens you to defeat," Katsu-shima said, standing above the little desk where Daigoro sat and wrote.

"Only if Lord Ōda has forgotten the virtues of *bushidō*."

"No. He need not abandon them; he need only be dis-tracted for a moment. Gold, *sake*, pettiness, grief; any of these might persuade him to forget his oath to you. He might come to regret his betrayal within the hour, but by then it will be too late."

"All right, all right," Daigoro said. "At least your ver-sion is easy to write."

Dipping his brush, he wrote three words. *I have it.* Then he folded and sealed the letter and they made ready to leave.

36

I have it.

You clever boy, Nene thought. He was right not to trust his messenger. Ōda Tomonosuke was a broken man. That much was clear by his windswept topknot and overlong fingernails. The man had managed to shave before meeting the most powerful woman in the empire, but that was all. The samurai prided themselves on bodily perfection, but even by a farmer's standards, Lord Ōda was a disheveled mess.

"Thank you so much for delivering this to me," Nene said, suffusing her voice with deference and respect. She found men tended to give her what she wanted if she spoke to them in the same way she spoke to the emperor. "I know carrying a letter is far beneath your station."

In truth that was almost all she knew about him. It was impossible to familiarize herself with all of her husband's allies; by now his sworn daimyo numbered well over a hundred. Even so, Nene made it her business to memorize everything she could, and in the case of Ōda Tomonosuke that was especially easy. The recent tragedies in his life were memorable: his son slain, his wife a suicide, his house destitute. The Ōdas were distant cousins to Oda Nobunaga, whom Nene audaciously considered a friend. Nobunaga had been the mightiest daimyo the empire had ever known, until that blackheart Akechi

Mitsuhide ambushed him, trapped him in a temple, and set it ablaze. Hideyoshi had been swift to avenge Nobunaga. He sent Akechi straight to hell, and with Nene's help he swiftly eclipsed his predecessor and mentor.

Nobunaga's great regard for Nene was one of the reasons Hideyoshi took her seriously. Or, put another way, if not for Nobunaga, Nene might have been just another wife. For that, the least Nene owed him was to remember the names of his cousins, even the little lordlings like Ōda Tomonosuke.

"It must have been hard for you, sitting down to tea with the man who killed your son," she said.

"More boy than man," said Ōda. "And we didn't sit down to tea. I gave him a clean bed and had my steward round up the healers, that's all."

"Healers? Oh, I do hope it's nothing serious."

Ōda winced. "Damn my flapping tongue. And damn the pact I made with that murderous devil. My lady, I promised I would not betray Daigoro to his enemies. I'll not name you an enemy, but . . . well, you understand. I was to bring you the letter, nothing more."

Ah, but you've told me so much, Nene thought. The ride from Ōda's home in Ayuchi to Nene's manor in the Jurakudai was about forty *ri*—a day's ride for a messenger on a fleet horse, at least two days' ride for a man of Ōda's years. Judging by his unkempt appearance, he was no longer a man with the energy and initiative to make the ride in two days. Call it three, she thought, and immediately she imagined how far the Bear Cub might have traveled from Ayuchi in that time. By sea, he could have returned to Izu, or sailed as far south as Shikoku. By the Tokaidō, it was hard to guess. There were too many variables.

"Well, never mind your healers; let's pretend I didn't hear that." She smiled at him sweetly. "I heard only that you are a noble and generous man, to go to great expense to shelter a boy who has done your family such harm. Why, just providing him horse fodder is no mean expense in times of war."

"Too true—as Daigoro knows damn well. He didn't even offer to pay."

So the Bear Cub travels on horseback, she thought. It made sense; she remembered the boy walked with a limp. Her map changed shape in her mind. The Tokaidō was well maintained and patrolled; riders could travel with little fear of bandits, *yamabushi*, or sudden holes where their horses might break a leg. Her own messages could travel nearly a hundred *ri* in a single day, but that was because Toyotomi couriers had relay stations all along the Tokaidō. No horse could cover that distance so swiftly on its own.

A lone boy, recently injured, on a well-fed horse. How far could he ride in three days? Would he risk the Tokaidō, or did he still fear spies on the great roads? If he still rode with that woolly-haired *rōnin* of his, the two of them might simply slaughter Shichio's bear hunters wherever they found them. On the other hand, Daigoro was not one to walk into a trap and then figure out how to cut his way free of it. The safer path was to ride the back roads.

Again the map changed its contours in Nene's mind. If he held to the great roads, he might be anywhere within, say, sixty *ri* of Lord Ōda's compound—including just outside my door, she realized with a start. Why was he not here already, and why had he not come with Streaming Dawn? That would have made matters so easy.

But there were no unwatched roads to Kyoto. Daigoro probably feared Shichio still had spies here. Nene shared the same worry herself; she could never be sure she'd rooted out every last one. No, the Bear Cub would not make himself seen if he did not have to. He would not come to her; she would have to find him, and that would not be easy. In all likelihood he traveled overland.

That would be slow going—and as the thought occurred to her, it dawned on her that she had no idea just how slow. Those pathways were entirely outside her ken. She knew how far her palanquin could bear her in a day, encumbered as it was by her entourage. She had a rough idea of how far her husband's troops could range on a march, and on a forced march. But how far a *rōnin* could cross the wilds? Nene could not even hazard a guess.

She needed more information, and poor Ōda had no defenses against her. "Didn't it frighten you to have this boy under your roof? I hear he's a ferocious warrior."

"Ferocious? He was half dead. No, his man Katsushima is the one to fear."

So Daigoro and Katsushima still ride together, Nene thought. And they are probably penniless, since Daigoro—a polite boy—did not offer to pay for horse feed. "I see. But once you were on the road, he wasn't your guest anymore, *neh*? You must have been worried about crossing paths with him then."

"Hardly. If he were riding west, he could have carried his own damned letter—oh, curse me for a jabbering fool. I should not have said that, my lady."

"Of course, of course. I'm frightfully sorry; I never meant to make a noble samurai break his oath. We won't speak another word of him—but I shan't let you go just yet. It's late, and I won't send you off without a good meal. Let's talk about something else, shall we? Something wholesome and innocent."

Even idle chatter about the weather divulged the information she needed to know. When Ōda told her he'd enjoyed cloudless skies on his ride to her home, he said by implication that Daigoro's little-used trails would be dry, not muddy. When Ōda said he hadn't seen any major storms since that typhoon last month, he might just as well have said that Daigoro would find every ford to be shallow and slow. Oh, you poor man, Nene thought. You have no flair for this game.

He'd come to deliver three words—*I have it*—and now he'd given Nene a soliloquy. Daigoro was badly hurt but on the mend, he and Katsushima rode together, the two of them departed Ayuchi three days ago, and now they were heading east and making good time. If Ōda had wanted to fulfill his promise to the boy, he should never have stepped out of the saddle. Better to trot through the gate, put the letter in Nene's hand, and leave like a stranger. The moment he opened his mouth, he was lost.

Purely out of habit she wondered what use she might

put him to. It was an old reflex, like a merchant biting a piece of gold to test it. In truth it embarrassed her. She ought not to think of men like Ōda as playing pieces. Naive nobility was still noble, was it not? He didn't deserve to be manipulated. But her husband's needs and the good of the empire took precedence over obligations to a dead friend's cousin.

The unfortunate truth was that this Ōda Tomonosuke was a useful tool. He was a sword master once, wasn't he? Nene questioned her memory for a moment, but one glance at Ōda's hands erased all doubt: they were meaty and strong, as callused as an oarsman's. Yes, he was a *kenjutsu* sensei after all. And who had just taken up the sword? Shichio.

She could be so kind to both of them. For Shichio, the only thing better than an expert sword master would be one with intimate knowledge of the Bear Cub. If Nene judged Ōda rightly, nothing would swell his sails like becoming a proper sensei again. Shichio would be a dismal student, childish and temperamental, but he would be a *paying* student. Clearly Ōda needed the money—and, come to think of it, he'd also benefit from the distraction. That much was genuine sympathy on Nene's part: Ōda was coming apart at the seams. Taking on a student might make him feel like a man again.

He could use a friend too, one who promised to write him regularly—a friend like Nene. He was too noble to knowingly betray Shichio, but she did not need him to be a mole. She needed him only to be himself, and to accidentally divulge all the countless details of Shichio's life.

"Do you know, I've just thought of someone you should meet," she said, deliberately sounding as if she had surprised herself. "My husband has a general who— you won't tell a secret, will you?" She lowered her voice to a conspiratorial whisper. "The men say he's better known for his penmanship than his swordsmanship."

"Disgraceful."

"*Neh?* But he wants to do better, and . . . well, I didn't think of it before because General Shichio is so far from here, but now . . . oh, I do hope you'll pardon me for saying so, but after your wife's passing, and your son's . . . I know it's terribly rude of me. . . ." She made herself sound weak and indecisive. Ōda would feel stronger if she gave him the opportunity to reassure her.

Inevitably, he took the bait. "It's all right, my lady. Please, speak your mind. You needn't be shy with me."

"Well, I wonder if it might do you some good to get away for a little while. If it's not too much trouble. This general is stationed all the way in Kanagawa-juku. But I'm sure he'll pay handsomely for a sword master of your caliber. Come to think of it"—she lowered her voice conspiratorially again—"my honored husband will pay you too. It shames him to have a general who hardly knows which end of the sword to hold."

A fleeting twinge passed over Ōda's face. Nene knew why. Her husband was no swordsman either. Like Shichio, he lacked the patience for martial art—though in his defense, Hideyoshi's impatience was not like Shichio's. Shichio was like a toddler throwing a temper tantrum. Hideyoshi was more like a randy teenager surrounded by naked women.

"Well, please consider it, Ōda-sensei. It would be my honor to recommend you—"

"And your recommendation is all the honor a man like me requires." Ōda bowed deeply. Already he seemed like a younger man. He came up from his bow with his shoulders squared and his chest puffed ever so slightly. "Do you know, my lady, just the other day I told that Okuma boy my warring days are behind me. Perhaps I spoke prematurely. It will be my greatest privilege to support General Toyotomi's war effort in whatever way I can."

"I do hope so," Nene said with a smile. "And please, do not take it amiss if I write you a letter now and again. If I am to blame for sending you into the back of beyond, then the least I can do is keep you abreast of what is afoot at home."

"It would be my honor and my pleasure."

"And you'll write back to me?"

That puffed him up even further. A strong man always wants the attentions of a woman, Nene thought. Even a woman he can never have, and especially a woman who knows she cannot have him.

"Oh, you've made me so happy," she said, speaking again with perfect honesty. "I'm sure there is no better place for you than at General Shichio's side."

37

"'*I have it*'? That's all it said? '*I have it*'?"

Nene's errand boy was holding out on him. Shichio knew it damn well. He misliked the look of this man from the moment he blustered through Shichio's gate. His name was Nezumi, and he had a cocky swagger unbefitting a common messenger. He wore clean white and darkest black, with a black *hachimaki* restraining his wild hair. His teeth were brown and broken, and he exposed their hideousness with a ready smile.

"That's all," Nezumi said. "But the courier said more than the letter."

Shichio sighed irritably. "Are you an actor on a stage? Is it your job to keep me in suspense? No. Out with it, or else it's out with your tongue and I'll have you write down anything more you need to tell me."

Nezumi bit his lip when he smiled, exposing those bestial teeth all the more. "Heh heh. That would be unwise."

"Because you're unlettered?"

"Because my lady likes me. There could be . . . what's the word? Reprisals."

I have no fear of Lady Nene, Shichio wanted to say. Now more than ever he wished it were true. If only she were a wife and not a sister-figure, he could have her killed and deflect Hashiba's wrath afterward. Perhaps he might even persuade Hashiba to punish him by stripping him of his swords. Once Shichio was demoted back to the peasantry, he could grow his hair back. As it was, he was forever worried about a sunburned scalp. He'd burned it once already and the pain was terrible.

Even now, standing on his veranda with this sweating messenger kneeling in his shadow, he worried about his shaven pate. He eyed Nezumi's dusty legs with disdain but bade him inside anyway. Once he was inside, Nezumi was a guest, so Shichio had no choice but to feed him. To do otherwise was unbecoming of a *hatamoto* of the great Toyotomi Hideyoshi.

"The courier," he said after a maid fetched a little tea. "What did he say?"

"Everything." There was that brutish smile again. "He vowed never to betray the Bear Cub, and to deliver that letter without saying a word. Then he ran straight to Lady Nene and told her all he knew."

"I like him already. Who was he?"

"Lord Ōda Tomonosuke. A swordsman of some repute."

"And more than an errand boy, unless I miss my guess. Couriers do not have lordships or surnames. So why should this one be reduced to carrying messages back and forth like a pigeon?"

"You mean like me? Heh."

By the gods, those brown teeth were hideous. "Yes, yes. Now out with it. Samurai are not known for their humility, and neither are they known to break a sworn oath. Why should this Ōda fellow deign to serve a crippled boy as a messenger, and why should he break his word?"

"Hard to say what goes on in another man's mind, but I expect he did the first one in order to do the second."

"Because?"

"The Bear Cub killed his son in a duel."

"Did he now?" That was an interesting development. This Ōda must have some personal connection to Nene, or else he would not have been granted an audience. Shichio could use a spy with Nene's confidence, and his hatred for Daigoro might be just the thing to sway Ōda's loyalty. Shichio had deployed spies, troops, ships, and a mountain of gold to capture the Bear Cub. If Ōda were to learn of that—accidentally, of course—then he might be manipulated into approaching Shichio to seek an alliance.

"I would like to speak with Lord Ōda. When you return to your mistress, you will tell her so."

"No need. He's coming to you."

"Oh?"

"Lady Nene sends him as a gift. She says he's better than the sword master you've got—"

"Curse that woman!"

Shichio didn't mean to say it aloud. It just burst out of him. How did she know he'd taken up *kenjutsu*? Did she know Wada-sensei by name, or was this just bluster? Was Ōda so fell-handed that even Wada couldn't stand against him? And did she honestly expect that Shichio would study under him? A gift, Nezumi said, but Shichio saw the truth: Ōda had to be Nene's spy. She knew he and Shichio shared the same hatred for the Bear Cub, and she hoped Shichio would befriend him on that basis alone—or if not, that his *kenjutsu* was strong enough for Shichio to keep him on as a sensei.

Well, that is a dance for two, Shichio thought. He would welcome Ōda after all, and learn what he could from him, not just of swords but of Nene. And when Shichio had wrung every last drop out of him—

"I haven't got all day," Nezumi said.

The ungrateful bastard might just as well have scratched his balls like a mountain monkey. He sat cross-legged now, as if he were in his own home and not sitting before a daimyo. Shichio could hardly believe his cheek. How gratifying it would be to don the mask and show Nezumi everything he'd learned of swordsmanship. But alas, he could not. He needed what this man knew.

"Well?" Shichio said. "Out with it. Your mistress sent you to pass along her secrets. Tell me what you know, then be gone from my house."

"The Bear Cub was wounded," Nezumi said. "Ōda's

healers nursed him back from death's door. Even so, the boy was hardly fit to ride when Ōda sent him away. North and east, that was his guess. Ōda's, I mean. He knows the boy didn't ride west."

"From where?"

"Ayuchi. Near Atsutahama. And he rode with that *rōnin* of his, the tall one with the woolly hair."

Shichio remembered the man. Katsuhiro? Katsuhama? Something like that. "When did they leave Ayuchi?"

"Six days ago. Maybe seven, maybe eight. I couldn't say for sure. I know when Lord Ōda spoke to my lady and I know my lady sent her pigeon within the hour. As soon as I received it, I came straight here—"

"Silence." Six days. More than enough time to find the whelp, if only Shichio's bear hunters weren't the most inept bunglers he'd ever had the misfortune to hire. How could that wretched boy elude every last one of them? Now he was wounded and *still* he managed to slip them by. Thanks to Nene, it was harder than ever for them to report to their master. So long as Shichio had stayed in Izu, he was rarely more than a half-day's ride from his informants. Now, banished to the barbarian north, everything took an eternity.

"I have been patient with you long enough," he said. "When do you plan to tell me what 'it' is?"

"Which 'it' would that be?"

"The letter, you fool. '*I have it.*' What is 'it'?"

Nezumi shrugged. "I couldn't say."

"Because Lady Nene didn't tell you or because she told you not to tell me?"

"Heh heh. Does it make a difference?"

It was all Shichio could do to leave his katana in its sheath. A good stabbing might improve this creature's manners. "I will share something with you, Nezumi-san. I think your mistress knows what 'it' is. I think she wants 'it,' or else the Bear Cub would have no reason to send the letter. It follows that the two of them have been in communication with one another." Which I can spin into charges of sedition, he thought. "It also stands to reason that they must speak again, or else the Bear Cub has no way to give her whatever 'it' is. Tell me, are you the one assigned to make contact with him?"

"Yes."

"You will tell me where and when."

Nezumi bowed. "That's why my lady sent me."

Shichio couldn't hide his skepticism. "Is it now?"

"Yes, my lord. When I find him, I'll arrange for a meeting. The boy has something to give Lady Nene, and she insists on seeing it for herself. Whatever it is, my lady has promised your head in exchange."

"*What?*"

"Of course." Nezumi sat back smiling, amused and bemused in equal measure. "I thought you knew."

"Make sense," Shichio told him.

"My lady is laying a trap. So you can kill the Bear Cub."

Shichio sneered. "Nene is not in the habit of giving me gifts. She is far more likely to help the Bear Cub take my head than to help me take his."

"Heh heh. You've got it wrong. Lady Nene wants you to have every contentment. She wants you to be so happy here that you never consider coming back to Kyoto."

Shichio studied Nezumi through narrowed eyes. Was this a bluff? No. A bluff rarely made perfect sense. Shichio reconsidered the ploy with Ōda Tomonosuke in a new light. He was Nene's informant, to be sure, but to what purpose? Was she devious enough to collect reports on Shichio's *happiness*?

Yes. There was no end to her cunning. But Shichio would not be taken in so quickly. "Suppose I believe you. Suppose your lady honestly wants me to live out my days here in the blessed north, with a certain boy's hollowed-out, gilded, jewel-encrusted skull as my chamber pot. If your mistress were to make this gift to me, how would she go about it?"

"She wouldn't. She is to remain an innocent party. But what you do of your own accord is not her concern." Nezumi reached into the sleeve of his over-robe and produced a small scroll. "See here," he said, flattening the scroll on the tatami. "On the southern flank of Mount Fuji there is another volcano called Ashitaka. On the southern slopes of Ashitaka there is a hamlet so small that even the villagers themselves have not taken the trouble to name it."

"Sounds charming," Shichio grumbled. He'd grown up in such a village, knee-deep in muck, eternally sweating, besieged by biting flies. He was all too happy to leave those memories by the wayside. A few years back, while campaigning with Hashiba, he'd razed his village to the ground. He had taken a bitter-tasting pleasure in lighting the first torch himself. And now he had come full circle: Kanagawa-juku was large enough to warrant a name on the map, but only just.

"The hamlet sits at the mouth of a narrow valley," said Nezumi. "Follow the stream up the valley and you will find Ōbyō Falls."

"Or I can stand on my own roof and have a piss." Shichio had never understood the commoners' fascination with waterfalls. He much preferred a book of poetry or an evening of kabuki. It was not mere beauty that captivated him, but artistry. "Make your point."

"At the falls there is a teahouse, as secluded as any place on earth. My lady will go there under the pretense of visiting a beautiful site. She will tell her husband she enjoyed her time in the north and wants to see more of it. The truth is that this teahouse is where I am to arrange a meeting between my lady and the Bear Cub."

Shichio scoffed. "I think not. If there is one thing that boy is known for, it is sensing a trap. What makes you think he will come?"

"He is a fugitive. He knows my lady cannot meet him in the open. Besides, I'll tell him it's safe. Heh heh." There was that ghoulish smile again. "What I won't tell him is that there is a rock shelf overlooking the teahouse, about halfway up the cliff. From below it is invisible; the spray from the waterfall makes the plants grow thick and lush. From the teahouse one only sees the cliff and the greenery clinging to it. If my lord were to lie in wait up there, perhaps with a platoon of archers . . ."

Then they might engage in a little more than bear hunting, Shichio thought. If Nene caught a stray arrow in the fracas, it would only serve her right for colluding with a known criminal.

No. Shichio would not be so lucky. Or rather, Nene would not be so naive as to place herself in harm's way, not while a host of Shichio's archers lay within bowshot. She would take shelter in the teahouse, surrounded by a ring of armored guards. She might even place troops of her own atop the rock shelf, to ensure Shichio's good behavior. It did not matter. Shichio would bring bodyguards of his own, in case she intended to play him false. But he would go. He knew he would never have a clearer shot at that damnable boy.

"When?" he said.

"My lady already rides for Ashitaka. She departed Kyoto some days ago. When I find the Bear Cub, I will send word to her, and when I hear back—"

"*How?* How, damn you, how can you find this boy when all of my hunters cannot?"

"Heh. I just sing his name." Nezumi gave Shichio a gleefully guilty grin. "Don't forget, Lord Kumanai, the boy wants me to find him. He's got spies of his own, thanks to that wife of his. Put the right words in the right ears and sooner or later he'll come calling."

"What then?"

"Then I'll send word to you, and to Lady Nene, and we'll all gather at Ōbyō Falls. The Bear Cub will never know what hit him."

And neither will Nene, Shichio thought. The woman knew him too well: if this was a trap, the Bear Cub was juicy bait. Shichio could not pass it up. But neither would he walk in blindly. He harbored no illusions: he was bait himself. Bear bait. He was the only prize that would draw out the Bear Cub. Nene intended to use Shichio and Daigoro as praying mantises, captured and tossed into a wicker cage. They were supposed to fight for her amusement.

So be it. The surviving mantis could still bite the fingers holding the cage. Shichio would not forgo his clearest shot at the Bear Cub, but if he must walk into this trap, he would not go unprepared. Kyoto was a long way from Ashitaka. Shichio would arrive first, and set his own traps in place.

"Be gone," he told Nezumi. "And be sure to thank your mistress for all of her lovely gifts."

He did not bother to see his guest to the door. He had too much planning to do.

38

"I know you," Daigoro told the woman threatening him with the knife.

She was a skeletal hag with skin like old leather. Her thick, yellowed fingernails matched her sharp, yellowed teeth. The knife quivered in her bony hand, but if she dropped it, she had seven more tucked into her belt. Not to mention the seven men with her, all of them armed to the hilt.

They had chosen their battleground well. It was late in the hour of the tiger, not long before sunrise, when Daigoro was still groggy. Katsushima insisted that they always set out before first light. He and Daigoro were safest when they were on the move, and Shichio's bear hunters were mercenaries—"a shiftless breed, the lot of them," according to Katsushima. "Never up before dawn. Even the *rōnin* among them lose their soldier's discipline. And why shouldn't they? There's no sergeant to whip them if they decide to have a lie-in."

Not this bunch. They must have stalked Daigoro to the bordello where he and Katsushima had spent the night. Now, just as Daigoro was saddling his mare, the scrawny harridan and her pack had formed a semicircle at the mouth of the bordello's stable. The only way out was to cut a path through them—no trouble at all, if only they were armed with knives like their ringleader. Daigoro and Katsushima had faced numbers far worse than four to one. But the other seven were archers, with seven arrows already drawn back to their ears. Daigoro could hear their bowstrings creak.

"You're Whalebelly's woman," he said.

"Who?" She laughed—an awful hacking sound—when Daigoro's meaning struck her. "Whalebelly! That name fits him as well as any. Well, Whale Carcass now, thanks to you."

"Daigoro, who is this creature?" Katsushima asked. Muffled by his words, his katana clicked as he loosened it in its scabbard.

"A *yamabushi* I met near Fuji-no-tenka. One who takes her coin from Shichio now, unless I miss my guess."

"You don't miss," said the woman. "Now you can come peaceful or we can stick you full of skewers."

And maybe roast a few skewers over a fire after it's done, Daigoro thought. She looked like she hadn't eaten in days. But maybe she always looked that way. Maybe that haunted look in her eye had nothing to do with hunger. She might simply have spent too long in the wild.

She stood no chance against Daigoro. His father's sword was nestled deep in his horse's pack, but his *wakizashi* still had superior reach over her knives. He'd already seen that she had a practiced hand, but a thrown knife was a weapon of desperation. It lacked penetrating power, and Daigoro was armored. Unless she hit him in the eye or the throat, he would be on her after the first throw.

And then a hail of arrows would strike him down. Some would blunt themselves on his armor, but not all. Two cornered swordsmen had little hope against seven archers. Even if he and Katsushima somehow managed to find cover, their hunters had only to set fire to the barn. There was no escape.

"How did you find me?" he asked.

"She had help," said the nearest of the archers. He wore a black *hachimaki* and an evil smile. Even in the twilight, Daigoro could see his teeth were stained and broken. "Not that it'll do her much good. Heh heh."

He loosed his arrow, but not at Daigoro. It hissed as it flew, and punched through the breastbone of one of the other bowmen.

That one let fly as he fell, but his shot wobbled and sailed wide. The rest went to pieces. Some froze in horror. Others trained their arrows on the traitor. Whalebelly's woman took her eye off of Daigoro just for an instant, to see what was happening. Then Daigoro cut her down.

Bowstrings hummed and men cried out. Katsushima was as fast as an arrow himself. Somehow he was in the fray before Daigoro even managed to pull his *wakizashi* free of its first victim. In no time at all, only three were left standing: Daigoro, Katsushima, and the traitor in the black *hachimaki*, who stood with his palms out in a peacemaking gesture. He'd tossed his weapon aside, and he eyed Katsushima's sword warily. "Easy now, gentlemen, I've come to help."

Daigoro didn't bother sheathing his *wakizashi*. "The last man who offered me his help tried to kill me." And damn near succeeded too, he thought. He was gasping for air even after such a short skirmish. His body still hadn't recovered from the bloodletting he'd suffered at the hands of the priest-assassin.

"Not the last one," Katsushima said, "the last two." He took a menacing step forward, driving the turncoat archer back. "Ōda broke his word, Daigoro. We've gone weeks without detection, but no sooner did we cross his path than this lot crosses ours."

"Heh heh," said the traitor. "It's a good thing he turned on you. This old bag's been hunting you since Yoshiwara." He nodded toward the dead woman still clutching her knife. "She came close too, before I found her. More talent than the rest of these put together."

"And you led her straight to me," said Daigoro. "You're Lady Nene's envoy, *neh*?"

"Nezumi, at your service." He bowed as deeply as he could without skewering himself on Katsushima's sword.

"And Katsushima's right? Ōda betrayed us to Shichio?"

"Not quite. You could say that was me. Ōda delivered

your message to my lady, she delivered it to Shichio—by way of the honorable Nezumi-sama, of course. Then he paid me extra to kill you instead of passing along her instructions."

How nice, Daigoro thought. The peacock never stops pecking at me. "Then I'm glad you're more loyal to her than to him. Now what do you want?"

"Only to do my duty. My lady wants to meet you and see . . . well, whatever it is you have to show her." He peered into the stable, perhaps hoping to spy something in Daigoro's pack. "She intends to make good on your agreement. In fact, all the arrangements are already in motion."

"Oh?"

Nezumi smiled an ugly, brown-toothed smile. "Yes. Lady Nene already rides north. She will meet you at a teahouse on the southern slope of Mount Ashitaka, at the foot of Ōbyō Falls. Do you know it?"

"The waterfall, no. The mountain, yes." Daigoro had seen it quite recently, in fact. It stood in view of Yasuda Jinichi's castle, Fuji-no-tenka.

"I have a map for you, if you won't cut my hand off when I try to reach for it." He looked hopefully at Katsushima, who took a half step back but did not lower his sword. Gingerly plucking a little scroll from the pocket in his sleeve, he said, "Lady Nene intends to meet you in the teahouse. It is a very old place, perfectly secure—except for one thing. There is a rocky shelf, hidden from below by all the greenery growing in the spray of the falls. It overlooks the teahouse and it's far larger than anyone would suspect. Large enough for Shichio to hide a platoon of archers up there, waiting for you."

Daigoro looked at Nezumi's scroll for a moment, wondering if he should touch it. A year ago he would have taken it without hesitation. That was before he'd felt the sting of a *shuriken* laced with contact poison, or had poisoned tea poured on his face by an assassin dressed as a priest. "Open it," he said, and only after he'd seen Nezumi handle every part of the scroll did he consent to holding it himself.

"Cagey bastard, aren't you? Heh heh. I like that." Nezumi pointed at the scroll. "I gave Shichio something similar, and I told him everything I'm telling you. But I left one thing out: that rock shelf isn't safe. It's halfway up the cliff, but you can't climb any higher from there. The rock's too brittle, and there's too much spray from the falls. But if a fellow were to come down the long way, from higher up on the mountain, he could walk right to the edge of that cliff and no one on the shelf would ever hear him coming. If he were a sneaky fellow like you, he might bring some of those Mongol grenades with him, assuming he knew someone resourceful enough to get his hands on them. Have you ever seen one of those?"

"No."

"They make an awful mess, believe you me. That gunpowder is the reason Emperor Go-Uda prayed for the *kamikaze* to sink the fleets of Kublai Khan. Wicked witchcraft, that stuff. Louder than thunder and it stinks like hellfire, but it gets the job done."

Daigoro knew that well enough. He'd taken a musket ball in the chest in the Battle of the Green Cliff. If not for his Sora breastplate, it would have burst his heart like a melon. And he'd read the stories of the Mongol invasions, of course. Kublai Khan was said to have deployed great iron wheels taller than a horse, full of black powder, spewing destruction everywhere they rolled. Daigoro wasn't sure how much of that to believe, but he'd heard of the handheld variety too. Globes of ceramic or iron, it was said, packed full of fire and death. They were the very embodiment of dishonor, capable of killing without the slightest need for discipline, strength, or skill.

He said as much. "Aren't you a choosy one?" Nezumi replied. "Heh heh. Go ahead, walk right up to the teahouse and announce yourself at the door. See how far your honor gets you then."

I may have to, Daigoro thought. If Nezumi instructed Shichio to hide on this unseen ledge, then that was the one place Shichio wouldn't be. He didn't have it in him to trust people, least of all Nene's own servant. He wouldn't place himself in a predictable position, and he certainly wouldn't box himself in. Looking at Nezumi's map, Daigoro saw that the teahouse itself was the only spot that offered an escape route back out of the valley. That was where Shichio would be. But that ledge would still be crawling with assassins.

"These Mongol grenades," he said reluctantly, "I don't suppose you happen to know anyone who's selling them."

"Clever boy. I have a crate of them for you, and the price is low: just one look at whatever it is you carry for my lady."

"No. Tell her to meet me at the Sora compound in Izu. She can see it there."

Nezumi huffed and threw his hands up. "No. She rides for Ōbyō Falls even as we speak."

"Then she won't have to ride much farther to reach the Soras. I will meet her there, nowhere else."

He returned Nezumi's defiant stare with one of his own. Daigoro had no intention of walking into a trap, and although he knew he and Lady Nene had a common enemy, there was a limit to his trust. Besides, he had to make good on his word to Lord Sora. Yasuda Kenbei and that she-wolf Azami still had a financial stranglehold on House Okuma, and they were relying on Sora's support to tighten it. With luck, Sora would see Streaming Dawn as not a gift but a curse. Then Daigoro could give the knife to Nene and still retain Sora's loyalty.

In the end Nezumi was the one to break eye contact, and Daigoro knew he'd won. "Have it your own way," Nezumi said. "I'll find my lady on the road and tell her to meet you at the Sora compound. Then you'll see how she reacts to taking orders from the likes of you."

39

Lord Sora's prisoner was a stringy, flea-bitten wretch. He was as pallid as a cave-dwelling creature, pinching his eyes tight against the sun. Daigoro wondered how long it had been since he'd seen daylight.

The prisoner hung limply from his bonds, a portrait of defeat. Not that struggle would have done him much good; the ropes that held him were thick and sure. His jailer had bound him wrist and ankle to a stout length of pine that was planted into the ground in the center of Lord Sora's courtyard. A considerable crowd had amassed around him, some out of duty, others out of curiosity. Rumors had spread of Streaming Dawn's power. Gruesome as it was, many of these people wanted to see it for themselves.

There were orange-clad Sora samurai, servants in faded blues and grays, Daigoro and Katsushima in their armor of white, Lady Nene in resplendent purple, her honor guard in Toyotomi red and gold, her handmaids dressed to complement their mistress in shades of lavender, lilac, and plum. The colors were radiant in the bright noon sun, which warmed the dwarf pines surrounding the courtyard and filled the air with their scent.

Even such a beautiful day could not lighten Daigoro's mood. "Lord Sora," he whispered, "is there no other way?"

Sora Izu-no-kami Nobushige stood with his guests not two paces from the poor soul bound to the stake. He dwarfed Daigoro and Nene, and the broad yellow shoulders of his *haori* made him seem all the larger. Even in his winter years he had strong, heavy arms. He wore the armor that had made him famous, impervious steel lacquered in the colors of sunset. His white eyebrows stood out starkly against his red face, and he arched one of them skeptically at Daigoro. "Are you so delicate that you can't stand the sight of blood? I had thought as much of Lady Nene, but not of you."

Lady Nene replied with a cold, superior smile. "Have you ever seen a man crucified, Lord Sora? It is a ghastly sight, and also one of my honored husband's latest fancies. I assure you, a little bloodshed will not trouble my sleep."

"It is honor, not blood, that concerns me," Daigoro said. "What were this man's crimes?"

"He broke a blacksmith's arm in a fight," Sora said. He spoke too loudly; a lifetime of hammering steel in the forge had dulled his hearing. "He cost a good man his livelihood."

That was hardly true; a broken arm would heal quickly enough. But Lord Sora was partial to blacksmiths. Armoring had been his highest martial art. Because the prisoner and the smith had fought on his lands, Sora was sovereign to give any punishment he saw fit. Daigoro saw no need to kill this man, much less to torture him in full public view, but he had no say in the matter.

"I will not have a *rōnin* lecture me on questions of honor," Sora said. He strode forward, slid Streaming Dawn from its sheath, and pushed it slowly into the prisoner's gut.

Gasps and whispers filled the courtyard, barely audible over the prisoner's agony. He wailed and cursed but did not bleed.

"Well, now," Sora boomed. "I will confess this is something I did not expect."

"Nor I," said Lady Nene. Daigoro could hear the wonder in her voice. He was awestruck himself, even though this was not the first time he'd seen the blade's witchery. He found himself unable to take his eyes from the bloodless wound.

The prisoner pulled mightily at his bonds, perhaps in

the hope of drawing the knife from his gut. But the cords held fast. He could only kick at the ground and howl.

"Young Daigoro-san tells me he suffered the blade's bite himself," Lord Sora said. "It was quite painful, *neh*?"

"More painful coming out," Daigoro muttered. He was accustomed to a *sama* from Sora Nobushige, but that was before he'd surrendered his name and station.

"What of subsequent wounds? Does Streaming Dawn make them any easier to bear?"

Sora drew his *wakizashi* and traced a shallow, experimental cut across the prisoner's throat. It cut veins, tendons, arteries, but not so deep as the vocal cords. The prisoner cried louder than ever, but impossibly he still lived.

This raised another chorus of astonished gasps. It drew one from Lady Nene as well. "My, my," she said. "Lord Sora, your weapon is most extraordinary."

"Mine? No. If this is the cost of immortality, then I will pass it by." He looked at the bloodless prisoner and did not suppress a shudder. "Take the dagger if you wish, my lady, but take it far from here."

With that Sora yanked Streaming Dawn from the doomed man's flesh. It loosed two hot red torrents, spurting at once from neck and belly. The prisoner died almost instantly.

Sora raised a finger and two serving men dashed forward to kneel in the dust. "Clean this," he said, handing one of them Streaming Dawn. "And find something to wrap it in—something beautiful, mind you. Her ladyship deserves our finest silk."

Nene graced him with a smile. "You are too kind, Lord Sora."

That was sufficient indication for the gathered host that the excitement was over. Servants hurried about their duties and soldiers returned to their posts. Lord Sora made use of the commotion as a rare opportunity to lower his voice. "It is no kindness, my lady. Unless young Daigoro is mistaken, this blade comes with more than a curse. He took it from a *shinobi*, which means somewhere a *shinobi* clan knows it is missing. They will come for it. I make this gift to you because Daigoro-san asked it of me, but if you take my advice you will cast this weapon into the sea. You may keep the silk."

Daigoro studied him with a suspicious eye. In all their dealings together, he'd only known Lord Sora to make matters needlessly difficult. This was going far too smoothly.

Sora noticed he was under scrutiny. "I haven't forgotten you, Daigoro-san. You've made good on your word. Despite your earlier insult, you will find I am a man of honor. Since you delivered the blade, I will support you against that money-grubbing rat in the south."

Daigoro hated to raise the question he knew he must ask. "If I may, Lord Sora, what do you mean by 'support'?"

"Hmph! Trust a renegade to drink of a man's *sake* and then question its quality! I mean just what I said, boy. Yasuda Kenbei wants me to call in all my debts with you. I pledge not to. What more could you require?"

You might actually take my side, Daigoro thought, instead of walking away from the field of battle. But that was too much to ask. "A thousand pardons, Sora-sama. You are most generous."

"Hmph."

The awkward moment was broken by the return of one of the manservants, who came bearing an elegant box of polished Chinese rosewood. The servant knelt before Lady Nene, raising up the box with both hands and bowing his head as low as it would go. Lord Sora rose to the occasion, overcoming his righteous indignation long enough to show courtesy to his guest. "Streaming Dawn," he said, opening the box for her. "In my wife's calligraphy case, I see. There will be hell to pay when she finds it missing, but I will happily give you the case if you will cast that evil knife away. My forges are stoked and ready; you have only to throw it in."

"Your chivalry is admirable," Nene said, "but no. I thank you for your gift. Daigoro-san, I thank you as well, for negotiating this exchange. . . ."

Daigoro scarcely heard her. His attention was fixed on Lord Sora, who was far happier than he should have been. A petty man did not part easily with such a lordly prize. There was only one explanation, but Daigoro dared not voice it aloud—not in Sora's own home, right in front of the most honored guest he'd ever received. He'd already seen how Sora punished those who offended him.

"My lady," Daigoro said, thinking quickly, "do you know the story of Prince Yamato?"

Nene regarded him with puzzlement. "Of course. Everyone does."

"I was just thinking of how he defeated the bandit kings. Their armies were so dense that he could not march against them, so instead he went on his own, disguising himself as a woman." Daigoro felt silly saying it aloud. Nene was quite right to say everyone knew the tale, but he was not retelling it for her benefit. It was Lord Sora's reaction that mattered most.

"In Prince Yamato's day it was a cunning tactic," Daigoro went on, "but today . . . today I am not so sure. We are no longer plagued by bandit kings; these are nobler times. Is it still in the way of *bushidō* to resort to such blatant deceit?"

Sora's face grew redder with every word; he seemed angry enough to burst into flame. "What do you mean to imply, boy?"

"Nothing. Nothing at all. I was just thinking of what I should have done from the beginning, as soon as I took Streaming Dawn. Since *shinobi* are certain to come for it, perhaps I should have disguised it. If I had a second *tantō* forged in its image, I could have passed off the counterfeit and kept the genuine Inazuma for myself. But no, what am I thinking? I am no weaponsmith, and I have no forge."

Nene's gaze rolled slowly toward Lord Sora's smithy. Sora himself had eyes only for Daigoro. "Speak carefully, Bear Cub. I can arrange for you to become intimately familiar with the forge."

"I mean no offense, Sora-sama. I was only thinking of what I might do in your stead. My Akiko has a jewelry box to rival your wife's calligraphy case. Suppose I had placed Streaming Dawn in it, and offered it to Lady Nene just as you did. If I had been wiser . . . well, if I'd fashioned a false Inazuma, I could keep the true blade for myself. It's what Prince Yamato would have done, but is it what *bushidō* would have me do?"

Lord Sora studiously avoided looking at the rosewood case. That by itself told Daigoro everything he needed to know. Sora glared at him, red-faced, breathing loudly through his nose. Daigoro wondered whether the two of them would come to blows then and there. He released all the tension in his arms; looser muscles made for a faster draw.

It was Lady Nene who intervened. She calmed both of them just by clearing her throat. "Daigoro-san, shame on you: you've offended your host. Lord Sora, I apologize on the young man's behalf. Sometimes we must forgive the youth; they have not the wisdom of our years."

"They certainly don't," Sora grumbled.

"And sometimes men must forgive women for their pettiness," Nene said. "I am ashamed to have accepted your generous offer of this beautiful calligraphy case. It belongs with your wife. Please, forgive me for being so selfish. Take it back, I beg you. I should be happy to carry Streaming Dawn in a rice sack."

Daigoro could hardly contain his astonishment. He'd never had close dealings with the aristocracy; this was the first time he'd seen their weapons deployed so artfully. She could have ordered Lord Sora to prove the knife he'd given her was the genuine article—by stabbing himself, for instance. Daigoro was certain he'd bleed. Instead, she caught him in the act and she still found a way for him to retain his honor. He bowed, thanked her on behalf of his wife, and returned with the manservant to the house. "To find some other vessel worthy of Streaming Dawn," he insisted.

That left Daigoro and Katsushima alone with Lady Nene—or rather, as close to alone as anyone was allowed to be with a woman of her station. Her honor guard and ladies-in-waiting were ever-present walls behind her. She approached Daigoro in her small, shuffling steps. He hadn't seen her in the daylight before; she was quite beautiful in her white face paint. She smelled of flowers, and her cloth-of-gold kimono glinted in the sun. It spoke volumes of her trust in him that she was willing to stand within sword's reach.

"That was cleverly done, Daigoro-san. You have impressed me, and not for the first time. I believe my envoy promised you a gift? From Mongolia?"

"Yes, my lady."

"You shall have it. Is there anything else you require of me to complete our pact?"

Daigoro glanced around, a little nervous about what he was about to ask. But he had given it considerable thought. "Well, yes. Your . . . your kimono is most beautiful, my lady. I wonder if you might be willing to give me one."

Nene tittered like a child. "Oh, my dear boy. Even now you have the presence of mind to think of gifts for your wife?"

"Not quite, Nene-dono."

In the end Nene would not give him a garment of her own, but she did ask her handmaid to give him something. The boy was so small that it was not hard to find a girl of his height.

He had an intriguing plan, worthy of Prince Yamato in the tales of old. Now that is a fine thing to think of a samurai, Nene thought. How many men today could be likened to Yamato himself? Like the legendary prince, Daigoro was courageous and cunning. But fortune had always sided with Yamato; not so with Daigoro. She feared this time the boy might be too clever for his own good.

It was a pity, sending a boy his age into that valley—especially a boy as brave and unlucky as this one. But if anyone stood a chance against Shichio, Daigoro was the one. She hoped he would survive. He might make a fine ally for her husband one day.

In any case, he was still an excellent subject for a haiku. The bear that was a bear trap. But better to wait until after the battle at Ōbyō Falls before she wrote it. She had to know whether the bear survived.

BOOK NINE

HEISEI ERA, THE YEAR 22

(2010 CE)

40

"You do understand," Mariko said into the phone, "I'm not fucking killing anyone."

"You've made that quite clear," said Furukawa. The son of a bitch sounded like he was smiling, as if he found her moral principles cute. Mariko hated this idea more than ever, but she didn't know what else to do. On her own she had no resources to bring down Jōko Daishi, or to find the thousand-and-some-odd first graders he'd kidnapped. The news anchors bumped up the number by the hour. Mariko had a sneaking suspicion that the final tally would be 1,304.

She mussed her still-wet hair with a towel; a quick shower had woken her up a bit and cleared her mind. A stripe of pain sang out when she ran the towel over the stitches in her scalp. "Ow. So what happens next? Thanks to you, I don't have a badge. Kind of hard for a detective to do much detecting without one."

"Not to worry. I can provide whatever resources you require—including a badge and sidearm, if carrying them illicitly doesn't offend your sensibilities. If it's computer access you need—"

"I get it. You've already hacked the department's system. That's a felony, you know."

"Oh, quite."

Mariko could think of a few things she'd like to do

with invisible access throughout the TMPD's network. Ending Captain Kusama's career would be a good start. Furukawa had the hackers to do that sort of thing—assuming, of course, that Kusama hadn't already done the deed himself. The press wouldn't forgive him for bullshitting them about Jemaah Islamiyah and covering up what he knew about the Divine Wind. At the moment he sat safely in the eye of that particular storm; this mass kidnapping made everyone forget about everything else. It was just his style to find some positive media spin even in a crisis like this.

"I told you before," Furukawa said, "I sought you out because you are ideally placed for our purposes. First, if your departed sensei was right, then your destiny is to kill Koji Makoto with Glorious Victory Unsought—"

"Which I'm not going to do."

"Yes, yes. Second, you have unique connections with police, drug dealers, and yakuzas—"

"Which you have too, so why drag me into this?"

"We're king-makers. Street-level criminality is not our milieu."

"So much for 'no place you cannot reach.'"

"On the contrary. We have you."

She heard crystal clink against crystal—a decanter gently bumping a whisky tumbler, if she had to guess. "This crisis will not be resolved in the halls of power," he said. "It will be resolved when someone sees a panic-stricken child waving frantically from a window. Your people make their living by knowing what happens on the streets. Talk to them. Find out what they've heard, what they've seen."

Mariko didn't need to think about that for long. "Well, maybe you shouldn't have disgraced me with my department, huh? A lot of cops won't want to take my calls right now. I can talk to my CIs, but I have to tell you, my guys know dope, not kooky cults."

"This kidnapping was a massive effort. Koji-san must have employed hundreds of people to carry it out—"

"And you're hoping for a blabbermouth in the group.

Keep hoping. These are cultists. Fanatically loyal. Some are willing to blow themselves up."

"Detective Oshiro, you have a pernicious habit of interrupting people. I must say I don't care for it."

"Gee, sorry."

He took a sip of whatever he was drinking. "As I was saying, Detective, he must have deployed many hundreds. Our intelligence indicates his entire cult is fewer than a thousand strong. Not all of them can be in his inner circle. One of them will talk."

"We can hope. But I don't like our chances. Start looking at traffic camera footage. Maybe we can spot . . . no, you've tried that already, haven't you?"

"Yes. The entire system underwent a 'routine software upgrade' at a quarter of eight this morning—seven hours *after* it was scheduled to happen, and about ten minutes before the first report of an abduction. We trained Koji-san too well."

"You think?"

Mariko threaded her arms awkwardly into yesterday's blouse, shifting the phone from one ear to the other and back, then pinching it between her ear and shoulder as she buttoned up. "Okay, but he took them by car, *neh*? Like, a lot of cars. It's the only way to move that many kids. So what if—?"

"Let me stop you there. The answer you're fumbling for is traffic helicopter footage. We've already captured it and we're analyzing it now. He was very careful; thus far we have detected no anomalies."

"Okay, fine," she said. "So you've thought of everything. I'll talk to my people, for all the good it will do. But word gets around about cops, so some of my CIs will know I've been suspended. They may not be willing to talk."

"You can tell them you've been reinstated. You'll find a badge and identification waiting for you in a box on the porch. A pistol and holster too; you prefer a SIG-Sauer P230, as I recall."

"How did you—?"

"There is no place the Wind cannot reach."

Mariko groaned. "What if I hadn't called this morning? You were just going to leave it sitting there?"

"Oh, but you did call."

"Whatever. I'm not taking the pistol."

"It's not illegal. I took the liberty of creating a permit for you."

"I said I'm not taking it."

"Jōko Daishi is dangerous. You should know when it comes time to face him: he is extraordinarily difficult to kill."

Face him? Mariko had no intention of doing that. She'd find him, keep eyes on him, and call the cops. Regardless of whether Furukawa was right about all the fate stuff, it was clear that Mariko and Jōko Daishi were on a collision course. She couldn't be tempted to pull a gun on him if she didn't carry one in the first place, and then she couldn't accidentally fulfill the destiny the Wind had planned for her.

Even so, something Furukawa had said made her curious. "You told me something like that before. You said he's almost bulletproof. Why?"

"There was an ancient weapon. Streaming Dawn, it was called. It had . . . oh, shall we say, *unusual* properties."

"I know. Yamada-sensei wrote about it in his notes."

"Well, now! You've been quite the diligent student, haven't you?"

Mariko let out an exasperated grunt. "You don't have to sound so surprised."

"Oh, pleasantly so. A historian's scribblings hardly make for exciting reading material. If you'll pardon my saying so, I didn't know you had the patience."

"Thanks. That makes me feel so much better. What's the deal with Streaming Dawn?"

"Ah, yes. The blade that heals. Well, after a fashion. The Wind unlocked its secrets some years ago. Do you know what we found? The blade needn't be whole to exercise its remarkable power."

"And?"

"It was broken. Four shards, none of them as potent as the original, yet each one has the power to stave off death. The *shōnin* bestow them upon an operative when they deem he is too important to lose."

Mariko nodded. "And they gave one to Jōko Daishi. Got it. I'll toss it in an evidence bag when I arrest him."

"I'm afraid it's not that simple." Furukawa breathed heavily into the phone; Mariko couldn't read the emotion there. "Streaming Dawn had to be embedded in the subject's body to be effective. That was the curse entwined with its blessing. The fragments are no different, but the *shōnin* found an alternative to stabbing oneself. Their solution was . . . well, more permanent, shall we say."

"Yeah?"

"The shards are surgically implanted."

Mariko squirmed. The thought of having a shattered knife stuck in her body made her shudder. "Eww."

"Yes. It's quite painful. Nevertheless, I must urge you to carry that pistol, Detective. You needn't fear killing him with it; your bullets are only likely to slow him a little. But slowing him might make the difference between your survival and an excruciating death."

"Right," Mariko said. It was exactly what he'd like her to believe if he wanted her to kill Jōko Daishi.

"I warn you, Detective Oshiro, his martial training is considerable. You must not face him unarmed."

"I'll take my chances. Good-bye, Furukawa-san."

She finished getting dressed and headed downstairs, where she found Shoji-san in the kitchen over a little pot of rice. "Some breakfast before you go, dear."

"I can't," Mariko said. "I've really got to run. Um . . . listen, I've got to ask. Do you know where I can find your son?"

Shoji deflated a little. "No."

"I promise I won't hurt him. Furukawa wants me to. He says I'm supposed to kill him. With Yamada-sensei's sword, no less. So here's the deal: I'm not going back to my apartment. I won't even set foot in the same room as the sword. And I'm going to give you the gun that Furukawa left for me on your porch. I swear to you, Shoji-san, I'm not going to do their dirty work for them. I'm not going to hurt your son."

Shoji's unseeing eyes gazed blankly at the steam rising off the rice. "I know."

"I can't say *they* won't. But I promise you this: I will do my best to see your son brought to justice. He's going to have a judge, a jury, and a defense attorney. From there, I have to tell you I hope he spends the rest of his life in prison. But he's not going to be executed by some assassin. Not if I have anything to say about it."

"I know, Mariko-san. I don't want to tell you. . . ." Shoji cleared her throat and blinked back tears. The way her eye scars bent at the corners made her seem sadder. "My child or all the others. For my whole life I've chosen mine. Today . . . Mariko, don't go after him. I see him wearing the mask. You have the sword in hand. He can see it coming. Do you understand, Mariko? He has seen his death coming. He sees it as a bright light, as bright as the sun. You'll try to ambush him. You'll fail."

"Am I going to . . . ?"

Mariko couldn't bring herself to finish the question. It was better not to know. If she got the wrong answer, she might have trouble seeing this through.

"I've got to go, Shoji-san." Mariko hurried for the door.

41

By ten o'clock the numbers were in: 1,304 public elementary schools in the Tokyo school system; 1,290 kids taken; thirteen botched attempts; two fatalities after one of the kidnappers got himself killed along with his abductee in a stupid, preventable car crash; zero sightings of Jōko Daishi, the Divine Wind, or the kidnapped children; nineteen attempts on Mariko's part to get something useful out of a contact or confidential informant, with zero results to show for it.

Every school was locked down, not just in Tokyo but Chiba, Yokohama, Saitama—every major city in the region. Not just the grade schools, either; all of them, public and private, from kindergarten through twelfth grade. There weren't enough police to cordon every school—not even close—so principals and teachers were left to fend for themselves. The advice they were getting from the National Police Agency was to lock down the campus completely. The NPA needed head counts from every classroom, and the counts had to be pristine. Well-meaning parents were being arrested for trying to take their kids home. The arresting officers had no choice; there was no way to tell between an earnest mother and a cultist of the Divine Wind.

Tokyo was crippled. Its hospitals were plague zones,

its roadways were death traps, its airports and train stations were targets. If there was a positive side for Mariko, it was that getting around town had never been easier. Traffic was light, and though the sky was swarming with police choppers, they were hunting for kids, not speeding drivers. Mariko didn't own a car, but Furukawa had left the white BMW parked outside Shoji's house, with the keys in the same box as the pistol, badge, and ID. As promised, Mariko left the gun in Shoji's foyer, unloaded and safetied. She kept the false badge, knowing it could get her in trouble but predicting greater trouble if she went without it. It hadn't done her much good thus far; none of her contacts had asked to see it, and even if they had, none of them knew anything.

Most of the kids hadn't been yanked screaming off the streets. That much was clear. There were trusted adults involved here, coconspirators, but Mariko couldn't let her thoughts wander that way. That was police thinking. There would already be over a hundred detectives tasked with identifying the kidnappers and figuring out how they were connected. It would take weeks to reach the conclusion Mariko already had in hand: they were all members of the Divine Wind. What she needed to know was where the hell they went, and that was where she was drawing a blank.

Furukawa was right: Mariko was in a position unlike any of his other operatives. Very few people could move as fluidly between the police and the criminal element. Any cop who knew of Mariko's suspension also knew it was a major indiscretion to keep her up to date on the details of the kidnapping investigations, but Han didn't care about rules like that. She had connections he didn't, so for him it was a simple quid pro quo. At the same time, she wasn't handcuffed by everything that usually limited a detective on duty. She could harass CIs with open-ended questions that had nothing to do with a real live case. She could even coerce them if she felt like it, and most importantly, if she broke any laws she could only be charged as a civilian. It was impossible to charge her with official misconduct, the felony that would end her career.

She pulled the Beemer into the parking garage of a posh Ebisu high-rise and slid it on squealing tires next to a giant red Land Rover. A hulking, sour-faced man was waiting for her. His arms were big enough to test the tensile strength of his ill-fitting suit jacket, and his chest was even bulkier. Mariko saw not just muscles there but also the outlines of an armored vest under his shirt. She got out of the car and said, "Hi, Bullet. Where's your boss?"

A darkly tinted window rolled down in the backseat of the Land Rover, revealing the broad, square-jawed face of Kamaguchi Hanzō. It was his ruthless tenacity, not just his sharp teeth and pronounced underbite, that had earned him the nickname the Bulldog. He maintained that reputation by never backing down from a fight, and by ripping people's throats out when they crossed him. Even by yakuza standards he was a bloodthirsty brute.

"Well, look at you," he said. "My little *gokudō* cop. Someone kick your ass, honey? You look beat to hell."

"Thanks."

"Come around this way. Let me see if you been keeping that tight little ass in shape."

There was a reason Mariko kept her car between herself and the man she'd come to see. The Bulldog was unpredictable, prone to fits of anger. She wouldn't get within arm's reach if she didn't have to. The fact that he couldn't ogle her as easily was just an unexpected perk.

"You know why I'm here," she said. "Kidnapped children. I want to know where they went."

"Depends. What are they worth?"

"What?"

"Can I buy them? Can I sell them? No. So I don't give a shit where they are."

Lovely. He was every bit as charming as she remembered. "Don't be naive," she said. "Thirteen hundred kids is a hell of a lot. You want to tell me not one yakuza's kid is in there? I thought you people took care of your own."

"Not my kid, not my problem. Plus, your friend did his homework. He didn't touch anyone who shouldn't be touched."

Go figure, Mariko thought. Jōko Daishi had planned

for everything. And he probably used the Wind's resources to do it. She still couldn't believe she'd gotten into bed with Furukawa.

"Look," she said, "you have a lot of people in this town. Someone has to have seen something. Help me this one time." Hating herself for saying it, she added, "I'll owe you one."

"Owe me one? What do you think you got? I hear you're on the outs with the cops."

Mariko flashed her badge. "I'm back in. Why else would I be investigating the kids?"

"Beats me. Maybe it's got something to do with those sweet wheels." His mouth widened into a smile, a hideous expression on such a cruel face. "Is that a real badge? Get over here and give me a closer look."

"Go fuck yourself, Bulldog."

"Heh. Still think you're pretty *gokudō*, huh?"

Not today, Mariko thought. She could use a little bad-ass mojo. But when dealing with a bulldog, if you didn't have it, you had to fake it. "You know what I think? I think you're not holding out on me at all. I think you don't know shit. All those cons you're running, all those front companies, all the sharks you've got collecting protection money, and what are they good for? Not one of them has seen a damn thing."

The Bulldog snarled. "Honey, this is a dangerous game you're playing."

"Is it? Prove me wrong. Show me the Kamaguchi-gumi can still get it up."

Even Bullet bristled at that, and usually he was about as expressive as a meat cleaver. Kamaguchi flung his door open and stepped out of the Land Rover. By the sound of it, his door left a pretty good dent in the side of Mariko's BMW. He wore a silver-gray suit, and brushing his jacket aside, he jerked a stubby stainless steel revolver out of a hip holster. "You're an annoying little cunt, you know that? I ought to blow your fucking brains out."

That was when Mariko knew she was safe. The Bulldog wasn't long on self-control. If he was going to fly into a rampage, he would have pulled the trigger already. The fact that he was talking, not shooting, meant this was pure theater. So Mariko played her role too. "Come on. Shooting a cop in your own parking garage? You're smarter than that."

It was the exit he needed to back down and still save face in front of his bodyguard. "Smarter? Yeah, this time. Next time you come around here, don't press your luck."

"Have a nice day, Kamaguchi-san."

He got back in the car and slammed the door. Bullet drove him away, leaving Mariko in a stinking haze of diesel fumes. Neither of them decided to shoot her on their way out, and exactly that much had gone right today.

Her phone vibrated irritably in her pocket. She knew who it was before she even looked at the screen. "Yeah?"

"Status report." Furukawa sounded tense.

"The same as it was half an hour ago. Except now I've exhausted *all* of my best leads, not just most of them. Oh, and I pissed off the most violent man in Tokyo. And now I'm a big fat oh-for-twenty, instead of oh-for-sixteen or seventeen or whatever I was the last time you called. What about on your end?"

"About the same."

"So much for all your 'no place we cannot reach' crap."

"That's precisely the trouble, Detective. We have too much data and not enough filters. That's what you're for: to narrow the search parameters. Find me someone who has seen something."

Mariko slipped into the Beemer, put Furukawa on speakerphone, and dropped him in the passenger seat. Then she massaged her eye sockets with her thumbs. She'd already tapped all her best resources. She was running out of ideas and those kids were running out of time. In a kidnapping case, the most important events usually happened within the first three hours: a kidnapper was identified, probable destinations were targeted, and most crucially, the kidnapper decided whether or not to kill the child. The great majority of abductors were family members, they usually stuck to their regular hangouts, and they almost never resorted to murder. But when they did, they almost always killed within three hours of the abduction.

Nothing was typical about this case, but Mariko had a gut-chilling feeling that the three-hour rule still applied. These kids had been gone for just over two hours. If they were still alive, and if Jōko Daishi meant to kill them, all the statistics suggested he'd do it soon.

Mariko's heart fluttered so erratically that it made her queasy. She feared Jōko Daishi had left himself no choice but to kill the children. The longer he kept them alive, the more likely they were to royally fuck up his plans. His people might have signed on for some screaming and crying, but by now they'd have piss and shit to deal with too. They'd had time to build a bit of sympathy for the kids, and maybe for their families as well. The initial adrenaline rush would have given way to exhaustion, unless he dosed his people with uppers to keep them alert; either alternative could lead to a moment's inattention. With the whole city looking for them, Jōko Daishi couldn't afford to let even one child slip away. Mass murder was his safest option.

Though it horrified her to think about it, her mind immediately leaped to modus operandi: how would he go about killing thirteen hundred children? The Nazis could teach him a thing or two. He knew his chemistry; building a gas chamber was well within his expertise. In fact, he'd built one already; Mariko and Han had stumbled across it out in Kamakura. It was a bona fide sex dungeon that doubled as a hermetically sealed suicide chamber for the Great Teacher and his closest disciples. Could that have been just a maquette? Was the full-scale model lying in wait? Or—she could hardly forgive herself for thinking it—was it already jam-packed with frightened kids?

The mental image sickened her, but it also gave her an idea. "What if we're going about this the wrong way?" she said. "We've been thinking about finding someone who saw something. What if we turn it around? He can't keep these kids just anywhere. He needs a hell of a lot of space."

"And?"

"He needs to minimize exposure, *neh*? That rules out a bunch of smaller locations. He'll want one big location, two at most. Somewhere remote, but easily accessible for vehicle traffic."

"Not remote. We're already looking at schools."

"What? Why?"

"Hiding in plain sight, Detective. It's his way—or rather, it's our way, and he learned it all too well. This country has been coping with negative population growth for decades. We've closed over a hundred schools in Tokyo alone. Every one of them is specifically designed to contain large groups of children."

"Come on. Aren't the locals going to notice a bunch of screaming kids at a school that's been deserted all year?"

"Dead children don't scream."

The thought froze Mariko's heart. What a perfect image for Jōko Daishi's next sermon: an ordinary school, ordinary classrooms, ordinary little desks, with a dead child sitting at each one. Then logic kicked in: how would he move the children there? Toss the bodies in the back of a van? One of those police choppers would have spotted them by now: a logjam of vans leading straight to an abandoned school. No, don't go there, she thought. Don't try to figure it out. Jōko Daishi thought all of this through already. You don't need to understand his logistics; you just need to find the kids.

She started the car. "I'm in Ebisu. Text me an address and I'll—"

"Don't bother," said Furukawa. "We've already eliminated all the schools in your area. Continue to work your contacts. What did you hear from Kamaguchi, by the way?"

"Nothing useful. He doesn't give a shit. Not his kids, not his problem. That's what he said."

"Hm. Disappointing."

"That's it? 'Disappointing'?" Mariko picked up the phone and turned it off speaker. "Why don't *you* have insiders in the Kamaguchi-gumi? You're in the king-making business, *neh*? The yakuzas have kings too. Why don't you make another magic phone call?"

"Oh, but I have. Detective Oshiro, if you think I am sitting back enjoying a fine whisky and waiting for you to solve all my problems, you're very much mistaken. You are not alone in this. You are not even very important in this. Please, do your part and I will do mine. Are you certain you can glean nothing more from Kamaguchi?"

"Yes. He left."

"Then I suggest you visit whoever is next on your list."

He hung up, leaving Mariko with a dead phone. *Not very important,* he said. She'd see about that.

42

Despite being a general scumbag, Bumps Ryota had a special place in Mariko's heart. He wasn't the first perp she'd converted into a confidential informant, but he was her first *narcotics* CI, and since Narcotics was her dream job, he was a merit badge of sorts. He'd also leaped to the defense of Mariko's sister, Saori, in a desperate attempt to prevent the yakuza enforcer Fuchida Shūzō from taking her hostage. Bumps got only partial credit for that; it was brave, but it didn't offset the fact that he'd sold meth to Saori for years. That said, he'd taken a through-and-through to the gut from Fuchida's sword, and since Mariko had suffered an identical wound, she supposed that made them scar buddies.

With all of that in his favor, it still had to be said that he lived in a shithole. Mariko found him just as he was leaving a dingy elevator in the dingy lobby of his dingy apartment building. The instant he saw Mariko, he turned and ran. Since he was tweaking, he didn't think it through, which didn't work out all that well for him. He spun face-first into the elevator door just as it was sliding shut. Mariko saw blood and guessed he'd broken his nose. Not to be daunted, and capitalizing on the fact that the impact with his face triggered the door's retraction reflex, he stumbled into the elevator and stabbed the DOOR CLOSE button with the relentless speed of a sewing machine. It didn't help him. Mariko calmly walked the three or four meters to the elevator, stepped in beside him, and said, "What floor?"

"Oh. Um. Nine?"

"Nine it is. Looks like you broke your nose, Bumps."

He touched a bleeding nostril with one hand while the other rubbed absently over his long, perm-stiffened, peroxide-orange hair. Mariko guessed the elevator wouldn't smell great empty, but standing next to Bumps it stank like the bottom of a sweat-moistened laundry hamper. "Bumps, when's the last time you changed your clothes?"

"Uh . . . I'm not for sure on that."

Mariko shook her head in disgust. As far as she knew, Bumps was playing by the rules of their CI arrangement: he provided regular intelligence leading to arrests and he wasn't dealing hard stuff on the side. But nothing about their agreement said he had to stay sober.

"Fuck this, we're getting off here." She hit the THREE button just in time for the elevator to stop there and open up. The musty carpet in the hallway didn't smell any better than the cockroach spray in the elevator, but both of them smelled a whole lot nicer than Bumps.

He floated in the hall in that strange, weightless, tweaker way, as if gravity had only a tenuous hold on him. Between the perm and the peroxide, his hair was as stiff as paintbrush bristles, and since it didn't spill down normally, it reinforced the illusion that he might blow away at any moment. "So, uh, what can I do for you, Officer?"

"You spend time by the harbor, *neh*? Lots of business down that way?"

"Sure. But I'm not, you know, like . . . I mean, we got that agreement."

"Yeah, I remember, Bumps. What time did you wake up this morning? Have you even been up long enough to know what's going on?"

He nodded hugely, his eyes wide. "Those kids? Heavy shit."

"Yeah. So here's the thing: the guy who took them,

he's got to be hiding them somewhere. Somewhere with a lot of room, with no windows, ideally with only one exit. And it has to be a place not a lot of people ever have reason to go. You follow me so far?"

"Uh-huh."

Mariko had her doubts. But she had greater doubts about Furukawa's reasoning. She could buy Jōko Daishi hiding in plain sight; what she didn't buy was that he'd hide exactly where Furukawa expected him to. The image of a school full of dead kids was terrifying, but she just couldn't derail the logical part of her mind that wanted to know how he'd get all the kids in there without being spotted. Today of all days, people were going to call 110 if they saw something suspicious going down in a schoolyard.

Maybe there was a decommissioned school being torn down somewhere. Maybe Jōko Daishi had planned for that months in advance. With the Wind's resources, he could have bought out a construction company, secured the demolition contract for a school, and filled the whole job site with his cultists. That would give him a perfect front for moving kids in a few at a time. All of that was possible. Even so, Mariko thought it much more likely that Furukawa's closed school idea was bogus.

"Here's my theory," she told Bumps. "Shipping containers. No windows, one entry, and once it's locked there's no way for those helicopters up there to spot the kids." And easy to fill with cyanide gas, if that was the way Jōko Daishi wanted to play it. She didn't have the stomach to say that aloud. She felt stupid indulging in a childish superstition like that, but if ever there was a day not to jinx something, today was the day.

Bumps walked to the end of the hall, where a dirty window commanded a less than beautiful view of the harbor. Mariko followed. "A lot of containers down there," he said.

"Exactly. So get down to the waterfront and talk to your people. Have them talk to their people. I'm interested in unusual traffic patterns. Moving these kids is going to take hundreds of cars, so someone's got to have seen—hey, are you listening to me?"

"Huh?" Bumps flinched when Mariko snapped her fingers in his ear. "Yeah. I got you. It's just . . ." He laughed ruefully, and surprised himself as much as Mariko when a tear rolled down his cheek. "Today's not going to be a good day to have a drug problem, know what I mean? If shit goes bad, I don't know if they got enough meth in this city to get me through it."

Mariko took a step back. She actually needed to find her balance; his words struck her like a tsunami. Somehow she'd just assumed that people like Bumps were disconnected from current events, and that these attacks on her city passed right over their heads. Bumps showed her a deeper truth: Jōko Daishi had shaken her city all the way down to the gutters. But if even Mariko and Bumps were on the same side against him, he'd also created a sort of citywide unity.

"Let me know what you hear, Bumps. And do it fast; the clock is ticking."

"Yeah. Totally. Wait . . . does it have to be shipping containers?"

"No. That's just a pet theory."

Bumps chewed his lower lip with his gray meth-mouth teeth. "How about train cars?"

"Maybe, yeah. What are you thinking?"

"I know a guy. A car thief. Specializes in rental cars. Because the insurance is good, *neh*? The customers don't take it personal, and—"

"Get to the point, Bumps."

"Okay, you know what an Elf is? Like, an Isuzu Elf? Boxy little truck?"

"Sure."

"Well, my guy has a thing for them. They're super-popular rentals. The chop shops give him a real good price on—"

"The *point*, Bumps."

"His girlfriend likes E. He used to buy from me. This morning he calls me and says he wants to buy everything

I got. She has some friends coming over or something, and they like to party, and he's all excited because he's got a line on all these Elfs. They're coming by Shinagawa Station one after the other. That's where he lives, down by the rail yard—"

Mariko's least favorite part about dealing with meth-heads was that when they were tweaking they just couldn't shut up. "Did he see any kids in these trucks?"

"Well, you can't really see inside them. The back is just a big box, you know?"

"Exactly. Did he see them stop anywhere?"

"He didn't *see* them, no. . . ."

"So he didn't see anyone take a bunch of kids out of the back, did he?"

"Um . . ."

Mariko wanted to smack him in the head. "Then what the hell does this have to do with anything, Bumps? I told you the clock is ticking."

"Oh yeah, the train cars. See, there's a bunch of them in the rail yard. Like, hundreds. Parked, just sitting there, you know? No one ever goes back there, because why would they? The cars are all empty. So my guy, he's wondering, how come all those Elfs are going into the rail yard if there's nothing back there?"

Bingo, Mariko thought. Hiding in plain sight, but not where Furukawa expected. And who would suspect foul play if they saw delivery trucks coming to meet cargo trains? The two went together like rice and shoyu.

She punched the elevator call button, then decided that way was too slow; she'd take the stairs. "Shinagawa rail yard. You're positive?"

"Yeah, pretty much."

She wasn't going to get anything more conclusive than "pretty much" from a tweaker. "Thanks, Bumps. Be seeing you."

She sprinted down the stairs, jumped in the car, and gunned it. Shinagawa Station was well within Bumps's turf, just a few blocks away from his rattrap apartment. When she got there, she pulled onto a skinny, little-used frontage road running parallel to the train tracks. It occurred to her that she'd spent her entire adult life in Tokyo and she'd never been here before. She passed through Shinagawa Station dozens of times a year, yet she'd never ventured as far as the rail yard, just a few hundred meters north of it. Not that there was much cause to come. There was nothing to do, no one to meet, nothing to shop for. The sightseeing consisted of dirt, gravel, weeds, kilometers of steel rail, and a few hundred train cars. It was all fenced in, and she had to drive around a bit before she got to a place where authorized personnel could pass through a gate and get into the yard itself.

Beside the gate, a uniformed rent-a-cop sat in a box not much bigger than one of those huge American refrigerators, manning a radio and minding his own business. At the sight of him it dawned on her that she had no idea how to proceed. Usually she'd have her badge, gun, radio, and probably a partner. Had she come in a squad car, dispatch would know right where she was, and given the severity of the situation, by now she probably would have called for a tactical team. As a civilian, she had none of those assets. The safest thing to do—in fact, the only intelligent thing to do—was to dial 110 and wait.

Mariko wasn't very good at waiting.

Furukawa could fake the dispatch call and get a tac team down here. But he might send assassins instead. Besides, Mariko wanted this to be a win for the TMPD, not the Wind. She called Han.

"Hey," he said, "what's up?"

"You said quid pro quo, *neh*? I've got something for you. Shinagawa rail yard, lots of trucks moving in and out all morning. I'm sitting outside a gate looking at about a million tire tracks leading in and out of the yard—"

"And you'd badge your way through it and go snooping around, except you're not carrying a badge today. Got it. I'll be there as soon as possible."

"Call—"

"SWAT," he said. "I know."

"I was going to say HRT. Well, SWAT too, but if we're lucky and this is a hit, it's really a job for hostage rescue."

"Good idea. I'm on my way. Oh, and Mariko?"

"Yeah?"

"Ahh, never mind. I was going to tell you to do yourself a favor and don't go in there. No chance of that, huh?"

"Nope."

"Then do yourself a different favor: don't get caught."

43

Mariko's method of not getting caught was a little unorthodox. She drove right up to the gate guard and said, "Hey, I'm pretty sure I heard a crying kid back there."

He looked down at her with an apprehensive look, but not the kind she expected to get. He wasn't worried about a kid in danger, or how a kid got past him, or how completely screwed he'd be if his boss found out a kid got past him. Mariko would have read any of those easily enough, and she'd have sympathized with all of them. This was different. He seemed more concerned about Mariko than anything else.

Usually flashing a badge sped things along in this sort of situation, but this guy was giving her a different vibe. She leaned in, lowered her voice a bit, and said, "We don't want anyone hearing those kids, do we?"

"What?"

Uh-oh, Mariko thought. Maybe she'd misread him entirely. But she'd already grabbed the tiger by the tail; the only thing to do was hold on. "What if some random person on the street hears one of the kids? That could ruin everything, *neh*? So maybe one of us ought to head back there and have a look around."

His suspicion deepened. "Who are you?"

"Relax," she said, saying it as much to herself as to

him. She'd read him correctly after all. "I'm with you, brother. A servant of the Purging Fire."

He loosened up, but only for an instant. The two of them spoke the same language; that was what set him at ease. But he had been placed here to carry out his holy errand; the thought of duty strengthened his resolve.

"Say the words," he said.

Mariko gulped. Her only weapon was her Pikachu, but the cultist was well out of reach. He was armed with a radio. That was all he'd need to contact whoever was watching the children. Mariko was certain this gate guard wasn't alone. He would have been the one to admit all the trucks, but there had to be someone on the other end to direct them. One quick call and all of those kids were as good as dead—if they weren't dead already.

"Say the words." His voice was ice cold. He picked up the radio.

"There is no place the Divine Wind cannot reach?"

Mariko's breath froze in her lungs. He put the radio to his mouth. "One coming down," he said. Then, to her, "Car thirteen oh four. You can't drive that, though. People will see. Take one of the carts."

She looked in the direction he was pointing, and used the brief moment facing away from him to recover from fright. Her situation wasn't rosy yet, but at least she'd kept it from going right to hell. She gave the guard a nod, then pulled the BMW into line with the row of little electric carts he'd indicated. They bore Japan Railways logos and they all had keys in the ignition. Mariko hopped in the first one and zipped off into the rail yard.

It occurred to her as she drove along that a lone undercover officer posing as a cultist might actually have been the TMPD's best bet against that gate guard. Much safer than a fully armed tac team, she figured. Cops weren't military; they weren't allowed to shoot just because a suspect raised a radio to his mouth. Jōko Daishi had trained his people with code phrases; surely they'd have one that meant "kill the hostages." Mariko had seen his handiwork at the house in Kamakura. Pull one lever and the death chamber flooded with hydrogen cyanide gas. There was no reason he couldn't rig a train car the same way.

It took her a long time to find car 1304. The cars were linked together in huge parallel lines, five or six rows deep, each one hundreds of meters long. Boxcars, mostly, but there were passenger cars and tankers too. She had assumed 1304 would be in the middle of the middle, well out of public view, but it wasn't. It was close to the end—hiding in plain sight—one of a string of rust-brown boxcars that had all seen their day. The cars could have been identical octuplets, and unlike the rest of the cars on this end of the rail yard, they were coupled to a locomotive. It rumbled restively, a massive noise compared to the wimpy electric purring of Mariko's cart.

She overshot 1304 the first time, and a guard had to whistle at her to draw her back. Like the last one, he was dressed as a JR worker. No, Mariko thought—they *are* JR workers. Cultists have day jobs too. And Jōko Daishi needed insiders, people who wouldn't seem out of place if they were seen here day after day. An operation of this scale hinged on having the right people in all the right places. It was just the Wind's style to put sleeper agents in key positions months before they were needed. Mariko figured the Divine Wind followed suit.

She stopped the little cart and twisted around to face the man waving her toward car 1304. "Where's everyone else?" she asked.

"At the new church, with the first ones."

First ones? Was that a religious term, like Daishi or Purging Fire? Furukawa would probably know. Mariko cursed herself for not asking; she should have demanded a full briefing on the Divine Wind. Whoever the first ones were, it was a bad sign that they'd left only one man behind. This guy couldn't manage hundreds of children by himself—not live ones, anyway. And there was no noise coming from within the car.

She wanted to break into a run, to rip the huge sliding door aside and look inside the boxcar. She had to press her body into the seat just to keep herself inside the cart. She wheeled around and came to a stop at the foot of the cultist, who stood on a little platform above the couplers.

"I can't believe they left you here alone with all the kids."

The cultist shrugged. "These ones aren't going anywhere. And Daishi-sama needs as many as possible to help with the purification."

First ones. New church. Purification. All of it sounded ominous. At least he'd done one favor: he'd confirmed that he was alone out here. "I want to look inside," she said.

"Not a good idea."

Why? Because opening the door would release a cloud of cyanide? Mariko sniffed but couldn't smell anything out of the ordinary. Did that mean anything? A boxcar wasn't airtight, but what if the kids had been gassed with something odorless?

"Good idea or not, I'm looking." A quick glance at the space between the cars confirmed what she expected to see: no doors there. A rusty ladder ran up to the top of the car, but Mariko didn't expect to find openings up there either. The point of a boxcar was to protect its cargo, not to give curious detectives easy access. She looked at the big sliding doors and saw they were padlocked. "Give me the key."

"No," he said.

So you do have the key. She thought it was quite gentlemanly of him to confirm this for her before she drew the Pikachu.

It was still in its cigarette case, so for him the first sign of trouble only came when Mariko hooked the back of his heel with her free hand. He had the high ground, so she had to reach up to hit him in the inner thigh. With his heel hooked, the Pikachu worked just like a takedown. It slammed him to the metal platform, knocking him cold as soon as his head made impact.

She hopped up on the platform, patted him down, and found a phone, a Makarov semiautomatic, two sets of keys, and a radio on a belt clip. She took all of it. One of the key rings was obviously apartment keys and such, so she started on the padlock with the other one. The last key was a match, but once the lock popped open, she wasn't sure what to do. If the car was full of gas, opening this door might kill her. It might also set off a booby trap or an alarm. On the other hand, it might free hundreds of children—and then what? She hadn't thought of that. It wasn't safe to set them loose in a rail yard.

The doors already sat a centimeter or two apart. It wouldn't hurt anything to take a peek.

She pressed her eye to the narrow gap and found herself face-to-face with a sleeping child. Sleeping, not dead. The girl's lips fluttered softly with each exhalation.

Relief swelled in Mariko's chest, so strong it made her want to cry. She realized belatedly that she'd been holding her breath.

She put her ear to the gap and heard snoring. These kids weren't dead—or not yet, anyway. Her best guess was that they'd all been dosed with some kind of sleeping agent as soon as they were taken. They'd be safe enough until the cops came—and if they weren't, if they'd been poisoned with something that put its victims to sleep before it killed them, it wasn't as if Mariko could do anything more to help. She'd already called in the cavalry. She'd leave it to the bomb squad to figure out how best to open the boxcar, and they'd leave it to the medics to figure out what to do next.

Mariko couldn't wait that long. She'd be in deep shit if Kusama ever found out she was here. Besides, she still had a couple of cultists to deal with. She took one last look at the little girl inside the car, to confirm that the girl really was just sleeping. Then she went back to the cultist she'd knocked out.

It wasn't his lucky day. The padlock's shackle was just long enough to accommodate a thumb and a ladder rung. She had to force it a bit to snap it shut. He grunted, but the pain wasn't sharp enough to bring him back around. His thumb would be pretty numb by the time Han arrived with SWAT, but if he sat still he wouldn't hurt himself. She tucked one hand up inside the sleeve of her blouse, and used the blouse to wipe the fingerprints off everything she'd touched. Then she jumped back in the electric cart, tossing the padlock keys well out of the cultist's reach but still in plain view. Adopting her deepest man's voice, she clicked on the radio and said, "One coming out." Then she turned it off, wiped it clean, and tossed it by the keys. The cell phone went alongside it, and after some consideration, the Makarov too. She couldn't help but think that this was fate once again, trying to put a lethal weapon in her hand.

Speeding away in the cart, she felt more than ever that she was on a collision course with Jōko Daishi. The words *first ones* and *purification* still hadn't left her mind. They didn't bode well. Wherever this new church was, she'd find Jōko Daishi there, ready to do the purifying. She could only hope she got there before the bodies were piled high—

"Oh no. No, no, no."

She jammed on the brakes. The last of 1304's octuplet siblings stood silently next to her, locked up tight. She jumped out of the cart, ran to the boxcar door, and looked inside. It was empty. So was the next one in line.

How many kids could fit in one of these cars? Two hundred? Three? Not thirteen hundred, that was for sure—not unless they were dead and stacked to the ceiling. She had been so relieved to find the kids alive that it didn't even occur to her to do a head count.

She couldn't go back now. The cops would be here any minute. Sliding back into the cart, she mashed the accelerator to the floor. Its puny engine whined in response, drawing a barrage of filthy invective from Mariko that on any other day would have made her blush. She wanted to call Furukawa, to get a magical Q-Branchy calculation of how many first graders could sleep in a standard boxcar. She wanted to call Han, to ask him . . . ask him what? To find the rest of the kids for her? Thousands of cops were already on it, with no success. Han couldn't help her. She was on her own.

She parked the cart, traded up for the Beemer, and looked herself over in the mirror. She was sweating. The guard in the gatehouse would notice. She cranked the AC to full blast and sat there for as long as she could stand to sit still. That lasted less than a minute. Then she dabbed herself dry with a tissue and drove up to the gate-house.

"Everything's in order," she said. "I want to speak with Jōkō Daishi. Do you think he'll be with the first ones?"

He gave her a puzzled look. "Of course. But you'll never get there in time. Once the purification starts, you can't interrupt him. His sermon must be heard."

Sermon? The last time she'd heard a sermon from Jōkō Daishi, it was about blowing up the Korakuen subway station—

Oh no.

The first ones weren't First Ones, like his first disciples or first rank of priests or something. They were the first batch, the first kids to receive purification.

And Jōkō Daishi had already collected them in whatever passed for a church in the Divine Wind. Mariko and Han had shut down one of his "churches" already, back when they first brought him into custody. That was just an empty mattress store, which he'd converted into a bomb-making workshop. It was abandoned now. She'd find no leads there.

Her phone buzzed. She glimpsed at it and saw a text from Han. It said *get out NOW*. Even via text, they shared a thought pattern that verged on telepathy. He wasn't one of those people who said *now* when they meant *soon*. If he was texting, not calling, it was because unwelcome ears were nearby. That meant he had a bunch of cops in tow and they were right around the corner. Even as she peered down at the phone, she heard the first of the helicopters.

She wanted to squeeze the gate guard for more information, but there just wasn't time. She peeled away, hit the street, and made her first turn just as the armored SWAT van rounded the corner. She was safe.

But the kids weren't. They'd never heard of the three-hour rule. They had no way of knowing their three hours were up. Wherever this new church was, hundreds of children were waiting like lambs for the sacrificial knife. Jōkō Daishi was heading straight for them, and Mariko didn't have a damn clue where to find him.

BOOK TEN

AZUCHI-MOMOYAMA PERIOD, THE YEAR 21

(1588 CE)

44

Just as he expected, Shichio found the teahouse far more beautiful than the waterfall behind it. Yes, the cascade and its pool were picturesque, but that only accentuated the artistry of the carpenter who built the teahouse. His first masterstroke was the choice of location. Like the largest stones in a rock garden, the teahouse could not be placed just anywhere—or rather, it could be, but only by a witless cretin with no appreciation for composition. Finding just the right setting, and then just the right size, the right shape, the right facing, then choosing the angle of the roof, the thickness of the beams and joists, even the age of the wood—there were a hundred decisions to be made before anyone ever picked up a saw.

Shichio had stopped in the hamlet at the mouth of the narrow valley to make inquiries about the teahouse. If the villagers had it right, it was built over a century ago by the Zen master Ikkyū. If so, then the tiny house was a testament to his *satori*. A hundred decisions, a hundred perfect choices made by an enlightened mind. Constant spray from the falls might have led to mildew, but instead the interior smelled only of the red cedar planking. The wood had grayed with age, but Shichio suspected fall colors would bring out the red. He vowed to come back and see for himself—perhaps on his triumphant return to

Kyoto, after Nene and the Bear Cub were dead and he could put all of his nightmares behind him.

Perhaps he could even rid himself of his dreaded, beloved mask. At the moment he held it in one hand, stroking it with his thumb. The better part of him wanted to throw it in the pool and never think of it again. But it was the smaller voice that held sway, the one that said appetite and lust were nothing compared to the need of the mask. Satisfying that glorious need was better than the most soul-shuddering orgasm. What higher pleasure could there possibly be than wearing the mask while stripping the Bear Cub of his pelt? Even Nene's death would pale in comparison.

The thought of Nene made him recall the image of fighting mantises locked in a cage. This teahouse was the most exquisite cage imaginable, but Shichio had no doubt that he was boxed in. Ōbyō Falls might just as well have been the end of the world. The cliff face was too brittle to climb. Recent rockfall was in evidence right in the middle of the pool, where sharp-edged slabs lurked like sharks just under the surface. The largest of them lay directly under the cascade, sending white spittle hissing in every direction. To the right of the falls, a line of thick, spray-spattered bushes seemed to cling to the cliff face with thick-fingered roots. Shichio knew this to be a trick of the eye. In fact, they grew on the lip of a rocky shelf, the only level surface between the base of the cliff and the crest. Behind the greenery, a host of Shichio's archers lay in wait.

The walls of the valley were not quite as steep as Ōbyō's cliff, but there were still places where even the most tenacious tree roots could not find purchase. Naked rock peered out here and there from the bamboo like slate gray islands in a sea of green. Shichio had contemplated deploying some of his bear hunters there, with orders so simple that even the most feckless of them could obey: remain hidden from any who enter the valley, and kill all who attempt to flee. Shichio's own people would not run, and that left only Nene, her retinue, and the Bear Cub.

But in the end he decided the bear hunters could only spoil the ambush at the falls. They'd failed him at every turn thus far; he would not rely on them now.

Shichio could not deny feeling vulnerable here. He'd intended to encamp with an entire platoon, but once he reached the waterfall he saw that would be impossible. The only place for them to stand was in the pool. That was part of the genius of the teahouse: it was tiny, just large enough to seat a tea master and three or four participants in the ceremony. It took up what little horizontal ground there was, yet it was not obtrusive; it seemed to have fallen there, just like the giant slabs that nature had strewn around the water.

So Shichio hid six of his samurai behind the shuttered *fusuma* of the teahouse, and had no other choice but to send the rest of his platoon in single file back up the trail. Their orders were to stand guard in the nameless hamlet at the valley's mouth, to offer Nene an escort to the teahouse if she allowed it, and to kill the Bear Cub on sight if he happened to show his face.

Shichio knew he would not. The whelp had been careful so far. Shichio did not expect to see Nene either. Quite to the contrary: it was her man Nezumi who chose this place for their meeting, and he would have told her there was no escape. Nene would send a trusted envoy in her stead.

That was all right. The Bear Cub only needed to see *someone* waiting for him. Shichio hoped Nene sent a woman—one of her handmaids, perhaps, some delicate flower the Bear Cub could not possibly find threatening. And a bodyguard or two, maybe even that vile Nezumi. That would be delicious, to see him die in the ambush as well. Nene wouldn't send many; she would not trust Shichio not to kill them.

Shichio intended to do just that. As soon as the Bear Cub showed his face, Shichio planned to fall back behind the six in the teahouse, with Ōda Tomonosuke at his side. He did not count Ōda as a bodyguard per se—he hadn't known the man long enough to place that much trust in

him—but the aging lord had already proved himself an
able sensei and a deadly sword hand. He had provided
helpful intelligence about Nene as well—quite accidentally, of course, but Shichio did not count that as a mark
against him. As a sword master he did not approve of
Shichio's mask, but neither did he mock it, and he begrudgingly allowed his student to wear it while training.
As well he should, Shichio thought, since I am his only
income. Ōda hadn't yet given him cause to mention this
aloud, another testament to his new sensei's wisdom.

"She is here," said Ōda, nodding toward a twittering
flock of sparrows startled from their roost. Once again
the man proved his usefulness. Since he was Nene's confidant, Shichio decided to keep him at his side; if she sent
archers or arquebusiers, fear of hitting her friend might
make them reluctant to let fly.

"What do you think?" Shichio asked. "Will she come
herself, or will she send an envoy?"

Ōda gave him a puzzled look. "Her messenger said she
had to see this gift with her own eyes. Isn't that what you
told me?"

"Yes, it is." And you believe every single thing you
hear, Shichio thought. Poor man. "Soon enough we'll see
if she is as good as her word, won't we? Yes, we will."

Soon enough, her horse came into view—but not with
Nene. The woman in the saddle was chubby, almost barrel-
chested. A huge parasol rested on her shoulder, and a
silken veil shielded her against the armies of biting insects
that made the valley their home. She wore lilac and lavender, not Nene's finest colors, though Shichio recalled seeing her ladies-in-waiting dressed that way. The man
walking ahead of her horse, leading it by the rein, was flailing at a cloud of mosquitoes. Shichio recognized him by
his black *hachimaki*. Nezumi. He wore a sword on one hip
and a quiver on the other, and swatted uselessly at the
mosquitoes with a long, black bow.

"I do not think that is Lady Nene," Ōda said.

No, Shichio thought, and perhaps you might also like
to announce whether you think that bright disc in the sky
is the sun or the moon. "Well, what do you know? She

broke her word to us. Later we'll have to talk about how often she does that."

"This one must be a trusted handmaiden."

Yes, Shichio thought, and it's the sun, by the way; the moon comes later.

"Lord Kumanai," Nezumi called. "My lady sends her greetings. And I bring you tidings: the Bear Cub still lives."

Shichio bit back a frustrated growl. "You know this because you found him? Or because you are wasting my time with an idle guess?"

"Heh heh. I found him right enough. I meant to kill him too, and collect your bounty, but your bear hunters botched it. Don't you worry, though. When he shows up here, I'll be the first to put an arrow in him—and then I'll expect the rest of the reward you promised."

Expect a few arrows of your own, Shichio thought. Nezumi's eyes flicked down to the mask, and Shichio realized that imagining those piercing arrows must have heightened his ardor for it. Now he cradled the mask in one hand and stroked it with the other, just like a pet. One finger traced the rim of an eyehole, running around and around and around.

"Your reward," Shichio said, snapping himself back to the present. "Yes. You're sure he'll come?"

"Heh heh. You tell me. How much does he want to kill you?"

Shichio nodded, granting the point. Nezumi smacked a mosquito, squashing it against his forearm and leaving a bloody smudge where it died. The sight of blood usually sickened Shichio, but today it titillated. The mask was unusually hungry—perhaps because triumph was so close at hand? No. This was something else. Something familiar. But he could not place it.

Nezumi stopped the horse some six or seven paces away, and when the girl in lilac tried to dismount, she slipped out of the saddle. Shichio caught only a glimpse as the veil fluttered away from her face, her mouth open in a dumbstruck O. He imagined her embarrassed blush under that white face paint. A delicate courtier like this one had probably never ventured so deep into the wild. Shichio knew everyone thought of him as effete, but at least he knew how to step in and out of the saddle.

No doubt Nezumi also thought of him as effeminate, and saw Ōda as the only threat here. So much the better. Shichio glanced up to the falls, verifying that all of his bowmen remained invisible, but something drew his attention back to Nene's errand boy—or rather, to his sword. It was the mask that called to him. It seemed to writhe in his hand, waking a lust that slithered through Shichio's body like a nest of snakes. He'd never felt its need so acutely before, but—no. He had. Once. At the Okuma compound.

Only Inazuma steel could arouse the mask this way. Glorious Victory Unsought was nearby. That meant the whelp was too. But where?

The mask made him acutely aware of Nezumi's swords, and Ōda's, and his own. Even the samurai in the teahouse seemed to resonate to him, like a bell's lingering tone long after it was struck. But there was Inazuma steel too. Where? He scanned the pool, the rocks, the bamboo clinging to the valley walls. There was no sign.

Where was the Bear Cub? And what was that hanging in the air? It looked like smoke, a faint blue ribbon of it, rising up from the ledge where his archers lay in ambush. No—not rising up *from*, but falling down *to*. Now there came another, fluttering down from the very crest of the cliff. Shichio could just make out the little iron ball sputtering flame.

45

When people told the story of Prince Yamato, they never mentioned what a difficult time the prince must have had moving around in women's clothing. Daigoro found the lilac kimono terribly confining, not because it was too small for him but because a courtly woman wore her garments so tight that she could hardly breathe. Daigoro didn't suffer that particular problem— his Sora breastplate gave him adequate breathing room— but the silken kimono still made it hard to move. As difficult as it had been getting up into the saddle, somehow he'd given no thought to what would happen when he tried to get back down.

The moment he fell off the horse, he was certain the ruse would fall apart. Shichio looked him right in the eye. But with the makeup, and with his hair down, and with the veil and head ornaments and everything else, Daigoro supposed Shichio must have seen only what he expected to see. And if there was one benefit to wearing such tightly constricting clothes, it was that they made his limp invisible. Since he was confined to small, shuffling steps, it was as if he limped from both legs.

He'd hoped to walk right up to Shichio before the first explosion. Now he could only hope Katsushima would understand what it meant for him to fall from the saddle. They had prearranged the signal yesterday afternoon:

when Daigoro dismounted, light the first grenade. That was the last time they'd spoken. Katsushima had spent the whole night hiking up the neighboring dell. Some time early this morning, he would have looped back down to reach the cliff top overlooking Ōbyō Falls. Daigoro had allowed him plenty of time, because they had no way to communicate—nor any way to discuss whether tumbling out of the saddle counted as dismounting.

Looking up, he saw Katsushima had arrived at the top of the cliff after all. Right on cue, he'd lit the first grenade. Even now, Daigoro saw the second one fall, trailing a string of blue smoke behind it. It was clear from his bewildered look that Shichio saw it too.

Daigoro jerked his *tantō* from a sheath inside his *obi* and cut away the lilac kimono. As he reached for the fallen parasol, a thunderclap punched him in the ear. It was the loudest noise he'd ever heard in his life.

Smoke consumed the ledge where Shichio's archers were hiding. In the same instant, a shuddering *bang* almost knocked Shichio flat. A lightning bolt could not have been louder. Then came a second *bang*, and this one did knock him down. Behind him, a horse screamed and reared. He turned, hoping to see the horse running away instead of trampling toward him. Instead he saw the Bear Cub.

The whelp had cut himself free of that ludicrous lilac kimono, and now he was scrambling for the parasol. No, not a parasol. Glorious Victory Unsought, in the thinnest disguise imaginable. Shichio could not believe he'd fallen for the ruse. "Loose, damn you, loose!" he shouted. "Kill them! Kill them all!"

The world fell into chaos. The peacock shrieked like a frightened maid, shouting at his hidden archers. Nene's horse nearly stove Daigoro's skull in. It bucked and jumped, spinning with a dexterity Daigoro wouldn't have believed possible. Then it fled for its life.

A third Mongol grenade exploded, filling the valley with thunder. Still Shichio screamed for his archers, not realizing in his panic that all of them were dead. Tatters of the damned kimono still clung to Daigoro's knees, hobbling him as he struggled to reach Glorious Victory. He wasted a precious moment cutting the last of the kimono asunder, then looked up to see the teahouse erupt with armored samurai.

Scrambling on his hands and knees, he reached his father's sword. Over his shoulder he caught a glimpse of Nezumi drawing a blade—too late. Ōda Tomonosuke lunged for him, slow but with peerless form. Nezumi fell, clutching the red gash where his eyes used to be.

Shichio's samurai advanced in unison—warned, perhaps, that they stood no chance against Daigoro if they faced him one-on-one. Daigoro drew Glorious Victory and struggled to his feet. This would not be like the Green Cliff. There he'd taken his enemies by surprise. These ones were waiting for him.

But not for the smoking iron ball that fell in their midst. A trail of thin blue smoke arced behind it, all the way back up to Katsushima. The explosion was deafening. Men flew in every direction. Daigoro caught a faceful of shards, both metal and bone.

He could not let it slow him. Half blind with blood, he lashed out and took a man's leg at the knee. Something chopped him right under the arm, ringing off his Sora *yoroi*. He chopped back. Someone screamed and died.

His sudden onslaught bought him a moment's reprieve, just long enough to wipe the blood from his eyes. There was no sign of Shichio. Four samurai lay dead; Daigoro only remembered felling two of them. Two others still stood, spreading out to flank him. Nezumi rolled on the ground, howling and clutching his face. Daigoro glanced over his shoulder and saw exactly what he did not want to see: Ōda Tomonosuke, a broken and vengeful man, a man with nothing to live for, yet one who had made his name as an expert swordsman.

Daigoro was alone, surrounded on three sides. He could not see Shichio anywhere.

*   *   *

Everything had gone to hell. Shichio had no idea what happened on that rock shelf, but all of his archers were dead. Dead before loosing a single arrow. The air tasted of mud and burnt gunpowder. Half of his samurai were dead, maybe more. He didn't dare look. Nezumi screamed piteously. His cries echoed off the cliff, even louder than the waterfall.

Shichio cursed himself for a craven. He hadn't even managed to draw his sword. He cowered behind the teahouse, the water just ankle-deep, but since he was crouching he was in to his balls. Cold and dripping, safe but humiliated.

Only his mask could restore his courage. As he tied it in place, the huge Inazuma blade sang out to him. It was visible even through the wooden walls of the teahouse, glowing like the sun through closed eyelids. The mask saw the other swords too, and one thing more: a little globe sailing through the air.

Shichio looked up and saw the thing. It smoked and sparked as it flew. Totally without thought, acting solely by reflex, he swung at the flying orb. He couldn't even say how his sword came to be in his hand. Guided by the mask, the flat of his blade hit the globe and sent it right back where it came from.

Halfway there, it vanished. Smoke and fury took its place. The noise was enough to buckle Shichio's knees. A thousand fragments pierced the surface of the pool. A thousand more hit the cliff, the teahouse, the mask. Some flew upward too. Shichio heard a grunt from above, and for the first time he noticed the shabby *rōnin*.

The explosion sent some of its deadly claws into the *rōnin*'s face, and since he'd shielded his eyes, the claws tore up his hands too. Now he bled freely. Either the wounds did not pain him or he was too much the samurai to cry out, but Shichio could hear him curse.

Good, he thought. The son of a bitch would have a front-row seat to the Bear Cub's demise.

*   *   *

Daigoro heard a metallic *clang* from the pool. An instant later a Mongol grenade exploded in midair.

It took everyone by surprise. It was also just the distraction Daigoro needed to cut his way free of his fate. But by the time he realized that, the others did too, and they were all right back where they started—with one crucial difference: Katsushima was out of the fight.

Daigoro didn't need to see him to know his friend was hurt. Hearing Katsushima's curses, he knew they came through gritted teeth. That was all the attention he could spare for his closest friend, for he had enemies encroaching on three sides.

"Ōda-sama," he called, "this is not your fight. I killed your son; don't make me kill you too."

A cold, cruel light filled Ōda's eyes. "You forget: I asked you to kill me."

He was right: Daigoro had forgotten. Now Daigoro reassessed that look in Ōda's eye. It wasn't cruelty: it was total detachment. Ōda no longer cared whether he lived or died. It was a fearless, deadly state of mind.

"You could marry again," Daigoro said. "Have more sons. Continue your family name. Don't be the last of the Ōdas."

Ōda lowered his blade. It was still a fighting stance—upward cuts were best for slipping underneath armor—but it was not especially aggressive. For a moment, Daigoro thought he meant to stay clear of the fray. But then, in a soft, calm voice, Ōda said, "I will press the attack. You two, cut for the hamstrings. And beware his reach."

Daigoro took a deep, centering breath. His fingers tightened on Glorious Victory's grip. Time slowed to a crawl. His enemies settled deeper into their stances, coiling to spring. Daigoro feinted and all three leaped back. That was good. They were afraid of him.

But that would only work once. Even now they crept closer, one slow footstep at a time. Daigoro understood how a wounded deer must feel when the wolves circled in.

Then he remembered Katsushima's watchdog, Kane, and the moral that came with that story: *Arrogance in the face of impossible odds. That's the way to win a fight.*

To hell with it, he thought.

He threw himself at the closest samurai. Inazuma steel cleaved helmet, bone, and brain. Behind him, Ōda shouted a *kiai*. Daigoro spun, his *ōdachi* reaching long and low. Glorious Victory sheared off Ōda's katana at the hilt.

Ōda pressed on, heedless of death. Daigoro side-stepped, let him pass, cut for the spine. The second samurai spoiled his cut. Steel flashed at Daigoro's face. He parried and counterstruck. Glorious Victory cut deep but did not kill.

Now Ōda was on him again, *wakizashi* in hand. Daigoro chopped at Ōda's hand. He missed, but he cut the *wakizashi* in two. Weaponless, Ōda was no threat. Daigoro rounded on Shichio's last remaining samurai and pressed a furious assault.

Sword-song echoed in the valley. Daigoro stumbled on wet rock. The samurai moved in for the kill. Daigoro's knee buckled completely. He fell, but Glorious Victory did not. Daigoro held it fast, like a spear set to meet a cavalry charge. The Inazuma blade caught the samurai under his breastplate and punched out below the shoulder blade.

Then Ōda kicked Daigoro in the back of the head. The world went dark.

46

Daigoro woke to crushing pain. His hands were tingling, almost numb. Something bit down on his wrists with the malice of a dragon.

His eyes fluttered open. A devil stood before him, and Daigoro wondered if he was in hell. Blinking hard, he cleared the spots from his vision. It was not a devil after all, but rather a devil mask. Solid iron, pitted with rust and age, too small to conceal Shichio's triumphant smile.

"Ah, at last he wakes," Shichio said. "But let's wait for Ōda-san before we get started, shall we? He's earned his place at the table. Yes, he has."

Daigoro had to blink again to drive the spots away. Gradually he took in his surroundings. He was in the teahouse, bound hand and foot to something vertical. Craning his head, he could just make out what it was: a support beam. The waterfall thundered endlessly behind him. The wall was open, the *fusuma* pushed apart to either side, but no sunlight came in. Crickets and frogs sang to each other in the night. A cold breeze made Daigoro realize he was naked to the waist.

He looked down to find his body wrapped in coils of hempen rope. The same rope crushed his wrists, which were stretched so high above his head that Daigoro's shoulders felt they might twist out of their sockets. He could not move his wrists at all, and his ankles were held just as fast, but the rest of his body was free to twist and squirm. The rope coiled randomly up and down his arms and torso, crossing itself many times over. There were many knots, all of them tied artfully, and the coils were pulled so tight that Daigoro's flesh bulged up between them. But why? They wrapped only around his body; they did not hold him fast to the beam. What use were bonds that did not bind?

"I usually use a table for this," Shichio said. "A very special table. Your friend General Mio could have told you all about it, if only I hadn't cut out his tongue."

A terrible vision flashed in Daigoro's mind: Mio Yasumasa quivering on his deathbed. His whole body was coiled with thin purple bruises. Huge ovular cuts festered, as if an animal had taken bites out of him. Before, Daigoro had never understood what could inflict such bizarre ropelike bruises. Now he understood all too well. Yet the bleeding, festering wounds were still a mystery. What could cause bitelike wounds, not ragged but smooth-sided, like the cuts of a razor? He could only imagine, and his imagination terrified him.

"Usually I strip my victims naked too," Shichio continued. "It makes them wonder how long I'll allow them to keep their manhood. But you . . . by the gods, that leg! How can you stomach it? I'd sooner cut it off than wake every morning to the sight of it. How can you let it share your bed?"

He shuddered and unsheathed his *wakizashi*. "Of course I could cut it off for you, but what would be the fun in that? You'd bleed to death right away, wouldn't you? Yes, you would."

In the center of the room, a brazier glowed as red as a demon's eyes. Now a new source of light drew near, orange, fluttering, crackling. Ōda Tomonosuke slipped out of his sandals and stepped into the tearoom, a torch held high in his left hand. He looked at Daigoro with disgust.

"The torch you requested, Lord Kumanai."

"Yes, yes, bring it closer." Shichio beckoned with his sword. Then, stepping onto the veranda overlooking the pool, he shouted, "Are you there, *rōnin*? Can you see your friend? Or have you abandoned him like everyone else?"

A quick slice, and a gobbet of flesh hit the floor. Hot blood ran down Daigoro's back. Shichio's blade was sharp; there wasn't much pain—at least not physically. But Daigoro had never been so scared in his life.

"Sharp, isn't it?" Shichio said, eerily echoing Daigoro's own thoughts. "It's Hashiba's, you know. General Toyotomi's. He gave it to me when he made me his *hatamoto*."

Daigoro smirked. Arrogance in the face of impossible odds. He would not let Shichio see him afraid. "Yes, I heard. 'Lord Kumanai,' is it? The same *kuma* of Okuma, I think."

"Yes. *Kuma-Nai*, 'No Bears.' And also 'No Okumas.' Do you like it?"

Daigoro threw out a laugh, loud enough to echo off the cliff. "I love it. You want to be rid of me? You named yourself after me!"

Shichio's grin curled into a snarl. He set his blade against Daigoro's belly and sliced. This one hurt. Shichio made sure of that. He drew the blade slowly, and left the bleeding slab dangling by a flap so it tugged at the wound.

"Laugh at me again and I will cut out your tongue," he said. "Just as I did with your friend Mio. Just as I'll do with your *rōnin* up on the cliff, as soon as I catch him. Now why hasn't he come for you yet? At sunset he was still up there. I expected him to ride in to your rescue. Yes, I did. Why hasn't he come?"

Because he's a full day's hike from here, Daigoro thought. Or a quick jump, if only the pool weren't so shallow. Katsushima had brought a length of knotted rope with him, and also a great bow and quiver; the fact that he'd used neither meant he must have injured his hands. If he could have joined the fight, he would have. And since he couldn't, one thing was certain: he'd stay as close to Daigoro as possible. Daigoro could not turn his head far enough to see atop the cliff, but he knew Katsushima was up there, watching helplessly. The man who had loved him like a father now had to watch on as Daigoro was tortured to death.

That thought wounded Daigoro more sharply than his own pain. He could not do that to Katsushima. "Face me, you coward. Cut me loose and face me."

"With what? With this?" Shichio picked up Glorious Victory Unsought. The mighty blade had been resting in the corner, along with Daigoro's *wakizashi* and the rest of his effects. Now Shichio unsheathed it, and took a nick out of the rafter because he was not used to the *ōdachi's* reach.

"Oh no," he said, and his eyes shot up to the scarred rafter. His sympathy for the rafter startled Daigoro. The peacock studied Glorious Victory's edge, then the ceiling again, then the steel. "Oh, thank the gods. I didn't blunt the sword."

Daigoro looked at him in horror. Until now he hadn't realized the depths of Shichio's depravity. This man felt more for works of art than he did for human beings.

The same horror showed in Ōda's eyes. "Lord Kumanai, the boy is right," he said. "Cut him loose and make him kneel. If he's too cowardly to open his belly, I'll behead him for you. But this . . . this is no way to kill a samurai."

"Oh, but our Bear Cub isn't a samurai, is he? Okuma Daigoro—now there was a samurai if ever there was one. But this whelp? Look at him. Does he shave his pate? No. Does he fight honorably? No. He comes dressed as a woman. Even now the smears of face paint linger, despite all the sweat and blood. He looks like a ghost."

Shichio returned to the heap in the corner, where Daigoro's clothes and armor were strewn. Lying atop the pile was Daigoro's *wakizashi*, until Shichio kicked it across the room. The sight was more than Daigoro could bear. That was an Okuma blade. It once belonged to Daigoro's father, and to his grandfather before him. Now this peacock had sullied it with his foot.

Shichio kicked it again. "What makes a samurai? The topknot and swords, *neh*?"

"Honor," said Daigoro.

"Well, yes," Shichio said, "that too. If you count a reign of terror as honorable. You'll forgive me; I've only been samurai for a month. I haven't quite worked out which acts of butchery our honor code permits."

He kicked the sword again, rolling it toward Daigoro's feet. "I understand the bit about the swords, though. Only samurai are allowed to wear the *daishō*. So if you're not samurai, this *wakizashi* of yours is illegal, isn't it? Yes. Yes, I think it is."

Glorious Victory rose and fell. It sheared right through Daigoro's *wakizashi* and into the tatami. The Inazuma was unharmed, but the Okuma blade lay in severed halves. Daigoro felt it as bitterly as if Shichio had cut off his arm.

"There," Shichio said. "I have two swords and you do not. I have a surname and you do not. I have lands, and lordship, and this ghastly topknot. What does it matter which one of us has honor? I am samurai forever more. You will die a common criminal."

Daigoro could stand no more. He pulled at his bonds but only succeeded in digging the ropes deeper into his wrists. Shichio enjoyed the show. He left Glorious Victory stuck in the floor, jutting up like the mast of a listing shipwreck. Stepping gingerly around it, he came to stand at Daigoro's side. Then, in a sickening act of kindness, he caressed Daigoro's cheek.

It was a lover's caress. Daigoro pulled his head away, but there was only so far he could go. "My dear boy," Shichio said. "We're just getting started. These bonds will slow your bleeding considerably. And you're a tough one, *neh*? Yes, you are. This could take until morning."

Shichio drew Hideyoshi's *wakizashi* again, and laid it against a strangled bulge of muscle just above Daigoro's armpit. The blade was so close that Daigoro could see his panicked breaths misting on it. He watched as the blade glided smoothly through skin and sinew. Dark blood spilled from the wound, steaming on his skin. The sight made him gag.

He was not alone. Even Shichio seemed sick. Lord Ōda actually ran from the room, his torch guttering loudly. He retched in the darkness. The sound redoubled Daigoro's urge to vomit.

"Samurai!" Shichio said with a snort. "Savages and hypocrites, that's all you are. Ask you to kill a thousand unarmed monks and you set about it with a will. But make it one of your own kind and it's a different story, isn't it? Render *you* unarmed, render *you* helpless, and all of a sudden the bloodletting is 'dishonorable.' *Neh?* Only now does it make you sick."

"You too," said Daigoro. "I can see it. You're turning green. I guess you're one of us after all."

Shichio slapped him. "No! And . . . and yes." His head sagged, pulled down by the mask. It was as if the mask had doubled in weight—and perhaps it had, not physically but morally. He was a different man wearing it. The pettiness was gone, replaced with a thirst for blood. He gripped his sword like a half-starved dog clamping down on stolen food. His whole body spoke of desperation.

"It *is* wrong," Shichio said. "I know it is. And yet . . ."

"Take the mask off," Daigoro said softly. "Free yourself of it." And then free me so we can fight like men, he thought.

"No!" Shichio snarled, baring his teeth. "I will not take orders from you. Command me again and I'll cut out your tongue."

"Do it," Daigoro said. Better to drown in his own blood than to die one slice at a time. "I command it."

Shichio took another piece out of him, just to show he could. Daigoro heard a grunt of dismay and realized Ōda had returned. He hadn't noticed before, which meant Ōda must have doused his torch before coming inside. If he was to be a spectator to Daigoro's torment, perhaps he did not want to see quite so vividly.

"Lord Ōda," Daigoro said, "look at the man you've taken sides with. He is a monster. You know this—and you are *better* than this. Remember your pride, my lord. Remember you are samurai."

"Silence!" Shichio raised his sword as if to open Daigoro's throat. Daigoro welcomed it; anything was better than dying piece by severed piece. "You killed his son! Have you forgotten?"

"No," Daigoro said. "I remember. I took his son. I took his livelihood. But no man can take your honor, Lord Ōda. Your enemies can take everything else from you, but you give up your honor of your own free will."

He wished he could see Ōda, to know whether his words had any effect. He could hear the man's breathing, but Ōda stood somewhere out of sight. Daigoro had little ability to look for him, for he could not move his head freely—not without cutting himself on Shichio's razor-sharp sword.

"What's this?" Shichio said. A smile spread behind those iron fangs. "Is that fear I see? Yes, it is. You don't like the look of my blade, do you?"

He took it back as if to sheathe it, then raised it so its tip hovered just in front of Daigoro's right eyeball. It edged ever closer, until at last Daigoro's eyelash brushed the very point of it, freeing a drop of blood that melted into Daigoro's eye.

"I would scoop that eye right out of your head," Shichio said, "if only I didn't want you to see what comes next—"

He cut himself short. His sword fell mercifully away as Shichio sniffed the air. "What is that? Do you smell it?"

Daigoro did. Wood smoke. Now that the sword no longer dominated his attention, he noticed an orange glow in the back of the teahouse. It could not be approaching torches; the light was too low to the ground. And now it was much too loud. Daigoro could hear it crackling.

"Fire!" Ōda said. "My lord, look!"

Shichio wheeled around just in time to see the flames crawl into the teahouse. A cold breeze came in off the water; the flames drank deeply of it, then sprang up the walls. They cloyed to the rafters and danced across the tatami. The heat was enough to beat back the breeze, filling the air with smoke.

"How?" Shichio said. "How is this possible?"

"The black powder," said Ōda. "It smolders sometimes. This damned wind must have rekindled it. My lord, this teahouse is over a hundred years old. Its timbers are as dry as an old wasp's nest. We must go."

Shichio twisted around like a snake, looking at Daigoro. He eyed the ropes binding Daigoro's wrists and ankles, then looked back at the fire. Already the blaze had begun to blacken the ceiling. "Yes," he said. "This will do nicely."

47

Shichio had never seen a fire spread so fast. Already it had claimed three of the four walls for its own. It must have crawled along the outside of the teahouse before it ever ventured indoors, yet somehow it had gone undetected. Ah, yes, he thought. The breeze. That was the culprit. It had fended off the smell of smoke, and probably eddied behind the teahouse to fan the flames.

His only route of escape was to leap from the teahouse into the pool. His feet slipped on the slate when he landed, slamming him onto his tailbone. Ōda followed, equally graceless, holding his swords high so he would not land on them. Shichio realized he should have done the same, then noticed Hashiba's *wakizashi* was still in his hand, naked and gleaming. The pool had washed all the gore away.

He looked up and saw the Bear Cub wriggling like a worm on a hook. It was no use; he was bound fast. Shichio hoped the wind would keep the boy from choking to death on the smoke. Usually that was how people died if you burned them. But if the breeze stayed steady, the flames would take their fill of him before he died.

Shichio had burned buildings before. People too. He'd put his own village to the torch, and had watched from a distance when Hashiba razed a Jōdo Shin temple that harbored a suspected Ikkō Ikki rabble-rouser. He'd never heard of black powder setting off a blaze like this, but he did know the stuff was fickle. A single fire arrow could kill an entire musket platoon if it pierced the right barrel.

Shichio shuffled awkwardly to shore, moving distract-edly because he did not want to peel his attention away from the Bear Cub. Already the whelp grunted and cursed. The squeals would come soon. Then there would be noises piteous enough to turn Shichio's stomach, sounds so inhuman that there were no words to describe them. They would float all the way to the top of the cliff, leaving that old *rōnin* with the choice to burn them into his memory or throw himself over the precipice, to deafen his ears forever.

Shichio looked up there, and was rewarded with the orange glimmer of firelight on armor. His mask could see the *rōnin*'s swords, and a clutch of arrowheads too. That sort of thing was hard to make out by daylight, but at night the mask's vision was clearer.

Relishing in the mask's second sight brought to mind that brief moment of satiety, the one he'd felt just as his fingers closed around Glorious Victory Unsought. The mask and the sword were born for each other. Shichio knew it the moment he first touched the sword, right af-ter watching Ōda kick the Bear Cub in the back of the head. That was a delight to see, but not half as satisfying as the touch of Inazuma steel. As soon as his fingers curled around its grip, the mask's hunger was gone. Sated. Fulfilled.

It had stayed that way while Shichio tied up the boy, and if it began to stir, he had only to touch Glori-ous Victory and—

"No!"

He surprised himself with his ferocity. Ōda jumped too. "The sword!" Shichio screamed. "Glorious Victory! It's still inside!"

He could not believe he'd forgotten it. The flames were so hot, the threat of pain so near. And his moment of triumph was at hand. The Bear Cub, helpless before him. Fear and exultation, swelling so swiftly that they drowned out even the mask. Now it shrieked at him, biting at his mind with cruel iron fangs.

"It's priceless," he sobbed. "That beautiful, beautiful sword . . ."

Ōda Tomonosuke grimly presented his *daishō* to Shichio. "Here," he said.

"Fool! You think these shoddy, rust-bitten—"

Ōda punched them into Shichio's chest, so he had no choice but to take them. "They are not for you," Ōda said, his voice like ice. "I am going to get your sword."

Shichio looked at the blaze, which was bright enough now that the waterfall itself had become a fountain of yellow light. The wind had died and black smoke roiled from under the teahouse roof. Shichio could not see the whelp, but he could hear wheezes, coughs, and cries. No sane man could possibly set foot in that inferno.

Ōda shed his belt, then his *hakama*, leaving his legs naked. He kept his *kosode*, but slipped his arms out of the sleeves so he wore it like a cape. He strode into the pool, the heavy fabric floating behind him like a shadow until at last it absorbed enough water to sink. Halfway to the teahouse, he dove under the surface, the long garment vanishing behind him like the tail of a sea dragon. The dragon emerged just where the teahouse veranda hung over the water. Ōda pulled himself up in one smooth motion, hiked the sodden *kosode* all the way over his head, and crawled into the flames.

His father had taught him never to cry, but tonight Daigoro failed his father.

The smoke chewed at his eyes with hot, stinging teeth. Its claws would tear out his throat if he let them, but the air was too hot to breathe. He wanted to simply squeeze his eyes and lips shut and wait bravely for the end, but his body betrayed him. It would not allow him that dignity. So he bucked and twisted, and only managed to grind blood-soaked ropes against raw skin. He thought his skin was already as hot as it could get without actually catching fire, but the raw patches burned hotter still. It was as if the flames could smell his blood. They had a taste for it.

At last he could hold his breath no longer. He inhaled through his nose and singed both nostrils. It was not enough air. He inhaled through his mouth and burned his throat. Now the smoke shoved its fist down his gullet. Coughing expelled what little breath he had left. He grew faint. His legs gave out. He sagged from his tormented shoulders; he'd long since lost feeling in his hands and wrists. So much the better; at least they would not make him suffer when they burned.

A black devil crept across the floor. Daigoro did not know what else to call it. It clambered out of the smoke, shapeless and steaming, faintly reminiscent of a manta ray. Then it sprouted a human hand. The hand seized Glorious Victory Unsought by the grip and ripped her out of the floor. The devil rose to its full height and enveloped Daigoro in blackness.

Cold, wet fabric pressed against Daigoro's forehead. It was the most beautiful thing he'd ever felt. He risked taking a breath, and though the air remained hot and foul, it was not quite so cruel as before. Daigoro closed his eyes, relishing the cold before the fire sapped it away. When he opened his eyes again, to his great surprise he found himself face-to-face with Ōda Tomonosuke.

Ōda had draped the two of them under a sodden blanket—or something like that, anyway; Daigoro's head was spinning too fast to make sense of everything. He was only sure that he was still alive, and that he had Ōda to thank for that. But instead of thanking him, all Daigoro could say was, "Why?"

"Honor."

Daigoro did not understand. Ōda fixed him with eyes hotter than the fire. "You were right. I could not stand by and let him kill you. Not like that."

"So you . . ."

"Set fire to the house. Yes."

Daigoro struggled to make sense of that. Ōda had left holding a torch and come back without it. He'd stayed by Shichio's side long enough to see Daigoro bound hand

and foot, but left as soon as he saw what Shichio had in store for him. Had he stayed out of sight long enough to set the building ablaze? Daigoro couldn't remember. He'd lost all sense of time.

As those thoughts swam confusedly in Daigoro's mind, a careful swipe with Glorious Victory freed his legs. His bonds had strangled all feeling out of his feet, and now they were not strong enough to hold his weight. Ōda learned that as soon as he cut Daigoro's hands free. Together they fell to the tatami, and for the first time in an eternity, Daigoro caught a breath of clean air.

Raw heat pummeled him from above. Blinding light seared his eyes even through lids pinched tight. Then the world grew dark and wet, and if not cool, then at least not hot enough to kill. Daigoro opened his eyes to see Ōda turtled above him, taking shelter under the wet cloth. "The sword comes with me," Ōda said. "As do you. We will fight, with no interference from that simpering pansy. You will kill me or I will kill you. That is how this ends."

"Agreed." No one had ever struck a fairer deal. "Ōda-sama, I once asked you if you are a samurai or a coward with a topknot. You have proved your mettle, my lord. Let no man call any Ōda a coward."

Ōda scowled. He had no patience for praise from the boy who had killed his son. "Can you stand?"

Daigoro tried and failed. "Soon, I think."

"Make it sooner."

Outside their dark little world, the fire roared like a dragon. Something heavy moaned like a falling tree. Whatever it was, it cracked, and then the whole floor shuddered. Flying embers pelted Daigoro's legs, and he realized he could feel his feet again.

He curled himself into a ball under Ōda's huddled form. His feet were shot through with pins and needles, incapable of supporting his weight. He decided they did not need to. He gave Ōda a nod, then got to his elbows and knees and crawled toward the pool. Ōda moved with him, a human turtle shell.

Another moan and a crack, this time without warning. Something crashed down, slamming Ōda in the back. He fell to his knees and knocked Daigoro flat. Then the whole damned roof came down.

When the roof caved in, it sent ten thousand fireflies swarming into the night. The flaming ruin belched forth a wall of heat that struck Shichio hard enough to stagger him. Shielding his face, he looked up to see a black form flying from the blaze. It streamed smoke and embers behind it, and it hissed when it struck the surface of the pool.

The sea dragon. Lord Ōda. He'd made it after all.

Shichio gaped unblinking at the cold, black water, waiting for Ōda to surface. Yellow and orange rippled across the water. No one emerged.

With the power of the mask Shichio could see a luminescent line glowing like a long, curved ember under the water. Glorious Victory Unsought. It had to be. It rested at the bottom of the pool, lying perfectly still for a very long time. Had Ōda dropped it? No; if he'd survived, Shichio should have seen him surface by now. More likely he'd drowned with it—better than burning to death, Shichio supposed—and now his stubborn dead samurai hand still clutched the heavy sword like a chain fixed to an anchor.

No matter. Shichio knew how to swim. For anyone else, finding the sword in ink-black water would have been impossible, but Shichio's mask would show him the way. But—wait. Was it moving? Yes. He would not have to go to the sword after all. It would come to him.

Cold water breathed life into every pore. Feeling came back to his hands and feet. His eyes opened, and the chill washed the sting and soot from them. In time Daigoro remembered he was a man, and not a dying creature.

When all was said and done—if he was still alive an hour from now—he would wait for the teahouse to burn away, then collect whatever was left of Ōda Tomonosuke. A worthy foe deserved a worthy funeral. If there was any death worse than seppuku, it could only be dying by fire. Ōda had thrown himself into that fate with the same detached resignation, the same unshakable courage, of a man driving a knife into his abdomen. He would be given a samurai's farewell.

Daigoro came slowly to the awareness that his lungs were burning—not from the heat of the fire but for want of air. Releasing his father's sword, he rose slowly to the surface. He breached like a sea turtle, with only his eyes, nose, and mouth. The cold air tasted like heaven. He could not see Shichio ashore—spots of fire still dotted his vision—but he knew the peacock was out there. Giddily watching the fire, in all likelihood, hoping Daigoro was burning to death inside.

Daigoro had to surface three times more, and wriggle underwater thrice more, before he freed his arms of Shichio's ropes. The water had swelled all the knots, but his skin was slippery now, and he had his hands free. Once his arms were unbound, he untied all the coils around his chest. By the time he was finished, he could see normally again. The next time he surfaced he saw Shichio, watching not the fire but the sword. Daigoro had forgotten: somehow that mask enabled him to see it. But the peacock didn't spot Daigoro; black water, brightly reflected flame, and the constant churning of the waterfall made the face of the pool a rippling cloak of camouflage.

The wisest thing to do was to flee, leaving his father's sword at the bottom of the pool. Second best would be to let Shichio's fixation on the sword distract him, then sneak out of the pool, creep up on the peacock, and stave his head in with a rock. But Daigoro was in no shape for a fight, much less a silent ambush. He was burned head to toe and bleeding badly. By now he must have tinged the whole pool red with blood. Besides, the Inazuma blade was his only weapon. Everything else he owned, including his Sora *yoroi*, was burning in what remained of the teahouse. A rock was no match for Shichio's *daishō*. Daigoro would fight with Glorious Victory Unsought or he would not fight at all.

Then he realized the awful, inescapable truth: he could not win. Glorious Victory Unsought would not allow it. The blade guaranteed victory only when he did not want to fight. More than anything in this world, he wanted Shichio dead. Glory be damned, he thought, but by the gods and buddhas, this is the one victory I cannot go without.

Drained, burnt, and bleeding, he stood no chance. His own sword would fight against him. But what choice did he have? The way of *bushidō* was to dash in headlong. And maybe there was a way to get Shichio to defeat himself. The peacock was no swordsman. He also had no patience, nor any control over his temper. If Daigoro could provoke him, the peacock might grow reckless. The footing was treacherous here, slick and uneven; it would be easy to slip and fall. Daigoro might not have to *defeat* Shichio; he would only have to lift his heavy sword above his foe, then let the blade do what it wanted to do.

He dove back down, found his sword, and found Ōda's *kosode* too. He would sustain the camouflage for as long as he could. With what little strength he had left, he dragged his heavy cargo into shore. When the water was shallow enough, he pulled the *kosode* over his head, struggled to his feet, and limped out of the pool. Glorious Victory Unsought rested on his right shoulder, a bright orange tiger stripe in the firelight. Just before he reached the shore, he let the cloak drop.

"You!" the peacock screeched. "Impossible! You should be dead!"

"Lord Ōda found his courage. He died a samurai's death."

Shichio backed away, terrified. Daigoro could only imagine what the peacock saw in him: skin burned as red as a demon's, but with a face streaked white like a ghost's. His hair hung long and limp, like a drowned man's. He even moved like a dead man, his steps slow and stilted, yet he bled like the living. What Shichio saw emerging from that pool was a condemned soul walking out of hell.

"You should be dead," was all Shichio could say. "You should be dead."

"You *will* be dead. Soon."

"No!" Shichio's katana whistled as it flashed from its sheath. "Look at you! You can barely stand."

He squared himself in a proper *kenjutsu* stance. That was the moment that Daigoro knew he'd lost. Shichio had been training. He couldn't have learned much, but a stable stance was the only advantage he needed. The treacherous footing wouldn't turn against him after all; it would turn against the half-dead boy with the crippled leg.

"Father, what should I do?" He breathed the words, too low for Shichio to hear. And his father answered: in his position there was only one thing a samurai *could* do. He had an enemy before him and a sword in his hand.

Daigoro lowered Glorious Victory Unsought to a ready position. His left hand caught the pommel just in the nick of time; the sword was so heavy, and Daigoro's arms so tired, that he nearly dropped his weapon. Shichio settled deeper into his stance. He would wait for Daigoro to press the attack—or else for Daigoro to simply pass out from exhaustion. Daigoro could not afford the luxury of patience. Yet another advantage in Shichio's favor.

The Inazuma blade reached for him and Shichio retreated. The two fighters moved inland. Daigoro tried to circle, to drive Shichio toward the fire, but Shichio seemed to feel it coming in advance. He chopped at Daigoro's hands. Daigoro parried, and Shichio used that instant of reprieve to correct his course.

"It's the mask," Shichio said. "It sees your sword. No matter what you do, I will feel it first. You're fighting two of us, not one."

Three, Daigoro thought, if you count my father's sword. Four against one, counting the terrain, or five, counting Daigoro's own exhaustion. He feinted high and cut low, and nearly lost his hands. Shichio's blade passed just short of them.

"Call out to your friend," Shichio said merrily. "The one up on the cliff. Ask for advice. Or bid your final farewell."

He'd almost forgotten Katsushima was looking on. No doubt Katsushima himself would prefer to be forgotten, because now that he was on Daigoro's mind, he was a distraction. How awful it would be to watch helplessly as a good friend got killed—and cut down by an honorless coward, no less.

Daigoro lashed out, aiming for Shichio's sword. Shichio hopped back, just out of reach. Now they fought on the narrow trail leading back up the valley. The trees pressed close on either side. Glorious Victory's reach would soon be a disadvantage.

Let the blade do what it wants to do, he thought. That was his best strategy before. It was the only idea he had left. The alternative was to fight a running battle all the way back to the valley mouth. Somewhere along the way, Shichio would get lucky and Daigoro would fall.

With a great *kiai*, Daigoro pressed the attack. Huge overhead swings should have cut his opponent in two. Each time Shichio turned them away. Ringing steel sang in the vale, scaring the birds from their roosts. Daigoro hacked and stabbed, and Shichio parried every blow. Deep in the trees now, Daigoro put everything he had into one last slash. He let the blade do what it wanted to do.

More than anything, he wanted Shichio dead. Glorious Victory knew it. It pulled him off balance. Shichio ducked, and the Inazuma blade sailed harmlessly over his head. It buried itself in a dead tree trunk. Daigoro could not pull it free.

When Shichio came for him, Daigoro met his assault. Unarmed, he grabbed Shichio's sword arm, then raked the demon mask down over his eyes. Then he yanked Shichio's *wakizashi* out of its sheath and gutted the son of a bitch with his own weapon.

Shichio cried and bent double. His katana rolled rustling through the underbrush. He fell to his knees. His hands, suddenly weak, pawed at the sword in his gut. His fingers rolled bonelessly off its grip.

Daigoro peeled the mask off his face so the two of them could see eye to eye. Shichio was pale, quivering like a leaf. "Ironic," Daigoro said. "You're unworthy of the twin swords, and now, because you're wearing both, you'll die on the one you never deserved."

Shichio sobbed. Pain wracked him, twisting his whole body around the blade. "I'd like to leave this sword in your belly," Daigoro said. "You'd be a long time in dying. Probably all night. But a man spared me from dying a dog's death tonight, and so it's my karma to spare you."

He stepped around Shichio and kneeled down behind him. "If you want to be samurai, you should die like a samurai," he said. "I will help you."

He reached around, took the *wakizashi* in both hands, and pulled it all the way in to the hilt. Shichio's screams reached the heavens. Daigoro rolled the blade over, turning it spineward. With agonizing slowness, he drew it across Shichio's belly.

Performed correctly, seppuku required a second. When the condemned man plunged the blade into his gut, the second stood with sword raised, ready to behead him. That way the condemned could not disgrace himself by crying out in his final moments. Shichio did not have the luxury of a second. He left this world screaming like a lamb at the slaughter, and died facedown in his own entrails.

48

The Green Cliff stood as strong as ever, its verdant moss glistening in the westering sun. A persistent drizzle hung over Izu, never quite turning to rain, never quite fading away. The horses bore it miserably, but Daigoro found it soothing. The teahouse fire had given him the equivalent of a whole-body sunburn, and though full-fledged raindrops would have stung like needles, the misty sprinkling came as cool relief.

"We've made it," Daigoro said, shooting his friend a worried look. Katsushima's arms ended in ugly stumps, for both hands were swaddled halfway to the elbow in dirty, bloodstained bandages. He claimed he could still feel his fingers. That was good, but Daigoro misliked the smell. Those bandages needed replacing, and soon. Daigoro hoped Old Yagyū was still at Lord Yasuda's bedside, because if anyone could save Katsushima's hands, it was Yagyū. The worst-case scenario did not bear thinking about. Katsushima had wedded himself to the sword; if his *kenjutsu* days were over . . . Daigoro could not even bring himself to finish the thought.

Getting out of the Ōbyō valley had not been easy. On his way in, Daigoro spied the platoon Shichio had stationed at the mouth of the vale. If their commander did not return, sooner or later they would have to send a scout to look for him. Daigoro had planned for this possibility; Katsushima had carried a knotted rope with him, which he could have bound to a tree if only he'd had two good hands. In the end he'd managed to tie a knot using his teeth and the crooks of his elbows, and found an angle to toss down the rope where the spray of the falls wouldn't soak it through. It had taken Daigoro the better part of the night to muster enough strength to climb that damned rope.

As weak as he'd been, he couldn't manage the weight of his father's sword, so he had to pull it up behind him. Tied with it were the remains of his Sora *yoroi*, which he'd wrapped in a makeshift bag made from a fallen samurai's kimono. Everything not made of metal had burned away, but the most important piece was still intact: the scarred steel breastplate. It was supposed to be lacquered in white, the color of death. As soon as Daigoro had picked it up from the embers of the teahouse, the lacquer disintegrated, blowing away like so many cherry blossoms on the wind. There was a poem to be written there, Daigoro thought.

Tied to his *ōdachi* and armor was one last encumbrance: his new *wakizashi*. Since Shichio destroyed Daigoro's short sword, Daigoro had replaced it with Shichio's. In addition to having a certain sentimental value—namely, Shichio's bloodstains—the sword also had a lineage not far shy of Glorious Victory Unsought's. It had once belonged to Toyotomi Hideyoshi himself.

"How is it that you come by such noble swords?" Katsushima had said when he saw it. "That makes two for you and none for me." When Daigoro pointed out that Hideyoshi's katana lay somewhere in the underbrush, Katsushima laughed ruefully. "Let the weeds have it."

They'd returned together along the meandering trail that had first led Katsushima up to the cliff overlooking Ōbyō Falls. From there they'd shuffled on weary feet to the first homely house that would take them in—a brothel, not surprisingly. Katsushima was a veritable homing pigeon when it came to finding whores. The madam had promised she could get them the rest of the way home if the price was right, but neither Daigoro nor Katsushima could bear the indignity of how she meant to send them. She had a good packhorse with two large baskets slung on either side of the saddle. "The baskets are most comfortable," she'd insisted. "My girls travel this way all the time. Their feet are as soft as a babe's."

Raw and blistered though they were, Daigoro still thought his feet were tougher than a baby's, and on no account would Katsushima allow himself to be seen sitting in a basket like a heap of laundry. Instead, the two of them opted to keep their rooms for a few nights, lingering until Daigoro felt he'd recovered strength enough to ride. His wounds never stopped weeping, though, and in the end he overruled Katsushima's counsel of patience. As soon as the *rōnin* started showing signs of a fever, Daigoro's concern for Katsushima's hands outweighed any concern he had for himself.

Now, approaching the great stronghold of House Yasuda, Daigoro found he could hardly keep himself ahorse. A dull ache had penetrated his thighs and belly and back. That was just from the effort of staying in the saddle; his burns and cuts pained him still more. He couldn't help but remember the last time he'd ridden through the Green Cliff's gate, when Katsushima had to tie him into the saddle just so Daigoro could stay on his horse. This time felt much the same, except Katsushima was in no state to tie knots.

As the great gate yawned open, Daigoro mustered the last of his strength to hold himself tall and proud. He would not have Kenbei and Azami see him loll drunkenly in the saddle. In the courtyard he saw the master and mistress of the house, and also Yasuda Jinichi, Kenbei's elder brother and lord of Fuji-no-tenka. Daigoro saw his mother there as well, holding her little lord and husband, Gorobei. Akiko stood beside them, looking radiant in red. She'd chosen a bright yellow *obi* to emphasize the child growing so swiftly in her womb. Daigoro wanted to leap off his horse and kiss her belly.

But the fact that so many were in attendance did not bode well. No doubt they had come to pay a final visit to Yasuda Izu-no-kami Jinbei, master of the Green Cliff, patriarch of House Yasuda. Daigoro could imagine other reasons they might have come—Jinichi to escort his money to his venal brother, Aki to see Daigoro a half-day sooner—but in all likelihood, Lord Yasuda had taken a turn for the worse.

Aki blanched when she saw Daigoro. As well she might, he thought. He was burnt as red as a boiled lobster, and Shichio's bonds had left raw, suppurating cuffs around his wrists. The cuts Shichio had taken out of Daigoro's back, arm, and stomach had never closed properly, and all the rocking in the saddle had cracked the scabs open. Red spots seeped through his borrowed kimono. That was to say nothing of the eggplant-purple bruises coiled around most of his body, which she would only see later, once he disrobed. What she saw now was enough to stop her heart. "Get Yagyū!" Aki cried. "Daigoro, what happened to you?"

"I'll be all right," Daigoro said. His voice sounded weak even to his own ears. He tried to sound more like his father. "Yagyū should tend to Goemon first. I—"

"No," Kenbei announced. "First you two will speak to me. I will not harbor fugitives, and I would have you tell me how many Toyotomi soldiers are on your heels."

"None," said Daigoro. "My quarrel with the regent is over. The peacock is dead. The pact we signed died with him, and that means my only remaining tie with Hideyoshi is the treaty he signed with my father."

With a flick of the rein he urged his horse closer. "Do you remember it?" he asked. "It said the lords protector of Izu would maintain a united front, and would pose no threat to Hideyoshi's expansion. In exchange for political stability, he promised us our independence. Do you understand, Kenbei-san?"

"Yasuda-dono," Azami corrected. "We will also accept Yasuda-sama."

"You'll accept what I give you."

Daigoro stepped out of his saddle, and hoped beyond hope that his right leg wouldn't buckle when he hit the ground. It didn't; Aki was there to support him. On any other day, he might have felt shame—a man was not supposed to need a woman's help for anything—but a few nights ago he'd nearly been tortured to death, then nearly burned to death. Even the sword fights paled in comparison. If the embrace of his beloved was supposed to be shameful, then shame was the least of his injuries. The simple truth was that he thought he'd never feel her touch again. Now the smell of perfume in her hair nearly brought him to tears.

"Akiko, will you marry me?"

The question took her utterly by surprise—and not just her. Everyone else too. He supposed it should have, since this was the bluntest, clumsiest, most inept proposal ever uttered. A man did not ask such a thing of a woman; he asked it of her father. Even then, custom demanded a lengthy conversation, and usually a long bartering process as well. The last time Daigoro and Akiko were married, it was to cement a relationship between their houses. That was before they'd really known each other, and certainly before they'd fallen in love. This was something else entirely.

"You idiot," she said. "I told you from the start: if you want to divorce me, you'll have to grab hold of me and throw me out of the house. Otherwise, I don't care what you sign with foreign lords. Here in Izu, you're my husband and you always will be."

Another couple might have kissed. Far more romantic for Daigoro and Akiko was for her to keep an arm around his waist, and for him to keep a hand on her shoulder, just so he would not collapse.

"There you have it," Daigoro told Kenbei and Azami. "House Okuma does not recognize my divorce. In fact, there is no one left alive who does. That means I was very much mistaken when I entered here. I thought my name was Daigoro. In truth it is Okuma Izu-no-kami Daigoro. House Yasuda has loyally served my clan for generations. Now, Kenbei-san, will you serve or will you not?"

The furrows in Azami's brow grew deeper. Kenbei's eyes, the color of storm clouds, threatened lightning. "Daigoro or Okuma Daigoro, it makes no difference," said Kenbei. "Your coffers are empty. Your clan is destitute. My brother's pity for you outweighs his coin. Lord protector or no, you are in my debt."

"Then I ask you to forgive the debt. As my loyal vassal. Will you obey?"

"What if we don't?" Azami snapped. "We have heard from Lord Sora. He does not support you; he has only promised to stand clear of the fray. The same goes for Lord Mifune in the north and Lord Inoue in the south. What does it mean if your own father-in-law will not stand by you?"

"My father-in-law is not here. I will demand his fealty later. Today I demand yours."

"No," Kenbei said. "Izu is no longer your home, Bear Cub. You have no support here."

"He has *my* support," said a reedy voice behind him.

Yasuda Izu-no-kami Jinbei looked more ghost than man. His face was almost as pale as his snow-white top-knot. He clutched a railing with bone-thin hands, but a fire burned in his eyes. Before leaving his sickroom he'd even taken the trouble to don his swords. Wracked by ague, he could scarcely bear their weight, so he kept his feet only through sheer force of will. He was, in short, the living spirit of *bushidō*.

"He has *our* support," the aging lord said. "Young master Daigoro is the third Okuma lord I have served. I had not thought to live long enough to kneel before a fourth, but by the gods, Kenbei, I would have guessed I'd live to serve a hundred more before I guessed one of my own sons would betray our closest friend."

"Father, I—"

"Shut your mouth!" Kenbei shriveled like a dead worm in the sun. Azami remained adamant, balling her fists. "And you," Lord Yasuda told her, "I have been patient with you for far too long. I have called you a she-bear before, but now I see you for what you are. Your tongue drips venom into my son's ears. Now you have made him one of your own: a viper."

"Wrong," she shouted back. "If I were a viper, I'd have poisoned you ages ago."

"Azami!"

No one expected her husband to strike her, least of all Kenbei himself. Evidently he still retained enough filial devotion to take offense when his wife insulted his father. The whip-snap sound of his slap across her cheek seemed to hang in the air. He was well within his rights as a husband, but clearly it was a line he'd never crossed before. He froze like a rabbit, stunned at what he'd done.

Azami all but growled and bared her teeth. The breath came loud and long through her nostrils. Then she punched him in the jaw.

The woman had the forearms of a blacksmith. Her fist caught him on the tip of the chin and knocked him cold. If Kenbei's slap made everyone gasp, Azami's punch rendered all of them speechless.

Except for Lord Yasuda. "Be gone! And drag my fool of a son with you! Find a new hole to make your den; you are not welcome here anymore."

The outburst was enough to make Lord Yasuda light-headed. He swooned, but his white-knuckled grip on the railing prevented him from falling over. Before he could right himself, a fit of coughing bent him double.

His eldest son, Jinichi, rushed to his side. Daigoro wanted to as well, and with Aki's help he made a few hobbling steps in that direction. Lord Yasuda waved all of them off. "I'm all right—or if not *all* right, then at least right enough to keep my footing. Damn this demon in my lungs! And damn you, Jinichi, for letting things go this far."

Jinichi kneeled and bowed. "I'm sorry, Father. When you made Kenbei steward of the Green Cliff, I thought—"

"You thought what? That he was fit to lead? I stationed him here so I could keep an eye on him."

All eyes turned to Kenbei, who still lay as limp as a wet rag. Azami proved she was not quite as heartless as Daigoro supposed. She did not drag her husband across the flagstones, as Lord Yasuda had commanded. Rather, she left Kenbei lying there to gather raindrops, and stormed off to their quarters to collect her things.

The wizened little lord bowed to Daigoro as deeply as he could manage. "You have my most abject apologies, Okuma-sama. I knew Kenbei was trouble from the moment I first met his sons. Mountain monkeys, all of them. I cannot imagine where he learned his fathering instincts, but I pray to all the gods and buddhas that it was not from me. I should never have agreed to marry his grandson to your mother, but you were in such need, and it seemed such a clever idea at the time. . . ."

"No apology is necessary," Daigoro said. Together he and Aki finally made their way to Lord Yasuda's side. "I asked a favor of you and you granted it without hesitation. What more could anyone ask? Azami spoke the truth: of all the lords protector, the only one to stand by the Okumas was you."

"The only one to make trouble for the Okumas was me."

"No, Yasuda-sama—"

"Enough with that *sama* nonsense. You are Lord Okuma Izu-no-kami Daigoro again. Now you listen. You will not know it, Okuma-sama, but once I was young like you. I used to go out drinking and whoring with my friends." He gave Katsushima a knowing wink, which Katsushima returned in kind. "I used to get good and drunk in those days, but if I was ever so drunk as to mate with a monkey, I cannot remember it. It must have happened, though, because I do not know how else Kenbei came to be so unlike his brothers."

Daigoro chuckled. "As direct as ever, Yasuda-san."

"Ha! Laughter. That's more like it. Now introduce me to this bride of yours. I don't believe we've met."

In the end, Aki and Daigoro stayed at the Green Cliff for three days. It was long enough for a Shinto priest to marry them—redundantly, as Aki insisted—and long enough for the old man to embrace Aki as a granddaughter. Since Jinbei was so welcoming of her, Daigoro thought he ought to show House Yasuda similar generosity. "Lord Yasuda," he said as they were readying to leave, "may I ask you to reconsider Kenbei's fate? Even if you got him on a mistress, and even if your mistress was an ape, is he not still your son? You're within your rights to turn him out, but . . . well, he is a Yasuda. Must he become a vagabond?"

Yasuda coughed. "It seems to me being a vagabond toughened you up some. He could do with a bit of that."

Daigoro smiled and shook his head. "I suppose he could at that. But even so—"

"If he makes the same request, I'll grant it. If not, he deserves to wander, or else to find a new den with that she-bear of his—or viper, or whatever it is I'm calling her these days."

The old man laughed, which brought on a fit of coughing. Daigoro decided it was time to go, since his departure would remove Lord Yasuda's last excuse for staying out of his sickbed. They bade their farewells and Aki and Daigoro called for their horses. Katsushima rode with them, and Old Yagyū too; his two new patients required more care than Lord Yasuda. Yagyū was optimistic about Katsushima's hands, less so about keeping Daigoro's gaping, bitelike wounds free of infection.

Daigoro's mother and her infant husband sat in the shade of a palanquin, and an honor guard from the Okuma compound had ridden up to accompany them. They had brought one of Daigoro's mares with them, wearing one of his old saddles, the kind that accommodated his withered leg. Sitting in that particular saddle, surrounded by that particular landscape, facing south on that particular road, it finally dawned on Daigoro that he was going home. Not merely the place of his birth but *his* house, *his* home, where once again he would sit as head of the clan and Lord Protector of Izu. He was Okuma Daigoro again. At the end of this ride, he would not just come back home; he would come back to himself.

He had the whole ride home to think about everything that meant for him—and not just for him, but for his unborn child, for the memory of his father and brother. When at last he reached the Okuma compound, riding through the great gate felt like stepping back into his own body. He swung out of the saddle, set foot in his courtyard, and said, "I'm back."

BOOK ELEVEN

HEISEI ERA, THE YEAR 22

(2010 CE)

49

Mariko stubbornly dialed Han's number again. He'd ignored the last four calls—or rather, he was tied up in the middle of a SWAT operation and didn't have the attention to spare for personal calls. Mariko rang him anyway. It gave her something to do.

Otherwise, she was stuck sitting in the BMW, not four blocks from the Shinagawa rail yard. She'd have driven farther if only she knew where to go. The unfortunate truth was that she had no idea where Jōko Daishi was or where he was headed. Her only clear idea was of what he'd do when he got there. He intended to purge close to a thousand children of their impurities. Or sacrifice them to purge Tokyo of its impurities, or some damn thing, anyway. Mariko didn't know what the Divine Wind called it. Her term for it was mass murder.

Her call went to voice mail, so she called Han again. And again. On the eighth call he finally picked up. "What?"

"Car thirteen oh four," she said. "Go to the north end and work your way back south; otherwise it'll take you forever to get to it."

It wasn't lost on her that neither of them made any attempt at witty banter. It spoke volumes about how frazzled they were. She saw no need to correct it, and neither did Han. "Thirteen oh four," he said. "You got anything more specific for me?"

"It's a boxcar, brown and rusty, in a big string of eight identical cars. Somewhere in the middle—the fourth or fifth, maybe? Screw it, just look for the one with a guy padlocked to it."

"Padlocked?"

"Yeah. Don't open the doors; call the bomb squad first. I don't think the car is rigged—I mean, they trusted a total idiot with the key—but you never know. Oh, and call paramedics too. You can tell them you think the kids were dosed with sleeping pills."

"Mariko, how the hell am I supposed to explain where I got this information? People are going to ask."

"Anonymous tip from a concerned citizen?"

"Concerned citizens don't take down a suspect and leave him physically attached to the crime scene. You know who does that? Spider-Man."

Mariko couldn't help but laugh. "Then tell them Spider-Man did it. Hell, Han, I don't know. You'll figure something out."

"Yeah, maybe, but it's got to be something that doesn't put you at the scene for assault—"

"And criminal trespassing and a million other charges. I know. Let's take care of the kids first. Tomorrow we can talk about whether we can still pull my ass out of the fire."

He didn't take long to think about it. "Anonymous tip it is."

"One more thing, Han. Get me a head count on the kids as soon as possible, okay?"

"It's not twelve ninety?"

"No. Way less. I'm not sure how many, but if you can give me a number, it might help me narrow down the places I go looking for the others."

Han was silent for a moment. Mariko heard a rasping noise and could picture him scratching his cheek where a long sideburn used to be. "Look, Mariko, I have to ask. Where are you getting this stuff?"

"All I can say is trust me."

He sighed. "All right. But we'll talk about this later, *neh*?"

"You bet. Oh, and Han? Hurry."

She killed the call and pounded the steering wheel in frustration. A lot of detective work was done on the phone, and on most cases she didn't mind. But on this one she felt every second bleed away as if it were a drop of her own blood. She had to find that "new church," but how? It could be anywhere, and Mariko had no one in the Divine Wind to question. The only members she knew by name, Akahata Daisuke and Hamaya Jirō, were both dead, and the only others she knew about were in that rail yard and probably in custody by now.

No, there was one more. She put in a call to Furukawa. "Status report," he said.

"That's not why I'm calling. I need to talk to Norika."

"All things in due time. Status report."

"Fine. I found a couple hundred kids in the Shinagawa rail yard," she said. "I think they're all alive; I sent cops that way to make sure. Now here's the important bit: they're keeping the kids in different groups. I think that's why you didn't pick up anything when you analyzed traffic patterns: they're not all going to one place."

"How many locations?"

"I don't know. I know Jōko Daishi is on his way to the first batch right this minute." If he's not there already, she thought. If the slaughter hasn't already begun. "He's going to some place his people call 'the new church.' Norika was close to him, *neh*? Like his concubine or something? Put her on the line; she might know where this church is."

"Young lady, you need to learn your place. I will not be ordered about by a—"

"Save it. I get enough of that shit at work." Mariko kneaded her temple with her free hand. A tension headache was settling in; it felt like steel cables pulled taut under her skin. "Look, either she knows where the 'new church' is or she doesn't. Which is it?"

"Norika-san has given a full report about the Divine Wind's internal structure. This includes the locations of many churches. I have people investigating each one, including the newest."

"How long is that going to take?"

"You're a detective, Oshiro-san. You of all people

ought to know how hard it is to answer that question. It takes as long as it takes."

Those steel cables pulled tighter. She needed a list of the locations Norika identified. Then she could figure out which ones could house a thousand kids and a bunch of whack-job cultists. As soon as the thought struck her, she realized it wasn't especially clever. Furukawa must have thought of it already, and performed the same process of elimination she would have carried out, except much faster, with many more resources. The only question was how much he was willing to share with Mariko.

"Have you found him already?" she asked.

"No."

"If you had, would you tell me?"

"Of course."

It was a stupid question and a hollow answer; if he was lying, she had no way of proving it. But it didn't gain her anything to assume he was holding out on her. "Look," she said, "I don't think we can wait any longer. If we can't find Jōko Daishi, then we have to make him come to us."

"Oh? What do you have in mind?"

"He needs his mask. He wants my sword. Let's give them to him."

"Hm." Furukawa sipped something. Ice clinked against crystal. "He does have people watching your apartment—or at least he did when last I checked. If we move the mask, he should learn of it soon."

"Make sure. Let it leak throughout your organization. You said he still has moles in the Wind, *neh*?"

"We must assume so, yes."

"Then get the word out."

Mariko felt something release in her chest, like a fist loosening up. It felt good to make progress, even if she hadn't actually accomplished anything yet. At this point, even an idea was good enough.

"It's a dangerous gambit," Furukawa said. "He believes the mask gives him divine power. And he is very clever. If he manages to steal the bait from off the hook, he may go on to do much worse than we've seen so far."

"How can it get worse than kidnapping and murdering over a thousand children?"

"How could it get worse than bombing an airport? Before this morning, Haneda was the worst we'd ever seen." He took a sip from whatever he was drinking, and much too calmly for Mariko's liking. She would have liked to hear those ice cubes jingling, as if held by a nervously quivering hand. "You ask how much worse it can get? I ask you, do we want to leave it to Jōko Daishi to answer that question?"

Now Mariko's hands were shaking. "Good point. But I don't see any other choice. I don't want to just sit back and wait."

"No, that isn't your style, is it?" Furukawa was almost jovial. He seemed to find her impatience adorable. "Very well. We'll do it your way. There's a pool hall called Kikuchi Billiards. Do you know it?"

"Is it anywhere near Kikuchi Park?"

"Across the street, in fact. We maintain a safe house there. I'll send the mask and sword. Can you beat them there?"

"I'll leave right now. I'll see if I can get a SWAT team on site too."

"And if not?"

"Then I'll see how many yakuzas I can have waiting for him. It's all pool balls, *neh*? The Bulldog is as bloodthirsty as they come. If he isn't willing to help me find Jōko Daishi, maybe he's willing to take a shot at him if I put the fucker in front of him."

"Well, now. That's most insidious of you, Detective Oshiro. You may be one of us after all."

Absolutely not, Mariko thought, but I'm counting on you being right about all the destiny stuff. She'd promised Shoji not to harm her son. If Shoji and Furukawa were right about Jōko Daishi's fate, then Kamaguchi firepower *couldn't* kill him. Neither could SWAT. Only Mariko could do that. But if they were wrong, she had practically called for Jōko Daishi's execution. Not a bad outcome, Furukawa would say, but Mariko made a promise to a friend and she didn't intend to break it. Besides, she'd be right there with him; she might end up in the cross fire herself.

Her phone beeped and she saw another call coming in. She hoped to see Han's name there; instead she saw the last name she'd expect.

"Hang on," she told Furukawa. "I have to take this." Then she clicked over to the other call.

"It's me," said the Bulldog. His rasping voice was unmistakable.

"Long time, no hear," Mariko said. "What's it been, half an hour?"

"Don't get cute. I changed my mind about those kids, but if you decide to fuck with me, I'll change it right back."

He sounded angry. "Are you okay, Kamaguchi-san?"

The breath came loud through his nostrils, blowing harshly over his phone's mouthpiece. "Those sissies who poisoned all those people at the hospital, they're the same ones who took the kids?"

"Uh-huh."

"Then fuck 'em. I'll help you bury them."

"Um . . . can I ask why?"

Another snort into the phone. "I got a girlfriend. Turns out she was pregnant. I didn't even know. She never told me; she just went to the hospital to have it taken care of. You understand what I'm saying?"

"Yeah."

"She came out of there sick. Like I said, I didn't even know she went in. Now I get this fucking phone call telling me she didn't make it. Looks like ricin."

"Oh." That brought the ricin death toll to twenty-four. No one would even hear about it, not in the shadow of the largest mass kidnapping in history. "I'm sorry, Kamaguchi-san. That's horrible."

"Here's what's going to happen," he said. "I'm going to help you find these cocksuckers, but for a price. I want the ringleader. I'm going to beat him to death with his own fucking mask."

Mariko had some experience with that. Unconsciously

she ran a finger over the line of stitches Norika had left in her scalp. "You know I can't make that deal."

"No? Then there's no deal. Simple as that."

"Come on, Kamaguchi-san. You're asking a cop to turn a blind eye to premeditated murder. You have to know that's not going to fly."

His nasal breath roared like an airplane engine over his phone's tiny receiver. "I'm asking a *suspended* cop. That's why you're calling me: because you can't call your own people. Am I wrong?"

"No." There was no point in lying. He had his police connections, just as she had hers in the *bōryokudan*.

"Then we play it my way. I been asking around, seeing if my people seen anything you're looking for. You want to find a place that'll hold thirteen hundred kids, *neh*?"

"Or close to it, yeah."

"I'm thinking somewhere out of the way—somewhere not too many people are going to notice when those kids start screaming."

"Yes." Mariko shivered; his cold logic gave her the creeps.

"Last thing: it's got to be somewhere that no one will look twice if a bunch of vehicles show up out of the blue— say, a bunch of light trucks."

"You know something. Tell me."

"You're going to love this." Kamaguchi paused as if waiting for a drum roll. "Haneda airport."

"What?"

"Some pretty cherry contracts went out for the cleanup and reconstruction. I made sure a Kamaguchi company got a couple of them. Heh. We're going to make a million yen a day out there."

"How nice for you. Get to the point."

"Women! Always so damn touchy." She could almost hear him shaking his head. "All right, here it is: Terminal 2 is huge, *neh*? Those bombs really only took out the lobby, but they had to shut down the whole terminal. It'll be months before anyone can fly out of there again. That leaves plenty of places to hide—big, dark places where no one's got any reason to go. So my foreman down there, he sees a bunch of trucks running in and out of the south end this morning. He doesn't think anything of it until I ask him, but then he says yeah, he hasn't seen them before."

"It's brilliant." Mariko just blurted it out. She didn't want to think it, much less say it, but Jōko Daishi was a genius. He'd taken hiding in plain sight to a new level. First he transformed Haneda into an international symbol for terrorism, then he camped out right inside it. But the Bulldog was right: strange vehicles would be running in and out of there for months to come. No one would think twice about them. And since all the reconstruction efforts were centered on the bomb site, no one there had any cause to explore the rest of the terminal.

"South end of Terminal 2," she said. "You're positive?"

"Yes, I'm fucking positive. What did I just say?"

"And you say *I'm* bitchy and temperamental. Chill out, Kamaguchi-san. I'm just doing my job."

"Then do it. And when you find that cocksucker, you bring him to me. That's the deal."

"I'll do you one better," Mariko said. "Kikuchi Billiards, across the street from Kikuchi Park. You know the place?"

"What about it?"

"Jōko Daishi's on his way now," Mariko said, hoping to hell that she could get cops there too. If not, she had just set up a hit. "You head there, you'll find him."

"Done," said the Bulldog.

He hung up. That brought Furukawa back on the line. "Norika's churches are a dead end," Mariko said. "The 'new church' is in the south end of Terminal 2."

"Terminal 2?" Furukawa sounded alarmed. "You don't mean Haneda?"

"No, McDonald's. Of course I mean Haneda. He's using the airport bombing as a smoke screen to hide the kidnapping."

"Oh, *very* good. Bravo."

Mariko rolled her eyes. "You're disgusting. Look, I have things to do. Figure out what to do about Terminal 2. Whatever you do, only use people you trust; as soon as

Jōko Daishi finds out we're onto him, he'll start killing kids."

"Don't worry. We'll be very careful."

"You better. One more thing: usually this would go without saying, but with you . . . look, try to solve this without murdering everyone, okay?"

"As you like, Detective Oshiro."

He said it as if she'd asked him for extra sprinkles on her ice cream sundae. Mariko shook her head, sighed in exasperation, and hung up. Then she put the BMW in gear and doubled back toward Shinagawa Station.

She called Han along the way. "Hey," she said, "you find them?"

"Three hundred and sixty-five of them," said Han.

"Jesus." Did Jōko Daishi plan to kill one a day for an entire year? Or set one free every day? Or did he just want everyone to leap to wild conclusions, and to be perpetually terrified of what would come next? Mariko supposed it didn't matter. These kids were safe; the Divine Wind wasn't getting them back. But that still left over nine hundred children unaccounted for. With luck, they'd all be in one place at the south end of Terminal 2. But so far all the luck was blowing Jōko Daishi's way.

"How soon can you get out of there?" Mariko asked.

"Right now, I guess. Why?"

"Come out to the sidewalk. I'm picking you up." Her engine roared as she gunned it through a yellow light.

"Mariko, tell me what's going on."

"I'll explain everything on the way. How long do you think SWAT's going to be tied up with those kids?"

Han thought about it for a second. "The area's pretty well clear. We should leave a couple of guys to watch the train car. Everyone else . . . I don't know, fifteen minutes?"

"Too long. We'll have to call another team." She downshifted and punched it around a big, slow newspaper truck. "You came in that SWAT van, not a cruiser, *neh*?"

"Yeah . . ."

"Damn. My car doesn't have lights or a siren. We'd get there faster if we could run code the whole way."

"What? Since when do you have a car?"

Just ahead, she saw Han jogging out from the access road to the rail yard. Mariko jammed on the brakes and the BMW skidded to a stop in front of him. "Holy shit, Mariko, where'd you get this?"

"Long story."

He ran around to the opposite side and jumped in. "Nice wheels."

"Thanks."

Mariko peeled out into traffic. Han grabbed the door for stability, then hurriedly snapped his seat belt shut. "Okay," he said, "you mind telling me what the hell is going on?"

"We're going to a pool hall over by Kikuchi Park. You need to make some calls and get a SWAT presence over there, because the Kamaguchi-gumi is sending a bunch of guys with guns."

"What? Why?" Han shook his head as if trying to shake off a knockout punch. "Mariko, I know you think we're on our usual wavelength, but I have to tell you, I have no idea what you're talking about."

"Sorry. Here's the deal. Jōko Daishi still has his eye on his demon mask. I'm going to put it right out where he can reach it, and I'm going to hope his obsession with the mask overrules his desire to kill hundreds of innocent children. I think this is going to be our best shot at him."

"Hell yeah. Nice work."

Mariko punched it through another yellow light. Then she looked at the speedometer, realized a hundred kilometers an hour was double the posted limit, and released the accelerator. "The thing is, there's a little bit of a hitch," she said. "I wasn't totally sure I'd be able to get enough cops on scene to catch Jōko Daishi."

"Uh-oh. What did you do?"

Mariko winced guiltily. "I may have called the Bulldog. And I might have told him the cult leader who stole his mask is going to be at Kikuchi Billiards."

"Oh."

"Yeah. So basically, the mask is the cheese in the mousetrap. The Kamaguchi-gumi is the mousetrap. And you and I are the great big human hand that's going to try to grab the mouse before the mousetrap kills him."

Han nodded reluctantly. "Major style points for the analogy, but this is pretty risky, don't you think?"

"Hence the need for you to call in SWAT."

"Right. Because this situation definitely needs a lot more guns."

"Exactly," she said with a laugh. It was nice to be back to their old repartee. "Hey, at least these guns will be on our side, *neh*?"

"If they get there in time. That's a major if, Mariko. I already have plenty of SWAT guys giving me funny looks about the last call. Car thirteen oh four, start looking on the north end, it's the one with the suspect padlocked to it. Remember that?"

"Then do it through Sakakibara. Just make it happen. We'll be there any minute."

50

Makoto looked on the faces of the sleeping children and his heart swelled with pride. Their sacrifice was so small in comparison to the truth they would illuminate.

These ones slept in a classroom, drowsing dreamlessly under the effects of a sleeping draft Makoto had developed himself. It was one of many concoctions he'd created for the Wind, some lethal, some not, back when he was still trapped in their clutches. In those days he did not liberate, he merely killed. Today he was glad to have put the Wind's murderous ways behind him.

He looked in on the next classroom, and was comforted to see dozens of little ones sleeping softly. The deluded soul saw children as the heirs of the future. The truth was that there was no future. There was only the now. Deluded people might fear what the future held in store, or eagerly await it, or be in doubt about it, but fear, anticipation, and doubt existed only in the now. To embrace that was to be liberated from all of them. What a simple thing it was to die, and what a monumental thing to deliver freedom from dread and doubt! The thought of such a noble transformation almost brought Makoto to tears.

Pain speared him in the temples. Any swift change to his emotional state, anything that induced a change in his pulse rate, stabbed sharp icicles through his skull. He'd suffered the headaches ever since the harlot shot his father and took him away. They were not as acute as they had been a week earlier, but they were not pleasant. Makoto had faith that his father could dispel the headaches, if only they could be together again. Until then, he only had his chi gung to control the pain.

If only his father could be here, to witness the Divine Wind's finest hour. This was his father's vision, greater and grander than any of Makoto's aspirations. So tragic that they could not realize that vision together.

"Daishi-sama," a voice called behind him. "A message for you."

He turned to see one of his disciples, a loathsome man with a scar across his left cheek. Makoto would not have called upon him for this sacred day if he'd had any other choice. Sending all of these children to the Purging Fire was a monumental task, and he needed every pair of hands he could muster. That included this disciple, who first drew Makoto's ire in the earliest days of planning this sermon. When Makoto nominated the airport as the newest church, this man had the temerity to suggest that the baggage handling system was perfectly suited for moving hundreds of child-sized corpses. "They are heralds of the truth," Makoto had said. "Divine servants of the Purging Fire. They shall be held in the highest honor, not tossed aside like so much luggage." Then he'd back handed the man, breaking a tooth and leaving that scar under his left eye.

The disciple was graceless then and he was graceless now. "A message," Makoto said. He kept his voice low, so as not to disturb the children. "Now? On the eve of my most important sermon? Use your head, child, and mind your tongue. This is the hour for listening, not speaking."

"It concerns your mask, Daishi-sama."

Makoto brightened at that. "Where is this messenger?"

The loathsome disciple kneeled, pulled a cell phone from his pocket, and presented it with both hands, holding it as high as he could manage while also bowing his head.

Makoto took the phone. "Yes?"

"Furukawa is moving the mask and the sword," said the voice on the other end. "They are no longer in the woman's apartment."

"Moving? Why?"

"He fears you are likely to come for them. He says you are more active now than you have ever been—his words exactly—and next you will take back what is yours. Since you know where it is now, he says it must be moved to a safer place."

"Which place?"

"Kikuchi Billiards. Daishi-sama, I fear this is a trap."

Of course it is, Makoto thought. The pool hall concealed one of Furukawa's safe houses. Makoto was not supposed to know the safe house existed. If he hadn't known of it, then it would have been the perfect place to hide his father and Glorious Victory Unsought. The fact that Furukawa thought it was safe made it all the easier to take what was hidden there. But Furukawa was crafty. If he suspected Makoto thought of the safe house as an easy target, then it was the ideal place to set a trap.

And yet . . .

Makoto longed for his father. Alone, he was only Koji Makoto. Reunited with his father, he was Jōkō Daishi, Great Teacher of the Purging Fire. It should be Jōkō Daishi that liberated these beautiful children. That was only fitting.

But was it worth the risk? Perhaps. Furukawa had not yet discovered the new church. If he had, Makoto would have heard about it. He had a disciple looking over Furukawa's shoulder. Furukawa was looking everywhere Makoto predicted he'd look. The old man had his agents inspecting every closed school in Tokyo, but he'd forgotten that there were other places with classrooms.

Not many people knew an airport had classrooms. They were not marked on the maps provided to travelers. But the flight crews needed a place to do their training, and Haneda International had designated rooms for that purpose. There were also quiet quarters here for weary crews to catch a little sleep. Every airline had its own accommodations, modest but functional, and after the Haneda sermon all were locked up and left behind. Makoto had found just enough space to house nine hundred and twenty-five children.

Not for much longer. The Purging Fire would claim them soon. Just as the classrooms and break rooms were abandoned, so too were the pumping stations at each of Terminal 2's gates. These connected via underground pipes to the millions of liters of jet fuel in Haneda's massive fuel depot. Makoto had a barrel set aside for each roomful of children. Deluded souls found death by fire to be utterly terrifying, but Makoto would show them the truth. Pain and death were merely states of being.

His father would be proud of this sermon. He had the right to see his vision brought to fruition. "It is my holy calling," Makoto said. "I must retrieve him, no matter the risk. So let us be wary of the trap and move boldly nonetheless."

"This is Furukawa," his disciple said. "He has tried to kill you before."

"He has his ploys and I have mine. What he does not have is a divine mandate. The light of the Purging Fire blinds his eyes. He has no idea how close my servant has drawn to him. When the time comes, faith will rule over cunning. My servant will return my father to the fold."

"It shall be as you say, Daishi-sama. There is one more thing: you know whose hands the mask and sword will go to."

"Yes, I know. She must not be allowed to live. Make sure of it."

51

"This is taking too long."

Mariko drummed her fingertips on the bar at Kikuchi Billiards. They fell in a steady, galloping rhythm, three beats at a time because the nub of her trigger finger wasn't long enough to reach the bar. Part of her wished she had a gun. The better part of her was relieved to be unarmed. What she really wanted was a few dozen cops with guns, and then a nice cold beer and a safe place to sit back and watch all the action unfold. The last thing she wanted was to be in the same room with Jōko Daishi and a lethal weapon. Fuck fate, she thought.

Han was nervous. He paced between the pool tables, leaving a haze of cigarette smoke in his wake. At one end of each pass, he glanced out the front door and onto the street. At the other end the sunset glow at the tip of his cigarette brightened like a warning light.

Kikuchi Billiards was a lot like Billiards Bagus: low ceilings, few windows, with most of the light coming from electronic dartboards or the boxy fluorescents hanging over the blue-green fields of the pool tables. The front wall was mostly comprised of heavily tinted windows, but at this time of day, steeped in shade, they did more for ambience than illumination.

"This is taking too long," she said again. "Where the hell is everyone?"

"Seriously?" Han said. "You're impatient about maybe getting shot at?"

"Well, it's weird, *neh*? You called Sakakibara. He called SWAT. The Bulldog probably called a whole damn army—"

"Leaving one big question: who did *you* call, Mariko? When are you going to tell me how you've been working all this magic?"

Mariko didn't want to answer that, and she didn't want to sit and do nothing anymore. "Screw it, I'm getting myself a beer."

She slid down off her stool and went behind the bar, which was unmanned; Furukawa had sent all of his people home. They had Suntory Malts on tap, so she poured herself a tall one. "I'm pretty sure that's against regs," Han said.

"Only if you're a cop on duty. I'm suspended, remember?" She raised her glass in a toast.

"You can't dodge me forever, Mariko. Tell me what's going on."

She took a long drink, steeling her nerve. "I made some deals with some bad people."

"Like who? The Bulldog?"

"Yeah."

"And the ancient ninja clan too, huh?"

"Yeah."

"That is so damn cool."

"Han, these guys do some seriously bad shit."

He shrugged and puffed on his cigarette. "You know I'm a Giants fan, *neh*? You know what I say when someone hits a home run against my Giants?"

"What?"

"I say that was a hell of a shot. These guys you teamed up with, they've got some serious swat. Let's keep them in the lineup, at least until this game is over."

Mariko shook her head. "This isn't a game, Han—"

Her phone quivered in her pocket, distracting her. She pulled it out and saw it was a call she had to take. "Where are they?" she said. "You told me they'd be here by now."

"The mask and sword will arrive shortly," Furukawa

said. "I'm afraid there has been a complication. They will arrive in the hands of a double agent."

"What, you mean Jōko Daishi's?"

"Yes. I sent word that the relics were to be moved, then monitored communications between Endo-san and Norika-san. It seems they are not as trustworthy as I expected."

"Perfect timing," Mariko said. At that very moment, someone was pounding on the door. "I have to go, Furukawa-san."

Han was at the door before Mariko could warn him away. "Well, hello there," he said. He stepped aside to admit Norika, and checked her out as soon as her back was turned. Then he caught Mariko's attention and mouthed the words *I'm in love.*

Usually Mariko had no trouble admitting when another woman looked good. Norika was the exception, for two reasons. First, she'd tried to kill Mariko once. Second, Mariko only had eyes for the bags slung over Norika's shoulder. Both were taken from Mariko's apartment. The smaller one was a muslin shopping bag, which contained something heavy and pointy. It had to be the mask. The larger one, tied to the first, was lavishly embroidered silk, very slender, almost as long as Norika was tall. In fact, it was a sword bag, formerly Yamada-sensei's, and it could only contain Glorious Victory Unsought.

The only thing Mariko could think of to say was, "You're not going to swing that mask at my face again, are you?"

Norika gave her a falsely sweet smile. "Keep hiding behind that bar and you won't have to find out."

Once again Mariko wished she had a gun. She wanted to tell Han to lock the door and draw down on his new ladylove, but she couldn't do that without revealing the fact that Furukawa had just outed Norika as the double agent. Mariko wasn't even sure Furukawa had it right. Wasn't Norika the one who shot Jōko Daishi and stole the mask in the first place? That was the story she told Furukawa, anyway. Could she have been lying? Yes. She was a *genin* of the Wind; she could lie about anything. The larger question was whether there was some ulterior motive in giving Mariko the mask. Was there anything so important that it trumped Jōko Daishi's need to keep the mask for himself?

If there was, Mariko couldn't imagine what it could be. She wished she had more time to think. Norika could see Mariko had doubts about her, because she stopped halfway to the bar. "What's wrong?" she said. "You don't trust me?"

At the same time, Han looked back out the doorway and said, "Hey, aren't you Endo Naomoto?" Then a lot of things happened at once:

Endo came in, his baseball bat hanging heavily in one hand.

Norika turned and smiled at him.

Han said, "You used to play right field for the Bay Stars, *neh*?"

Mariko figured out who the double agent was.

Then Endo took a homerun swing at Norika's head.

The bat caught her in the base of the skull. It caved her head in. She hit the floor face-first, limp as a wet rag. "For Daishi-sama," Endo said.

Han was stunned speechless. For a fateful half second, he forgot to draw his sidearm. Endo wheeled around. His bat swung high and fast at Han's forehead.

Fortunately, Mariko had figured out one second earlier that Endo was the enemy. She was already in motion. The only weapon she had in hand was her beer, so she threw it at Endo as hard as she could. Some deep-seated ballplayer's instinct made him duck away from anything pitched at his face. His flinch reaction pulled his swing off kilter, and Han twisted just enough to take the bat in the shoulder, not the temple.

Mariko grabbed a pool cue on her way to Endo. A cue stick was no match for a baseball bat, but baseball was no match for *kenjutsu*. She rushed him with a bellowing *kiai*, hoping to draw him away from Han. It worked. Endo spun, his bat a speeding blur. Mariko stutter-stepped. The bat flew past her. She flicked her makeshift sword at Endo's eyes.

She hit his cheek, not his eyeball. It still caused his head to snap back. Her cue stick flicked like a whip, striking the throat, the ear, the eye. With every blow she drove him back, and every time she stepped up to strike again. Han dove aside, and Mariko drove Endo right into the wall.

"Mariko, down!"

It was Han shouting. She didn't think; she just ducked and rolled.

Bullets smashed through the door, sending a shower of glass into the pool hall. Mariko had expected the possibility of gunfire, but from Han, not from outside. There was only one person reckless enough to fire blindly into a place of business. The Bulldog had arrived.

He brought friends, too. Holes of sunlight opened in the front wall. Han and Mariko scrambled under the nearest pool table. Endo dove for the floor too, then Mariko lost track of him. She rolled behind one of the stout, broad table legs just in time to see it shudder as two bullets struck home. She heard more rounds skipping off the tabletop.

The whole front wall came down in a tinkling cascade. Light flooded the pool hall. Mariko looked around for Endo but couldn't spot him. She didn't dare stick her head out from cover.

More gunfire erupted outside. These were different weapons, smaller in caliber, and they came from farther away. She heard shouting, and then the weapons that had been slinging rounds her way started shooting in a different direction.

She peeked out from behind the heavy leg of the pool table. There was the Bulldog, crouched behind his Land Rover's engine block and letting fly with an AK-47. Bullet was with him, along with six other yakuzas, all of them blazing away like they were in a video game. They were shooting away from Mariko, toward a small park on the other side of the street. Mariko couldn't see who they were firing on, but she guessed it wasn't cops. The Kamaguchi-gumi had no interest in starting a shooting war with the police; they were happy with the status quo. By the same token, cops wouldn't have just opened fire; they would have ordered the Kamaguchis to drop their weapons first.

"Who the hell are they shooting at?" Han said. "It's not SWAT."

Mariko loved that she and Han thought along the same lines even in the midst of a firefight. "I think the Divine Wind just got here."

A stray round from the park hummed over their heads, hit the light above their pool table, and brought it crashing down. "Dumbasses," Han said. "Don't they know they're shooting at their own guy?"

"I don't know if they are. Can you see Endo?"

Both of them scanned everything they could see without leaving cover. "No," said Han. "Did he make it outside?"

"Probably. He was right by the door. If he's still alive, he'll have to come back for those."

She nodded toward Glorious Victory and the mask. There they were, safe in their bags, surrounded by shattered glass and bullet-riddled barstools. Norika's body lay next to them, staring blankly at the mask. "Damn," Han said. "Karma's a bitch, huh? She who clubs people in the head gets clubbed in the head."

"I don't think that's how that verse goes."

Mariko hoped Endo was alive. If he was, he'd do everything possible to take the mask to Jōko Daishi, and Mariko and Han would follow him. If he was dead, then the odds against Mariko were long. She'd need someone else to follow back to Jōko Daishi, which meant the Divine Wind would have to win the gunfight outside. That wasn't likely; the Bulldog was a savage fighter. If the Kamaguchis won the battle, then Jōko Daishi wouldn't be so stupid as to walk up and demand the mask. He'd abandon the plan and come back for it some other time—*after* killing hundreds of innocent children.

In all likelihood, Endo was dead, splattered on the sidewalk just out of view. His brothers and sisters in the Divine Wind still sent stray bullets into the pool hall. Mariko risked a peek and saw the Bulldog drop behind the Land Rover to slam a new clip into his Kalashnikov. The man was clearly in his element. He even took a moment to pull a cigar from his jacket pocket. As he lit it, he accidentally made eye contact with Mariko. Seeing her made him do a double take. "Hey, sorry," he shouted. "Didn't know you were in there."

Mariko was too stunned for words. In her vocabulary, "sorry" didn't offset pumping forty or fifty rounds in someone's direction. But she got lucky; someone else in her profession decided on an appropriate response. *"Throw down your weapons,"* blared the megaphone, and Mariko heard tires squealing to a stop. A police cruiser. It had to be.

Then came a second set of braking tires, and a second voice shouting commands over a loudspeaker. Mariko heard a helicopter too, low and coming lower. Now sirens rang out on all sides of the park. The cultists were effectively caged. The cavalry had come. It wasn't SWAT; they must have been tied up elsewhere. This was general patrol. Tokyo's police had never been stretched thinner, yet somehow they'd still managed to respond in minutes. They made Mariko proud to be a cop.

Even as she felt that swell of pride, everything went to hell.

Yakuzas had the good sense not to shoot at cops. There was no money in it. But cultists didn't care about money. They didn't care about good sense, either. One of them popped a round at a squad car. It was a terrible mistake.

The cops in the squad shot back, just as they were trained to do. The cultists returned fire. Every other cop on scene took aim and fired on the cultists, just as they were trained to do. Some hit; most missed. One of those misses punched right through two doors of the Land Rover and hit the Bulldog in the hip.

Once the Kamaguchi guns lit up, it was a free-for-all. The Bulldog was shouting at his own guys to calm the fuck down, but it was hard to hear him over the sound of gunfire and a raging testosterone rush. Then, as if he'd been waiting all along just for this cue, Endo Naomoto reappeared.

After the initial fusillade, Han and Mariko had taken shelter under their pool table, behind one of its broad, wall-like legs. Endo had been hiding behind the other leg the whole time. Now he dashed past Mariko, grabbed the bags holding the mask and the sword, and ran for the shot-out windows.

"Stop! Police!" Han shouted. Endo didn't stop. Han took aim and put a round in his hamstring.

Endo crumpled, tumbling out of the pool hall and onto the sidewalk. The Bulldog heard Han's shot and came around with the AK-47. Mariko yelled for him not to shoot—too late. As Endo limped to his feet, the Bulldog pulled the trigger.

The round took Endo through the lung. It should have drilled straight through him, killing Mariko next, but it must have taken a funny bounce off a rib, because it winged off in a random direction instead. Endo fell to his knees. In his right fist he held the mask and the sword as if they were trophies—as if by holding them high he could show defiance to his tormentors. His whole body quivered with the effort.

No one noticed the motorcycle until it was too late.

Jōko Daishi shot past, a deafening blur of white and yellow. Then he was gone, and so were the sword and mask. Endo must have held on a little too tightly, because the handoff whipped him around hard, slamming him to the sidewalk. The bike's high-pitched whine filled the air, though moments earlier the helicopter and the gunfire were all anyone could hear.

Kamaguchi was the first to react. He raised the rifle to his shoulder and spat round after round at the motorcycle. There was no mistaking the sound of a Kalashnikov; his shots slugged the air like giant metal fists, loud and slow and heavy. They stood no chance of hitting their target. Kamaguchi was a bully, not a marksman. He didn't know anything about stance or breathing; he just shot stuff until it fell down. And Jōko Daishi was *fast*. He might have slowed to fifty kilometers an hour when he grabbed the bags, but he'd be closer to a hundred and fifty by now.

But Han responded almost as quickly as Kamaguchi. By the time Mariko got out onto the street, Han had drawn a bead and braced himself against the corner of a wall. He fired once. More than a block away, Jōko Daishi's back tire blew out.

It was an impossible shot, one in a million. The bike fishtailed like mad. Somehow Jōko Daishi brought it under control. He couldn't ride it, but he brought it to a stop before it killed him. He dropped it in the middle of traffic and started to run.

Mariko sprinted up the street, slapping Han on the shoulder as she passed him. She didn't turn around to see if he would follow; his footfalls told her everything she needed to know.

She was so intent on Jōko Daishi that she forgot she was running right through a firefight. A cultist's three-round burst reminded her. It spanked off a squad car's windshield, so close that Mariko could hear the ricochets whistling past her. She ducked and reeled away but she didn't stop running.

Ahead she saw a little traffic jam. A bunch of panicked motorists had slammed on their brakes at the sound of gunfire, and when the people behind them did the same, there was no backing out to get away. The smart civilians ducked as low as they could. The clueless ones poked their heads out for a better view.

Mariko ignored all of them; the only thing she cared about was the motorcycle stopped at the back end. The rider, guilty of felony stupidity, had pulled out his phone to film the gun battle. "TMPD!" she shouted. "We're taking your bike!"

"We're what?" Han said. "You know how to ride one of these things?"

"It's been a while," Mariko admitted. It was true, but not the whole truth. She'd learned to ride in central Illinois, where, apart from romping around on dirt bikes, ATVs, and snowmobiles, there wasn't much to do. The last time she'd ridden a motorcycle, she was twelve years old.

But nothing else was agile enough to catch up with Jōko Daishi. Mariko tore off, gunning it too hard and almost dumping Han off the back. When she shifted into second, she released the clutch too quickly and got a head butt in the back of the head. After that she was stable, at least until she hit the first curb. Her turns could have been smoother. Weaving between pedestrians went as well as could be expected, inasmuch as no one broke any bones. But at least she caught sight of Jōko Daishi.

He wasn't fast on his feet. He limped with a rolling gait, and he'd made it only as far as the nearest subway station. Mariko got a glimpse of his bushy hair just as he ran down the stairs.

In the movies, she would have jumped the bike all the way down to the first landing. In her youth, she might have had the guts to try riding it down the stairs. But Mariko wasn't a stuntwoman, and it had been a long time since she'd attacked the back hills of downstate Illinois. She jammed on the brakes, nearly throwing Han again, and stopped a few centimeters shy of sending Han, herself, and the bike in an avalanche down the stairwell.

They sprinted down, taking the steps two at a time. There was Jōko Daishi, muscling his way through a sparse crowd. Han had no clear shot and Mariko had no weapon. They ran after him.

Jōko Daishi vaulted the turnstiles, far more nimble than someone his age had any right to be. He hopped sidesaddle onto the next railing and slid out of view.

Mariko jumped the turnstiles; Han slipped under them in a baseball slide. Mariko snagged her toe on the way over, spiraled in midair, and landed on all fours. Han popped right to his feet, taking the lead. He slid down the railing with Mariko not far behind.

Downstairs, she could hear a train stop and open its doors. If Jōko Daishi got on board before Mariko and Han could reach him, they were done for. But it wasn't as if Mariko could make herself slide any faster.

She lost sight of Jōko Daishi, then of Han. By the time she caught them, they were embroiled in a fistfight right next to the train. There weren't many commuters—the whole city was on lockdown—and the few that were there had all fled the man with the demon mask. Mariko wasn't sure when he'd taken the time to put it on. Glorious Victory Unsought was slung across his back, still in its sword bag, though that had come untied. A wild light shone in his eyes, and a childlike grin turned the corners of his mouth, even in the midst of a brawl.

Han punched him in the chin. Jōko Daishi caught it, rolled with it, and slammed Han face-first into the side of the train. Han came away dizzy and bleeding. Then Mariko was in the mix. She hit Jōko Daishi with a flying tackle, but somehow he turned with her. She found herself upside down and airborne, and she hit the ground three meters away. The department's aikido instructors would have been proud of her breakfall. The cold tiles of the platform didn't knock her out, didn't knock the wind out of her either, and she rolled back to her feet.

Han threw three fast punches. Jōko Daishi parried all three, then head-butted Han. His demon horns drew blood. Mariko came up from behind, looking for a sleeper hold to end the fight. Without even turning around, Jōko Daishi stiff-armed her with a palm to the face. It laid her out flat.

She drew the Pikachu. Han reached for his sidearm. Jōko Daishi snagged Han's hand before it reached the pistol. With a quick twist he wrist-locked it, cranked it over, and sent Han flying right on top of Mariko. The Pikachu went spinning away.

The train doors closed. Exactly that much was right in the world. Jōko Daishi might still escape, but not on this train.

The problem was, he didn't seem to mind much. Instead of trying to stop the doors from closing, he pulled Han's handcuffs from his belt. He snapped one bracelet on Han's wrist and the other on the steel handle bolted beside the train door. Then the train began to pull away.

Han slid off of Mariko, dragged by the cuffs. Mariko

had no keys. Han did, and he dug for them, but to no avail. He and Mariko both looked past him to the end of the platform—or rather, to the heavy steel guardrail that was soon to stave Han's head in and tear his arm off at the shoulder.

Jōko Daishi watched with boyish anticipation. Mariko made him pay for his inattention. She kicked his bad leg with everything she had. Nothing broke, but at least she made him fall. She scrambled on top of him, planted both palms on his face, and put all of her bodyweight there. It pinned him and allowed her to spring to her feet. Then she tried to stomp on his head. He rolled aside easily enough, but that was the reaction she wanted. He exposed his back. She drew Glorious Victory Unsought from its scabbard.

"It's him or me," Jōko Daishi said, looking at the sword. He even stretched out his neck a bit.

Mariko ignored him and ran after Han.

The train was picking up speed. Mariko dug in hard, running for all she was worth. Her sword swung wildly with her pumping arms. Han still pawed at his right pocket with his left hand, digging for the handcuff key. His eyes wide with panic, he looked at Mariko's sword, then at the guardrail.

Terrified of losing his arm, he made a last desperate gambit for the key. He ripped the pocket right off. His key ring bounced away. He snatched it out of the air just before it fell. By some miracle his fumbling left hand managed to find the handcuff key among all the others. He reached up with the key, but the keyhole was too far. It bounced and jittered, a couple of millimeters out of reach.

"Do it!" he shouted, and he cringed away from his taut right arm.

Mariko's hands found their grip. She raised her sword and unleashed her loudest *kiai*. Then she struck.

The Inazuma blade slashed right through the handcuff chain, never touching flesh.

Han skidded along the platform and smashed into the guardrail. It rang like a tuning fork but he didn't hit it hard enough to hurt him. Impossibly, he even had the presence of mind to draw his pistol. He pointed it feebly in Jōko Daishi's direction, but it was a long shot, left-handed, and his whole body was trembling. He fired and missed.

But at least he was still alive, and well enough that he wasn't going to pass out. He gave Mariko a weak nod, and she turned and charged Jōko Daishi. He jumped down onto the train tracks and limped into the tunnel.

Thoughts of Shoji-san entered Mariko's mind. She sometimes spoke of the forces of destiny roaring in her ears. Mariko felt something like that now. Her whole body was tingling—adrenaline, not destiny, her rational mind insisted. She had refused Furukawa's pistol, rejected his invitation, insisted she'd never kill Jōko Daishi, and now here she was, chasing Shoji's son with a lethal weapon in hand. Furukawa had even said she'd kill him with Glorious Victory Unsought.

But what else was she supposed to do? Just toss her sensei's sword on the ground? The country's most dangerous criminal was at large. She knew where he was. She had no other weapon and he'd proven he was the superior fighter. He could kill her at will. Glorious Victory Unsought was her only defense.

But if he could kill her at will, why hadn't he? Was it faith in destiny? The first thing he'd ever said to her was that he had seen the hour of his death, and that he would die by the sword. But Mariko didn't buy that. It was just the hallucination of a sick mind. Besides, if he really believed in it, he could have stood his ground instead of running. He could have spread his arms wide and asked her to kill him. So what was his game? Was he just toying with her? Or did he mean to kill the kidnapped children, and only then let Mariko cut his throat?

It didn't matter. Mariko couldn't let him go. She jumped down onto the tracks and followed him into the darkness.

5 2

I see him wearing the mask. You have the sword in hand. He can see it coming. Do you understand, Mariko? He has seen his death coming. He sees it as a bright light, as bright as the sun. You'll try to ambush him. You'll fail.

Those were Shoji-san's words. Mariko remembered them with unusual clarity. She also remembered the question she wanted to ask next, the one she stopped herself from asking because she was afraid of the answer: *Am I going to die?*

She figured she understood the vision well enough. That mask allowed Jōko Daishi to see Glorious Victory, even in total darkness. It glowed for him—glowed like sunlight, she supposed. Mariko was counting on it. She wasn't likely to find him down here. The farther she got from the platform, the darker it got, and once she rounded the first curve she could see almost nothing. But the mask instilled an obsession for the sword. If Mariko could just get close to him, maybe the mask would draw him out.

It was cold in the tunnel. A distant rumble forewarned her of a coming train. It seemed far away, but even so, the sound terrified her. The reptilian part of her brain instantly demanded that she look for shelter. There was a narrow walkway on one side of the tunnel, a concrete ledge little wider than the length of Mariko's shoe. It would be of some use in getting passengers out of a stalled train, as they could keep a steadying hand on the train itself. Balancing on it while a train rushed by was a terrifying prospect. Still, Mariko had no choice. She climbed up onto the ledge, then pressed her back to the wall and hoped the wind from the train wouldn't knock her loose.

The train never came. It was going the opposite direction, on another track. "Do not worry," an eerie voice called from farther up the tunnel. "It will not be a train that claims my life. I do not think it will take yours either."

"Come on out," Mariko shouted. "We know about your church at the airport. Those kids are already safe." She hoped to hell it was true. "There's no way out for you. My partner already called for backup." She hoped that was true too.

"Your partner relies on law and order," said Jōko Daishi. "They will fail him, just as they have failed you. But you, you have abandoned your former keepers. You have fallen into the den of iniquity that is the Wind."

His voice echoed weirdly in the tunnel; it was impossible to tell if he was near or far. Mariko tightened her grip on Glorious Victory and settled her weight into her feet. It wasn't easy, balancing on this ledge while holding something as long and heavy as an ōdachi. She wanted to angle the sword toward the tunnel wall, erring on the side of caution; if a train came, just nicking it with the tip of her sword would knock her off the ledge. But if Jōko Daishi was closer than she thought, angling the sword that way would allow him to trap it against the wall, leaving her defenseless.

She didn't know what to do. She'd never trained for a situation like this. And now a low rumble shivered throughout the tunnel. Another train was coming.

"They are deceivers," Jōko Daishi said. "Purveyors of false truths."

"So are you. They trained you."

"Born of the Wind, yet not of the Wind. That is my nature. I am the light. I am the brightest fire."

For a moment Mariko thought she saw him glow. A faint light brightened the far end of the tunnel. It came from just around the bend. Then Mariko snapped out of it. The truth was simple: crazy people didn't glow. Train headlights did. But just for a moment, she'd been so scared that she actually started to believe him.

"Where are you?" she shouted. "Get on the ledge! Let me bring you out of here alive."

"You do not understand life. You do not understand death. I will show you their true nature."

She couldn't tell if that was a threat or the prelude to a sermon. She took sliding steps forward, her feet grating through years' worth of dust and grit. The ledge quaked under her feet, not from the train but just from the noise of it.

"You're sick, Koji-san. Let me help you. Just tell me where you are."

"I am everywhere. I am the light that disperses all shadows. Come to me, child; I will show you."

A wall of air hit Mariko in the face. A rumbling came with it, growing louder by the second. Glorious Victory shuddered, cutting the wind just like a rudder. The sword wrestled against her with a will of its own. A trembling glow grew brighter and brighter around the bend. Light consumed the far side of the tunnel, pitching Mariko's side deeper into shadow.

"Let me help you!" She had to shout at the top of her lungs. "Where are you?"

"I am here."

He stepped out from the shadow right in front of her, close enough for Glorious Victory to touch him. In the instant he stepped forward, the train rounded the curve. Its lights hurled his shadow at her, so vividly that she actually had to jump back.

When she landed she lost her balance. The ledge wasn't wide enough for a decent *kenjutsu* stance. She teetered on the edge, millimeters from the train cars that would smash her bones to pulp.

Jōko Daishi stepped forward. With one hand he brushed Glorious Victory aside, pressing it toward the wall. He was inside her reach now; she was defenseless. But his push moved the sword like a counterweight, allowing Mariko to regain her balance.

She twisted the sword, trying to drive the edge into him. He stepped in, grabbed her hand, and twisted back. Now she was locked into his range. She should have been two meters away, taking him apart piece by piece. Instead she was close enough to punch him—close enough for him to reach out and grab her by the hair.

It wasn't a great hold. It didn't even hurt that much. Mariko knew three different escapes from it, including one that would break his wrist and end the fight right there. But for that she needed mobility and she needed to be able to reach him. Her right hand was stuck, clamped on to Glorious Victory by Jōkō Daishi's iron-hard grip. With her left she could reach the hand that was grabbing her, but she couldn't hit any vital targets. She tried kicking him, but that was when he started pulling her head toward the train.

The train cars lit his face stroboscopically, so she got a good look at the childlike curiosity in his eyes. Every moment was frozen like a film cell. He was like a little boy with a bug under his thumb, pushing slowly just to see what would happen.

If she kicked him, she'd compromise her balance, and then she'd go headfirst into the train. She couldn't punch, couldn't elbow, couldn't bite him or gouge his eyes. She had no weapons left, except for Glorious Victory Unsought. The train was close enough that she could feel it hit her hair.

Yamada-sensei always taught her to keep her sword between herself and her opponent. He also told her the only response to failure was to try again. So she did. She couldn't get her sword free, so instead she wormed her way behind it. In effect she treated it like a guardrail, putting it between herself and the train. Because of the way he'd trapped it, Jōkō Daishi was on the train's side. He had her skull and her right hand totally locked down, but she was free to move everything else, so she put everything else behind Glorious Victory Unsought.

Now it wasn't trapped. Now it was a lever.

She pushed.

The train hit his shoulder blade first. Everything after that happened much too fast for Mariko to see. He hit the train, the wall, the ceiling, bouncing like a rubber ball in a blender. Sparks flew whenever the mask struck something solid.

When the train was gone, its stroboscopic effect left with it, so Mariko was left in the dark. Soon after that, she was left in silence.

53

Mariko collapsed on the ledge and took the biggest, deepest breath of her life. She sat that way for a while, just breathing, her head lolled back against the concrete wall, legs dangling off the lip of the ledge. Let another train come, she figured. It can't be worse than the last one.

In time she was ready to stand again, and she started walking back toward the platform where she'd left Han. She couldn't see a damn thing, so she held Glorious Victory one-handed, letting it rest on her collarbone, while the other hand lightly brushed the wall. It dawned on her that her scalp hurt. When she prodded it her fingertips burned what they touched, then came away sticky. Jōko Daishi had taken a big chunk of hair with him when he got hit.

"Ow," she said.

"My child," said Jōko Daishi.

Mariko practically jumped out of her skin. Glorious Victory sprang to the ready, almost of its own accord. Tightening her bloody fingers around the grip, she realized he could see her and she was still blind. She probed the darkness with the tip of her sword, her back pressed flat against the wall.

"My child, please," Jōko Daishi murmured.

He sounded half dead. His words burbled in his throat.

Wheezing breaths came slowly, as if passing through a slice in a piece of paper.

Mariko realized she had a light with her. After all her years with an old-school cheapo clamshell phone, it was easy to forget her new smartphone could double as a flashlight. She got it out, pointed Glorious Victory in the direction of Jōko Daishi's voice, and turned the light on.

The man in front of her was a mangled, broken, jagged, bleeding heap. He lay between the rails, crumpled like paper, his body knotted into impossible shapes. But his eyes were bright and white, blazing behind that evil mask. The mask had finally drunk its fill; every crease and furrow ran red with blood.

"Please," he mumbled.

He should have been dead. Hell, he should have been dead ten or twelve times over. And since he wasn't dead yet, he'd probably be a long time in dying. A long time suffering, too. It was clear from his face, from the twitches and shudders, from the sick sucking noises his body made when he breathed. Every moment was torture. If he were an animal, only a sadist would wonder whether or not to put him down.

Mariko realized she wasn't the only one who could see that. Shoji could see it. Somehow she shared a profound connection with her son, something far stronger than blood. She knew his future. At this moment, did she see hours of agony or did she see an end? Mariko could decide that for her. She could decide right now.

I shall die by the sword. That was what Jōko Daishi told her the first time they met. Shoji knew it. Furukawa knew it. If Furukawa could be believed, even Yamada-sensei knew it. He knew it well enough to keep Glorious Victory Unsought for himself, so no one else in the Wind could use it to kill Shoji's son. And now here it was, the fateful blade in its fateful place, with Mariko's hand on its grip.

She thought of the *kaishakunin* of old. When a samurai committed seppuku, he had a second to behead him if his suffering became too great. But Mariko was no samurai, and Jōko Daishi didn't deserve a samurai's death.

Then she remembered what Furukawa had said about Streaming Dawn. Maybe she wouldn't have to play the *kaishakunin* after all. Maybe she could just pull out the shard that was keeping Jōko Daishi alive. But Furukawa never told her what to look for or where to look. That was probably deliberate; no doubt the Wind planned to steal it from the body once Jōko Daishi was in the morgue. Not that it mattered. She wasn't about to start prodding a pulped, mangled man in hopes of finding the shard. No, there was only one way to end this painlessly.

Pity and resentment came to blows in her mind. She hated destiny, and she hated the fact that it wouldn't be destiny that killed Jōko Daishi. It would be Mariko. She wouldn't even be able to assuage her guilt by saying fate guided her hand. This was a deliberate, willful, fully conscious choice, and the worst part was that Mariko already knew what it was going to be. Apparently fate did too.

"Goddamn you," she said. "I don't want to do this."

She said it in English, not intending to. Now she couldn't tell if she meant to say it to herself or to Jōko Daishi.

Maybe he deserved his pain. Maybe he deserved hours and hours of it. He'd certainly caused enough pain. But for Mariko that was irrelevant. The only thing that mattered was that an old woman had suffered enough. Shoji would spend the rest of her life grieving over what her son had done and what she might have done to prevent it. If Mariko could ease her burden even a little, then that was what she ought to do.

She set down the phone. Even that sickened her, deliberately positioning it so she could see what she was doing. Her sensei's sword had never been so heavy in her hands. She lined up the cut. Jōko Daishi closed his eyes.

Mariko raised the sword and let it fall. She wasn't sure she could ever pick it up again.

54

Han came for her just before she reached the platform. Paramedics hadn't arrived yet, or else his right arm would have been in a sling. There was no way his rotator cuff could have survived being dragged by the train. Not having a sling, he just carried his right arm in his left. He had a nasty limp too. In fact, the whole right side of his body must have been bruised to hell. He didn't need a sling; he needed a stretcher, a neck brace, a backboard, and a quick route to the nearest emergency room. But he came for Mariko instead.

She watched him grit his teeth and groan as he lowered himself down to the tracks. He was backlit by the red taillights of the train, which stood parked and empty at the platform. Behind him, all the passengers were being directed up the stairs. The whole station was a crime scene now. None of them could see Mariko—the red light didn't penetrate that far into the dark tunnel—and she waited until they were gone.

"Mariko!" Han doubled his pace as soon as he saw her, though it obviously hurt like hell to do it. "I called for them to stop all the trains. I called them as soon as you went in the tunnel. I swear—"

"It's okay."

"I called them. I swear I did. I said stop every train,

there's an officer on the tracks. Then I heard that damn thing coming, then I saw it—"

"I'm all right. I wasn't hit."

She wanted to hug him, but he was beat to hell and couldn't use either arm. She settled for squeezing his good shoulder. She was so happy to see him that she almost cried. Only now did she fully understand how close she'd come to dying. Fear was strange that way, catching up only after the danger had passed. The fight with Jōko Daishi had terrified her, but it wasn't until she saw Han that she understood everything she could have lost.

"What happened?" he said.

"He . . ." Mariko swallowed. "He hit the train. And then I did something I shouldn't have done."

Han studied her closely, trying to make sense of the tears welling in her eyes. Then he saw the thin trickle of blood oozing down the length of Glorious Victory Unsought. "Oh," he said.

Mariko just nodded. She tried to speak but nothing came out.

Han nodded back. He tucked his left lapel into his right hand, which couldn't do much other than grab onto whatever he put in it. Now that it had a good hold, his right arm could serve as its own sling. With his left hand he ripped off the tattered remains of his torn pants pocket, then reached up and cleaned the blood from Glorious Victory Unsought. He did it carefully and thoroughly. Then, rather than tossing the bloody rag aside for evidence techs to find, he stuffed it in his remaining pocket. "It'll be all right," he said.

"Han, I can't ask you to—"

"You didn't ask me for anything. You didn't do anything you shouldn't have done. And we don't have to talk about this now. Let's get you home."

55

A week passed and life settled into what could only
be called the new normal. The most mundane
tasks were a part of Mariko's life again. This included checking her e-mail, which for her ranked on par
with shaving her legs: pointless, time-consuming, never
the way she'd prefer to be spending her morning, but necessary because it was just what people expected you to
do. This week the chore was much larger than usual. Her
in-box had all the usual garbage—officer safety bulletins,
policy reminders, a retirement announcement, the day's
menu from the commissary—plus seventy-five messages
from individuals in the department, most of whom she'd
never met, all offering congratulations.

From this she gathered that word had got out about the
commendation she was to receive. The Medal of Honor
was the highest award the department had to offer. The
thought of it made her sick to her stomach.

Getting praise at work had never been easy for her, in
either sense of easy: it was tough to come by, since most
of her superiors thought of her not as a cop but as a lady
cop, and it was tough to accept, because thanks to her
weird self-esteem issues, she found compliments to be a
form of embarrassment. She had always been her own
worst critic. In this case it was especially hard to accept
the accolades because she knew what she'd done to

achieve them. She got into bed with the enemy. She broke the law. And now she was a rock star.

Just by virtue of taking place in public, the shootout in Kikuchi Park was automatically on YouTube. A couple of videos showed Mariko hauling ass on her commandeered motorcycle. Inevitably, her sister, Saori, found all of them and sent links to everyone she knew. But the clip that went viral was a ten-second snippet that some brainless little prick at Japan Railways pirated from their security feed. His title: COP OUTRUNS SPEEDING TRAIN AND CHOPS IMPOSSIBLY SMALL CHAIN IN HALF WITH GIANT SAMURAI SWORD.

Mariko objected on numerous counts. She didn't outrun the train, she'd only caught up to it. And it wasn't speeding either; at best it was speeding up. She had to concede the point about the five-centimeter chain and the *ōdachi*, but it would have been nice of the guy to call the TMPD and ask for her permission before royally fucking up any chance she'd ever have at working undercover again. That stupid video collected eighty thousand hits on its first day.

After that, Mariko could hardly blame Saori for pinning it to the top of her Facebook page. She begged Saori to change her status, and Saori complied, though not in the way Mariko had hoped. She deleted "My sister is a superhero!" as requested, only to replace it with "My sister is a Jedi Knight!"

Mariko wasn't in the mood for high fives, though she had to admit she'd played a big part in a big win. Of 1,290 kidnapped children, 1,284 were returned safely to their homes. Six died in their sleep, the result of an overdose of whatever Jōko Daishi concocted to put them under. It was a common risk with anesthesia of any kind, which was why people had to go to school for anesthesiology in the first place. The most callous news analysts said six out of thirteen hundred was statistically quite good; the number could have been much worse.

That was no consolation to the six grieving families. In fact it added insult to injury, because while they were left with their pain, the rest of the country actually felt relieved. In any other year, a serial killer overdosing six children would be too horrific for words. The bereft families would find an outpouring of sympathy on a national level. But in the wake of Jōko Daishi, popular consensus could actually make sense of the grotesque phrase "*only* six dead children."

Tokyo's Purging Fire, the international media were calling it. Mariko despised them for giving Jōko Daishi that much credit, using his term instead of coining one of their own. But these were the same unthinking drones who used the phrase "ethnic cleansing" instead of "genocide," blithely ignorant of the implied premise that some ethnicities *were* dirty, or else they could not be "cleansed."

A hundred and twelve dead at Haneda, four in the intentional head-on collisions, twenty-four poisoned at St. Luke's, a child and a kidnapper dead in a car crash, six more children killed by overdose. SWAT and HRT shot and killed seven cultists in the course of freeing the children held in Terminal 2—perfect justice, some said, for the seven kidnapped kids who never made it back home. Four more cultists died in Kikuchi Park, along with one of the Bulldog's enforcers, who took a bullet through the liver and died in surgery. A hundred and sixty all told, with three times that many injured. Koji Makoto was consciously left out of the count. Captain Kusama, in his final public address, said the TMPD would not sully the names of the other victims by including Jōko Daishi among their number.

Kusama had almost everything he needed to keep his job. He was well connected, graceful under pressure, and demonstrated a unique capacity for turning ugly truths into flattering semitruths. Striking preemptively, he made Mariko's demotion and suspension public knowledge, but claimed the department had never lost faith in her. He said she had unique knowledge of the Divine Wind, which was true. He said that if she was to accept a special assignment to investigate the cult, she couldn't afford the distraction of having other officers report to her—also true, though of course he neglected to point out that there was no such assignment. He also failed to mention that he'd formally barred her from the Haneda investigation. On the other hand, he did highlight her central role in the rescue of the three hundred and sixty-five children in the Shinagawa rail yard. This got Han off the hook for his seemingly miraculous "anonymous tips," and it absolved Mariko of everything she did while under suspension. She would even be restored to her previous rank. The only cost was that Kusama got to take credit by proxy for everything she'd accomplished.

Yes, Kusama was as slippery as an eel. He even managed to pass off the Jemaah Islamiyah fiasco as a deliberate misinformation campaign, intended to offend Jōko Daishi and coax him out of hiding. The only thing he couldn't overcome was Japanese culture itself. When an organization failed, someone at the head of that organization was expected to fall on his sword. Not so long ago, that was the literal truth. Even today, the top-ranked sumo referees carried a *tantō* in the ring, the knife traditionally used for seppuku. It symbolized their willingness to commit suicide if they should ever make a bad call. No one expected seppuku of them anymore, but they were expected to commit professional suicide: if one of their calls was ever overturned, they had to tender their resignation immediately. Police work was no different. The TMPD had failed Tokyo. A hundred and sixty people were dead because of it. A prominent leader had to take a fall, and no one had cultivated a more prominent profile than Captain Kusama.

This was the new normal. Captains fell and disgraced detectives got their sergeant's tags back. Mariko was to be decorated for honor too. Hence the seventy-five e-mails. She ignored them. Sooner or later she'd have to write a blanket reply, but she wasn't up to it at the moment. Instead, she sent a short message to Lieutenant Sakakibara, asking him to delay the medal ceremony another week. She claimed she wanted her bruises to heal before everyone took photos.

Another week passed and she sent another e-mail. Terribly sorry, she said, but I forgot all about my class A's.

It was sort of true. She hadn't exactly *forgotten* her dress uniform; it was the most expensive clothing she'd ever owned, and she'd shredded it beyond repair during the relief effort at Terminal 2. That wasn't a hit her bank account could simply forget. She also hadn't forgotten that regulations prescribed class A's for all ceremonial proceedings. What she did forget—willfully—was to place an order for new class A's, which was another way of putting off that commendation for one more week.

Six days later she was standing in front of Sakakibara's desk. "Sir," she said, "I lost a fistful of hair in that fight. I mean literally a fistful. Look." She took off the baseball cap she was wearing and bowed her head down so he could see the huge scab in her hairline. "He practically scalped me. Give me a month to grow it out. Otherwise it'll look like the TMPD hires chimps to do its haircuts."

Sakakibara frowned. "Seriously, Frodo? Bad hair day? That's a pretty girly move. Not really your style."

Mariko managed not to blush. She was afraid he'd say something like that.

His frown took a slightly different shape—puzzled, not annoyed. "You got a problem with getting a commendation, Frodo?"

"No sir. Why would I?"

"Damned if I know. You get that uniform yet?"

"It's supposed to arrive tomorrow, sir."

The grumpy frown came back. "You didn't pull any bullshit with the order, did you? Just the pants, not the jacket? Nothing like that?"

"No, sir." She wished she'd thought of that.

"Then it comes with a cap. So put your damn cap on, cover up your damn hairdo, and show up tomorrow to receive your damn commendation. Got it?"

"Yes, sir."

She invited her mom and her sister to come to the award ceremony, but Han was the only one she asked to come to her apartment first. She wouldn't admit it to him, but she didn't want to be alone when the uniform arrived.

It was only polite to come bearing a gift, and Han brought what he always brought: cold beer in a six-pack. Bottles this time, for a change of pace. He would have been a gentleman and picked up the big cardboard box waiting on her doorstep, but he couldn't manage the beer and the box with one hand. His right arm was still in a sling.

His "little train ride," as he called it, had sprained, strained, or dislocated pretty much everything in his right arm. On the positive side, his physical therapist was hot, and he got to see her three days a week. "But only so she can hurt me," he said. "Does it make me a sicko if I kind of like it?"

"Yes." She took the drinks first, opening one for him because he couldn't manage it one-handed. She took a swig of her own before returning to the hallway for the box. It ended up on her kitchen table, which wasn't much bigger than the box itself. That was as close as she'd get to opening it for now.

They drank the first two beers talking about nothing. The big news in Han's life was that a former Chicago Cub named Matt Murton broke Ichirō Suzuki's single season hit record, which Han thought was relevant to Mariko because she used to live in Illinois and in his geographically challenged mind Illinois and Chicago were more or less synonymous. Mariko didn't really care about baseball, but she found his enthusiasm entertaining nonetheless. For the first time in two weeks, she laughed.

"It's about time," he said. "What's gotten into you?"

"Can I ask you something? When you shot Jōko Daishi's tire out, do you ever think about what would have happened if you hit him instead? I mean, that was a hell of a long shot."

"I was aiming for him."

"Huh?"

Han shrugged, an asymmetrical gesture given the state of his right shoulder. "You think that was an amazing shot? It wasn't. I missed. I was trying to hit *him*."

"Doesn't that mess with your head? I mean, you could have killed somebody. What if you hit a civilian?"

"I didn't." When he saw that answer didn't do anything for her, he said, "I don't know what to tell you. I spend as much time on the range as anyone. Well, okay, maybe not as much as you, but as much as any sane person. If I thought I was going to hit a civilian, I wouldn't have taken the shot."

"But you just said you missed."

"Honestly, I don't know what to tell you. I don't think about it a lot. I guess I'm lucky I don't have to. What's this all about? What's eating at you?"

She closed her eyes, steeled herself, and took the plunge. "You saw the medical examiner's report on Jōko Daishi?"

"I sure did. 'Cause of death: massive blunt force trauma.' Score one for the good guys."

"Han, you and I both know what happened down there."

"Yeah. We do. Is that what's got you bent out of shape?"

Mariko didn't expect to see legitimate surprise in his face. "Of course it is. That and everything that led up to it. All that shit with Furukawa, with the Wind . . ." She'd given him most of the general outlines by now. "Did I tell you about the Bulldog's girlfriend?"

"No."

"They killed her. Get this: I go to the Bulldog, looking for information about the kidnapped kids. He tells me to go fuck myself. Not his kids, not his problem, that's what he says."

"Sounds about right."

"Neh?" Mariko cracked open another drink. "Except half an hour later, he calls me back. He's the one who gave me the tip on the kids in Terminal 2. If not for him . . . I mean, we don't know what would have happened, but it could have been pretty bad."

"So why the change of heart?"

"He said his girlfriend was the latest case of ricin poisoning. Said she was pregnant and didn't want to keep it, so she went to St. Luke's."

"Hm." Han wrinkled up his face at that. "Pretty convenient timing."

"Right. Ricin takes, what, four or five days to kill? She's sick for *days* and he never hears about it until the minute I need him to?"

"You went and checked St. Luke's, didn't you?"

Mariko nodded. "I went to Organized Crimes first, and asked them for all the Bulldog's known associates. They gave me the complete list: girlfriends, exes, all of them. I ran every name through St. Luke's. No hits."

"So what are you saying?"

Mariko's hands were shaking now. "Furukawa killed her. He killed her and made the Bulldog think it was ricin. He didn't even bother forging a medical record, Han. He could have hacked St. Luke's computers but he didn't bother, because he only needed Kamaguchi to believe the story long enough to help us."

"Holy shit." He thought about it a minute, scratching unconsciously at his cheek. "So what are we going to do about it?"

"What can we do? The guy is a ghost in the machine. Not just him; his whole damn organization."

"There's got to be something—"

"What? Call the cops? He *is* the cops, Han. He's whoever he wants to be. I've seen how these people work. They can make and break people with a phone call. I have half an idea that they're the ones who toppled Kusama."

"Seriously?"

"Look at how it went down. Kusama's as slick as they come. He dodged everything the media threw at him. No, he did more than just dodge it. They pelted him with shit and he turned it into snowflakes. He came away as clean as can be. And *then* the top brass push him out?"

"Mariko, I don't know—"

"Okay, fine, I don't know either. Call it a theory." She took a drink. Focusing on how cold it was helped cool her flaring temper too. "But if that's how it happened, it might be Furukawa's way of thanking me. He knows I think Kusama was a sexist prick."

"He *was* a sexist prick. Good riddance." Han raised his beer in a toast.

Mariko obliged him; they clinked their bottles together. "You see what I'm saying, though, *neh*? I don't think we have what it takes to burn down Furukawa."

"We know he exists. That's a start."

"Okay, good point." Mariko allowed herself a wry laugh. "It might be more than a start."

"Uh-oh. What did you do?"

"I might have visited the Bulldog in prison." Kamaguchi would be behind bars for a long time. That was what you got when you fired an AK-47 in a public park. It didn't matter where the bullets went or how many soldiers you had to stand tall and plead guilty for you. "I might have let Furukawa's name slip. Along with his description. And everything else I know about him."

Han grinned. "You're a bad girl."

"See?" She smacked him. "This is what I'm worried about. We shouldn't laugh about this. I shouldn't feel good about it. I should feel guilty as hell."

"Why? Because one bad guy is going to fuck over another bad guy? Let them. It's what they do."

"*I* helped, Han. Don't you get that? I helped."

She scowled at the brown cardboard box that contained her new class A's. "This is why I don't want that damn medal, Han. You were there when I broke into that strip club. That was criminal trespassing at best. Felony burglary as soon as I walked out the door with that printout. And that was *before* I fell in with the Wind. Since then . . ." She pinched her eyes shut and took a long drink. "Han, I lie awake at night listing all the crimes I committed for these people. It's dozens. Maybe fifty, maybe a hundred. I'm too scared to write them all down."

"Mariko—"

"We took an oath. That's the difference between a cop and a civilian, you know? You swear an oath, and then all of a sudden you're different. But I'm not. Not anymore. And now I don't have the guts to open that stupid box."

"Mariko, you *are* different—"

"Han, I killed a man. Not in self-defense. He was just lying there, and I killed him, and then you and I covered it up."

He tried to put an arm around her. She shoved him away. Instantly she regretted it; jostling him shot pain through his ruined right arm. "Dammit, sorry," she said. "You see my point, *neh*? We got away with it. 'Cause of death: massive blunt force trauma.' And now I'm supposed to accept a medal for heroism in the line of duty."

Mariko finished her drink. Han didn't give her a new one. "You know what the worst part is, Han? The worst part is I've been here before. But Fuchida was different. Akahata was different. Those guys . . . I mean, they train us to take down guys like that. But this . . . this was *cold*, Han."

"Good."

It was the last thing she expected him to say. She couldn't even think of anything to say in response. He'd short-circuited her brain.

Han met her gaze head-on. "Why did you do it? Because he deserved it?"

"No."

"Because you were pissed off?"

"No."

"Okay, so you weren't playing vigilante and you weren't a hormone-raging PMS monster. That's what Captain Kusama thought of you, *neh*? Turns out he's full of shit."

Mariko nodded reluctantly. "I guess."

"No, you don't. You know. Now tell me, what's the real story? Why did you kill Jōko Daishi?"

Mariko didn't want to tell him about Shoji, or about psychic links and foreseeing the future. She felt too weak. Instead she said, "This is kind of hard to believe, but I know his mom. Jōko Daishi's, I mean. She's a friend of my old sensei, Yamada."

"Whoa. Weird."

"You could put it that way. Anyway, I figured I owed it to her. He was her son. I mean, you saw the ME's report. You saw the photos. How could I just leave him like that? I couldn't do that to her."

"So you . . ." He looked at Glorious Victory Unsought, which hung in its wall-mounted rack above her bed.

Mariko nodded somberly. She couldn't speak. As soon as her thoughts ventured toward what happened in that tunnel she flinched away, as viscerally as if she'd touched a hot stove.

Han was dumbstruck too, at least for a while. Finally he said, "You're amazing."

"Huh?"

"You're face-to-face with a guy who killed over a hundred people—a guy who tried to kill *you*—but you, your first response is compassion."

Mariko hadn't thought of it like that.

Leave it to Han to show her what was going on in her own brain. She supposed he was right. He had to be; all the evidence supported his conclusion, and Mariko believed what the evidence told her to believe. She was a detective, after all.

She *was* a detective. She'd never stopped being one, not even in her darkest hours—not when she was wiping her prints off a pistol and a padlock, not even when she let her friend wipe a dead man's blood off her sword. The unnerving truth was that being a detective made her better at being a criminal. Everything she'd done for the Wind she was just as capable of doing on her own. But compassion had to count for something, didn't it?

It did. She saw that now. Furukawa tried three times to recruit her. What tipped the balance wasn't some new argument on his part: it was hundreds of kidnapped children.

Would she do it all over again? She didn't want to think about that. She wasn't afraid of a yes; she was afraid of what it might mean if the answer was no. Now wasn't the time to think about it anyway. She was in too fragile a state for that. Besides, she had things to do.

She sniffed, wiped her nose, and got up to open the box. The cap was on top. She plopped it on her head, covering her ridiculous mostly bald spot, and held the jacket up in front of her as if to imagine herself wearing it in front of a mirror. "Well? What do you think?"

"I think you're fucked. You're not planning on wearing that to the ceremony, are you?"

"Um . . . yeah?"

"Right out of the box? Mariko, you're supposed to have it dry-cleaned."

Mariko thought about that for a second. No one had ever worn this uniform. It wasn't dirty. It didn't stink. She was missing something.

"Wrinkles!" Han said. He'd have thrown his hands up in despair if only he had two good hands. Instead he managed a kind of flailing motion. "It's a dress uniform. It's supposed to look, you know, *dressy*."

"I don't really do dressy."

"No shit." He flailed again. "You're unbelievable."

"I thought you said I was amazing."

"You're a jackass is what you are."

Mariko laughed out loud. It had been a long time since she'd done that. "You think Sakakibara will give me one more day?"

"Are you kidding? He'll skin you, stuff you, and use you as a punching bag. His words. He said he'd hang you in the police academy gym so all the new recruits could whale on you."

Mariko laughed again. "Okay, so what now?"

Han shoved the last of the beers in her hand. "Drink this. Fast."

"Han, I can't show up drunk to the ceremony."

"Trust me, you'll sober right up when you find out how much one-hour dry cleaning costs."

"It's about damn time," Sakakibara said when Mariko showed up in her spotless, wrinkle-free uniform. Mariko's eyes flicked frantically to the wall clock, afraid she was late. Then, seeing she was five minutes early, she realized he meant she should have done this two weeks ago.

It hadn't occurred to her how many people would be involved in this ceremony. She figured the usual: someone getting pinned, someone to do the pinning, maybe a photographer or two. Her mother, Saori, and Han should have doubled attendance. The department's pressroom wasn't big, just a nice little stage and a few dozen seats. Most of those seats should have been empty.

Instead it was standing room only. A complete press corps filled the front row. All the top brass were there. The governor himself was on stage, chatting idly in the wings with the chief of police. No wonder Sakakibara was pissed about rescheduling this thing.

At the chief's insistence, three reporters were moved to stand in the aisle so Mariko's mother could sit front and center, her little pocket camera at the ready. Saori sat to her left, Han to her right. Mariko could see them through the door, which she'd opened just the tiniest sliver.

"You ready for this?" Sakakibara asked.

"Hell no, sir. What are all these people doing here?"

He shut the door. "Frodo, you took down the most dangerous criminal this country has ever seen. That's the kind of thing the governor shows up for. So for once in your life, pay attention to etiquette. He's going to give you a very deep bow. What are you going to do?"

"Bow back even deeper, sir?"

"Damn right, you will. You'll accept your medal, you'll accept your sergeant's tags, and you'll do it without freaking out or getting weepy. Is that clear?"

Mariko smiled. "Yes, sir."

He scowled at her, but it was a different kind of scowl than she'd seen from him before. "One more thing," he said. "I suppose you think I'm pretty proud of you."

"Are you, sir?"

"Hell, no. You did your damn job. What do you want, a cookie?"

Her smile broadened. "No, sir."

"All right, then. Let's get your damn medal."

GLOSSARY

Amaterasu: sun goddess and goddess of the universe, from whom the Emperor of Japan is said to be a direct descendant

arare: rice crackers usually flavored with soy sauce or seaweed

Bizen: a style of unglazed pottery

bokken: solid wooden training sword, usually of oak

bōryokudan: the term used by police, and in the media at the behest of the police, for organized crime syndicates in Japan (literally "violent crime organization")

bunraku: a traditional art of puppetry using ornate, lifelike puppets

bushidō: the way of the warrior

chūnin: a midlevel lieutenant in a ninja clan (literally "middle person")

CI: Confidential Informant

daishō: katana and wakizashi together, the twin swords of the samurai (literally "big-little")

dono: an honorific expressing great humility on the part of the speaker, more respectful than -san or even -sama

foxfire: magical lights said to be carried by foxes or fox-spirits

fusuma: sliding divider, usually wooden and covered with cloth or paper, usable as both door and wall

gaijin: foreigner (literally "outsider")

geisha: a skilled artist paid to wait on, entertain, and in some cases provide sexual services for clientele

genin: a low-level operative in a ninja clan (literally "low person")

Gion: a district in Kyoto known for its geisha

goze: blind itinerant female, usually a musician, said to have the gift of second sight

gumi: yakuza clan (as in Kamaguchi-gumi)

Hachiman: god of war

hakama: wide, pleated pants bound tightly at the waist and hanging to the ankle

haori: a Japanese tabard (i.e., short, sleeveless jacket) characterized by wide, almost winglike shoulders, often worn over armor

hatamoto: bannerman, the highest rank of retainer in a lord's service

hitatare: a robe associated with the samurai class, worn over a kimono and under armor

IAD: Internal Affairs Division

Ikebana: the art of flower arrangement

Ikkō Ikki: a peasant uprising, largely disorganized and only nominally Buddhist, whose political and economic influence endured for over a hundred years

Irasshaimase: a welcome greeting said when customers enter a place of business

jizamurai: a low-level samurai not wholly removed from farming life

Joseon: a Korean kingdom of the fourteenth to nineteenth centuries

kaishakunin: person charged with decapitating someone who must commit seppuku; also called the "second"

kama: a short-hafted sickle for farming or gardening

kami: creative natural forces, often called "spirits"

Kansai: the geographic region around Kyoto, Nara, and Osaka, and the locus of political power for nearly all of Japanese history

katana: a curved long sword worn with the cutting edge facing upward

kenjutsu: the lethal art of the sword (as opposed to kendō, the sporting art of the sword)

kesagiri: in Japanese sword arts, a downward diagonal cut to the left shoulder

ki: life energy

kiai: a loud shout practiced as a part of martial arts training, usually uttered upon delivering a strike

kiri: a paulownia blossom, the emblem of Toyotomi Hideyoshi

koku: the amount of rice required to feed one person for one year; also, a unit for measuring the size of a fiefdom or estate, corresponding to the amount of rice its land can produce

kosode: a long garment similar to a kimono but with smaller sleeves

kote: the wrist, as a target for sword practice

kote-uchi: a strike to the wrist

Kura-okami: dragon-god of rain and snow

MDA: methylenedioxyamphetamine, a hallucinogenic amphetamine

mugi-cha: roasted barley tea, usually served cold

naginata: a polearm consisting of a curved sword blade on the end of a long haft

ōdachi: a single-edged great sword, curved like a katana

ri: a unit of measurement equal to about two and a half miles

rōnin: a masterless samurai (literally "wave-person")

sama: an honorific expressing humility on the part of the speaker, more respectful than -san but not as humbling as -dono

sarariman: "salary man"; a man with a white-collar job

satori: Buddhist enlightenment

seiza: a kneeling position on the floor; as a verb, "to sit seiza" means "to meditate" (literally "proper sitting")

sensei: teacher, professor, or doctor, depending on the context (literally "born-before")

seppuku: ritual suicide by disembowelment, also known as hara-kiri

shakuhachi: traditional Japanese flute

shamisen: traditional Japanese lute

shinobi: ninja

shoji: sliding divider with rice-paper windows, usable as both door and wall

shomenuchi: in Japanese sword arts, a downward vertical cut to the head

shōnin: the highest level of commander in a ninja clan (literally "high person")

shoyu: soy sauce

shōzoku: the bodysuit, hood, and mask that ninja were (erroneously) said to have worn as a sort of uniform

sode: broad, panellike shoulder armor, usually of lamellar

southern barbarian: white person (considered "southern" because European sailors were only allowed to dock in Nagasaki, which lies far to the south)

Sword Hunt: an edict restricting the ownership of weapons to the samurai caste; there were two such edicts, each one carrying additional provisions on arms control and other political decrees

tantō: a single-edged combat knife, curved like a katana, ritually used in seppuku

tengu: a goblin with birdlike features

tetsubin: a traditional teapot made of cast iron

Tokaidō: the "East Sea Road" connecting modern-day Tokyo to modern-day Kyoto

torii: a gate signifying the entryway to a Shinto shrine, usually composed of two pillars connected at the top by either a lintel or a sacred rope (shimenawa)

wakizashi: a curved short sword, typically paired with a katana, worn with the blade facing upward

yakitori: grilled chicken served on a skewer

yakuza: member of an organized crime syndicate; "good-for-nothing"

yamabushi: ex-soldier dwelling in the wilds as a criminal (literally "mountain warrior")

yoroi: armor

yukata: a light robe

AUTHOR'S NOTE

If you've gotten this far, you're three books in and you're expecting a third author's note. Dear reader, I shall not disappoint.

The first question to address in this book is *where's Kaida?* Don't worry; you'll see more of her. She had a storyline in this book all the way up to the very last draft, but in the end the manuscript was just too long. It made more sense to give Kaida her own lead role than to whittle her down along with everyone else in order to trim the book down to fighting weight. So now she's the star of *Streaming Dawn*; I hope you catch up with her there.

The next set of questions concerns the historical stuff. Toyotomi Hideyoshi is the most important historical figure in the novel, and as you may remember from *Year of the Demon*, he was the second of the Three Unifiers, the three great lords who united Japan in the late 1500s. His predecessor, Oda Nobunaga, was a ferocious fighter who brought a third of the empire to heel before being assassinated by one of his inner circle. His successor, Tokugawa Ieyasu, sat back and waited for Hideyoshi to bring all the Japanese islands under his rule, then ousted his heirs. Ieyasu built a house on Hideyoshi's foundation, creating a shogunate that would last more than two and a half centuries.

One of Hideyoshi's most important political advisors

was his wife, Nene. Intelligent, genteel, and politically savvy, she was by all accounts an extraordinary woman. She commanded not only Hideyoshi's respect but also Nobunaga's, who wrote to her fondly and even took her side when Hideyoshi complained about her. Nene and Hideyoshi exchanged letters throughout his campaigns, and when she criticized his policies, he was known to change them. It is hard to overstate what a stunning accomplishment this was; Hideyoshi was no feminist, and the Azuchi-Momoyama period was not an era of enlightened gender politics.

In some ways theirs was a strained marriage, for she bore him no children and he did take other wives and concubines. When he died, his proclaimed heir was his son by his second wife, and one factor that allowed Tokugawa Ieyasu to cement his power was that Nene backed Ieyasu, not her own husband's son. Thus while she cannot properly be called the Fourth Unifier, she was influential for all of the other three. No other woman in Japanese history can lay claim to a similar position.

Other events in Hideyoshi's biography are also as I portrayed them here. He did boast that he would someday conquer China, and he went so far as to invade the Korean peninsula. (The conquest was short-lived.) He was ugly as sin, but quite charming in spite of that fact. To prevent civil uprising he issued a Sword Hunt that disarmed the peasantry, and this would have included the *kama*-wielding *yamabushi* that Daigoro faces in the hills near Fuji-no-tenka.

Yamabushi were a fixture of Japanese life in the sixteenth century. They came in two varieties, because the word is a homonym. In one sense, the *yamabushi* are "ones who lie in the mountains," a monastic tradition of ascetic hermits. In Japan the tradition of seeking enlightenment in the mountains dates back to the eighth or ninth century and still lives on today. In the other sense (written with a different kanji for *bushi*) the *yamabushi* were "mountain warriors," packs of soldiers, *rōnin*, and martially trained monks who had turned to banditry.

They plagued the countryside, and even the great daimyo were hard-pressed to manage them.

Fuji-no-tenka is fictional, but Atsuta Shrine is not. You can still visit the Shrine today; it is one of Japan's most venerated sites. It is said to have been founded in the second century to house the remains of Prince Yamato and his fabled Kusanagi no Tsurugi, the Grass-Cutting Sword. Prince Yamato is a legendary hero whose story is told in the *Kojiki* and *Nihon Shoki*, the earliest chronicles of Japanese myth and history. His most famous episode is his defeat of the bandit kings Kumaso and Takeru, whom he ambushed in their tents by disguising himself as a serving maid. In another famous adventure, he was caught in a brush fire and survived by cutting down all the grass around him so the fire could not approach. Then he used his sword to redirect the wind, sending the flames back toward his enemies. (If it were me, I'd have called my sword Weather Dominator, not Grass Cutter, but different strokes for different folks, I guess.)

I make brief mention in the book of two other historical figures: Akechi Mitsuhide, who betrayed Oda Nobunaga, and Takeda Shingen, a daimyo renowned for his ferocity, craftiness, and general badassery. I think I need to write a book about him one of these days. Mongol grenades also appear in this book; they were real, and by Mongol standards they're maybe the tenth-coolest thing in the arsenal. When Kublai Khan invaded Japan, he brought flamethrowers, mortars, and even primitive rockets. He also brought his death-dealing war wheels, huge iron monstrosities that were filled with black powder, ignited, then sent rolling downhill into the ranks of the enemy. Even the samurai could not stand against them; if not for a pair of timely typhoons that raked the Mongolian fleets, Japan would almost certainly have become a protectorate of the Mongol Empire.

A final note about medieval Japan concerns women. Legally speaking, they had little say in matters of marriage and no rights whatsoever when it came to divorce. A man could divorce his wife by writing a short letter (three and a half lines long, to be precise), citing whatever reasons he liked. If she refused to leave, he could throw her bodily out of the house and no one could gainsay him. A woman could not rely on the law to protect her from an abusive husband, but by custom she could take shelter in a convent; two or three years as a nun effectively annulled her marriage.

This was but one of many double standards, almost all of which were to the woman's disadvantage. The one counterexample in this book concerns ritual suicide (which, if you'll recall, is the way Lady Ōda ended her life after she learned Daigoro killed her son in a duel). Men of the samurai caste were expected to commit seppuku, or self-disembowelment. This was held to be the most painful form of death imaginable, and since samurai women were not deemed strong enough to go through with it, their method was different: they placed a knife point upward on the floor, then fell throat-first onto it. The idea was that if they lost their nerve at the last moment, they would have already lost their balance and their fate would be sealed. Whether women were not brave enough to perform seppuku, or simply not stupid enough to do it when given a better alternative, is a judgment I leave to you.

The most important historical discrepancy in this book is also the most obvious: no terrorists ever blew up Haneda's Terminal 2. There was no ricin scare in Tokyo hospitals, nor any conspiracy to cause traffic deaths. The Divine Wind's activities aside, I took 2010 as it was given to me. Matt Murton did break Ichirō Suzuki's single season hit record, Jemaah Islamiyah was the most feared terrorist organization in East Asia, and there really is a pool hall called Billiards Bagus near Yamada-sensei's home in Machida.

Incidentally, I know where Yamada's house is—or rather, I've chosen which house is his on Google Earth, and I map Mariko's comings and goings from there. For Daigoro's peregrinations I use Google Earth and also period maps from his era. You can find a link to the best of these maps on my website, www.philosofiction.com, where you'll also find links to armor diagrams, descriptions of period clothing, and other items of historical interest.

This brings me to another point. In talking with readers—which I very much enjoy, so please do send me an e-mail—one of the topics that often comes up is the degree of research required for these books. It has been suggested to me that I could get away with doing a lot less digging. You can imagine the Venn diagram mapping the sets of 1) people who read my books; 2) people who know so much about the Japanese educational system that they'd correct me if I had said Tokyo had 1,403 public elementary schools and not 1,304; and 3) people who will publicly lambaste me for getting the number wrong. These are not huge populations we're dealing with here.

Nevertheless, I did spend a night researching Tokyo public schools. In 2010 the count was 1,304, and this probably has no influence whatsoever on the review you're planning to post on Goodreads. So why bother with the research?

Part of it is that I also write as an academic, and so it's ingrained in me to cite a source for just about everything I put to paper. (I'm always tempted to put a footnote after my name, citing my own birth certificate as the reference.) Another part of it, as I'm sure my friends and family will attest, is that I like to be right about stuff. The largest part is that worldbuilding is very important to me, especially when I'm building a world in which you're supposed to believe in the supernatural. And then there's the last part—a tiny part, I swear: if I get the rest of the details right, I figure you're less likely to catch me when I tell you bald-faced lies.

For instance, Google Earth will not show you a Kikuchi Park in downtown Tokyo, for the simple reason that there isn't one. I wanted a first-floor pool hall across the street from a public park, and when I couldn't find one, I made it up. I named it Kikuchi Park because I'd just seen *Pacific Rim* and I really enjoyed seeing Rinko Kikuchi kick ass with a bo staff.

Many of my characters get their names this way. Mariko is the name of Logan's great love in the *Wolverine* comics, and also the name of Miyamoto Usagi's love interest in *Usagi Yojimbo*. Daigoro is both named and nicknamed after Ogami Daigoro, the Wolf Cub in the cult classic samurai series *Lone Wolf and Cub*. Furukawa Ujio shares his initials with another great schemer, Francis Underwood of *House of Cards*. Captain Kusama's last name is one letter away from *kisama*, Japanese for "son of a bitch." Three characters are named for my former Japanese professors. Others are named for friends.

Finally, the Kamaguchi-gumi shares all but one letter in common with the Yamaguchi-gumi, Japan's largest yakuza clan. In the earliest drafts of *Daughter of the Sword*, my yakuzas did belong to the real-world Yamaguchis, but upon further consideration I decided this might well be suicidal. Yakuzas have been known to take punitive actions against authors who malign them in their books. So I'll reiterate: my Kamaguchis are not based on any real live Yamaguchis, not one teeny bit.

—Steve Bein
Austin, Texas
September 2014

ACKNOWLEDGMENTS

Many mahalos to everyone who assisted in the research for this book: Alex Embry and Diana Rowland for the cop stuff, D. P. Lyle for the medical stuff, and the Codex hivemind for every other topic under the sun. Alex was especially helpful in orchestrating police responses to a massive terrorist attack. Charlie Bee and Jess Sund were instrumental in figuring out the mechanics of Streaming Dawn. Luc Reid served as literary tech support, helping a technophobe and Luddite write intelligibly about computery stuff. Special thanks for proofreading go to my mother, and also to Tim Robinson.

My deepest gratitude goes to all of my readers. I think it was Mark Twain who said every time you choose to read a book, you choose not to read all the other ones. That makes picking up a new book an almost sacred decision. Thank you for putting that faith in me.

Thanks also to my beta readers, including Kris Bein, Kat Sherbo, Luc Reid, Kati Strande, and most especially my illustrious agent, Cameron McClure. Special thanks to my extraordinarily patient editor, Anne Sowards, who extended my deadline when plotting this book got hairy, and again to Cameron for helping to comb out the tangles. As with past books, Cameron and Anne were crucial in tightening the manuscript and making this the best book it could be.

I have been remiss in my last two acknowledgments pages for not thanking Allison Hiroto, who narrates the audio books and turns in one beautiful performance after the next. Chris McGrath continues to produce covers that make other authors envious. The beautiful and talented Sayuri Oyamada models for the cover, and made me feel really good about myself when she wrote to me via Facebook. All lifelong nerds should have the pleasure at least once in their lives of getting personal messages from a professional model.

Begrudging thanks are due once more to Michele, this time for getting me on Twitter, and once again, sincerest thanks for everything else.

ABOUT THE AUTHOR

Steve Bein teaches philosophy at the University of Dayton. He has a PhD in philosophy, and his graduate work took him to Japan, where he translated a seminal work in the study of Zen Buddhism. He holds black belts in two American forms of combative martial arts and has trained in about two dozen other martial arts. His short fiction has been published in *Asimov's Science Fiction*, *Interzone*, and *Writers of the Future*, and he has been anthologized for use in college courses alongside the works of such figures as Orson Scott Card, Larry Niven, Isaac Asimov, and H. G. Wells. His Fated Blades saga includes *Disciple of the Wind*, *Year of the Demon*, *Daughter of the Sword*, and the novellas *Only a Shadow* and *Streaming Dawn*.